D1343349

BRIGHT SWORD

THE BYRHTNOTH CHRONICLES: BOOK 1

CHRISTINE HANCOCK

The Book Guild Ltd

First published in Great Britain in 2018 by
The Book Guild Ltd
9 Priory Business Park
Wistow Road, Kibworth
Leicestershire, LE8 0RX
Freephone: 0800 999 2982
www.bookguild.co.uk
Email: info@bookguild.co.uk
Twitter: @bookguild

Copyright © 2018 Christine Hancock

The right of Christine Hancock to be identified as the author of this
work has been asserted by her in accordance with the
Copyright, Design and Patents Act 1988.

All rights reserved. No part of this publication may be
reproduced, transmitted, or stored in a retrieval system, in any form or by any means,
without permission in writing from the publisher, nor be otherwise circulated in
any form of binding or cover other than that in which it is published and without
a similar condition being imposed on the subsequent purchaser.

This work is entirely fictitious and bears no resemblance to any persons living or dead.

Cover Design by Cathy Helms (www.avalongraphics.org)
Cover image © Jacek Wojnarowski

Typeset in Adobe Garamond Pro

Printed and bound in Great Britain by CPI Group (UK) Ltd, Croydon, CR0 4YY

ISBN 978 1912083 404

British Library Cataloguing in Publication Data.
A catalogue record for this book is available from the British Library.

For my mother.

WINTER 937

1

They told me to wait. They left me, all alone, and told me to wait outside the door, a door so tall that the top was lost in darkness. Strange figures, animals and birds, climbed the solid oak posts. In daylight they would glow with bright colours, but now only the gleam of sharp teeth or the curve of grasping claws was visible. I reached out, running a finger along the back of some hunched creature. Was it gold?

"Is this the right door?"

Startled, I looked round. A boy stood nearby. Where had he come from? No one else was in sight. He gave a hesitant smile and I caught a glint of dark eyes below a mass of tangled black hair. I turned back to the door, looked left, then right. "There isn't another."

The boy nodded. He was smaller than me, only skin and bone. He was dressed in a collection of rags but seemed oblivious to the cold. My tunic was old but it had been good quality. Mother had complained about how quickly I grew out of clothes. But I mustn't think of that now. I tugged at the hem, but I still felt cold. I pointed at the animals.

"Is that gold?"

"Probably. It is the king's hall."

"Is it?" I took a step backwards.

"Didn't you know?"

"Someone told me to wait here." I looked out into the darkness; there was no one there, just us. "I've come a long way." I paused remembering the journey. "I'm hungry."

"There may be food in there." We stared at the door. Light filtered round the edges and we could hear the shouts of many voices. They sounded cheerful.

"It will be warm as well," he added.

The door was flung open. A man stood there, gulping in the cold night air. His large belly bulged over a thick leather belt, and plump red cheeks glowed above a chin of grey stubble. He gave a large belch and noticed us.

"What are you doing out here?"

We backed away. Neither of us spoke.

"You'd better come in." The man held the door wide.

I felt a rumbling inside my stomach as the smell of roast meat teased its way out past the man. Whatever was inside couldn't be worse than the cold and hunger out here. I took a step towards the light. I looked back at my companion.

"I'm scared." He turned, as if to run.

"Don't worry, I'll look after you." I held out my hand. He took it.

We walked through the great door together. I was no longer alone.

Inside, the blast of noise almost knocked us backwards. So many voices shouting at the same time, like a battle was taking place. I felt my new friend's hand tighten in mine.

"At least it's warm," I said. After the cold outside it was almost too hot. The thick smoky heat carried with it the smell of many bodies, dirty straw and spilt ale. Best of all was the smell of food; the wonderful smell of roasting meat.

Long boards stretched either side of the hall with warriors seated at them. Nearest were young men, clad in shades of brown or grey with only a glimpse here and there of more colourful embroidery. Further away were the older men, wealthy thegns, with richer clothes. So many colours, like a summer meadow. The bands of embroidery were wider and more intricate. Gold rings flashed as arms moved, and jewels glinted from knife hilts. Everyone was shouting, mostly in good-humour; toasts and bragging, snatches of drinking songs. There were arguments, which never quite developed into fights. Someone would pull the men apart and pour more ale from the large jugs scattered liberally along the boards.

The far end of the hall was invisible. Hidden by the smoke of the fire pits; not just one hearth that you might find in an ordinary hall, but a whole line of them. Over every one a carcass roasted or a cauldron bubbled. Servants carved slabs of meat from the great roasts, cleverly avoiding the flames leaping up from the fires. Others rushed around with plates of meat or baskets full of warm crusty bread.

Someone thrust some meat into my hand before dashing elsewhere. It was golden brown and crispy on the outside, still slightly bloody inside. I had never held so much meat in my hands. Before anyone could change their mind, I tore off a piece and handed it to my companion. He ripped at it like a half starved dog, gulping it down in chunks. I bit into the fragrant meat, the fat running down my chin. I had never tasted anything so delicious before.

I was licking the last of the juices from my fingers when the door opened again. It was the man who had let us in.

"You two still here? Someone's given you something to eat?"

I nodded, fearful we had done something wrong.

"Come with me. I'm Oswald, you'll be seeing a lot more of me."

Close to the door sat two men. They waved us on when they saw we had no weapons to hand in. Behind them was a vast collection. Knives and sharp seaxes lay neatly on a bench, some sheathed, others gleaming in naked menace. In the corner stood axes, firelight glinting from the vicious blades. Bundles of spears like sheaves of corn leaned against the wall. Then I saw the swords. I stopped and stared. They hung from hooks, some marked by the badge of their owner, sheathed in scabbards of different lengths, some plain leather; many dyed glorious colours and inlaid with gold, silver or decorated with precious jewels. The sword hilts rose proudly from the scabbards, matching them in decoration. Some were new, highly polished, crying out their owner's status. Others were old, handed down through some great family, pommels worn smooth by the hands of generations of warriors. Automatically my hand fell to the small plain knife that hung from my belt.

"Don't worry. Eating knives are allowed." One of the guards smiled at me.

I hung my head and hurried away.

"You'll have a sword one day," he shouted after me. I looked back. His grin broadened and he nodded before giving me a wave. As I followed Oswald along the side of the hall, I felt a sudden thrill. A sword. Could I ever earn a sword of my own? Had my father, whoever he was, owned a sword?

We reached the far end of the hall, an area partitioned off from the rest of the building. It was near the top table and less noisy; the royal party had retired to their private quarters. The space was filled with straw and a few dirty sheepskins, a storage area. There were other boys there, all about my age. I had reached the age of seven years last spring. Several pairs of eyes stared up at us but most were asleep. Guarding the room was an elderly woman. Her back was bent as she focused on the sewing in her lap.

"Didn't you hear me?" Oswald shouted, "two more have arrived. Had to bring them all the way from the door myself."

"How do you expect me to hear you with all this racket?" The woman hardly glanced up. "Anyway, I'm supposed to stay here."

"And I'm not supposed to leave the door."

"Keep your voice down, these babies are trying to sleep. You could have sent someone else with them."

"Everyone's drunk. I'd better get back." He pushed us into the room. "Find somewhere to sleep."

He hurried back down the hall, pausing only to grab a cup of ale from a table.

We pushed and shoved, found a corner and settled down.

"I wonder what's going to happen tomorrow?" I whispered.

"I don't know, and I don't care. I just want to sleep."

"What's your name?"

"Wulfstan."

"I'm Byrhtnoth." There was no reply.

I lay gazing up at the shadows moving in the smoke far above, imagining the battles I would fight, the sword I would wield, one day.

2

I woke up scratching. My new friend was lousy. He smelt as well, although that could have been the ancient sheepskins that formed our bed. I edged carefully away from him.

The hall was dim. Embers glowed dark red in some of the hearths. A spray of sparks erupted when a servant swept the remains into a neat pile. Others carried armfuls of wood that they arranged carefully around the debris of the previous night's blaze. Somewhere a door opened and the draft made clouds of silver ash rise in the air. A woman shouted and the sound echoed round the space. The door slammed shut and the dust settled.

"Come on, you lot. Up you get." Oswald had drunk too much the previous night. He was not happy to be awake this early. He grabbed boys only half awake and pushed them in the direction of food left over from the feast. I followed and helped myself to some bread and a chunk of cheese. I slipped more into my pouch in case I was offered nothing later and looked around.

Servants were clearing tables, collecting cups and throwing leftover food into baskets. Buckets of water appeared and rags were whisked across dirty boards. Men who had slept slumped at the board had their head roughly lifted, then dropped with a thud back onto the cleaned wooden surface. I took a bite of cold meat and washed it down with a mouthful of ale, before Oswald herded us out into the fresh air.

It was a cold, crisp morning and the weak sun had little effect on the frosty ground. Oswald led us through empty streets. In the distance a cock crowed, then squawked in alarm as someone threw something to silence it. We arrived at an empty animal pen on the edge of the town. The previous occupants had vacated the area very recently, probably for the fires of the night before. Oswald gathered us together.

"Does anyone know why you are here?"

Most shook their heads. I wasn't the only ignorant one then. Someone mumbled something.

"Come on, speak up."

"They told me I would be trained. Taught to be a warrior."

It was a neat, well dressed boy.

"That is correct." So it was true, suddenly the day brightened.

"Quiet! You know about the great battle that took place recently?" There were a number of blank faces.

"This is going to be a harder job than I thought." Oswald scratched his close-cropped head. "First lesson. This summer our Lord Edmund and his brother Athelstan, King of the English... You must have heard of him?" Some boys nodded. "Thank goodness for that. They fought a battle against the Kings of Alba and Strathclyde and the King of Dublin and others. And they defeated them all." We cheered. "It was at a place called Brunanburh, it's in the north. It will be remembered for all time."

I recalled men leaving the village to serve their time in the fyrd. That must have been where they had gone. Not all had returned.

"Were you there? Did you fight in the battle?"

Oswald shook his head. "My time of fighting battles is past. But I know many men who were there. If you behave yourselves, I'll ask them to tell you about it." The boys started talking, excitedly.

"Calm down. It means that Athelstan is now king of the whole of England, and there will be peace in all this land."

"If there is peace, why does he want more warriors?" I asked.

Oswald thought for a moment. "Such a large country needs many wise men to help rule it; to uphold the laws and punish the evil-doers. That is what warriors do. They don't just fight."

There were groans from the group, but my new friend, Wulfstan whispered, "I wouldn't mind doing that. First of all I'd..."

"Silence," Oswald shouted. "You will be educated and trained in weapons. That's my job. You will be fed and clothed and, as long as you obey the rules, you will have a glorious future. Rule number one is that no-one talks unless I tell them to!"

The chattering died down.

"First let's find out what we've got here. Form a circle."

We shuffled apart. I tried to get away from my companion, even in the fresh air his smell was noticeable, but he stuck to my side.

"Everyone must give their name and where they come from."

A plump boy, better dressed than the rest of us, stepped forward.

"I said no-one was to speak until asked."

The boy shrank back to his place. Oswald surveyed the rest of us.

"You first." He pointed at my smelly friend.

"My name is Wulfstan."

"Wulfstan. Not very big are you?"

"I'm sure I'll grow."

"I'm sure you will," said Oswald, dryly. "You're very dark, not a slave, are you? Or Welsh, which is nearly as bad. Who are your parents?"

Wulfstan's grin faded. "I don't have any parents. I've lived in many places."

"You must be an escaped slave. We must find out where you came from and send you back. We can't have slaves in this group."

"I'm not a slave. I'm not." The boy was terrified. I had promised to protect him.

"Of course he's not a slave." I moved closer to him. "We came together. You remember, you opened the door for us last night?"

Oswald nodded.

"I know him. He wasn't a slave in my village." That much was true. He might have been a slave, but not in our village.

"And who are you?"

"Byrhtnoth. My mother died recently."

"And what is your father's name?"

I took a deep breath. "I don't know. It was a secret. My mother said she would tell me when I was older, but she died quickly, there wasn't time."

"We know what that means, don't we lads? She didn't know who his father was."

There were sniggers round the circle. Nothing had changed. I was still to be punished for something I couldn't help. I felt my head going down but then Wulfstan spoke up.

"I knew his mother and there was never any scandal told about her. She was the most beautiful and honourable lady in the village."

Oswald stared hard at him, nodded, then continued round the circle, a group of orphans, younger sons and dubious characters. Finally it was the turn of the well-fed boy. I had taken an instant dislike to him. He reminded me of the bully back in the village who had made my life hell.

"My name is Egbert, and I am a relative of the king." He puffed himself up, looking like a pompous frog. "I will be your leader."

"Correction, this is Egbert." Oswald scowled. "He is wearing one of the tunics that you will all be given later today. My wife made them. You met her last night."

Egbert opened his mouth to protest, but Oswald cut him short. "Leadership of this group must be earned. At the moment you are all equal." He looked around the animal pen. "This is

11

going to be our training ground. It needs cleaning up. Egbert, you know your way around. Go and find some shovels. The rest of you divide the area into sections. When he comes back, you will remove all this muck. When it is clear, you can go for a bath and receive your new tunics."

Egbert shuffled off to find the shovels. Oswald strolled over to Wulfstan and me.

"I don't believe a word either of you said."

I glanced at Wulfstan in alarm.

"Don't say anything. I admire initiative and I liked the way you stuck up for each other. That's what this group needs. Keep your noses clean and we'll say no more about it."

He walked away to talk to some of the other boys.

"What was that all about?" I asked Wulfstan.

Wulfstan just grunted and bent to his work. "We'd better get on with shovelling this shit."

3

Oswald herded us into a wooden building, close to the hall. Inside his wife leaned over a barrel, which steamed gently. She was the woman who had looked over us during the night. Behind her, a large cauldron hung over a fire. Servants were pouring buckets of water in. We were hungry from our exertions. Once we had cleared the pen we had done exercises: running, jumping and wrestling in pairs. Were we going to get some food? The scent of herbs hung in the air, but there was no smell of food. I was glad I had saved something from earlier.

"Get your clothes off. Who's going first?" We all hung back. A few moved towards the door, worried they were about to be cooked for the next feast.

"What's the matter?" said Oswald. "You won't get any food until you've had a bath. They won't let you into the hall smelling like that."

A bath? In hot water? I spotted piles of clothing, laid out on a bench. I'd give anything for some new clothes. They might even fit me properly. I stepped forward but was beaten to it by another boy. He was the one who had known about the training. I watched him carefully.

"There's nothing to worry about. I've had baths like this

before, back at home." He undressed, folded his clothes carefully and climbed into the barrel of hot water. He sat down. We all craned forward to see what would happen. The woman scrubbed him and poured water over his head, as if basting a joint of meat. When she decided he was clean enough, she let him go. I didn't think he had been dirty to begin with.

"Who's next?"

"I'll have a go." I stepped forward with more confidence than I felt. "You come next," I whispered to Wulfstan, "I imagine that water is going to get dirty very quickly. Might as well make the most of it while it's clean."

I stripped off my tunic and threw it into the corner of the room. It wasn't fit for anything else and I was glad to get rid of it. I stepped gingerly into the warm, fragrant water. I soon realised how pleasant it was. There was the sharp smell of rosemary and other herbs. I would have liked to spend more time wallowing in the fragrant heat but after my head had been dunked under water, I was forced to leave, spluttering. I beckoned to Wulfstan and then whispered to the woman.

"Make sure you get his head right under. His hair is full of lice."

I hurried over to where the first boy was sorting through the clothing. "Anything in my size? What's your name? I'm Byrhtnoth."

"I'm Elfhere. I was sorry to hear about your mother. When did it happen? This tunic looks as if it might fit. It's good thick material as well."

I held it up, and then pulled it over my head. I felt warmer already.

"Back in the summer." I managed to keep my voice steady. "I hardly think about it any more."

"Of course not." Elfhere patted my back, smoothing down the tunic. "Where did you live? I'm from Mercia."

"I don't know the name. It was just the village." I remembered the cold journey. "It took a long time to get here. I didn't know the way."

"If you can't remember where it is, they can't send you back," Elfhere said cheerfully.

"I suppose not." I didn't want to go back.

Oswald had overheard my mention of lice. "Good idea. I imagine most of you are crawling with them." He rummaged in a bag, produced a battered comb and tossed it to me. "You're in charge. No-one's allowed out until they've been checked over."

Elfhere produced his own, elaborately carved, comb and handed it to me.

"Use this one, I don't want that old thing near my head."

I did as he ordered and then Elfhere offered to do my hair. I didn't think I needed it either, but just the thought made me itch. I bent so Elfhere could reach my head. I had noticed that I was the tallest one there, I wasn't sure if that was an advantage or not. We had nearly finished, when Wulfstan approached, coughing and choking.

"What did you say that for? She gave me a really good scrubbing."

"I thought you'd want to get rid of the lice."

"Why would I want to get rid of them? I'm used to them. Sometimes they've been my only friends." He stood, shivering miserably in a pool of water.

"Find some clothes, then I'll give your hair a good comb. You've got real friends now."

"Have you known him long?" asked Elfhere, as he shook out the comb.

"No, we only met last night, but somehow I've got the job of looking after him." I started on Wulfstan's thick curls.

"Where did you get all this hair from? I can't get the comb through it."

"How would I know? It's always been like that. Ouch!"

"Perhaps we should cut it all off. Anyone got some shears?"

"No!" Wulfstan pulled away. He dragged his fingers through the unruly mop. "It's all right as it is."

I gave up and grabbed another head. "If I see you scratching, you're not coming anywhere near me."

Soon the room looked like a vision of hell. Flames from the fire mingled with the billowing steam from the cauldron and bath. Wet, naked boys ran wild, flicking wet clothes at each other and shouting. Shrieks from the washing and the combing punctuated the foggy air. Wulfstan helped the old woman with the bath, ducking everyone with enthusiasm and asking about the herbs that she had used.

Suddenly a loud, desperate scream rang out. Had someone fallen into the fire? Attention turned to the corner of the room, where Oswald loomed over a small figure.

"I don't need a bath." The boy wriggled as Oswald grabbed an arm and pulled him towards the water.

"Everyone else has had a bath. It's not so bad."

"But I'm quite clean, I don't need it."

"You do. You've been out with the others. I saw you myself, rolling in the dirt, winning that wrestling bout. You're going to make a good fighter."

"Will I?" The boy stopped struggling and looked up at Oswald with a happy smile.

"Of course. Now let's get these clothes off and you can join the others." He took hold of the boy's tunic to pull it over his head.

"No! You can't." The boy fought back frantically, biting and scratching.

"He is a good fighter," Elfhere commented with approval. I shook my head, something was wrong.

There was a sound of ripping cloth and Oswald was left with a handful of torn material. The small figure stood before him, naked. There was a gasp. "It's a girl."

The words rippled round the room. She didn't try to hide; it was too late for that. I was close enough to see her teeth bite her lower lip, trying to stop the tears that threatened to fall.

Oswald slapped her, and blood trickled from her mouth.

"How dare you." He thrust the ruined tunic at her and pushed her towards the door. "Get out." She was crying properly now.

"But why? I only wanted to train with the rest." She looked round the circle of hostile faces. Elfhere was closest. "Please?"

"Girls don't fight." He turned away.

She moved her gaze to me.

"I'm sorry. You were good." There was nothing else I could say. She gave a sad smile and walked slowly to the door. She looked at the ruined tunic in her hand. She tried to wrap it round her thin body. It hung open from her shoulders. I ran to the corner, picked up my discarded tunic and gave it to her.

"Thank you." She wiped the blood from her mouth with the back of her hand. "What will I do now?" Tears swam in her large grey eyes.

"You'll find something." I reached into my pouch. I had no money, but gave her the bundle of bread and cheese. "It's not much, I haven't anything else."

"At least I won't have to beg for a while." She walked towards the door then looked back at me. "Good luck. I hope you get what you want."

"You too."

She shook her head and walked away. I could sense Oswald looking at me but I kept my head down.

Order was restored and we were lined up and inspected. Everyone was clean and mostly dry, hair slicked down and for the moment tidy. We all wore new tunics and trousers. We had even been given shoes; I curled my toes at the restriction.

"You are starting to look like proper warriors. Tomorrow we will begin your training, but now, let's get some food."

"Why can't girls fight, become warriors?" I asked Elfhere as we followed the others out.

"Because they can't, it's not allowed." He shrugged. "They do other things."

"You were brave," Wulfstan said.

"No I wasn't. I just did what I thought was right."

"It's brave to go against what other people think."

I looked around the empty room. My life had changed but I thought I would enjoy it. What would the girl's life be like?

LATE WINTER 943

4

I sucked the cold winter air into my lungs. My hand tightened in the shield grip. I pushed forward, my whole weight against the board. My companions on either side moved with me, years of training aimed towards this one moment of impact. The helmet I wore muffled the shouted threats and the clatter of swords on shields. My view was restricted. It didn't matter. I waited for that brief flicker of the eyes that would tell me a blow was coming. I could feel the panting breath of my opponent on my face. My feet were steady on the frozen ground, but the trampling by so many feet would soon turn it to mud. It must be done quickly.

I glared into the eyes of the enemy.

"Push!"

The whole line moved forwards another pace. The opposition wavered. I checked my shield still overlapped my neighbour's then I dropped it slightly. The enemy took the bait and swung his sword. It flashed down towards my head. I was ready. I raised my shield to deflect the blow. The blade crashed against the wood and slid away, harmless. From beneath my shield, my sword snaked out and into the belly in front of me. Eyes registered the shock, before he fell away. I stepped over the body and screamed in triumph. My companions followed me through the gap. The enemy's shield wall had broken.

A horn sounded and the lines broke up.

"Help me up. You knocked all the breath out of me."

I bent and pulled Elfhere to his feet.

"You're lucky we were using wooden swords," I told him. "Your guts would be all over the ground by now."

"Yes. But you forgot to finish me off before you stepped forward." Elfhere grinned. "I would still have had enough life in me to attack you from below. That would have made a nasty mess and we'd both be dead."

I would remember next time. I unbuckled my helmet and pulled it off together with the padded lining and ran a hand through my sweat-drenched hair.

"Hot work." A servant offered me a jug. I drained some of the ale and passed it to Elfhere. The others joined us and we discussed the tactics of the battle. It just came down to who pushed the hardest.

"When's the next event?"

"Not long now. They're raising the targets for the mounted battle."

Someone asked me if I was taking part. I shook my head. I was not keen on horses.

"I'll sit it out and watch the rest of you make fools of yourselves."

"At last. A chance for someone else to win something." Elfhere inspected the empty jug and looked round for another. "You must have taken all the prizes so far. The king is coming to congratulate you personally."

"Let's go and see if Wulfstan needs any help. It's the only event he has a chance in." I handed over my helmet and added the wooden sword to the pile waiting to be collected, then walked rapidly away.

"Don't you want to be honoured by the king?" Elfhere asked, catching up with me.

"There'll be enough of that tonight, at the feast." I disliked receiving praise. I knew from experience it wasn't worth the jealousy it caused.

***

We found Wulfstan at the horse lines, brushing his horse. It was difficult to say what colour the animal was. The shaggy winter coat was white, but not the bright white of some of the other horses or a gentle smoky grey. It was the dirty white of soiled linen abandoned by a washerwoman. Darker patches of black and brown scattered the rough coat at random. He always looked half starved, his head too large for the spindly legs. It was the ugliest horse anyone had ever seen.

"However much you brush, he's not going to look any better," I said as we leaned on the fence to watch.

The horse turned his head towards us and snorted.

"Oh dear. Have we offended him?"

Wulfstan stood back to look at the unfortunate animal. "Looks aren't important. Sleipnir is a very intelligent horse."

Hearing his name, the horse seemed to nod in agreement.

"Still got the same number of legs?" Elfhere counted slowly. "One. Two. Three. Still only four. He hasn't grown the rest yet then?"

Wulfstan shrugged, and returned to the grooming. He was used to the jokes. I always thought it had been a mistake to name the animal after Odin's eight-legged horse.

"Don't you have to go and get ready, Elfhere? The competition will be starting soon."

"If I can still get on a horse after the blow Byrhtnoth gave me." Elfhere hobbled off.

"You won then?" Wulfstan glanced at me before returning to the grooming.

"Do you think you've got a chance on this old nag?

Wouldn't you rather ride a horse like that?" Egbert was passing on a magnificent beast. Unlike the rest of the horses with their shaggy winter coats, this one had been clipped short. On its rump swirling patterns had been shaved into the hair. "That must have taken a lot of work, and he would have to have been kept undercover. Poor thing would freeze to death outside; he's already shivering."

Although Egbert was an experienced rider, he was having difficulty controlling the powerful animal. Wulfstan glanced at the sight and continued preparing his own mount.

"No. Too stupid."

I watched the struggle between horse and rider. "Egbert or the horse?"

Wulfstan thought for a second. "Both."

I laughed. "Good luck. You're going to need it."

"Oh, I don't know. I have a plan."

***

The crowd had thinned since my battle in the shield wall. Although the day was bright, it was cold standing around and some spectators had gone indoors for warmth, or to prepare for the feast to be held later. Twelfth Night was the highlight of the Christmas festival and the biggest feast of the year. I wrapped myself in my cloak, savouring my earlier victory and thinking it over; I must make sure Elfhere was dead, not just injured, next time.

"Stop thief." I turned at the sound and a small figure collided with me. I grabbed the boy by a bony shoulder. He tried to pull away, but I held him tight as one of the cooks from the fire pits approached. He stopped, panting and wiped his red face with a piece of cloth. He had been using it to protect his hands from the heat and a smear of grease joined the sweat that poured from his brow.

"Thank you, my lord." He took hold of the boy's arm and started to drag him away. "I'll give you a good whipping for that. Wouldn't be surprised if they don't chop your hand off as well."

I looked down at the boy. His thin cheeks moved as he franticly chewed something, then he swallowed, almost gagging as he forced the food down.

"I didn't steal anything." He defiantly held up his empty hands. "See?" I smiled at his audacity.

"What did he steal?"

"The best piece of the ox. I was saving it especially for the king. Nearly done to a turn it was. Turned my back for one moment and it was gone."

"That's a very serious crime stealing from the king himself." I looked down at the boy. Grey eyes stared up at me, innocently, but I could see the pleading in them. "Did you see him take it?"

The cook frowned. "Not exactly, but it must have been him. He was running away."

"The field is busy," I waved at the crowds, "and I can see at least a dozen running boys."

"Yes. But…"

"There is no proof that this boy took the meat." I noticed he was busy wiping his hands on his ragged tunic. "See, his hands are clean." Well, not clean, but there was no evidence of fresh grease on them. "Perhaps you had better get back to the fire before more meat disappears. It seems to be gathering quite a crowd."

"Thank you, my lord." He gave the boy a sharp glance and hurried away.

"Can I go now?" The boy attempted to escape.

"Not just yet." I looked him up and down. He was very thin and I wondered when he had last had a decent meal. "Are you still hungry?" He nodded vigorously. I remembered what it was like. "Let's see if we can find you something else to eat. Follow me." I let him go. He straightened his clothes, thought about running then followed me across the grass. There was not much meat left on the pig carcase that had been issued to our troop. I asked the servant to carve off as much as he could find.

"Still hungry, Byrhtnoth? Thought you'd had enough earlier."

"It's the cold weather. All that exercise gives you an appetite." I shoved a couple of loaves into a canvas bag, chopped off a chunk of cheese and added it to the haul. The servant handed me a plate full of pork scraps. He looked from me to the boy. "Want some ale with that?" He handed me a sealed jug, checking no-one was looking. "Enjoy your meal."

We found a quiet place and sat down on a pile of logs. I handed the boy some of the meat and a chunk of bread and watched him eat.

"There's no rush, no-one's going to take it away from you. There's probably enough here to last you a few days, if you're careful." Eventually he slowed down.

"I remember you. You gave me food before." I didn't recognise him and I wasn't in the habit of giving food away; I never seemed to have enough for myself.

"I think you must be confusing me with someone else."

"Yes, it was definitely you. Bread and cheese it was. A bit crushed, but still fresh. Long time ago." I shook my head. He did look familiar, but I couldn't place him. He put down the remains of the bread and wiped his mouth with the back of his dirty hand. He looked round to check no-one was near, then leaned forward.

"I was a girl then." A girl? He didn't look like a girl, perhaps with a bit more flesh on his bones he might. "They threw me out. Girls weren't allowed to fight, the big man said."

"Even though you were the best fighter there." I remembered now. My first day here, meeting the others, the bath. "What do you do now, apart from stealing?"

"Surviving. Working, when I can get it; holding horses, shovelling shit, fighting if someone wants a sparring partner. If they find out I'm a girl, a bit of whoring. That's good money but I don't like it much." I opened my mouth in shock, then closed it.

She must be my age. Some women were married by that age, but not many. I didn't like to ask how long she had had to do that. I made a decision.

"I've got to go now, my friend's competing in the riding competition." I thought for a moment. "There's a feast tonight."

"I know, lots of leftovers."

"Meet me outside, late, I'll try and find a job for you. In the kitchen or something. Then you won't have to do… that."

"You're sure? You can do that?"

"I promise. I'll find you, outside the hall tonight. I'll bring more food."

"If you bring gold, you can have a fuck."

"I've got to go. See you later."

"All right." She stuffed more meat into her mouth. "Thank you," she mumbled.

5

Horses and riders were collecting on the field, milling around, greeting friends or exchanging challenges with rivals. I spotted Wulfstan easily. There was Egbert on his new horse. I noticed how much taller it was than the other mounts. It must be one of the special horses being bred for battle. Fighting on horseback didn't seem right to me. Horses were useful to reach a battlefield quickly, but then you faced the enemy on foot, face to face. A horse could never defeat a shield wall, they were only good for the sick or old.

I never trusted horses but as I grew I disliked the small animals that forced me to drag my feet in the dust. On a bigger horse there would be space to swing a sword at least. I paid more attention to Egbert's horse, noticing how much higher from the ground he was. I realised the advantage it would give against a man on foot. That would not be honourable though. Not a proper test of one man against another.

The competition was about to begin. The crowd around were making bets on the outcome. I was sure that it would come down to a fight between Wulfstan and Egbert. Wulfstan was the better rider, but Egbert's new horse might make a difference.

It began with shooting arrows at targets hung from the surrounding trees. Three shots and the losers were eliminated.

Then again with spears. This was more competitive. The bow was a coward's weapon, useful only for hunting, but most warriors were proficient with a spear. The distance of the throw was lengthened and more participants were knocked out. Next was the race.

The remaining riders bunched together, jostling for the best position. The horn sounded and they were off. The course was through light woodland and the river of horses separated and came together as each took their favoured course. The low winter sun caught the flash of metal from a bridle. The hair of man and animal mingled as riders crouched low over straining necks. They chased their own long shadows to the first marker. Egbert's tall horse, with its longer legs reached it first, but Elfhere, close behind was quicker on the turn. Where was Wulfstan? I found him in the next group of riders. They rounded the marker, pushing and jostling. Several fell and the riderless horses continued with the others.

The crowd became noisier. Bets were getting larger. The riders thundered across the stubble fields beyond. The wide river became a swift steam as the competitors strung out. Sleipnir and Wulfstan were close behind the leaders. My shouts were drowned amongst the mass of spectators. Again, the bigger horse was slower on the turn and Elfhere overtook Egbert. They headed back to the start, directly into the sun. Through the trees the flicker from light to dark made it difficult to distinguish obstacles. The horses were tiring now and the pace fell. Reckless riders caught up with the more cautious and, as they burst onto the field, it was difficult to divide winner from loser. I thought that Egbert had just beaten Wulfstan.

***

When Elfhere found me in the crowd, he was limping.

"That's enough. I've spent enough time on the ground today. First you knock me down..."

"I didn't knock you down, you got a sword in the stomach," I corrected him.

"Yes, and I can still feel it. I'll have the bruises for weeks. Did you see who pulled me off? I'd have won that race if that hadn't happened."

"I think you fell off without any help. You tried to swerve round a tree and forgot to hang on to your horse. He went one way and you went the other."

"No, I'm sure someone grabbed at me," Elfhere insisted.

"Perhaps it was the tree." I craned over the heads of the crowd. "I think they've made a decision." The judges were huddled at the end of the field, arguing the final result. An announcement was made. It was as I had expected.

"Wulfstan against Egbert in the final," I told Elfhere.

We went to meet Wulfstan who was leading Sleipnir.

"Well done," Elfhere congratulated him.

"Thanks. What happened to you?"

"He was attacked by a tree," I said.

"It must have been a big one."

We watched as Elfhere tried to brush some of the dirt from his clothes.

"That was the ground, it came up and hit him."

"I see." Wulfstan tried not to laugh. "Will you hold Sleipnir for a moment? I won't be long."

He disappeared into the crowd.

"Just so long as he doesn't expect me to ride him." I stared at the horse and Sleipnir stared back. "Why do I always get the feeling that that horse thinks I'm stupid?"

"Because you are?" If I hadn't been holding the horse, Elfhere would have been flat on the ground again.

Wulfstan returned and wiped down Sleipnir with a piece of cloth.

"He's not sweating much. What was that for?"

Wulfstan just smiled and got back into the saddle.

"Time for our performance." He patted Sleipnir and trotted back to the centre of the field.

***

The two horsemen walked forward, stopping in front of the king and his attendants. I saw Wulfstan lean forward and whisper something to his horse. Sleipnir slowly bent one foreleg and then the other, until he appeared to be bowing before the royal party. The king clapped his hands and the audience cheered. The sudden noise upset Egbert's horse and he moved restlessly, the rider fought to keep control.

First there was a race to the far end of the arena where a pile of arrows and spears was scattered on the ground. The ends were blunt and tightly wrapped in cloth. They had been dipped in whitewash, left over from the regular painting of King Alfred's minster. Once retrieved, they could be used with a bow, or thrown. Egbert was still having problems controlling his horse. Whenever he tried to reach down for a weapon, the animal moved. It seemed that in this, the horse's height was a disadvantage. They made an easy target and Wulfstan was an expert with the bow. Both horse and rider became splattered with paint. Egbert lost his temper. He rode his horse straight at Wulfstan, but Sleipnir was agile and avoided him.

Next was a race, this time through the forest and with obstacles to jump. I expected Sleipnir's small size would be a disadvantage, but the bigger horse held back, reluctant to leave Sleipnir behind. I couldn't work out why. Egbert tore a thin branch from one of the bushes and desperately whipped the horse. In the end he won by a small margin but the audience disapproved of Egbert's rough treatment of his horse. Booing was mixed with laughter.

The final round was a fight between the riders, with sword and shield. Holding his weapons as well as the reins, Egbert was still finding it difficult to control his horse. The smooth hide was now marked by the whipping, streaks of blood and whitewash mixed with sweat. The horse's eyes rolled and nostrils flared. Hot breath steamed in the cold air. Egbert drove his heels into his horse's flanks. They galloped straight towards Wulfstan and Sleipnir waiting in the centre of the field. I was worried for Wulfstan. He was smaller than most of our group, with less strength. He tried, but the hard life before we met had taken its toll. Egbert screamed and whirled his sword around his head. Wulfstan sat there, relaxed. He didn't even raise his shield. The crowd shouted at him to defend himself, I shouted myself. Egbert brought down his sword with all his force.

He missed. With perfect timing Sleipnir stepped one pace to the side and the sword sliced through empty air. The force of it nearly unseated Egbert and he struggled to regain his balance. He dragged his horse's head around and attacked again. Wulfstan waited for him and again moved out of the way. Again, and again, each time to more cheers and laughter from the crowd. Egbert became more enraged as people shouted advice. Sleipnir ambled round the field chased by Egbert's horse, which somehow never managed to catch up.

Then Wulfstan decided he had had enough. He stopped suddenly in front of the king. Caught unawares, Egbert slid to a stop. He lost hold of the reins and desperately tried to grab the sweat-soaked mane. Wulfstan smashed his shield into the face of Egbert's horse. The crowd gasped. Outraged the horse reared. Egbert slid slowly backwards, down the long back, over the flowing tail and onto the ground. He hit it with a thump and lay there, winded.

The horse, relieved of his burden, dropped his front legs to the ground and stood, sides heaving and head hanging. He lifted his tail and deposited the contents of his bowels over the stunned Egbert. In the silence that followed, everyone heard Wulfstan's comment.

"Can't you control your horse, Egbert?"

***

Later, as we prepared for the night's feast, I asked Wulfstan about his win.

"How did you do it? Make such a fool of Egbert?"

"It was easy. Once you control the horse, you control the man. I must admit, that final flourish was just luck, although understandable in the circumstances." We laughed at the memory. "I knew that Egbert wasn't that good a rider, especially on that new horse. Once he lost control, I knew we'd won. I'd trained Sleipnir well. I knew he'd do whatever I asked."

"But how did you upset the horse?"

"The way you control any male, with a woman, or in this case, a mare. Once that stallion decided Sleipnir was an available mare, he couldn't think of anything else."

"But how did you...?" I remembered the cloth.

Wulfstan nodded. "A quick visit to the mares' stables and I dipped it in a bucket of urine. It was easy to transfer the scent. Then all I had to do was keep out of the way."

"But what would you have done if it hadn't worked?"

"Lost probably. Now, are you ready? I'm so hungry, I could eat a horse."

6

I walked down the hall, receiving congratulations from men I barely knew. It was the first time I realised how many people are happy to acknowledge you when the king has spoken to you. I clutched my new seax tightly, half expecting someone to take it from me. The bone handle, or was it antler – I hadn't had a chance to inspect it properly, felt smooth in my hand. I found my usual place at the board, far from the king and his household. Wulfstan shuffled along the seat to make room for me.

"I thought you might need this." He pushed a full cup of ale in front of me. I drained it and held it out for more. "That bad, was it?"

"You've decided to return and join us then? Thought you'd deserted us for the top table." Elfhere leaned to see the seax I had laid on the table. I put my hand on the hilt and pulled it closer. "We saw you, talking to the king. What did he say?"

I ignored the question and asked if there was anything left to eat. I hadn't had a chance to taste anything.

"You said you'd bring us back something special," one of the others complained.

"Sorry. I wasn't thinking about food, just worrying about

saying the right thing. The mead was good. It was poured by one of the king's relatives, I don't know her name."

"What did you talk about?" said Wulfstan.

"She didn't say anything."

"The king, stupid. What did you talk to the king about?"

I leaned back, trying to remember.

"He congratulated me on my success in the competition. He gave me this." I lifted the seax, admiring the way the light caught the blade. "We talked about weapons and fighting."

"What a surprise." Elfhere sounded bored but his eyes never left the knife.

"Then he had to discuss politics with some bishop. I had a long conversation with another man. Anyone know who he is?"

"Which one?"

They craned their necks to see the nobles sitting with the king.

"Sitting on the end. Soberly dressed. Thick grey hair."

Elfhere whistled quietly. "You're aiming high. That's Athelstan, Ealdorman of East Anglia. The one they call half-king. He's probably more powerful than King Edmund himself."

We stared up the hall, through the thick, smoky atmosphere. As if aware of the attention, the great man glanced in our direction and inclined his head, before returning to his conversation.

"Remember when we arrived here? Must be five years ago now. All this was strange and new."

"Byrhtnoth has had too much to drink again," Elfhere said. "Must have been all that mead."

I ignored his comment.

"Do you wonder what we will be doing in another five years?"

"I hope we'll all be sitting further up the table," said Wulfstan, "celebrating our victories in proper battles."

"We might be dead," someone said gloomily.

"In which case we will be feasting with the gods and the scop will be singing of our great deeds," Wulfstan picked up the harness he had been presented with earlier. The metal decorations jingled quietly against the wooden board, "and our great horses."

"What about the king?" I waved in his direction. "Edmund is barely twenty. He's only been king for, what, three years? Already he's fought the Danes in the north and won back most of Mercia. I hear that trouble is brewing in Northumberland; I expect he'll be off there next year. Don't you wonder if there will be anything left for us, when we are warriors? Will there be any battles left; for us to win glory?"

"Don't worry. There will always be battles." Elfhere refilled my empty cup. I picked it up, stared into the liquid and put it down. I had had enough to drink. I looked round for something to eat. "Perhaps we will be fighting in Frankia by then. Or Scotland."

"Don't want to fight in Scotland," someone added, "nasty cold place, full of savages." The discussion faded into the distance. I concentrated on the wooden board in front of me, grabbed it to stop it swaying.

"I think I need some fresh air. I don't feel well."

"You'll never be a warrior, Byrhtnoth, if you can't hold your drink."

"Will you be all right?" asked Wulfstan.

"I just need to clear my head." I stood up carefully. "Keep an eye on that." I pushed the seax in his direction then walked carefully towards the door.

I stopped outside the door, letting my eyes adjust to the darkness. Soon I identified the well-worn path to the latrines, my bladder bursting from the drink. Inside the wooden shack, the smell was almost overwhelming. I held my breath before beating a hasty retreat. I put one hand against a wall, to steady myself. A dark shape staggered past and I heard the creak of a door opening. The second blast of the foul smell was too much. I bent over and was violently sick. Feeling a bit better, I moved away and in the darkness found a barrel of water. I scooped handfuls over my head and rinsed my mouth several times, spitting the excess onto the ground. I moved away, further into the darkness. I had been too nervous to eat anything before I met the king. Then I had drunk too much mead, normally the horn rarely reached our part of the hall. The ale was the final straw. Now I just wanted to sleep. I looked up at the sky. Cloud was beginning to drift across; it would rain tomorrow. A rest day, then it would be back to the everlasting training. I stretched. I had better go back to the hall. I hadn't even had a proper look at my new seax.

Before I reached the door, a shape stepped out of the shadows.

"Hello Byrhtnoth." The man was old, but held himself upright. Dark sunken eyes gleamed behind a large bony nose. "Don't you recognise me?" I searched my memory. Was it someone from the village? I remembered him. He had left me in this very place, years before. "The steward. Edward?"

"Eadric. I have come to take you home. You are needed."

7

It felt strange to be back in the village. Everything was the same, yet different. Smaller. I had been a child when I left and now, if not quite a man, I was close to it.

I was hungry. How long had we been travelling since the few mouthfuls of food that morning? I glanced up at the sky. The sun was invisible; cloud the livid yellow grey of a half healed bruise stretched to the horizon, where it merged into the waters of the fens. The dreary expanse was broken only by the rusty black reeds, emerging from the water like the spears of drowned warriors. I shivered as the damp air invaded my body.

Below was the village, a scattering of houses on either side of the road. Not much of a road, more a dank muddy ditch. Dung-brown mud, studded with slime-green pools of water. My old home was somewhere down there, on the right I thought. It was impossible to distinguish from the other huts; they all looked the same, rotting grey mushrooms slowly sinking into the mud. Patches of virulent green moss glistened on thatch.

Where was everybody? There was not a soul to be seen. Perhaps they were out in the fields, a long walk from the village, ploughing the rich dark soil. Christmas was long past. If there had been revelry here, it had left no sign.

Why had I been summoned? Was I to spend the rest of my life here? When I left, I had been an extra mouth to feed. Now I would be a useful body, a strong back to work in the fields. Was it to be my future, after all that training? What had been the point? My friends and all the colour of the royal court were draining away. Sinking, like the village, into the glutinous grey mud of reality.

I would have to run away. I didn't know where, but I knew I couldn't stay here. I felt a mixture of anger and despair.

The continual drizzle had turned to rain. Heavy drops of water fell. I backed against the wall of the hall. I felt the spongy rotting boards against my back as they tried to pull me in. The dripping thatch reached down to grab me. It was too late. I would never get away again.

The door opened and Eadric appeared. "He will receive you now."

It was drier inside, but no warmer. A pot stood in one corner to catch drips from a hole in the roof. It had not been emptied for a long time. For every drip that fell, another spilled over the lip and ran down the side, to join a small stream that wound its way across the floor. The walls I remembered being whitewashed every spring were covered in patches of blue-black mould. Tables still bore the remains of the last meal.

Eadric opened the door at the far end and ushered me through. There was heat and light here, but no welcome. Flames rose from a brazier in the middle of the small room. Sweet herbs had been added to the fire, but they couldn't disguise the smell of sickness and death. From the walls, colourful cloths hung in the stagnant air and muffled any sound from outside.

Lord Toli lay on a bed to one side. At least I assumed it was him. Long gone was the strong vital warrior. In his place was a shrivelled old man. The shape of his body barely raised the blanket that covered it. I hesitated just inside the door, uncertain of my reception. A voice emerged from the body on the bed. That, at least, still retained some of its power.

"Come into the light. I want to see you."

I stepped forward and stood next to the brazier. I stared into the washed out blue eyes of the man who had sent me away, all those years before.

"Eadric tells me you are doing well at court." Toli glanced at Eadric. "You were right. He looks like his father."

"You knew my father?" Excitement swept through me.

"Oh yes, I knew your father. Who could forget one of the greatest warriors of his time? He fought at the side of Athelstan. And I was with him."

"Athelstan the king?"

"Of course King Athelstan. Who else? Grandson of the great Alfred, who proclaimed him his heir – so they say." Toli paused. "Strange family. You know Athelstan never married?"

"Some sort of vow?" I tried to remember the lessons we had been forced to sit through. "He was base-born and swore to defend the land until his half-brother was of age, King Edmund who rules now. That is why he never married."

I remembered his death, the uncertainty, then a new king; the king who had presented me with a seax a few days before.

"Perhaps that was the problem." Toli began to cough and Eadric rushed forward to help. Toli waved him away and closed his eyes.

"What problem?" It felt like I was getting answers about my life at last. I didn't want him to stop talking now.

"You." Toli's eyes opened. He gave a bitter laugh. "You were the problem. I suppose you need to know." He paused for a moment, thinking. "King Athelstan didn't marry. Perhaps there was no time for such things; the fighting was hard then. Perhaps he loved God more than any woman. His followers felt they should follow his example. Then your father met your mother."

"How? When?" At last I would know the truth.

"I'll tell you if you stop interrupting." Toli searched for the right words. "They married quietly and your father returned to

Athelstan's court. I was tasked with protecting your mother. He gave me this village, and others. They will be yours when I'm gone. He was sent to the North. I don't know where, or why. So many alliances made, and broken." I saw tears appear in his eyes. "He was never heard of again. Your mother refused to gave up hope, but when she caught the fever, it was too much, she gave up. Perhaps she went to meet him at last."

In the silence I remembered the sad woman of my childhood, her mind always elsewhere.

"There is more." Toli raised a frail hand towards a wooden chest that stood against the wall. "Fetch it."

"This is not the time." Eadric's mouth formed a stubborn line.

"I don't care what you think. While I still live you will obey me." Toli tried to sit, but fell back on the bed, panting. "He needs to see it." His voice rose. "Bring it out!" I looked from one man to the other. What was happening?

Eadric bowed his head reluctantly. He opened the lid. He folded back the contents of the chest and found what he wanted. He stood up with a sheathed sword in his arms. He hesitated.

"Give it to him!" Toli commanded.

With a look of dislike Eadric handed me the sword. It was heavy in my hands. The scabbard was old, battered and worn. I noticed the hilt had been well used. Golden decoration gleamed yellow in the firelight. A piece of the wire binding the shaft had become loose; it shone like a woman's hair, newly combed.

"Take it out." I barely heard Toli's excited command. I grasped the hilt and drew the sword from the scabbard.

It slid out easily, as if eager to join the company. I held my breath as it was revealed. The blade seemed to attract all the light in the small room and radiate it twice as bright. It drew the eye but was difficult to focus on, like a bottomless sea bathed in sunlight. I moved it slowly through the thick air. It was heavy. It would need a strong man to wield it properly, stronger than I. Despite the length and weight, it was perfectly balanced. It felt like an extension of my arm. The hilt fitted in my hand as if it had always been there. I studied the blade. The great men of the court owned such blades. I recognised the patterns created by the best blade smiths, but these were more beautiful than anything I had seen before. Rippling and turning like a gentle wave kissing a sandy shore. Surrounding the patterns were other, delicate markings, inlaid with gold. I gazed deep into the swirling metal, trying to grasp the message it was trying to tell me. Was it writing? If so it was no writing I recognised. I was on the verge of understanding when the light changed and the words, if they were words, transformed into something else.

I raised a hand to test the sharpness of the edge. I felt nothing, but now there was a smear of blood on the blade.

"She has tasted your blood. She will know you again." Was it Eadric who spoke?

I forced myself to tear my eyes away from the sword. It was like waking from a deep sleep. I started breathing again.

"It has a keen edge." Toli grinned at me.

"Where did it come from?"

"It is your father's sword." As he said the words, it was as if I felt my father, there, in the room with us. I resisted the temptation to turn and look for him. I grasped the sword tighter. I never wanted to let it go.

"It is a great sword, fit for a king. Does it..." I glanced at Eadric, "does she have a name?"

"She will tell her master her name, when the time is come." The voice echoed round the room, as if the sword spoke the words with him. Eadric took a deep breath. "Put it away. It is enough."

I slid the sword back into its sheath. It gave a whisper that sounded like a promise. The room dimmed. It felt as if something or someone very powerful had departed. There was silence as we mourned the loss.

I sank to my knees beside the bed.

"Thank you for showing me." I would never forget the experience.

"Too soon. But I wanted to experience it again, before..." The old man was drifting away. We both watched Eadric, who was carefully laying the sword back in the chest.

"Can I...?" I'm not sure what I asked.

"Trust him." The words were so quiet. I was uncertain if Lord Toli was completing my question or answering it. His eyes closed, blue tinged lids too heavy to keep open any longer.

"Wait. You haven't told me his name."

Toli's eyes flickered. "Whose name?" he mumbled.

"My father's name," I paused, remembering the sad woman of my childhood, "and my mother's."

"Ah, your mother." Toli smiled sadly. The next sound was a gentle snore.

"You will get nothing out of him for now." I felt the shadow of Eadric looming over me. He seemed pleased that I had not received an answer. "Once the poppy syrup has worked, it is impossible to wake him. Perhaps you will discover more tomorrow." He pushed me towards the door. "The day is over. The people will be returning. The evening meal will be served soon."

8

The door slammed in my face. I walked down the hall and sat down in my old place. Someone had lit a fire in the hearth and thin wisps of smoke rose from the meagre pile of sticks. It made little impression on the cold dampness of the building. I stared into the flickering tongues of flame and tried to make sense of what I had seen and heard.

Eadric emerged from the chamber, closing the door gently behind him.

"What are you doing there? You are the lord's guest. You should sit here."

He pushed a large ornately carved chair towards the board at the head of the room. I walked back reluctantly and sat down. The rough carvings dug into my back and the seat sloped at an uncomfortable angle. I noticed this part of the room was raised, only a few inches, but I felt exposed as people entered the hall. I supposed I was an important person in the village now, a big jump from a skinny boy with no father. Even if I still knew little about my father.

Conversations about the day's work ceased as the villagers noticed my presence; then resumed in quieter voices. Servants appeared and a young girl shyly put down a flagon of ale in front of me. I took a large gulp of the cloudy liquid. It tasted foul, but I was thirsty. I thanked her and took another sip.

I kept my eyes fixed on the wooden board, waiting for a certain voice. Then I heard it: the loud bragging of Godric, my childhood tormentor. This voice made no attempt to be quiet. It wanted to be heard, and by the whole hall.

"If it isn't the whore's skinny bastard, returned to honour us with his presence." I heard a smattering of laughter. "Come back to get what you can from the lord?"

My stomach churned. I could feel my hands start to tremble. I wanted to run, as far and as fast as I could.

Godric was a few years older than me. He had terrorised the younger children and I had been his main victim. Without a father to protect me, I had suffered beatings, until I learnt to keep out of Godric's way. This was partly why I dreaded returning to the village. A bowl of food appeared in front of me and I gripped the spoon tightly. There was a stinging in my thumb and a bead of blood appeared. It was the cut I had received from the sword.

Had I forgotten so quickly? I did have a father. I didn't know his name yet, but he had been a great warrior. I sat upright in the chair of honour. It felt comfortable. I raised my head.

Godric was no terrifying giant, just an ordinary man. I had fought, and won, against more impressive opponents. His body was running to fat, eyes sunk into his round face. The twisted, sneering mouth was the same, but it no longer frightened me.

"Hello Godric. Are you still here?" I dipped a spoon into my bowl. "The lord has told me about my father." I studied the contents of the spoon. "Have you found out who yours is yet?"

As I chewed on a piece of tough meat, I surveyed the room, at the men waiting for their meals and back to Godric. He stood up. His mouth opened, then closed. Laughter broke the silence and the bully's face turned red. The servant girl had just reached Godric with the jug of ale. She gave a nervous giggle. Godric swung and hit her violently across the face with the back of his hand.

"Shut up," he roared. The laughter died. The girl sprawled across the floor. The jug lay smashed beside her and liquid soaked quickly into the dirty rushes.

I'd had enough. I stood up.

"Come here, girl." She struggled to her feet. Blood dripped from her cut lip and her eyes were wide with fear as she stood before me. I asked her name.

"Hild, my lord."

"Please fetch another jug, Hild, I would like more ale."

"Leave my woman alone," Godric shouted.

"Are you his woman?" I asked Hild. She was rooted to the spot. I smiled and tried again. "Do you want to be his woman?" This time the girl shook her head.

"Don't worry, I'll sort this out. Go and get the ale." The girl scurried out.

I sat down and surveyed the silent room.

"I suggest we all get on with our meal. I'm hungry, even if you're not." Heads bent and the only sound was the scraping of spoons in wooden bowls. Godric was still on his feet, hands flat on the board. He breathed heavily, his head thrust forward, like an ox straining at a heavy load.

"Sit down, Godric." I added a hint of steel to the command.

Hild brought the new ale and filled my cup. She stood, uncertain what to do.

"Stay and talk to me. Tell me all the village news."

"Oh no, my lord, I have to serve the rest of the hall." She hefted the heavy jug, but didn't move.

"Someone else can do that." I called to Eadric who stood in the corner of the room, watching everything, "Find someone else to serve the ale. Or perhaps you can do it yourself?" Reluctantly the steward came and took the jug from Hild. With an expression as sour as the ale, he hurried away.

"That's got rid of him. Tell me, is the food here always this bad?" I prodded the lumps of gristle left in the bottom of my bowl. "I suppose things are short now Christmas is over."

"No, my lord, that's what we always eat." Hild had retreated behind the chair. She leaned forward and inspected the bowl. "You have the best bits there. If you don't want it, can I have some?"

I offered her the bowl. She grabbed a lump and chewed on it.

"I don't remember the food here being quite so bad. Did the harvest fail?"

Hild moved the lump of gristle into her cheek. "Last year was very good, but we don't see much of it, most goes to the abbey."

"Have the taxes increased?" I took another sip of the ale, frowned and put it down.

"It's not that. We must pay for the lord's medicine. Eadric told us it comes from far away and is very expensive." She glanced over her shoulder to check that the steward wasn't at his observation place. "We must sell as much as we can, to pay for it. Times have been hard – for all of us."

Not for everyone. I gave Eadric a thoughtful look as he returned to the room. I was certain some of the money stuck to his fingers. I glanced round the hall. Men with families were leaving for their homes. The single men were preparing to sleep.

"Do you have somewhere safe for the night?" I asked Hild.

"I'll find a corner in the kitchen."

"Good. Take the rest of the bowl with you. I can manage without for tonight." I stood up. I needed fresh air.

I stopped here and there to exchange a few words with men I recognised. They were all as tired and hungry as Hild, all except Godric. He still sat at the board, deep in conversation with his companions. I avoided them.

Outside, the rain had cleared and the sky was full of bright stars. It had turned colder and ice was forming on the edge of the puddles. The ground crunched under my feet. I stared out over the water. So much had happened since I arrived. Thoughts swirled around in my head. I needed time to make sense of it all but it would have to wait. I heard the sound of someone approaching, someone trying to make no noise. There was an intake of breath. I ducked. Something heavy missed my head by inches. I spun round and grabbed an arm. Within seconds Godric was flat on his back in the mud, my knife at his throat.

"I didn't think you'd be able to resist the opportunity."

The knife moved. I laughed at his expression as he tried to follow the point of the sharp blade. It stopped close to one of his eyes.

"I wouldn't struggle if I were you." His body froze. "If I find out you have bullied anyone, ever again, I will cut out this eye." I sketched small circles with the knife and then moved it to the other eye. "And if you hurt Hild, or any of the women, I will take this one as well."

I kicked away the heavy piece of wood that had nearly brained me, stretched and noticed the stars again. The day had ended well. Suddenly I felt tired. I walked back to the hall straight through the group of Godric's cronies, clustered just inside the door.

"I think Godric needs some help. He seems to have slipped in the mud," I told them. At the front of the hall I found my baggage. I wrapped myself in my cloak and was soon asleep.

I woke to the sound of screaming.

9

I lay still with eyes closed, assessing the situation, as I had been trained to do. Was the village being attacked? I decided it was some domestic crisis. I relaxed and opened my eyes slowly.

The door to Lord Toli's chamber was open; people crowded round the door.

"Dead!"

I pushed through urgently. Inside was Eadric, looking down at the bed.

"My lord is dead." He didn't raise his head.

I stepped forward and touched the thin white hands, lying crossed on the blanket. They were icy cold, like the rest of the room. I looked around. Everything had changed from the previous night. The brazier was empty and the shutters had been thrown open, to let the dead man's soul escape. Forgive me but my first thoughts were for myself. How would I find out about my parents now? My eyes were drawn towards the chest. Was the sword there or had it been hidden elsewhere? Would I ever see it again? I pushed its glowing image to the back of my mind.

"His suffering is at an end. He has gone to a better place." It was the only thing I could think to say.

"This is your fault. You killed him." I recoiled from the force of the hate in Eadric's eyes. I heard whispers in the crowd. Frustrated anger rose in me.

"His death has nothing to do with me. You brought me here. You had the care of him." I recalled Eadric's careful closing of the door last night. "You were the last person with him."

We glared across the silent corpse. Eadric was the first to drop his eyes.

"Has the priest been sent for?" I pushed the crowd of onlookers out of the room. "What has been arranged for the burial?"

***

The hall was full, everyone discussing events and speculating on the future. They barely noticed as Hild put down gruel in front of them. I thanked her when she gave me a bowl. At least she still did her job.

I lingered over the food. I had been given tantalising information about my parents. I had seen that wonderful sword; my father's sword. Now Lord Toli was dead. Had he clung to life just long enough to speak to me, or had someone decided he had said too much? I stared at the empty bowl. The villagers left the hall. I followed them outside.

The bright sun was dazzling. Ice filled the furrows in the village street. There was a new bustle about the place as people went about their business. The frost meant there could be no ploughing; there was no need to go out to the fields. The death of their lord had suspended normal life. They gathered in groups, glances were cast in my direction.

I wandered through the village. A man repaired a roof, arranging reeds across a thinning patch. He carefully lined them up and levelled them. He hammered bent pegs to keep everything in place.

"You're making a good job of that." The worker grunted. "Do you do all the thatching in the village?" I asked.

"Them as can afford it," the man paused in his hammering, "not many can, and I don't have the time."

"You know there's a hole in the roof of the hall?"

"I know it."

"Can you repair it? When you have time."

"I need instructions from the lord to do that and he's dead." He glanced down at me. "You the new lord?"

"I might be. I'm not sure. I think it depends on the abbey."

I thought about it for a moment, remembering what Toli had said the night before. "I rather think I might be." I grinned, realising my new status.

"I'll do it then." The man nodded.

As I walked slowly back towards the hall, I heard whispers as the news spread through the village. I hoped I hadn't said the wrong thing.

Down beside the water a group of men had gathered. Hild, the kitchen girl, was watching.

"What's going on?" I asked her.

Close to the water's edge was a large hole. Two men poked sticks into the churning water while a third held a sack nearby.

"They're catching the eels. It's part of our payment to the abbey at Ely. You'll be travelling there tomorrow, for the funeral. You can deliver them."

We watched as the men tried to catch the fish.

"I remember eating eels before I went away. It was my favourite meal. I don't know how they were cooked." I realised how hungry I was.

"My mother used to do the cooking. It was her secret recipe." Hild glanced up at me. "She taught it to me. Not that I get a chance to cook them nowadays. They all go to the abbey."

There was a shout. One of the men had dropped an eel and the dark shape slithered through the grass towards the open water.

"That one doesn't want to go." I stepped forward and put my

foot firmly on its slimy back. I drew my knife, cut off its head and tossed the body into Hild's empty basket. "More?"

She nodded. I thrust both hands into the tank. It was cold, almost frozen, slowing the ceaseless motion of the eels. I grabbed one, then another. I stood up with an eel in each hand. They writhed and twisted in my grasp.

"Will that do?" She smiled and nodded. They were soon dispatched and added to the basket.

"They will make a fine feast tonight, but what about the monks?" she asked anxiously.

"There are plenty left for them. They won't know that any missing unless someone tells them and we're not going to, are we?"

Hild shook her head and frowned at the eels in the basket. "We will eat well tonight, but..."

"What's wrong? Is there anything else you need?"

"How long will you be away at the abbey?"

"I don't know." I thought about it. "We will bury the lord. Then there is business to be done, oaths to be sworn. I expect we will stay a night, perhaps two."

"When you return you will require a feast, to welcome the new lord? Whoever he is."

"Don't worry, I'll think of something." I spoke with more confidence than I felt. "Get on with preparing those eels, I can taste them already. I'll help to get the rest of them in the sack."

***

I wiped my hands on some grass, trying to remove the eel slime. I had received a couple of bites from the sharp teeth, but they would soon heal. It was better to plunge straight in and grab what you wanted, rather than flap around thinking about it.

I noticed Godric, hanging around with some of his friends, near the boats.

"Just the man I need."

Godric turned, with a guilty look on his face. "I wasn't doing anything."

"Did I say you were? You and your friends appear to be at a loose end." A couple of the group muttered excuses and sidled off. "I remember you were a good hunter, catching wildfowl in the marshes. Do you still do it?"

"Not much, the lord makes us work hard." He stared across the water. "We never have time to hunt. Anything we catch is sold off or sent to the abbey. No point hunting if you can't enjoy the results of your own efforts."

"The lord is dead now. God rest his soul." I watched as they muttered a response. "When we return from the abbey, there will be a new lord, and he will need to provide a feast. Can I rely on you to find us something to eat?"

"We'll be needed in the fields. We've just started the ploughing," one of the men complained.

I glanced up at the sky. "This cold spell will last a day or so."

Godric scowled, then thought about it. "We could do it. What do you want?"

"I don't know. Anything you can find. Hild will tell you what she needs. She's cooking some eels for tonight's meal. I don't suppose you've had those for a while?"

"Her mother's old recipe?" Godric consulted the others. "We'll do it."

***

"Thank you, Hild, I don't think I've tasted better at the king's table." I leaned back from the board and surveyed the hall. The day off from work had improved the mood of the village and talk was animated. I noticed the bucket to catch the water from the leak in the roof had been removed and the wet patch was drying out.

I knew I should make some sort of a speech and the hall fell silent when I stood.

"Our lord has died." As I paused I heard someone mutter "Good riddance."

I cleared my throat. "Times have been bad recently, but that was not the fault of Lord Toli. God gave him great pain to endure, but now he is free from it. This is his funeral feast and we should celebrate his life. There is no scop in the village to sing his praises, so we must do the best we can." Some of the audience nodded, but most stared mutinously back.

"Without Lord Toli my life would have been bleak. He protected and supported my mother and when she died," I paused, remembering the feeling of utter loss, "he sent me away. I went to the king's court, to be trained as a warrior. I have been educated. I have been taught to fight." I noticed Godric nodding agreement. "I still have a long way to go, but in a few years I will be fighting for the king, defending my land, your land, from invaders. That is what Lord Toli did for me, and I am grateful." There was silence in the hall. "Does anyone else want to speak?"

A woman stood up. "Forgive me, my lord, for speaking, but it seems that the men of this village have short memories. I remember the lord a few years back, before he was struck down. There were good times, sometimes not so good, but he was always fair in his dealings. He looked after the less fortunate. Remember my old dad? When he got too old to work, the lord didn't cast him out. He gave him bread every day until he died. Said he had worked hard for the village all his life and deserved the reward. He was a good lord." She sank back onto the bench as the other women cheered. Others began telling their own memories of the lord and the mood softened.

I sat back and listened. A noise came from behind. Eadric had emerged from Lord Toli's room and taken up his usual place in the corner of the hall. His expression was impossible to read.

10

Wulfstan rode slowly through the trees. A particularly large and savage boar had been reported and a hunt had been arranged. He wasn't interested in the hunt, although he would enjoy the taste of the meat if a kill was made. He had heard about an ancient building in the heart of the forest and, ever curious, wanted to explore it.

He liked to be on his own. At the court there was always something going on, a job that needed doing, or the everlasting weapons training. When he did get a break, it was usually spent with Byrhtnoth, and he wasn't interested in anything, except fighting. His friend had no interest in finding out about the world around them or what had happened in the past. Only the future was important. He wondered how he was getting on. Would he find out more about his own past? Wulfstan would know soon.

The day was bright but little light penetrated the tightly packed trees. In summer it would be even darker when the trees were clothed in foliage. Spring plants still lingered beneath the earth. The only sound was the steady thud of Sleipnir's hooves. The shouts of hunters and barking of dogs had faded away. They had been drawn in a different direction. He spotted something through the trees. He turned Sleipnir off the track and deeper into the forest.

Wulfstan dismounted, leaving his horse to graze on any lingering greenery, and walked over to a ruined wall. It was tall, taller than him, even taller than Byrhtnoth could stretch. It must be very old, crumbling away among the trees. It was thick, a jumble of stones and reddish tiles. It ran for several yards and stopped at an archway. Only half the arch remained, hanging abandoned in the air. Was it part of a building, a doorway? He walked through. There was nothing but a few stones scattered about. He bent and picked up a piece of tile. It was battered and weathered; it had lain there a long time. How long?

He looked back. He had seen something like it before, where? It resembled the wall around Wintanceaster. That was old and enclosed a large area, much bigger than the present town. It was said the Romans had built it, long before the Saxons had arrived in this land. A tree grew from the base of the wall. An acorn must have found its way there when the wall was already ruined. Now it was a massive oak, stretching upwards, branches mingling with the other trees of the forest. So old, but the wall was older. He walked further through the trees, looking for more walls. Debris was scattered across the ground. Moss-covered lumps reared out of the ground but whether they were natural rocks or part of a building, it was impossible to tell.

He heard trickling water and followed the sound to a dip in the ground. He crouched down and carefully separated the clumps of grass. The water was flowing through a channel lined with square cut stones. Someone had built this, but why? It was too narrow for a millrace, only a few inches wide. Thirsty, he bent and scooped up a handful of the water. It was cool and refreshing. Perhaps Sleipnir would like some. As if in reply he heard the jingle of harness. With a sudden rush of wings and a hoarse cry, a raven flew from the wall. He watched the dark shape as it flapped away through the trees. He must get back.

It was only as he walked through the broken arch that he thought to wonder why he had not disturbed the ill-omened bird earlier. He felt a blow to his head and everything went black.

11

We wound slowly along the narrow path. Eadric was at the front, straight-backed on his flea-bitten nag. He must have travelled this way many times. Behind him was the bier, carried by two strong men of the village. Lord Toli's body was covered by his best cloak, the edges hung low, catching on the close-growing bushes, as if trying to delay this final journey. Next came a small group, the lord's closest servants and anyone else who cared enough to accompany him to his final resting place. Following them, a small boy led a pony with the eels hung in heavy baskets either side. I rode behind. My horse, rested after its long journey, was impatient, but was forced to adopt the slow pace of the others.

I suspected Eadric had positioned me there to put me in my place. I was to guard the valuable tribute for the abbey, although I doubted anyone would be out on such a miserable day. We had left at first light and the sky had not brightened much since then. Mist hung over the water. A distant view would appear suddenly and disappear just as quickly. Grey wisps of fog hung in the tops of trees like wool caught on a thorn and water dripped onto our heads. I stared ahead. Was the sky clearing? A milky glow had appeared, low in the sky. The sun, draped in cloud, surveyed us like the single eye of Woden. The clouds dropped and the eye slowly closed, bored by what it saw.

How little I knew about these people. We were travelling to a Christian burial but the old gods still lingered. Lord Toli was a Dane, one of the many families who had travelled to this land from across the sea. Would he have preferred a proper pagan funeral, buried with all his possessions and great feasting? But that would have meant that the beautiful sword would be lost to mortal man. Was it still in the chest back in the village, or had someone decided it should be buried with the body? I studied the draped corpse. I wouldn't put it past the crafty old steward.

The path widened and climbed gently uphill. Other paths joined and we arrived at the settlement that controlled the entrance to Ely. Across the still water was a low hill. Elsewhere it would not have been considered a hill, but here, amongst the flat waterlogged countryside, it stood out. Scattered amongst carefully tilled fields were small huts. A fence surrounded larger buildings. This must be the abbey. As we waited for a boat to ferry us across the water, Eadric drew me to one side.

"I have dealt with the abbey for many years. Perhaps I can offer you some advice." I listened politely. "If the Abbott confirms the will of Lord Toli, you will receive the lordship of several villages. You are still young and do not want to be burdened with the running of them. I would suggest that you donate one of the properties to the abbey. You will earn their good will. I can help, of course, with the management of the rest of the lands."

I thanked him for his advice. Whether I would take it was another matter.

Eadric accompanied the body across the water, while I shared a small craft with the eels. The proximity of the water made them restless and I heard slithering within the baskets.

A small group of monks were waiting to welcome us. We walked up a well trodden track and through the gate. Eadric and the men carrying Toli's body were directed towards the chapel. The eels were taken away to the fishponds. A young monk showed the rest of us to a nearby hut.

"You will want to rest after your journey and warm yourselves at the fire. The abbot requests that you join him for the evening meal. I will return to show you the way."

It was warm in the hut and we dried our damp cloaks before the hearth. I changed into my best tunic; I had not been received by such an important man before. The monk brought food and drink for the villagers and led me across the yard. We passed a low building, a byre judging by the sound of animals shuffling in the darkness. A flicker of candlelight filtered from small windows, high in the walls of the chapel. The monk pushed open the door of what I thought was a barn.

"Here is our young warrior, newly arrived from the king's household. Come. Sit here." The man indicated an empty space beside him. Had I been brought to the labourers' hall? This couldn't be the abbot's table; everyone dressed in drab working clothes. Although my clothing was not rich, I felt overdressed.

"You were expecting something different? We don't stand on ceremony here," the man welcomed me. "I'm Leofsige. They call me Abbot. The old abbey was burnt years ago, but the title remains. We'll get things up and running again one day, God willing."

He was younger than I expected, only a touch of grey mingled with the wiry dark hair that surrounded his tonsure. Heavily muscled arms ended in rough square hands, the nails short and ingrained with dirt. He noticed my glance.

"When you work in the fields all day, it's difficult to get clean." Leofsige shrugged. "Have some food, you must be hungry after your journey."

The food was plain but plentiful, and the beer much better than I had suffered at the village. I drank deep and asked about the history of the place. History didn't interest me but I knew Wulfstan would ask me when I next saw him. I might find out more about my parents too.

"The abbey was originally founded by Etheldreda. She was a daughter of Anna, King of East Anglia and she became a saint. The monastery was for men and women. Not together of course. They had separate buildings, but she ruled over all. We don't have women here now, only the occasional visitor to pray at the shrine. The Danes burnt the church she built. We have a small chapel. We built it ourselves to shelter the shrine, but that's all."

"That must be where they took the body of Lord Toli." I recalled the glow of candlelight. "Eadric will be standing vigil over him."

"Eadric the steward. We know him well. How are you getting on with him?"

"He is very..." I searched for the right word, "efficient."

"He is that; perhaps too efficient. I suspect part of the offerings he brings go astray on the way. Never managed to prove anything, mind. He makes me feel uncomfortable, staring down that long nose of his as if I were something he'd scraped off the bottom of his shoe."

I agreed, laughing at the image.

"It has been a long time since I was in Wintanceaster," Leofsige changed the subject. "How are things at court nowadays? I hear you are making quite a name for yourself." I wondered where he had heard that.

We sat talking and drinking for some time, until I realised the fire was burning low. I found it difficult to stifle my yawns. Many of the monks had left the board and were asleep against the walls.

"I think you'd better be away to your own bed." Abbot Leofsige smiled. "Michael. Show this lad back to the visitors' hut."

12

We met in the chapel in the cold light of early morning. The stone building, not much larger than the others, was set on the very top of the hill. Inside, all was colour.

Toli lay on the bier in the centre of the chapel, surrounded by candles, and close beside stood Eadric, straight and stiff as the candles. I joined him, guilty I had spent the night in warmth and comfort. But I knew Eadric would not have wanted me there, sharing that last night with his master.

Intricate carvings and painted scenes from the life of St Etheldreda surrounded us. Richly embroidered cloths covered the altar and the shrine itself. The abbot, dressed in rich robes, was unrecognisable as the bluff companion of the previous night. Leofsige led the singing of psalms in a surprising melodious voice. He was joined by the mingled voices of monks and villagers, sending Lord Toli's soul triumphant to heaven.

We lifted the bier, and followed him outside, accompanied by the procession of monks. Behind came the members of the congregation, the whole company singing. The grave was at the edge of the hill. The fog had cleared although the sky was full of cloud. A brisk wind set the colourful vestments swirling like the flags of battle. Behind us, the rising sun broke through the clouds and our long shadows streamed across the pink tinged water into the west, the land of the dead. The body was lowered into the grave and holy water sprinkled. Solemn words were spoken. Gradually the singing faded away. We stood in silence, lost in contemplation of death, and the afterlife.

***

"Are there enough free men here to witness the event?"

The monk called Michael nodded. He passed a sheet of vellum to Leofsige, who scanned the document as if he had not read it before. "Everything is in order." He gestured for me to step forward. I was aware of everyone watching, the monks with curiosity; I could not tell what the villagers thought.

"You are Byrhtnoth, heir to Lord Toli?"

"So I have been told."

"You are not sure?" Leofsige gave me a sharp glance.

"Since the death of my mother, many years ago, I have been alone." I took a deep breath. "I was summoned back to the village. Lord Toli told me that his lands, that had been my father's lands, would come to me. He died soon after." A murmur ran through the room.

"A man's deathbed words carry great weight. Is there a witness to this speech?"

I held my breath. Eadric stepped forward.

"That is settled then. Are you of age to swear the oath?"

"I reached the age of twelve winters last spring." I stood straight.

"The lord Toli expected that you would be a grown man before he died. He would have explained to you the reasons for this document." Leofsige glanced again at the parchment. "We are not to know the reasons why God took him, before that was accomplished, but you are of an age to receive his bequest." He looked around the assembly and several men nodded their assent.

"It is very straight forward. You are to receive all the lands, properties and responsibilities of which the Lord Toli was possessed at the time of his death." My throat went dry and I swallowed, wishing I had drunk something before the ceremony. Leofsige handed the document to Michael who read out the details. Several other villages in the area were listed. There was land in Essex, and even a property in Mercia. Mills were mentioned and rights to fishing and hunting. Where had all this come from and why did I now own it?

"Approach the altar." Leofsige swept the cloth away to reveal a large box. It was made of ivory, carved with intricate figures. I think there was the image of a queen amongst the tangle of fantastic animals and strange symbols.

"This box contains the immortal bones of St Etheldreda, founder of our house. Place your hand upon it." I felt the smooth surface beneath my fingers, sensed the great power contained within.

"Do you accept this bequest and do you swear to protect and preserve the lands now in your possession? Do you swear to maintain the laws and practises of each place as appropriate and administer justice without fear or favour? Do you swear to defend the lands from attack and produce the men or arms when required by your overlord to protect the realm?"

Such responsibility almost overwhelmed me but I didn't hesitate. "I do swear all this, in the name of God and St Etheldreda."

Leofsige led me back to the centre of the chapel.

"Does every man bear witness to what has passed here?"

"We do."

"You!" Leofsige pointed at a small boy, squeezed between the legs of the men. "What is your name?"

It was the boy who had led the pony on the journey from the village.

"Edward, my lord." He shrank back as the abbot towered over him.

"A good name. Are you freeborn, Edward?" The boy nodded. "Do you know what has happened here today?" Another nod. "Tell me." The boy was silent. "It's all right, you're not in trouble." Leofsige bent and spoke quietly to him. "Just tell me what you understand."

"Him," he pointed at me, "he's a great lord." Encouraged, he added, " Doesn't look like it though."

I agreed with him.

"No, he doesn't, but he will be." Leofsige smiled. He laid his hand on Edward's head and then got back to his feet. "You are the youngest here. You will remember the longest. You will bear witness to this day for the rest of your life." Wide-eyed, the small boy nodded.

"I think that is everything, unless anyone has anything to add." Leofsige turned back to the assembly. In the silence that followed, I felt Eadric's eyes drilling into me.

"I must say something." Now everyone was staring at me. "I am not yet of an age to take control of these lands. Not yet able to defend them as a man must. I have been advised that I should donate a suitable property to you, to this abbey, so that you will... favour me."

"That is a generous gesture," Leofsige replied. "Do you have any property in mind?"

"At this time I know nothing about these lands and have no way of coming to any decision." I saw Eadric move. Leofsige held up a hand.

"Let him finish."

"If I am considered too inexperienced to make such a decision, I am also too young to judge whether the advice I have been given is correct." I paused and took a deep breath. "I will delay any action until I have visited and learnt about these places. Meanwhile, until I am capable of ruling them properly, I place them under your personal control, to supervise and maintain them in a proper manner. Only then will we discuss this further."

Silence gathered in the chapel. Abbot Leofsige considered what I had said.

"It sounds like an excellent idea. Michael, make a note on the document, and on the copy for this new landowner. Now, it's time we went and broke our fast. I'm hungry after all this business."

He flung an arm round my shoulders and escorted me from the chapel. "You will be wanting to leave soon, if you want to be back before dark."

The rest of the monks and villagers hurried behind, chattering excitedly about what had happened. Eadric stood in silence, watching, before following us out.

13

The trip back to the village was much quicker. This time I led, the boy, Edward, followed on the pony and the village men, relieved of their burden, walked briskly behind. They talked quietly about what had happened, wary of Eadric, riding his horse, silently at the end of the procession.

As we neared the village, Eadric caught up with me.

"I will ride ahead. I must prepare for your arrival; instruct the servants on how to prepare the meal."

I ignored him for a moment, shading my eyes against the fiery orange ball of the sun as it sank slowly into the mist that was gathering again across the water.

"That will not be necessary. I made the arrangements before we left; the meal will be ready by the time we arrive."

Eadric fell back to the end of the line.

"I think my sister would like to know we are coming." The whisper came from the boy on the pony. He edged closer.

"Your sister?"

"Hild in the kitchen. She's my sister. She told me to come along and look after you."

"In that case, you'd better finish your job," I laughed, "it can't be far now." Edward shook his head. "All right, go and let her know we are close, if that mount of yours can go any faster."

The boy gave the pony a kick. Its head jerked up in surprise. Another kick and its speed increased. I slowed my horse as they jogged past and disappeared into the trees ahead.

***

"I'm glad you made it back in time." Hild spoke quietly as she served me. "I don't know what I'd have done with all this food. Godric had luck with the hunting. He came back with several geese. We could have had them cold tomorrow, but they're better hot."

I agreed. The thick slices of meat oozed juices into freshly made bread. I picked up a leg and tore at the succulent flesh. "And perfectly cooked."

Someone brought a jug and a thick golden liquid was poured into my cup.

"I've been saving that mead for a special occasion. I think this is it." Hild, face flushed, dashed off with the heavy platter to serve the rest of the villagers.

As I ate, I looked around the hall, my hall now. Everyone seemed pleased with the news of their new lord. It grew quieter as people ate. I relaxed. It had been a long day, several long days, in the saddle. The heat from the hearth made me sleepy. I sipped the mead slowly, savouring the rich, honeyed taste.

I jumped as something heavy struck the table. I hadn't realised Eadric had taken up his place behind the chair.

"We have buried the old lord and now we have a new lord." His voice was loud and echoed round the hall. People looked up from their food. "He has sworn before the abbot at Ely, and placed his hand on the sacred shrine of St Etheldreda. Now he must promise to protect us and we will swear our allegiance to him."

He produced a sword. I rose slowly from the carved chair.

Blood pounded in my ears and my mouth was dry. Why had I drunk so much mead? Was this the sword? Had Eadric decided I was worthy of it? I thought it unlikely. I took the worn, scuffed scabbard and grasped the hilt. Immediately I knew this was a different sword. I controlled my expression. I would not let him make a fool of me. I drew the sword and held it up in triumph. The room erupted in cheers. When the noise died down, I lowered the weapon and placed my hand upon the blade.

"I swear to serve this village and protect it from its enemies and administer justice to all," I paused, "to do this I must return to court, to the king, to complete my training. Until that day, someone else must care for you."

I swung the sword towards Eadric. I stopped just short of the steward's face, which drained of blood. I slowly lowered the blade.

"Eadric has served you for many years as steward." Everyone in the hall held their breath. "He will continue to do so, under the supervision of the monks at Ely."

A nervous laugh emerged from the watching crowd. I stared deep into Eadric's eyes.

"You will be the first to swear allegiance to me."

Eadric hesitated and I lowered my voice until only he could hear. "Swear to serve me, now, or die."

Eadric swallowed. "I am sorry, my lord, I was overcome by the honour you do me." He placed his hand gingerly on the blade. "I swear to serve you in all things. Everything I have is yours."

"Yes it is. Remember that."

14

It felt strange, waking alone, away from the companionship of a busy hearthside. When I had been escorted to the lord's chamber the previous night it had been dark and I was tired. Deep emotion along with the rich food and drink had sent me straight to sleep. I noticed the room had been cleaned and tidied while we had been away in Ely. The last time I had entered it Lord Toli's body had lain on this very bed. I rose quickly and opened the shutters, letting in the morning light. I went straight to the large chest against the wall that contained the lord's personal possessions. Everything belonged to me now. I knew the sword was no longer there. I recalled a whispered threat from Eadric, the previous night.

"You will never find it." Or had that been a dream? I lifted the heavy wooden lid and rummaged through the contents. So much. Rich clothing and thick warm cloaks, valuable rings and cups, presented at some long ago feast. It was overwhelming. I had never owned more than the clothes I wore and they had been handed down from someone else. I had only recently got a second tunic, for feasts, and I was already growing out of it. I sorted through the pile and found one I liked: tawny brown, the wool thick and soft. It was edged with a wide band of embroidery, a pattern of bright colours, red, yellow and green. Toli had been a big man once and it fit me well. I picked out a few more pieces of clothing, a fine linen undershirt that appeared unworn, a rare luxury, and hard-wearing trousers.

I put them to one side and turned my attention to another, smaller chest. It was roughly made, but strong; well travelled, the outside stained. Was it blood or something more innocent? This chest contained arms. There was a mail shirt, rusted into a solid mass. It would need a lot of work to bring it back to use, but it was worth a small fortune. I picked up a helmet, plain but serviceable, invaluable in battle. Its battered appearance showed it had protected its owner from injury many times. I tried it on. It was a bit loose; perhaps a padded lining would help. All this I would keep. The rich clothes were good to have but with these I would be a warrior. I found an empty scabbard that I judged would fit my new seax. It had remained wrapped up in my luggage since I had received it from the king.

There was a soft knock on the door and Hild entered with a cup of ale and some bread and meat left over from the previous night. She saw the open chests.

"Have we been attacked, or are you just exploring?"

I removed the helmet and combed my fingers through my hair.

"Just the person I need. Help me sort all this out." I explained what I wanted to do.

***

We carried a selection of Lord Toli's belongings into the hall and piled them on the table. The villagers, who had been breaking their fast, watched, curious about what was to happen. I had everybody's attention.

"Last night you swore allegiance to me. This morning I will give gifts, as a good lord should." I settled into the carved chair, the gift stool. I had no idea if I was doing the right thing, but the ritual felt right. "Eadric will be first."

I beckoned the steward forward. "You served the Lord Toli well and know his things. Choose what you will." I picked up a gold vessel inlaid with jewels. "What about this cup, an old and valuable object? Or perhaps a robe – this has fine gold embroidery?"

Eadric hesitated then shook his head.

"I will take this." He laid his hand on a shabby brown cloak. It had seen better days, but the lining of soft fur gleamed in the weak morning light.

"It is cold here in winter and my lord wore it often. It served him well and will comfort me in my old age."

"I understand." I draped the heavy cloak over Eadric's shoulders. "I give you this gift in exchange for your service to me from this day forward."

I stared into his eyes. He nodded. I breathed more easily, he had accepted my authority.

I called the headmen of the village, the men who had gone to Ely as witnesses, the eldest first. I handed them their gifts. Hild stood nearby and made suggestions. She knew everyone in the village, their rank and what the most suitable gift should be.

Then Godric shambled to the chair.

"Your hunt went well. We had a good feast last night," I told him

"We were lucky," he shrugged, "a flock of geese arrived as we waited. They had flown a long way and were tired. All we had to do was pick them from the water."

"God favoured you. I thank you anyway."

He stood up straighter. "There has been no hunting here for a long time. The birds have lost their fear." He raised his voice, so that the whole hall heard what he said. "The old lord is dead and we have a new one. He is young but he will be a good lord. Luck has returned to this village." Cheers rung round the hall. Cups were filled and toasts were made.

"Thank you, Godric." I was grateful for his words and happy to put our conflict behind us. I made a decision. "As lord of this village, I am obliged to provide men to fight for the king. Two mounted men and two more horses, I understand." Eadric confirmed it. "I am one man, or I will be in a year or so. Will you be the other? To fight in the king's army and serve me at his court?"

"Me? Why me, my lord. I'm..."

"The best fighter in the village. I don't think there is anyone here who would dispute that?" Godric's friends cheered. Laughter, mingled with a few groans, came from the rest of the room. "That's settled then. Unless you would rather stay here and work in the fields?"

"Oh no, my lord." He dropped to his knees in front of me. "I swear to serve you, always"

I presented him with his gift. It was Toli's own seax. The blade was long but rusty. It had lain unused for months, if not years. The hilt was covered in gold and inlaid with garnets. It was a beautiful weapon. I would have expected to keep this for myself, but I already had the seax given to me by the king. That I had earned by my own effort, not handed down to me by someone I barely knew. I wondered, for a moment, if it had belonged to my father. I dismissed the thought. I had a sword now, although not the one I longed for. I was too young yet for that. I would have to earn it for myself .

"Use this in my service," I told Godric.

He took the weapon, turned it in his hand, admiring the decoration, and stuttered his thanks. He stood up and moved to stand at my right hand.

"We need someone else, someone to help with the horses and other jobs. Do you have any suggestions?" Godric surveyed the hall. His friends waved and shouted, desperate to be chosen.

"Can I come? Please let me come with you."

It was Edward. The small boy had been sitting close by,

watching the gift giving. "I'm good with horses, everyone will tell you that."

"I don't know," I said, "you're bit young to be leaving the village."

"I'm not much younger than you were when you left. Please?"

"That is true." I didn't want one of Godric's companions, he needed a fresh start, away from his gang of troublemakers. "We will have to ask your family. I understand your sister is responsible for you."

"She'll be glad to get rid of me. I'm always getting into scrapes," he pleaded with a cheerful grin.

"He is young," Hild agreed, "but he needs someone to keep him out of mischief. You will look after him?"

"Of course I will," I promised. "What about you, Godric? Do you think we can cope with him?"

"I think we can knock him into shape." He saw Hild's worried face. "I didn't mean it like that. We'll protect him from any harm."

"You had both better go and get ready. We'll leave at first light tomorrow."

I finished handing out the gifts and then announced I would inspect the village lands. My role as lord was tiring and I needed to get out of the crowded hall into the fresh air.

Eadric took charge and showed me the boundaries and explained who farmed the adjoining lands. The village elders accompanied us and most of the rest of the village trailed along behind. Eadric said it was good for everyone to know which was our land and which was not. It prevented arguments. Soon he was going into the boring details of which crops were grown where and how many animals were grazed on which pasture. I nodded politely, trying not to yawn. How interested Wulfstan would have been. He would have asked questions about everything. I realised how much I missed him and the other boys. I would be glad to get back; I had so much to tell them.

15

Wulfstan's head pounded. He opened his eyes slowly and focused on the trees above, waiting for them to stop moving. He tried to get up. A wave of pain swept over him and he fell back onto the ground. He turned his head carefully, concentrating on the stones in the wall beside him, until the world steadied again. Had a Roman ghost attacked him? He was not sure that he believed in ghosts. Perhaps it was some animal; the boar they had been hunting?

Gritting his teeth, he attempted to sit up. It took him a while to work out what he saw, before he let himself lay back. His left foot was pointing in a strange direction and the white of shattered bone was visible within a mass of bloody flesh. Torn between vomiting or sinking back into the blackness, he swallowed hard and forced himself to think.

He would not be walking away from this place. He ignored the thought that he might never walk anywhere, ever again. He was alone in the forest; nobody knew where he was. It was late in the day. The sun, which had been high in the sky, was now low and its slanting rays lingered on the ragged stones on the top of the wall. It was cold and getting colder.

He heard a movement and turned his head. Was it friend or

foe? Sleipnir stood nearby. A friend then, but what could he do? Wulfstan called and eventually the horse approached. Something had scared him. His eyes rolled and he tossed his head nervously. Wulfstan saw blood on his hooves. Had someone hurt him? Or had he fought off the attacker? Wulfstan couldn't think more about what had happened. He needed to work out how to survive. He persuaded the horse close enough to grab the dangling reins, but there was no way he could get onto the animal. He slumped back down. He shivered and the movement caused ripples of pain to run through his whole body. To distract himself, he thought about other times, good times. Then he remembered the trick he had taught Sleipnir. It had worked in front of the king. Would he remember? Would he obey?

He tugged gently on the reins. "Down." The horse stood motionless, but his ears twitched at the words. More encouragement and he slowly bent first one front leg and then the other.

"Lie down," Wulfstan pleaded, until the horse was lying close beside him. He seemed to sense what was required and leaned his head protectively across Wulfstan's chest. Wulfstan wrapped his arms around the broad, warm neck and buried his face in the thick shaggy coat. He smelled the familiar horse smell of his friend and felt the thud of his hot horse blood. The life-giving heat drowned out the shivers and pain. He sighed and surrendered to the darkness.

He roused when the horse stood, disturbed by the sound of barking dogs. He was aware of shouts, blazing lights, pain, as he was loaded onto a makeshift litter. Then he was flying through the air. It was strangely soothing as he watched the branches pass overhead, flickering in the light of burning torches. The only disturbance was the sound of someone screaming. He wished it would go away, but it continued for a long time.

16

In the east the sun was rising. Godric and Edward were still arguing about the best way to load the packhorse. The old chest that contained the lord's war gear was balanced precariously on the animal's back. It started to slip and the horse stepped forward. Edward tried to tell Godric what to do, but he insisted he knew better. The rest of the village were helpfully offering advice.

"Get it sorted now, or I leave without you. Edward has done this before. Just follow his instructions, Godric."

Hild held the pony's head and soon the pack was loaded. She added a bundle of food for the journey. Eadric approached. What did he want? It was too early to deal with any more snide remarks from the steward.

"Good morning, Eadric." I tried to be polite. "You will be glad to see the back of us."

Eadric stood uncertain, then made a decision. He caught my eye then returned his gaze to my horse's neck.

"So like your father." Edric forced out the words. "Byrhthelm; his name was Byrhthelm." He scurried away without another word.

I watched him go. Was this the truth, or was he misleading me again? I couldn't think about it now. Godric and Edward were mounted and ready.

"About time. Let's go." I urged my horse forward. We trotted down the track and the road south.

***

The novelty of the journey soon wore off. Once we reached the old road they called Ermine Street, the way was wide and straight. There were few travellers at this time of year and the only obstacles lay in avoiding the ruts and potholes.

"Last one to that tree ahead, cooks the meal tonight." My horse leapt forward. Godric, jerked from a half doze, was not far behind. We reached the target and waited for Edward.

"It's not fair. Why did you do that? I never have a chance. Someone else should take a turn in leading this horse." Edward jerked at the leading rein. "I'll leave it behind next time."

"Don't worry," Godric laughed, "I'll give you a hand when we stop. Perhaps I can find you something fresh to cook."

I ignored the bickering. I had seen something on the road ahead. A long string of packhorses had stopped. One near the front of the column was lying motionless on the ground. Guards had turned towards the edge of the forest. Nervously they drew weapons. Men emerged from the trees. They were thin and their clothes ragged, but knives glittered in the low winter sun.

"Robbers!"

I drew my sword, checked the others had their weapons out, and set my horse galloping down the slope. Godric and Edward followed, shouting. A man with a thick staff swung it backwards and forwards, preventing the thieves from approaching. The rest of the defenders milled about, well away from the action. The leader screamed at the attackers, but was soon surrounded. One of the forest men ducked under the moving staff. Distracted by our approach, he was felled by the backswing and fell to the ground. His companions, seeing us arrive, slipped away and disappeared back into the forest like the cowards they were.

The man confronted us, staff swinging. I dragged my horse to a halt and lowered my sword.

"Are you all right? We saw the attack and came to help."

"Help." The man lowered the staff. He broke into a wide smile. "I grateful for your help." He was a big man, made larger by the layers of clothing he wore. Each layer was a different colour, or patchwork of colours. He threw back the hood of a striped travelling cloak. He had a bright blue cloth wrapped around his head, the end hanging over his shoulder.

"I am Coela. It is not my real name. It is what you call me in this country. It is your word for person with dark face?" He gestured towards his swarthy features. His eyes, dark as blackberries, shone in the folds of fat cheeks and his large hooked nose loomed above his broad grin. "And what is the name of my brave rescuer?"

I glanced towards the trees to check the thieves had gone and slid my sword back in the scabbard. "I am Byrhtnoth. This is Godric, and the boy is Edward. We are travelling to Wintanceaster." I dismounted. "Can we help you with anything else?"

"You are a boy as well, I think," he paused at my expression, "but nearly a man, and a brave man."

The guards gathered round sheepishly.

"Why don't you defend me and my property? I pay you enough silver." He prodded the body sprawled on the ground in front of him with his foot. "Get rid of this rubbish."

The men rushed to pick up the body. Brains spewed from the head as they carried it away. Coela approached the injured horse. An arrow had caught it in the stomach and blood pulsed slowly from the wound, together with a foul smell. Coela bent and stroked the muzzle of the doomed animal. He muttered a few words in his own language, then drew a knife and slit the horse's throat. When he stood up, his eyes were damp. "Help me get the packs off. She has been with me a long time. Never complained. I don't know where I'm going to put everything."

"We can help." I told Edward to take our gear off the spare mount. "There's not much. Distribute it between the other horses. Godric will help." As the packs were secured, I asked Coela where he was going. "You are heading to Lundenburh?"

"It is not many miles now," he said. "We were thinking to stop for the night, but I think we should leave this place."

I agreed. "I don't think they will attack again, but best to find somewhere a bit less exposed."

As we rode slowly south, I asked him how far they had travelled. It was unusual to find traders on the road at this time of year.

"I wouldn't be travelling if I could help it. We were delayed by the fighting in the north. We thought there would be peace after the great battle of Brunanburh, but still they fight. The Danes took all my best guards for their army, so I have to lie low until the roads are safe again. I thought things were going well; I lowered my guard too soon. I should have known the most dangerous part of the journey was close to Lunden. The evil men strike when you lower your guard."

"Did you see any of the fighting?"

"We kept well out of the way. Do you think this is good place to camp? The animals are getting tired."

"It's as good as we're likely to find." I looked around. "We'll camp over there."

The long train of horses left the road. With the ease of long practice, Coela's servants located and erected a small tent. The packs were piled up beside it and a fire was lit. A vessel was filled with water from a nearby steam and placed on the fire. I offered Coela a flagon of ale.

"I thank you, but no. I have my own drink." The container of water on the fire steamed in the cold air. From the depths of his clothing Coela brought out a small bowl and a bag. He opened the bag and sprinkled some dried leaves into the bowl. We watched as he added some of the boiling water. "Just mint." He swirled the contents around and tasted it. "It is better with honey, but we have run out." He blew gently on the liquid and took another sip. "That's better."

"My sister does that," Edward said, "it's medicine, different leaves for different illnesses. Always tastes horrible though."

"Do you know what leaves she uses?" Coela asked him.

"No, but she drags me out at all hours to collect plants. She says some have to be collected at night, some during the day. I think there's something to do with the moon as well."

"She is very knowledgeable lady, your sister." Coela called one of his servants, who brought a bag of dried peas. He dropped a handful into the container of water that remained on the fire. Another bag was produced and a few pieces of dried mushroom were added to the pot.

"She's a good cook as well," I said.

"Yes. This is some of hers." Godric had found a piece of bacon and was cutting thin slices and laying them on the hot stones around the fire. "Do you want some?" he asked Coela.

"That is the meat of a pig, I think. Thank you, but I cannot eat it. My god does not allow it."

"Which god is that?" Some people still worshiped the old gods. Places where Christianity had not reached, or which had rejected the teachings of the priests.

"He has no name that we can use, but I think he is a part of your god. We read some of the same books. Your priests tell you what you can and can't eat on holy days. Our priests tell us what we can eat. It is hard sometimes, but it is what we must do."

"You say that God sets different rules in different places?" Edward was puzzled. "In your land you can't eat pork? Here we eat fish on Fridays."

"Sounds to me it is the priests who decide the rules," I said.

"The boy makes a very good point. Perhaps it depends on the place, not the person. As your St Ambrose says 'When in Rome...'"

"But we're not in Rome. Are we?"

We all laughed at Edward.

The bacon was crisping on the stones. The delicious smell rose around us.

"I think I will try some of your pig meat, just a small piece. You can share my meal. Then we are proper friends, yes? If my god disapproves, I'm sure he will find a way to punish me." Coela laughed cheerfully.

"We have some bread as well. It's a bit dry." Godric tapped the lump with the hilt of his knife. It made a hollow sound. "Shall I add it to the pot?"

"Please, go ahead."

17

As we loaded the pack horses early the next morning, I asked what goods they carried.

"This and that; everything and anything. Whatever people are selling cheap in one place that can be sold elsewhere for more. These," he patted the bulging packages hanging either side of the small horse, "are cloaks. The best cloaks are made of the best wool, and that comes from the north of this country. They will travel on my ship across the water to Frankia. Perhaps I will sell them there. If the price is not good, I will take them further south until I get the price I want. Perhaps they will travel further, with another merchant, even to Byzantium."

"Byzantium. I have heard that is a wonderful place." I wondered if I would ever see it. "Have you been there? Is that your home?"

"My home is nowhere and everywhere. This year it is in your town of Lundenburh. Next year, who knows? Wherever there is a profit to be made. Perhaps Byzantium. Do you want to come? I need men who can fight, to guard my goods."

"We'll come as far as Lundenburh. Then I must return to the king's court."

"Perhaps we will meet again there. That is my first destination when I come to this country; the best market for the goods I bring. Fine silks from the distant east, to deck your beautiful women and precious stones to hang round their necks. I bring herbs and spices to flavour your food. Other things you cannot imagine. Tell me what you want and I will bring it."

"I don't think I could afford anything like that."

"Blades for weapons?" Coela was an expert trader. He knew his customers.

"I saw a blade recently." I paused, remembering it. "A sword, the most beautiful I have ever seen. Old, I think. I was told it belonged to my father."

"It is not yours?"

"I must earn it. That is why I have to go to Wintanceaster, to become a great warrior."

"If you become trader, you will be rich and buy any sword you want."

"I don't want any sword. I want that sword. Anyway trade is not an honourable profession."

"Perhaps not. But it is lucrative."

Sometimes I was still a boy, blurting out the first words in my head. "Sorry, I didn't mean..."

"Think nothing of it. I am used to such talk."

**

Later I asked Coela about the fighting in the north.

"You people, always fighting. You have such a beautiful land here. It is cold now, but in its season fertile; so productive. There is more than enough for everybody, but you destroy it with your fighting."

"There was a treaty. After Brunanburh, everyone swore to keep the peace. Athelstan made the country one land. It should have been for ever."

"But Athelstan died, young they say, and no heir to take his place. Strength is needed for peace."

"Edmund, his half brother was his heir. He is a man. He fought at Athelstan's side."

"A man, but only eighteen winters. Older men must test their strength against him."

"He beat them though. The boroughs belong to Mercia again; part of England. There will be peace now." I was sure of it.

"You are disappointed?"

"Of course, how can I win glory if the country is at peace?"

"Don't worry, boy. There will always be fighting. A few powerful men will become rich and others will envy them. Meanwhile the common people suffer. Even if they are not called to fight and die, their animals and crops are destroyed and they starve."

I remembered the village. People near starvation because one man took all the resources. It was my village now and I had sworn to defend it. When had everything become so complicated?

"Is there no fighting in your land then?" I asked him.

"There is always fighting. We must try our best to survive. And sell our goods to the winners."

***

From the top of a hill we saw the city spread before us. Beyond was the river, gleaming bright. It twisted its way like a great serpent into the heart of the country. In the distance were more hills. Coela pointed to the west, where a scatter of wooden buildings huddled at the rivers edge.

"That's Lundenwic, where the Saxons built their town. Your ancestors didn't like to live in the Roman remains. Perhaps scared of the ghosts."

"I'm not going anywhere there's ghosts," Edward said.

"That was long ago. The ghosts have gone now." Coela pointed down the road ahead. "That's the old city, Lundenburh, on the hill. It was abandoned for years, but people are moving back. They need the space."

When we got closer, I saw the Roman ruins, like bones sticking out of an old carcass. What appeared at first to be maggots consuming the body, gradually became men. They teemed over the buildings. Here a collection of stones was being rebuilt as a wall. There, precarious wooden scaffolding clung to a building and men, like ants, carried loads to the top.

The road became busy. Most of the traffic was leaving the city. Empty carts rattled over the rutted surface. Women trudged along, some with heavy bundles, others more cheerful. They shouted at Coela and his long train of pack animals.

"You're late for the market. Everything is sold."

"Perhaps they've arrived early for tomorrow."

"They won't let you in with all those animals," one warned.

Coela just waved at everyone.

"Where are they all going?" I asked him.

"To their homes. They live in the surrounding farms and villages. They bring goods to market in the morning, and go home in the evening. If you see what the women are carrying back, you can tell what is not wanted in the city, at least today."

The massive gate of red brick glowed in the low setting sun. The walls ran to left and right. In places brickwork had crumbled and been patched with wooden stakes. Elsewhere old wood had been burnt, and then repaired with new. Many enemies had attacked these walls over the years. Guards were preparing to close the heavy oak gates.

"You're too late. You must wait outside until tomorrow."

"Hello my friend." Coela rode up to the captain of the guard. "The sun has not yet reached the horizon. I'm sure the authorities would not approve of their laws to be broken."

There was a whispered conversation and coins changed hands.

"Be quick about it."

The column of horses threaded through the narrow gap and the gates slammed shut behind us.

It was already dark within the city. The walls and tall buildings cut out the remaining daylight. The roadways were narrow and crowded with people. Lamps were being lit in houses and we saw life continue inside as we passed. Some shopkeepers were closing for the night; others continued their business. A tavern, close to the gate, was already busy. Customers spilt out into the street, shouting cheerfully.

"Keep a close eye on the packs. It only takes one slash of a knife and something is gone. I spent enough time gathering these goods, I'm not going to lose them now."

Godric and I drew our weapons. Even Edward rode up and down, watching anyone who came too close. It felt good to be doing something. The streets became wider near the centre of the town. The houses were large, some surrounded by their own walls. A richly dressed man noticed us passing.

"Is that you, Coela? We expected you long ago. Thought you must have died in the north. What have you brought back from your travels?"

"Let me get home first. I must unpack. Come to dinner in a day or so. I will send invitation. I promise, you will have first pick." The man waved and disappeared down a side street.

The streets narrowed again and darkness closed in. Most of the properties here were workshops, now shut up for the night. In a few, a glimmer of light was visible behind a shuttered window. Now and then a whiff of the sea mingled with the smell of rubbish underfoot. We were near the river. A sleek brown shape emerged from the shadows. It stopped and turned towards us. It showed its sharp white teeth, shining in the gloom, as if grinning at us, then disappeared.

"A rat. Hate them, but it proves the place is thriving." Coela turned into a narrow alley. "Nearly there." The packs brushed the rough walls on either side. A damp breeze carried the scent of the river and we heard the gentle lap of water. Coela stopped at a sturdy wooden door and struck it several times with his staff.

"Open the gate. I'm home. Hurry up." The door opened to

reveal a young man. He bowed deeply and talked swiftly in some foreign language. Coela held up a hand. "How many times do I have to tell you? We try and speak the language of this country, especially when we have visitors."

The young man noticed us and bobbed his head. He shouted in the direction of the surrounding buildings.

"Come quickly. Uncle's home."

We dismounted and the man stood aside as we led the horses through the gate. Out of nowhere, more young men appeared, some carrying flaming torches. The flickering light revealed a large yard. On three sides were arched openings, some closed off by locked doors, others open. On the fourth side stood a high wooden fence. As each packhorse entered the yard, one of the men seized it. Coela directed each to one of the openings, where the packs were removed and stored. The gear from the horses went one way and the animals were herded through another gate. A boy took the reins of our mounts.

"Need rest and good feed, I think." He followed the pack animals. Doors slammed. There was silence. We stood with Coela in the middle of the yard as the young men lined up at the side and bowed.

"Very impressive," Godric whispered. I tried to look as if I were comfortable here, in this strange man's home, it was like nothing I'd ever seen before.

Coela inspected the line, exchanging a few words with one man, nodding at a boy.

"Very good. We will sort things out properly tomorrow. You may go."

18

In the central wall was a narrow doorway. Coela produced a key and led us up a flight of steep steps. At the top, another door opened out into an enclosed courtyard. Large pots were scattered around. The skeletons of trees emerged from some. In one corner was a sunken area, empty but for a puddle of water and a few dead leaves.

"Not much at the moment, but it is pleasant in summer." Coela threw open a pair of wide doors and it was as if that summer had already arrived.

There was a riot of light and warmth. Scents assailed our nostrils, some familiar, others more exotic. Flowers climbed the walls; so realistic that it took some time to realise they were only painted there. Cloths of every hue hung from the walls and large colourful cushions littered the floor. From them rose a flock of women, like brightly plumaged birds. They descended on Coela, screaming and cooing. When they noticed our presence, they retreated, pulling veils across their faces.

"Do not be afraid, these are my friends. I owe my life to them." Some of the girls whispered amongst themselves and looked curiously towards us.

"Godric. Close your mouth and behave yourself." I turned

to Coela. "These ladies are," I searched for the right word, "your nieces?"

"Wives, sisters, daughters and yes, I think some are nieces. I lose track sometimes." He beckoned one of the women forward. She was tall and stately, dark eyes ringed with black paint. "This is my first wife. I'm afraid she doesn't know your language." He spoke a few words to her. She nodded and after giving us a careful inspection, swept from the room. "She is in charge of my whole household. She very good cook."

The next woman he beckoned over had a voluptuous figure, barely contained by her clothing. Dark red hair tumbled down her back and her pouting red mouth was clearly visible through a transparent veil. She twined herself round Coela. "This is my second wife. She is good... at other things." He patted her rump and peeled her reluctantly from his body. "Later," he whispered to her, as she flounced to a cushion and arranged her body to best advantage. The sight enthralled even Edward. "Not a thought in her brain," Coela shook his head, "but that body... "

"Sorry I was slow to greet you. I was resting." Another woman had entered the room. She spoke in a soft, clear voice and her blond hair hung in a thick plait over her shoulder. The end rested on the bulge of her stomach.

"Ah my dear. You must be near your time." She glanced at us and a blush warmed her pale face. "This is my third wife. She teaches me your language and produces Saxon children, to run my business when I am gone."

"You have three wives?" Godric had regained his voice but he couldn't hide his astonishment.

"Of course. My religion permits a man to have four wives, if he can afford them. That is why I have to work so hard." He shrugged. "This servant will show you to your quarters." A man appeared behind us. "We are all tired. Food and drink will be brought to you. We will meet in the morning."

The man led us along a passage and into another room. Beds had been prepared and in the centre of the room was a wooden barrel. Servants were pouring steaming jugs of hot water into it.

I unbuckled my sword belt and dropped it onto one of the beds. "Good, a proper hot bath."

I watched as Godric and Edward took in the luxurious surroundings.

"Do you bathe often, at the king's court?" Godric asked.

"No. And if I do, I'm at the end of the queue and the water is cold and scummy." I dumped the last of my clothes in a heap on the floor and lowered myself into the fragrant water. It was a tight fit and my knees stuck up above the surface. Some of the water sloshed over the edge and formed a pool on the floor. It brought out patterns formed from small tiles that covered that area. I leaned back against the side of the cloth-lined bath and closed my eyes.

"I'm not sure about this." I heard Godric whisper to Edward.

A servant gathered up my clothes from the floor and left the room. Another attempted to help Godric undress. Edward sat on one of the beds and slowly removed his boots.

"This floor is warm." He leaned forward and put his hand flat against the tiles. "Definitely warm. How do they do that?"

"It must be some kind of magic." Godric was down on his hands and knees, feeling the floor.

There was no hearth in the room. There must have been at some time, in one place the tiles were cracked and burned. The only light was from oil lamps scattered around.

"Come back. Where are you going with those?" Godric had noticed the servant disappearing through the door with his clothes.

"For tonight." The man pointed at a pile of clean linen tunics on a shelf. He held the dirty well-worn clothes away from him and sniffed. "These need wash."

"Stop making a fuss, Godric. Just enjoy it." I stared up at the arched roof. Here and there patches of plaster clung to the walls and pictures of fish swam above me, moving in the flickering light. "This house must have been built by the Romans. I heard once that they had a system of heating their houses. Perhaps everyone has houses like this where Coela comes from. We'll ask him later."

I yawned, nearly asleep. I ducked my head under the water, and reluctantly stood up.

"You go next, Edward. There'll be no water left once Godric gets in." I was dressing, when a young woman entered the room. Godric stood rooted to the spot, desperately scanning the room for somewhere to hide. The woman put down a tray of food, looked the naked Godric up and down and gave a nod of approval. At the door she met another woman carrying a large jug and cups. They exchanged a few words and giggled. The second woman, not much more than a girl, also inspected Godric. His face had turned bright red. She put her hand to her mouth and followed the other woman out. We listened as the sound of laughter and chatter disappeared into the distance.

"I think they were impressed, Godric." I sat down and inspected the food. "Hurry up with your bath or there won't be anything left."

19

Wulfstan lay in the hut. He stared up at the thatch. The daylight filtered through the gaps and offered a little illumination. He knew what was there and no longer cared if he saw it or not. Was it better when it was cold and the thatch froze, or when it warmed slightly and water dripped onto everything? It didn't matter. He was too chilled to care.

He did not remember being brought here. All he remembered was the pain, like a maddened wolf tearing and ripping at his legs. He had waited for it to consume his whole body but it had withdrawn. Now, it was only when he moved suddenly that the wolf leapt from the shadows and gnawed at his bones for a while.

People had visited in the beginning. His companions were sympathetic and talked about what they were doing, but when the talk turned to the future, the conversation would die. They would make their excuses and leave. When people stopped coming, the fire had died and no food was delivered. He had tried catching the drips of water in an empty bowl, but he had become bored with that.

He knew why they avoided him. Although still boys, they had been taught that honour was everything. Failure was impossible and imperfection was a stain on the whole group. He wondered if

Byrhtnoth, his greatest friend, would have behaved the same way. He was the best, the brightest of them all and would not tolerate failure. Wulfstan was glad he was absent. He could not have stood his friend turning his back on him.

When the last of them left, he had heard them speaking outside. They did not know he heard, or perhaps they did and didn't care. One of them, Elfhere, he recognised the voice, said "He'd be better off dead."

Wulfstan agreed and so he would die.

As he waited, he wondered why whoever had done this to him, had not killed him outright. Who hated him that much? They had all blamed Sleipnir for the accident, but Wulfstan knew that he would not have done it. What had happened to his horse? He hoped they had not killed him. Even a horse as ugly as him must be useful for something. He remembered the competition they had won together, only a few weeks ago. Even now he could hear the cheering crowds and how the king had honoured him. How the fates must have been laughing.

He knew that he was not as tall and strong as the others, but he had found a place in the world, a home. Now it had been taken away. He remembered the time before. Before he had arrived outside the mead hall and met Byrhtnoth. The time he had been alone. When he had to fight or beg for scraps of food. Sleep under a hedge or on some rocky shore. He still had hope then. He could not do that again, not crippled and a butt of every man's scorn.

He remembered further back. How had he forgotten? There had been just the two of them.

***

"Please don't cry, little one, I'll find you something to eat."

He thought that there would be plenty of food left after Mama died, although she had eaten little enough herself. She lay down one night and never woke up.

"See the mound on the other side of the clearing? She is there. When spring comes we will put some flowers on it."

Perhaps his sister would be walking by then and they could go and find help. She was too heavy for him to carry, but already she stood up if he held her hands.

Mama had told him to protect his sister, but now he had to leave her. He gave her a piece of cloth to suck. It would keep her quiet, while he went to get them something to eat. He found a village. It was late and everyone was indoors, in the warm. He crept between the huts, searching for food. He found the rubbish pit, a few rotten vegetables. He stuffed them inside his tunic. There was a dog, tied outside one of the huts. It was asleep. There was a bone, still with scraps of meat attached. His mouth watered as the smell drifted towards him. He moved closer, his hand reached for the bone. The dog woke, it growled, a low rumbling like the sound in his stomach. He hesitated, too long. The door opened. The dog barked. He ran. Heard voices. Ran faster. More dogs barking as he zigzagged through the darkening trees. When he was unable to run any more, he hid.

Through the long night, he hid. Why hadn't he grabbed the bone? He felt the vegetables, slimy against his chest, but he mustn't eat them. They were for his little sister.

***

He tried to find his way back, but he was lost. He roamed the forest for days, searching for her, but she was lost to him. He had thought of her, all alone, crying for someone to help her. When he realised she must have perished, of hunger, or by animals, he lay, huddled beneath a bush in the forest. He cried for a long time, but in the end he stopped, and carried on with his life.

He lay there, remembering. If he had had the energy, he would have laughed at the fact that he would die in the same way as her. He wondered if the hunger and cold would get him first, or the animals. He heard then in the darkness. Not the wolf, but the real little animals that rustled in the thatch and pit patted their way across the floor. Sometimes he felt the touch of their fur in the night.

Perhaps he had been meant to die with her, he had just been delayed a while. Carefully he turned to face the wall. The wolf raised its head but then lowered it again. Wufstan felt the tears on his face, warm on his cold cheeks, as he searched for his sister.

"Where are you, little one? I'm coming."

He hoped he would recognise her when they met again.

20

The room was hot and stuffy. The others were still asleep. Our clothes had been cleaned and returned to the room. I dressed quickly and went in search of some fresh air. I found the courtyard we had crossed the previous night. A row of arches framed the grey light of dawn that was reflected from the river below. As I approached I saw that someone was sitting on a bench within a shadowed arch. I backed away.

"I'm sorry. I didn't realise anyone was here."

"Don't go. I would welcome some company."

I recognised the quiet voice of Coela's wife. The one introduced as number three. She re-arranged her warm cloak to hide the bulk of her pregnancy.

"I find it difficult to sleep in my present condition. It is peaceful out here, away from other people."

"It must be very..." I searched for the right word.

"Oppressive?"

"I was going to say warm." I cursed my lack of tact. "It is very cold out here."

A breeze had sprung up, stirring the dead leaves in the paved yard into a frantic dance.

"You don't know how wonderful it is to feel wind on your face."

She leaned further out the window and closed her eyes. The air caught a wisp of hair that had escaped the hood of the cloak. She lifted a thin, white hand and pushed the hood back. Her smooth hair shone silver in the early morning light. She opened her eyes and smiled sadly.

"Do you not go out much?"

She shook her head, and shifted her position.

"Not now. And not much before." She gave me a shy glance. "It is a long time since I had a conversation in my own language. Everyone here is very friendly. Some try to speak English to me, but it is too much of an effort."

"How long have you been in this house? How did you meet Coela?"

She pulled the hood back over her head, her face in shadow again.

"I don't remember how long. I was a young girl. A slave. He saw me in the market place and bought me to serve his women. When I became old enough, he took me. When I became pregnant, he married me. I am lucky."

"But are you happy?" It didn't seem to be much of a life.

"It is not my place to be happy, or unhappy. I serve my master." She stared across the river, towards the hills and forests beyond. "It's just," her voice so low I barely caught it, "sometimes I wish I had a normal life, with a proper husband. Someone like you perhaps, to work the land and live in freedom." She gave a sad smile. "But how many people live like that anyway?"

Before I could think of a reply, the doors opened and Coela appeared.

"What are you doing out here? It's far too cold." He pulled his cloak tighter. "Come inside and have something to eat. Are you feeling well, my wife?"

"I am fine; a little uncomfortable perhaps. Help me up, please?" She offered me her hand. She was nearly as tall as me. For a moment, she stared straight into my eyes, then she squeezed my hand. Her fingers were very cold.

"Thank you." Her lashes veiled the soft grey eyes and she turned to her husband. She rested her hand on her round stomach.

"It will not be long now. I must get my strength up. Do we have any eggs?"

"For you, anything. Now come into the warm." As he opened the door and ushered her through, Coela looked back at me. "Come along, it will be a busy day."

I told him I would follow shortly. I went to the edge of the courtyard and looked out across the river. Morning had arrived and small boats moved across the surface of the water, bobbing over the small white waves. Then I went in for breakfast.

***

People rushed to and fro. Bread and the other food on the table had been pushed to one side. Clerks sorted small pieces of parchment and scribbled notes on wax tablets. Godric and Edward were sheltering in a corner.

"Where have you been? Did you manage to track down one of those girls?" Godric leered, "Did you have a good night?"

I ignored him. "What's happening?"

"We don't know." Edward handed me some bread. "Everybody was eating, then there was shouting. Did you do anything?"

"No. Anyway, they're ignoring us. Can you find some ale to go with this bread?"

Edward fetched a jug and more food. Coela hurried up. His beard had been trimmed short and his hairless head shone.

"My friends! I apologise for the commotion. My son tells me that the weather has changed. Conditions are good for sailing. We must load the ship and depart. Other merchants prepare to leave and we cannot let them beat us to the markets in Frankia." A servant offered him a cup of fruit juice. He swallowed it quickly and handed it back. "I planned to show you the town, but I have too much to do here. I don't know if there is anyone else who can take you." He looked round at the frantic activity.

"Don't trouble yourself," I told him with relief, "I'm sure we can find our own way around."

Godric nodded. Edward shrugged, his mouth full of food.

"Are you sure?" Coela frowned, and then relaxed. "It is not that big a place. If you lose yourselves, just head towards the river. We are just down stream from that pile of rotten wood they call a bridge. Or just mention my name. Everyone knows me."

Someone approached with a handful of documents and a worried expression.

"I must go. We will meet later for the evening meal. I will introduce you to my sons."

***

"Which way?" The door slammed shut behind us.

"I hear some hammering in that direction." Godric pointed. "Perhaps there are swords we can look at."

It sounded like a good idea. "Let's go."

We visited several forges and explored more of the town. We watched the butchers, efficiently dividing carcasses into smaller useful joints, then pushed our way through the crowds to an area of better shops. Shoemakers and sellers of cloth, dark shops with dried plants hanging from the ceiling and boxes of mysterious medicines. Pigs mingled with the shoppers, snuffling through the rubbish that littered the ground.

The inhabitants were as exotic as the contents of the shops. Saxons and Danes, from the local shires, mingled in apparent peace. Veiled ladies in rich clothing jostled with rough women in from the country. Children darted through the crowds and crippled beggars sat in the mud. We marvelled at men with faces black as night and fur-clad giants from the frozen north. We stopped when we came to a massive circular building. We gazed up at the crumbling rows of arches that rose towards the sky and speculated what it had been used for.

Finally we noticed the sun was getting lower. "Come on, I want to have a look at the bridge on the way back."

***

The tide was out and water moved sluggishly between broad muddy banks. We walked cautiously out onto the wooden road that led across the great river. Some of the boards were old, spongy with rot. In places, the bridge was burnt black, like charcoal. Elsewhere, whole sections shone bright with new wood. We leaned over the edge to see enormous tree trunks emerging from the riverbed, as if they had grown there. Dark with age, they were wet from the water that had recently receded. Weed hung down, decorated with the rubbish brought there by the changing tides. The carcass of some dead animal, a dog perhaps, fell from the post into the shallow water. Birds gathered and squabbled over the feast, screeching loudly.

We dodged through the travellers to the other side of the structure. The crowds parted as a messenger on horseback galloped through, hooves echoing on the wooden surface. He would be heading for Wintanceaster. What news was he carrying? I turned back to the river, squinting into the low sun. To the west boats were pulled up onto the shore. Nearby, smoke rose from a collection of huts. Beyond, the river disappeared round a bend.

"It must be Lundenwic, the old town, that Coela mentioned."

"Do they bring those ships under the bridge?" Edward craned over to study the gaps between the massive piles.

"If they're small enough, and only when the tide is right." I had heard that the bridge was used to defend the city. "Large war boats can't get through to attack the lands up the river. But an army can cross the bridge from the south to attack the city."

"Perhaps that's why it's been burnt." Edward wiped his hand down his tunic, leaving a black mark.

"We'd better be getting back. Coela said something about a feast tonight."

21

"Please be seated."

Coela indicated a pile of cushions. Other men reclined round the low table covered with dishes of food. One sipped from a glass and studied us carefully over the rim. Coela clapped his hands and servants entered with jugs.

"Wine? Or perhaps some fruit juice for the little one?" Edward held out his glass for wine, but changed his mind when Godric cast him a fierce glance.

"Have you had a good day? Have you seen all the sights of the town?" Coela asked as we settled back against the cushions.

"I think so. We've walked far enough. It's an amazing place." I told him of the blacksmith who had told us all about swords. We had even helped in the making of one.

"There were so many people," Godric said, "there can never have been so many in one place."

"Not as many as some places I've been, but for this country it is big. May I introduce my eldest son?"

The man sitting opposite put down his glass carefully and inclined his head.

"I am happy to meet you. I wish to thank you for coming to the aid of my father. We would miss him greatly." He gave a thin smile.

"These are my sons. They all speak English. I have trained them well," Coela explained.

I acknowledged each in turn. "I see that they all have your good looks."

Coela roared with laughter and the sons laughed politely. He selected something from the laden table.

"Please, help yourself. You must be hungry. Is the wine to your satisfaction? It is the same that I supply to the king."

I took a mouthful from the glass and choked. Godric thumped me on the back.

"I apologise. I am not accustomed to drinking the King's wine." I told him that I sat too far down the royal table to be given anything but ale. "Mead on special occasions." I took another smaller sip. The warmth spread through my body. "It is very good."

I inspected the table, laden with small bowls. What to taste first?

"Try this." Coela passed me a dish. "It is one of my favourites; the meat of sheep, chopped finely and mixed with spices." I took one of the balls, sniffed it and took a nervous bite. The flavour exploded in my mouth. I tried to identify the spices, but there were too many. I stopped wondering and just enjoyed the taste. I took another and tore some bread from one of the flat round loaves. Other dishes caught my attention: rice studded with nuts and fruits like jewels, small fish in a crispy golden coating. Everything looked so tempting and everything was delicious. The wine in my glass never ran out, someone must have been refilling it, I didn't notice.

Soft music filled any pauses in the conversation; musicians playing a flute, some kind of stringed instrument. I lay back against the cushions, wondering if Coela had a scop, to recite stories of warriors and battles. Somehow I didn't think so.

Another musician entered the room. He had a small drum that added an insistent rhythm. The flute stopped with a flourish of notes and the drummer gave several loud beats. The men around the board stirred as women entered the room. Their faces were veiled, but their hair was unbound. It hung, dark or fair, luxurious to their waists, or even longer. Colourful robes covered them, from head to their bare feet. They started swaying. As their bodies moved, the thin material moulded itself to the shape beneath or separated to display a glimpse of smooth skin. The drum beat faster and the women spun, hair and clothing wrapping around their bodies.

As they turned, first one way and then the other, the whole room seemed to spin with them. I put my glass down carefully on the table. It was expensive and I didn't want it to fall and break. The beat slowed and the women's feet stopped, but their slim bodies continued to move, undulating like serpents, hips swaying suggestively. The beat became louder and faster again. The women came closer, circling the men. I became giddy, trying to follow the motion. As they bent and twisted, men reached out to catch them, some were left grasping only a scrap of fabric, others nothing.

One woman paused near us. Slowly she bent backwards, until her hands reached the floor. She raised first one leg and then the other. Her draperies fell to cover her upper body, leaving her shapely legs moving to the music. She came closer. One foot reached forward to stroke Godric's face, before she leaped away and back onto her feet.

Godric grabbed at the trailing material. The cloth ripped and he was left with most of the woman's costume in his hands. She glided away, nearly naked and the men applauded. She giggled as she escaped. I recognised her as the girl who had disturbed our bath the previous night. The music rose to a crescendo and the women spun. They collapsed to the floor and the music stopped. Cheers and applause rang through the room. I wanted to enjoy the sight, but the motion had made me feel ill. Godric, on the other hand, was transfixed as the girl raised her head. Her breasts heaved as she panted for breath and a trickle of sweat wound between them and down her smooth taut stomach. Behind the veil her mouth curved into a smile. Her eyes meet Godric's before her lashes dropped modestly. Silence fell. Godric stood up clumsily. He walked towards the girl. Everyone watched as he handed the clothing to her. He stood, at a loss at what to do next.

"Well done, my friend." Coela broke the silence. "You like this girl? I think she like you."

Godric nodded. He watched as she wrapped the material round herself. I heard someone groan as the naked flesh was veiled.

"She is yours."

There were cheers as the girl took Godric's hand and led him from the room. The other women moved to the table as the men offered refreshment, then they joined them on the cushions. Hot and confused, I found a jug of chilled water and poured some into my glass.

"And you," I realised Coela was speaking to me, "which girl would you like for the night? Dark or fair? I will get them to unveil if you wish to inspect them closer."

"Perhaps some other time." I took a drink. It soothed my hot throat and cleared my head. I could feel the start of a headache.

"Ah, I understand. You prefer the boys perhaps?"

I struggled to understand what he said.

"He is your boy, yes?" Coela pointed to Edward, who sat, open mouthed, watching the proceedings. Among the cushions, hands caressed bodies and explored beneath clothing.

"I have very nice boys, if you want a different one." Coela turned to a nearby servant.

I grasped what he was suggesting. My blood rose; if I had had a sword in my hand I would have killed him for the insult. I had found much to respect in this strange house, but this was too far from what I knew. I lifted the gaudy glass with a shaking hand; stuffing the other into the depths of the soft cushion, digging my nails into the smooth cloth, trying to keep calm.

"Certainly not. I don't like boys. I just don't want a girl. Not at the moment anyway. I think Edward ought to leave." I tried to stand up. "He is too young for all this. I will take him back to our quarters."

"There is no need." Coela clapped his hands and spoke sharply to his sons. The women left. Some men followed them out.

"I have told them that you are our guest and that your people do not behave in this way. Those of my sons who prefer the company of the women have gone with them. Those who are more serious and appreciate the talk of men remain."

I could breath more easily. Coela was just trying to be a good host, even if I found some of his ways unsettling.

***

We sat and listened to the musicians. One plucked liquid notes from a lyre while the other played the flute. The sounds mingled and separated like a conversation between lovers. One of the younger men joined in with a sad wordless song.

"It is a song of loss." Coela brushed a hand across his eyes. "Loss of family, home, a lover perhaps. A song for old men with regrets." He glanced at me. "You are too young to have regrets, yet the song speaks to you. You have lost someone?"

I stared into the empty cup. Light from the candles, burning low now, reflected the jewel colours from the glass. They swirled and moved with the music. Coela lifted the jug, but I refused more wine. I remembered the sword and how it too had seemed to move in the light.

"I lost a sword. But how can you lose something you've never had? Perhaps..." I struggled with the words. "Perhaps it's not the sword, but what it means."

"It was your father's sword?"

I nodded.

"What happened to him?"

"I don't know. I have no memory of him. I have been told he is dead, but where and when, no one will tell me. They say he was a great man, so how could he just... disappear. His name was Byrhthelm."

"A common enough name. Did your mother not tell you anything?"

"She died too, I barely remember her. I miss her."

The music faded to silence.

"I think you need to discover the truth about your father. Then you can get on with your own life."

"Perhaps, but not now, I need to sleep."

Edward was curled in a ball at the end of the table next to an empty plate. He clutched the last of the honey cakes in a sticky hand.

"I am sorry. He's made a mess of your cushions."

"It is not a problem. These things happen with children." Coela called a servant to carry the boy to bed. I stood up, swaying with weariness.

"Thank you for your hospitality. It has been an interesting meal." The exotic spices lingered on my tongue. "We must be up early. You needed help to load your ship? Then, I think, we must leave."

22

My head felt like a blacksmith had been hammering at it all night. My stomach lurched as I sat up cautiously. Edward was crouched in the corner being sick in the bucket. I splashed some water on my face and swallowed grimly.

"Have you seen Godric this morning?" Edward looked up and shook his head, before retching again. "I told you not to eat so many honey cakes. Go back to bed. You'll feel better later."

I followed the distant sound of shouting out into the courtyard. After taking deep breathes of the cold morning air, I descended the narrow stone steps. In the lower yard, wooden doors stood ajar, offering glimpses of the goods stored within. What I had thought to be a fence had disappeared. It had been lowered onto pilings in the river to create a dock. Cargo littered the area, waiting to be loaded. The tide was low and Coela's ship was moored in the narrow channel at the centre of the river. I watched as small boats clustered round it like piglets round a sow. Men climbed ropes and shouted.

"Don't stand there. You'll get run over." Coela's eldest son pulled me out of the way as a barrow with a large, well packed bale, rattled across the wooden boards. "Do you feel all right? You are a little pale."

"Nothing that a bit of hard work won't cure." I gritted my teeth. "What can I do?"

"We need someone to guard things; keep an eye open for any strangers trying to steal." Two slaves were struggling to lift the contents of the barrow. "Would you mind helping to get that bale into the boat?"

I strode over and grabbed the package by the ropes that wrapped around it, lowering it carefully to the man in a small boat that bobbed below. Once settled, he poled the vessel swiftly across the water.

"They have you working already? Did you sleep well?" Coela had replaced his son, who disappeared back into the yard.

"I slept very well. It was the waking that was a problem. Perhaps I'll join your religion. Too much wine is not good for me. Then there are all those wives."

"I don't think you would enjoy the entry conditions." Coela handed over some bread. "This will settle your stomach." We watched the activity.

"Sorry, I overslept." Godric joined us, yawning sheepishly.

"You managed to get some sleep then?" I grinned at him.

"Not much. You wouldn't believe the things that girl could do."

"She did seem to be very, athletic," I glanced at Coela, busy directing his workers. "Tell me about it another time."

***

Slowly the river rose, making it easier to get cargo into the small boats. As it got close to high tide the ship floated free of the river mud and swung on its anchor.

"We're not going to get away today. There's not much more to get on board, but it still needs to be properly stowed." Coela looked anxiously at the sky. "I hope the wind doesn't change." He went to discuss the conditions with his shipmaster, a broad weathered man with a bushy beard.

Other boats moved down the river, past the bridge; manoeuvring carefully between the ancient wooden pilings. They could use neither sail nor oars. They waited for the right depth of water then steered for the gap. With luck the current carried them through. Several were moored in the river nearby; crews busy stepping masts and repairing damaged woodwork. All were smaller than Coela's ship.

"He says the wind will hold. The next high tide is at first light tomorrow. If we work late, we should be ready to go by then. Would you mind sleeping on board tonight? To discourage any of our neighbours making off with anything."

"Not at all." As long as he remembered to let me off before they sailed. We really had to continue our journey.

***

I found a comfortable spot in the stern of the ship. The night was cold, the sky had cleared and stars shone bright. Warm in my cloak I leaned against a bale of woollen cloth. I could see the whole length of the deck. The ship's master was snoring under a makeshift canvas cover. He would get little sleep once they were at sea. We had talked for a while about the stars. How he used them for navigation and about some of the voyages he had made. Now it was quiet, I took the chance to get recent events into some sort of an order. Wulfstan would be jealous of my experiences and would want to know every detail. It would be good to get home again. I stretched, the loading had been hard work, but I had been neglecting my training. I walked the length of the boat and back. All was still quiet. I drew my sword silently from the scabbard, swung it left and right. I lifted it high and struck down at some imaginary foe, passed it from one hand to the other, bending and straightening. Finally, I re-sheathed the weapon and returned to my post. That would discourage any thieves. I sat and watched, enjoying the peaceful night.

***

The ship floated free and light appeared in the eastern sky. The first boats knocked gently against the hull and the crew came on board. They unwrapped the sail and pulled on ropes. I rowed back to the shore and hoisted myself up onto the quay. The area was crowded. Those travelling across the sea huddled in cloaks and grasped last minute bundles. Others waited to say farewell. Godric and Edward stood to one side, horses loaded for our journey. Coela bustled across the decking and flung his arms round me.

"What a night! Great news! I am father again. I have two Saxon sons. Twins. I will name them after my Saxon friends who rescued me. Byrhtnoth and Godric!"

"That is indeed great news. You do us great honour. And your wife? She is well?"

"Sadly she did not survive. She was so narrow and the boys were so big," Coela's face fell for a moment, but then he brightened. "No matter, there are plenty more women to father babies with."

I was shocked, but perhaps it was his way of coping with grief.

"I am sorry. I only met her briefly." That short conversation in the morning light. "We will delay our journey for her funeral. When is it to be held?"

"It is already done. We have our own customs."

"In that case." I had difficulty controlling my voice. "I would like to say a prayer for her, in our church. What was her name?"

"Her name?" Coela looked puzzled. "She was just called as my wife, I remember nothing else. Did anyone know her name?" he asked the gathered household. Some exchanged questioning glances; they shook their heads.

"It seems not. We waste time. I must get aboard the ship before the tide changes."

"Then we must be on our way as well. I thank you for you hospitality. I hope your business prospers." He was such a mixture

112

of hospitality and astuteness, but I couldn't stand his presence any longer. Without another word I strode across the yard. I jerked the reins from Edward's hand and swung up into the saddle.

"We are leaving." I dug in my heels violently and the horse leapt into action. We crossed the cramped space, scattering people and luggage in all directions. Ducking under the low gateway, I clattered away along the narrow street.

Godric and Edward caught me up before we reached the bridge.

23

Edward was asleep. His tiredness had triumphed over the excitement of our imminent arrival in Wintanceaster. I added a few sticks to the campfire and stared into the flickering flames. Leaning back against the broad trunk of a tree, I watched Godric preparing a place to sleep

"Do you remember my mother?" He was older than me; he must have seen her around the village.

Godric joined me, warming his hands at the fire.

"Not really. I only noticed the children. I remember you, skinny little runt. You could run though."

"I had to."

"Sorry about that." He squirmed a little with embarrassment.

"It was a long time ago, times change." I wasn't interested in that. "My mother?"

"All the women were the same." Godric scratched his head. "They didn't interest me." He inspected his nails. "Not then," he leered.

He sat, searching for memories in the fire. "Quieter than the others? Better dressed – cleaner. That's about it." He looked up. "Why do you want to know?"

"Coela's wife, the one who died." I wished I'd never started this conversation. "She reminded me of my mother."

"Can't say I noticed her. I was busy watching wife number two, what a body. Now there's a good memory to sleep with. Perhaps I'll dream about her."

"What about the girl you spent the night with?"

"She wasn't bad either. Perhaps I'll dream of them both. That would be a sweet dream." Godric closed his eyes and smiled. "Do you want to know about anything else?"

"No. Get some sleep now. I'll wake you later to stand guard."

I stared into the red embers of the fire, watching the pictures that formed and reformed. Did one of them resemble a thick plait of silvery hair?

***

The sky still held the last light of the sun when we reached Wintanceaster. We clattered over the wooden bridge near the mill, and through fields and gardens. Buildings started to appear on either side and our pace slowed. I pointed out a large shape that loomed white in the gathering darkness.

"That's the church built by King Alfred. They're building another beside it, even bigger. It will house his tomb."

"Why do they need two churches?" Edward asked.

"I don't know, perhaps they'll knock the first one down, when the new one is finished. We're nearly there now."

"What's that?" Godric pointed at a tall fence that ran along beside the road. Through a gateway, torches burned brightly. Crowds of people in colourful clothing hurried in and out.

"It's the entrance to the king's palace. The mead hall and other buildings are inside. We'll come back later."

"Isn't that where you live?" Godric peered back as we rode past the enclosure.

"We're up there." My horse recognised the scent of home and trotted briskly uphill, towards a small collection of buildings, huddled in the angle of the old walls. "Welcome home."

***

We left the horses at the stables and headed towards a long hut nearby. I flung open the door.

The room was nearly full. Work or training was over and everyone had gathered to prepare for the evening meal. Weapons were being sharpened; I dropped my hand to my sword hilt. Some were mending clothes, but most of the boys were lying on their beds or chatting with friends.

"You decided to come back, then?" Elfhere glanced up from his bed. He was relaxed, hands behind his head. "We wondered if we'd ever see you again." He sat up when he saw the sword. "Where did you get that?" Everyone crowded round, asking questions. Some tried to touch the sword; others cast curious glances in the direction of Godric and Edward.

"Let me get through the door." I pushed my way through the crowd and dropped my pack onto the bed.

"Where's Wulfstan?" His bed was unused, no clothes piled neatly on the self nearby. I looked round the room. "Is he busy somewhere?" He was probably off grooming that horse of his, but why the empty bed?

Silence fell on the room like a sudden frost. Elfhere returned to his bed and studied the ceiling as if he had never seen it before. Others turned away, busying themselves with jobs that were suddenly more important.

"What's wrong? Elfhere, what's happened?"

There was a long awkward silence before Elfhere replied, "I'm sorry Byrhtnoth, Wulfstan had an accident. He's not here any more."

"Not here? Where is he?"

Elfhere ignored my question and continued his contemplation of the ceiling.

"It's quiet in here." Oswald pushed open the door. "What's going on? The meal will be ready soon." He stopped when he noticed me. "Oh, hello Byrhtnoth, welcome back."

"Yes, I'm back." I was becoming angry. "This lot say Wulfstan has had an accident. What happened? Why isn't he here?"

"You'd better come outside."

Godric and Edward followed us out into the darkness, whispering together in confusion. This was not the reception they had expected.

"You've been gone a while, haven't you?" Oswald stated the obvious, as usual.

"Only a few weeks, less than a month." I noticed his eyes fall to my new sword and my hand that rested on it. "Get on with it."

"Just after you left, Wulfstan had an accident. Trampled by his horse."

"I don't believe it. Sleipnir would never do that."

"It appears that he did. He was badly injured, crippled." Oswald forced out the word. "He can't stay in the troop. I'm sorry, I know he was your friend." He turned away, to return to the warmth and companionship of the hut.

"Where is he?"

Oswald noticed the steel in my voice. "He might be in the gardener's hut, up by the wall." He gestured in the direction of a building standing alone, separate from the others. "If he's still alive."

I called Godric and Edward to follow me. "We must find out what's going on."

24

We paused outside the hut, I was afraid of what we might find. I slowly opened the rickety door. A foul smell billowed out of the darkness, forcing us away but I stepped forward to face it.

"Wulfstan?" It was completely dark now and impossible to see anything. I thought I heard a small rustle of movement and took another step. "Are you there? It's me, Byrhtnoth." A low rasping croak emerged from the darkness.

"Go away."

I moved towards the sound and tripped over something.

"We need light. Get a fire going, Godric. I think I've found the remains of a hearth." Where had Edward gone? The boy rushed up, holding aloft a burning torch.

"Thought this might come in handy."

"Well done." I took the torch and walked towards a pile of rags, heaped against the opposite walll. "Let's find out what's been going on." As the light got closer there was movement. Wulfstan turned his head away from the brightness. There was a jug lying empty on the floor. Nearby a bowl, a smear of whatever it had last contained dried in the bottom.

"We need food, and drink. Edward, can you find the kitchen?"

"With my eyes closed. I'll just follow my nose." He disappeared through the door.

Ignoring the stench, I crouched down beside Wulfstan.

"How long have you been here?"

"Don't know... Forever." His voice was faint, each word forced out with effort.

"Hasn't anyone been caring for you?" The only response was a feeble shake of the head.

"No food?"

"Sometimes," Wulfstan managed to say.

Godric had got a small fire burning. The heat began to push the bone-chilling cold from the room. The smell increased. I removed some of the rags covering Wulfstan.

"Leave me alone. I want to die."

"I can't do that."

Wulfstan wore only a thin under tunic. Was it covered in blood? No, unable to move and with no one to care for him, Wulfstan had been forced to soil himself. He had been left to lie in it. How long had he suffered like this? I told Godric to find some water and heat it on the fire.

"Use some of these rags to keep the fire going."

Godric headed for the door. I told him to fetch the gear we had left in the main hut, and some bedding. We were going to be here for some time. I turned my attention to Wulfstan's legs. That was where the damage lay.

His right leg didn't look too bad. It had been broken but was straight and healing well. The left leg was different. Someone had tried their best, but it had not been enough. The bones were too shattered to be properly set, the leg was twisted. As far as I could tell it was now shorter than the other. Oswald had been right; Wulfstan would never be able to fight. It would take a miracle for him to walk again.

"Everything seems to be healing well." I tried to sound cheerful. "Are you in much pain?"

"Yes," the answer came through gritted teeth.

"Can you move your right leg?" The leg rose slightly and was dropped with a grunt. "What about the other?" He shook his head.

I leaned over and ran a finger across the bottom of his left foot. The leg shifted and Wulfstan screamed.

"Sorry about that. Things could be a lot worse."

Before Wulfstan could reply, Edward returned. He carried a large basket filled with freshly cooked meat and a loaf of bread. A flask of ale was tucked in the side.

"I just mentioned your name. I said you were back from your journey, tired and hungry. They gave me all this. You must be popular."

I ignored him and poured some of the ale into the bowl. "Help me sit him up. Gently. He'll probably shout a bit." I put an arm round Wulfstan's shoulders to support him and handed him the bowl. "Take a good drink to keep you going. We're not having anything to eat until we get you clean."

***

The meat was not quite cold by the time we had washed Wulfstan and settled him on a proper bed. All the rags, which we discovered were old vegetable sacks, were on the blazing fire. Godric fed it with small pieces of rubbish he found.

"Feeling better now?" I asked Wulfstan.

"When I've got some of this food down me." Wulfstan was pale but tore at one of the pieces of meat, stuffing pieces into his mouth. "Pass me some bread."

I divided the loaf and handed him a piece.

"Don't eat too quickly, you'll make yourself ill."

"More ill than I already am, you mean."

"You're not ill, just injured. We'll soon get you back on your feet." There was silence as the others concentrated on their food. I could curse my mouth sometimes. "Sorry, I didn't think."

"Doesn't matter. I've had plenty of time to think. That's why I decided to die. Until you came and messed it all up. I can never be a warrior now. Everyone made that very clear. What else can I do? It is the only thing I've been trained for. All the future holds for me is as a beggar, dependant on charity."

"Don't worry about that now. We'll find something for you to do. We know a village that needs a good steward, don't we, Godric?"

"You haven't told me what happened while you were away. Who are your new friends? And where did you find something like this?" Wulfstan plucked at the fine linen tunic that he now wore. It was the one I had found in the chest.

"It's a long story. I was called back because Lord Toli was ill. I only spoke to him once, before he died. That was when I discovered that I had inherited all his lands."

"So, he was your father after all?" We had spent many hours speculating.

"Not at all. It's all much more complicated than that." I saw Wulfstan's eyes closing. "I'll tell you about that tomorrow."

25

"Something's been nibbling at this bread." Edward inspected the leftovers. "Wonder what it was? We'll have to get rid of it."

"It's just the mice," said Wulfstan, sleepily, "they were my only friends for a time."

"They must think they've died and gone to heaven, with all this food." Godric fanned the remains of the fire. He added wood that he had found from somewhere.

"I feel a bit like that myself." Wulfstan sat up, wincing from the pain. "You've got to find out what happened to Sleipnir. They say he did this, but I can't believe it."

"Neither can I. What happened?" I helped myself to some of the cold meat. We needed more ale. "Can you find some, Edward?" Reluctantly the boy left the hut.

"I don't know. We were on our own. Someone mentioned some ruins out in the forest, so I went to explore. Everyone else was hunting a boar. I found the ruins; everything else is hazy. I remember waking up and my head hurt."

"Sounds as if someone hit you. Even you couldn't bump into something hard enough to knock yourself out."

"It was cold and getting dark. My legs were..." Wulfstan paused. "Sleipnir was there. He kept me warm." His eyes widened.

"He saved my life, not destroyed it. You've got to make sure he's all right."

"Of course I will. Any idea who attacked you?"

"I don't know. I didn't see who it was. An outlaw in the forest?"

"Someone must have really hated you, to do something like that."

"But who? I don't know anyone who disliked me that much."

I could think of one person. "We'll talk more about this later." I stood up. "There are things I must do. The abbot in Ely gave me letters to deliver. I'll get that out of the way; then I'll find Sleipnir. Thanks, Edward, just in time." I took a deep draught from the jug and handed it to Wulfstan. "I'll be back later. Godric and Edward will look after you."

"I don't need anyone to..." I missed the rest. I was already through the door.

I had nearly reached the main path down to the town, when I heard footsteps.

"What do you want?" I turned to face Elfhere.

"How's Wulfstan?"

"Alive, just. No thanks to you." I turned to walk away, but anger took over. "How could you do such a thing? Leave him like that; alone in the cold and dark. After everything we've been taught about supporting each other."

"I don't know. I assumed he would be cared for," Elfhere whined. "He wasn't part of the king's troop any longer, not our responsibility."

I shook my head in disgust. Elfhere offered me a bundle.

"We found his things. Will you give them to him?" I stared at him.

"Not only did you leave him to die," I spoke slowly, trying to make him understand, "you stole his possessions as well." Elfhere hung his head.

"Give them to him yourself," I shouted and strode away. I stopped and looked back. "Where's Egbert? I didn't notice him in the dormitory last night."

"Egbert? I haven't seen him for a while. Not since just after the accident." He stopped abruptly.

"Exactly."

***

I had to wait a long time before Bishop Alphege found the time to receive me. I delivered the letters and answered questions about the monastery at Ely. Before I was dismissed, I asked if I might make a request.

"Go ahead. What can we do for you?"

"It's not for me. I have a friend who has been injured. It is Wulfstan, he won the riding prize at the competition during the Christmas court."

The bishop turned to speak to one of his priests. "I know the boy. I didn't attend, but I am told it was very entertaining." I noticed several of the attendants smiling. "What does he want?"

I took a deep breath. "He had an accident, he was attacked. He was badly injured, his leg broken. He is recovering but cannot continue his training as a warrior."

"That is unfortunate."

"Could you find a place for him in a monastery somewhere? He's very bright. We have all been taught to read and write, but he is the only one who enjoys it. I think he would be better as a clerk than a warrior." I paused and plunged on. "If it's a matter of money, I can pay towards his education. Please help him. He has survived great suffering and fears he will be left a crippled beggar."

"Can he not walk at all?"

"It is too early to tell, perhaps he will be able to walk with a crutch. I am sure God would not have allowed him to survive this trial if He did not have plans for Wulfstan's future."

"I think I am the person qualified to decide what God wants," Bishop Alphege chastised me, but smiled.

I was forced to wait as the bishop spoke to his attendants. A whispered discussion ensued. I worried I had said the wrong thing; had I offended the priest and destroyed any chance of success?

"We have come to a decision. The boy you speak of is still recovering. We cannot know if he will walk or not. Bring him to me," he paused as one of the attendants leaned in and offered some advice. "Bring him to us at Easter. If we then judge him satisfactory, we will find a place for him."

"Thank you, my lord, you are very generous, thank you."

"All right, you may go."

I managed to exit respectfully. However, once outside the cathedral, I started to run.

***

I burst into the hut.

"I've checked on Sleipnir. He's kept away from the other horses and he hasn't had a lot to eat. I'll bring him here. We'll find something for him."

"Thank you." Wulfstan bowed his head. "That is the best thing I've heard for a long time."

"That's not all. I've spoken to the bishop. He has promised that he would find a place for you in a monastery. All we've got to do is get you on your feet by Easter."

SPRING 946

26

"Vikings!"

Wulfstan urged his horse a few more yards and slid off its back. I rushed to help as he collapsed in a heap on the dusty ground.

"Where? Are they behind you?" I turned towards the gate.

"Gone. Attack. Bodies," he paused, "water."

"Bring some water; there's a bucket inside the fence." The others abandoned their sword practice, and hurried towards us. "Find Oswald," I shouted.

The water was warm and dusty from standing all day in the sun, but Wulfstan drank it gratefully.

"Give the horse some, he deserves it." He struggled to his feet and hung onto the fence, drawing on his strength to speak. "About ten miles back. Someone's attacked a group of travellers. There were bodies everywhere." He paused for another sip of water. "I don't think they stayed long; must have happened days ago."

"What's going on?" Elfhere asked.

"Tell Lord Elfgar there are raiders in Wessex. We'll come as soon as Wulfstan recovers." When he'd gone, I turned to Wulfstan. "Ealdorman Elfgar is in charge here in Wintanceaster. King Edmund is away with his new wife. You heard he'd married Elfgar's daughter?" Wulfstan nodded. "He's got another daughter, Elfgar, not the king... Where did you say this attack took place?"

"About ten miles south of here. On the road through the forest; the meadow beside the stream, where travellers camp?" I knew the place.

"Lord Elfgar sent his family home a few days ago. They would have travelled that way." I took a deep breath. "Were there any young women amongst the bodies?"

"I don't think so. The only woman I noticed was old."

"That would have been the nurse. It might not have been them. Perhaps they're safely home by now. If not, it means..."

"They're captives."

"Come on." I grabbed Wulfstan's arm and pulled him towards the palace.

We met Oswald near the hall. "What are all these rumours about Viking attacks?"

Lord Elfgar and his attendants swept through the door.

"There have been no reports of ships along the coast. Is this the boy who brought the news?"

"This is Wulfstan. He has returned from his monastery for the summer to train with us. It's bad news."

"Can't he can speak for himself?"

"Yes, I can, my lord."

I stepped back.

"Byrhtnoth told me your family was travelling home. It is possible that they were the group that were attacked." He described the scene. Bodies scattered across the ground, the tracks of many horses. "It appears that the raiders, together with their captives travelled west."

"Perhaps they came from Ireland," I suggested.

"I don't need your suggestions," Elfgar snapped. "It was your fault I had to send my daughter away. Now look what's happened."

I saw Wufstan's glance of surprise. I ignored him.

"It's too late to do anything now. We'll leave in the morning."

Elfgar frowned. "I don't know where we'll get men at such short notice. The king left enough to defend the town and there's no time to call for more."

"What about us?" It was too good an opportunity.

"I think you've done enough. Out of my way."

I stood firm. "Why can't we join the hunt? We've done enough training; we're ready for a real fight. What do you think?" I turned to Oswald for support.

"My lord, it is about time they stopped sitting around stuffing their faces and earned their keep. From what I heard, you will need people to dig graves. They've got plenty of energy and it's going to be a hard ride."

I could see Elfgar wanted to reject the offer, but it was the only option. "Be ready to leave at first light!" He swept back into the hall.

***

There was a lot to do. I strode away, thinking about what needed to be done. I shouted to Godric to fetch our weapons. "And tell Edward to check the horses. We'll need mounts for everyone, plus spares."

"Slow down."

"Sorry." I waited for Wulfstan. "Do you still use a stick?"

"I can manage without, but I move faster with something to lean on. Have you grown since last autumn? Your legs are longer than ever." I shrugged, I hadn't noticed.

By the time we reached the barracks, everyone was busy. Provisions were being gathered and packed into travelling bags. Godric was issuing weapons and instructing negligent owners to sharpen blades.

"Bring them back for inspection. If they're not up to standard, you don't come." He handed me my sword. "Nothing wrong with this one, but I expect you'll want to check it yourself."

"Thank you." I pulled it from the scabbard and inspected the blade. "Not bad, I'll put the final edge on it later." We stopped as Edward led a string of horses across the path. "Make sure they have all been groomed. Have you checked the hooves?"

"Already done." He gave a broad grin. "My lord."

"Have you seen to my mount?" Wulfstan asked.

"All done. Good to see you back. He was in a bad state. Monastery horses aren't used to being ridden like that. I was surprised you'd do that."

"Sorry. I had to get here as quickly as possible. He was as eager to leave that place as I was."

"What happened?"

"Death, bodies, the smell was…" Wulfstan's face grew pale and he staggered.

"You need some rest. And something to eat."

He shook his head. "The horse will be all right?"

"Couple of day's rest and he'll be fine." Edward waved and led the horses away.

I stopped a servant and asked him to bring some food. "And a jug of ale, or two." I took Wulfstan's arm and led him to the barracks. "You might not want anything, but I do. God knows when we'll eat again."

***

Wulfstan lay back on his old bed. The food and ale arrived. I grabbed a loaf and started to leave.

"Stay and talk for a while. I'm exhausted, but I don't think I can sleep. What's been going on since I left in the autumn?"

I poured him a cup of ale. "The usual things. Weapon practice, hunting, feasting." I broke the loaf of fresh bread and handed him some.

"Was that when you met this girl? She must be something special, for you to notice her. Apart from being the king's wife's sister."

"What do you mean?" I nearly choked on my mouthful of bread.

"I'm your friend. I know you. What's she like?" Wulfstan poured us some more ale.

I thought while I sipped it. "She's very beautiful, and I think she likes me. She comes to watch when we're training. She smiles whenever we meet."

"And have you spoken to her?"

"Not really. Her father doesn't approve. He thinks I'm not good enough."

"Well, she's related to the king. You'll need to earn a lot more honour and glory, before you can even think about approaching someone like that."

"She might be in the hands of the raiders now." I might never see her again.

"Perhaps her father will be so grateful when you rescue her, he'll change his mind."

"Perhaps." I took out my sword and found the stone to sharpen it.

"You've not used it yet, in anger?" Wulfstan reached for a piece of cold meat. His colour was coming back and I handed him the jug of ale.

"That's the only good thing about this attack." Not that Elfflaed had been captured, that was terrible news. "After all these years of training, we'll have the chance of a proper fight." I swung the sword, backwards and forwards. "I'll kill some Vikings and become a man, a proper warrior, win honour and glory."

"And get the girl?"

"That as well." I ran the stone along the already razor edge of the sword. "Any girls in that monastery of yours? I suppose not. What have you been up to this winter?"

Wulfstan put down his cup of ale and leaned back. "No girls. There's a nunnery next-door; big wall in the way though. Anyway I've been too busy."

I looked up from the sword. "How can you be busy in a monastery? It's all prayer and contemplation."

"Everyone has to go to services, but I haven't taken any vows yet, although I have to make that decision soon."

"What are you going to do?"

"I don't know. Perhaps this summer will help me decide. Meanwhile, I spend a lot of time writing; copying books and documents. You'd be amazed at the amount I've learnt, just reading the books in the library."

"Don't you get any exercise?" How boring to sit and read a book.

"I've been helping out in the monastery garden. They need someone strong to help with the digging. In exchange, the gardener there, he knows a lot about herbs, he's been teaching me about their uses. Did you know...?" I let him chatter on. Talking about his boring life would take his mind off the horrible experience.

I wiped the sword with a rag and slid it gently into the scabbard. "I'll leave you now. I must check everyone is ready for the early start. I'll see you when we get back."

"No." He sat up, "I'm coming too."

"Why do you want to come? You'll be safer here," I told him.

"I've had enough of being safe. You didn't find those bodies today. You want your honour and glory? Well I want revenge on the animals who did that."

I stared at his determined face. "I'll wake you when it's time to leave."

27

As the first glow of light appeared in the east, we waited, armed and mounted. If Elfgar was surprised to find us ready, he didn't show it. He nodded and we fell in behind his personal guard. The sun appeared and the early morning mist faded away. We rode silently through the forest, our shadows disappearing into the surrounding trees. It was a trip we had often made; hunts for game. This was different. No chatter about the prospects for the day, no boasting about our prowess or wagers on who would kill that day. Even the dogs, controlled by an experienced tracker, sensed the tense atmosphere and made no noise.

"Good to be back on Sleipnir?" I asked Wulfstan.

"He's getting fat, hasn't had much exercise."

Elfgar turned to see who was talking. We stared straight ahead.

"He'll get plenty on this expedition," I whispered.

The sun rose higher and it became hot. We must be getting close. Elfgar halted the column and beckoned Wulfstan forward; after a discussion Elfgar ordered us to dismount.

"Leave the horses here, no need to upset them. The site is just ahead." Some of the animals were restless, catching the smell of death on the breeze. Wulfstan calmed Sleipnir, then headed towards a stream just visible through the trees.

"Where's he going? The bodies are further along the road."

"Perhaps he needs a drink." I watched Wulfstan curiously.

"That's the wrong place for a drink." Elfgar studied the surrounding area. "It's downstream from the death site. What's he doing now? Picking flowers? Come on," he shouted, "we've got work to do."

Wulfstan waved and walked back towards us. He had tied a strip of linen across his mouth and nose.

"I knew there would be some mint growing down there. It'll help keep some of the smell out."

Elfgar snorted and strode away. Wulfstan's face was chalky white.

"Do you want to stay here with the horses?" I asked, but he shook his head. We followed the others along the road.

To one side of the road was a steep slope of trees; bluebells thick beneath the fresh green leaves. A vixen disappeared through the flowers, dragging something behind her. There were deep gouges, as if a giant cat had clawed the ground. The attack must have come from that direction. Men and horses sliding down the hill, catching their victims by surprise. Dead flowers were trampled into the surface of the road. Bodies were scattered across the meadow. Mostly men. Judging from the range of ages, it was not a band of warriors. Perhaps a group travelling together for protection. The only woman visible was old, skirts pulled up over her face and legs forced apart. One, or several, of the attackers had taken their pleasure of her. They had not deemed her worth taking with them. Her belly was ripped open, entrails strewn across the grass, some missing. Was that what the vixen had carried?

All the bodies were stripped of weapons and valuables. There were no other women or children among the dead. The scene spoke of only one thing: a Viking attack. They wouldn't have hung around for long.

There was a mound of fresh earth beside the road, on the edge of the meadow. Someone, at least, had fought back and killed one of the attackers. So, enough time to dig a grave, sort out the captives, rape a woman, then away. The small campfire near the stream must have belonged to the travellers.

Elfgar approached the low grave and stared down at it.

"You two." He pointed at me and Elfhere. "Fetch the shovels and dig up these heathens." We hesitated, why did he want them disinterred? There were so many other bodies to be buried.

"They don't deserve a decent burial. We need the grave for our own people, unless you want to dig a fresh one?" Elfhere hurried off. "The rest of you, search the area. Collect the bodies. Lay them here." He pointed to a spot at the edge of the road. "Make them decent, ready for burial." He turned to Wulfstan. "Someone told me you could write." Wulfstan nodded. "You're good for something then. Stay close to me and write down the names of the dead. This atrocity must be recorded."

Elfgar moved to the old woman and arranged her limbs into a semblance of normality. "She was my daughter's nurse. She was mine as well, many years ago." He crouched by the body, staring silently into the surrounding trees. "We will catch the animals who did this and kill them, as they have massacred these innocent people." He stood up.

"Your daughter is not here?" Wulfstan asked in a low voice.

"Perhaps it would be better if she was," Elfgar said.

"Elfhere said you needed help." Godric dumped a pile of shovels beside me.

"Trust him to disappear when there's work to do. Let's get started."

The soil was loose and the bodies had not been buried deep, just enough to keep animals away. As we cleared away the soil, the smell drifted up to join the stench of the other bodies that were being gathered. Elfgar came to inspect our work.

"Get them out and strip them."

"Strip them?" I stared down at the rotting corpses.

"They may have valuables on them, weapons. The clothes might be worth something."

I exchanged a glance with Godric. We did as we were told.

"String them up over there." Elfgar pointed to a tree with a thick branch overhanging the road. "Tie this round their feet." He handed us a length of rope.

We threw the end of the rope over the branch and pulled the bodies into the air. I wondered how long the bodies would hang before the rotting ankles gave way. If Elfgar wanted them to hang as a warning, perhaps they would last longer with the rope around their bodies. On second thoughts, I decided not to suggest it.

"Dig the hole deeper," Elfgar considered the line of bodies awaiting burial, "and longer." With a sigh I picked up my shovel and attacked the soil.

Finally the grave was to Elfgar's satisfaction. The bodies were laid carefully, side by side.

"We need a priest to say the words over the dead." Elfgar beckoned Wulfstan.

"I'm not a priest. I spend time in the monastery, but I am not ordained."

"Did no one think to bring a priest?" There was silence. "Then you are the nearest we have. You know the words?" Wulfstan nodded and stepped forward. He stared into the grave and closed his eyes. He spoke the words in Latin. None of the company understood the words but repeated, "Amen."

Elfgar stood for a moment and then moved away.

"Fill it in and get ready to leave."

"No." My clothes were caked with grave dirt and the smell of rotting flesh filled my mouth. "We'll upset the horses smelling like this; the dogs will be confused. I'm going to wash." I ignored Elfgar and walked rapidly towards the stream at the bottom of the slope.

28

The stream was shallow, a place where animals came to drink. It was only a few inches deep but chilled my feet. The riverbed was covered in small pebbles that gleamed in the sunlight as swift water ran through them.

I walked upstream, searching for deeper water to wash off the stench of death. The river narrowed and green weed, like the hair of drowned women, flowed towards me. The banks rose on both sides and trees closed in. The water grew deeper and overhead shafts of sunlight penetrated the leaves. Somewhere a crow croaked its displeasure at the loss of its feast.

Distracted, I stepped on a slime-covered rock. My foot slipped. I lost my balance. Arms flailing, I landed flat on my back with a tremendous splash. At least I was wet now. I scrubbed at my dirty clothes and ducked my head under the fresh, cool water. I struggled back to my feet and pushed wet hair from my eyes.

That was when I heard a small voice, calling my name.

I reached for my knife and scanned the bushes along the banks. Was it one of the others playing a trick on me? I heard them back downstream, splashing and shouting. It had sounded like a child's voice. Who knew me out here? There was a flicker of sunlight. I noticed a pair of dark eyes staring through the leaves. Carefully I waded over.

"Hello. What woodland animal has been watching me?"

"I'm not an animal." A scornful expression passed across the small face.

"Of course you're not. It's safe to come out now. The bad men have gone."

"I know they've gone; they went days ago. I'm stuck here. I can't move."

I put away the knife and found a gap in the bushes lining the river. I heaved myself out of the water and crouched down beside what I now realised was a young girl. Somehow she had crawled under a large thorn bush and was caught fast. I inspected the bush. Tufts of green leaves emerged from bare stems. One branch had reached the sun and small white flowers bloomed. The bush leaned sideways, growing towards the light. The main trunk was across the girl's back, pinning her down.

I searched the undergrowth and found a fallen branch. I tested it for strength then carefully pushed it under the thorny trunk. I put a shoulder under one end and pushed upwards.

"I'll be as careful as I can but this is going to hurt." I patted the girl's shoulder. "How did you get under there? Did you run when the Vikings attacked?"

"I don't run away. I was already in the woods. We were setting up camp and I left to... well... you know."

"Of course. So you don't know what happened?"

"I heard noises," she paused, "are they all dead?"

I gently detached the thorns from the back of her clothing. I lifted the branch higher.

"We don't know. Some are missing. They must have been taken by the raiders."

"My mistress, the Lady Elfflaed, is she...?"

"There was no sign of her. We can only hope she's still alive.

Don't worry, we'll find her." The girl's reply was interrupted by a muffled cry as a thorn racked across her back.

"Sorry. You serve Elfflaed? That must be how you know my name. I don't recognise you."

"You wouldn't. When she's in the room, all the men gaze at her, the rest of us are invisible." She was probably right.

"It's not your fault, it happens to everyone. I'm Saewynn. Ouch."

"Well, Saewynn, I think your back is clear now."

"I still can't move."

"Your hair is caught. If I raise the branch any higher it's going to hurt you more." Every movement of her head had twisted the long brown hair round the spiky branches. She was trapped, her face pressed into the leaf litter beneath. As I wondered what to do next, someone shouted from far away.

"Was that Elfgar?" The girl sounded scared.

"He's in charge of the expedition. We have to leave soon." I pulled at the tangled mass of hair and twigs. "There's only one thing to do." I took out my knife; Saewynn gasped as the sharp edge glittered in the sunlight. "I'm going to have to cut your hair." She struggled. I told her to keep very still. It was awkward, with the weight of the tree across my back. I cupped the back of the girl's head gently with one hand and with the other, sawed through the thick mass of her hair.

"That's it. Don't worry; it will soon grow back. Can you move now?" Gingerly Saewynn nodded. "Don't try and get up. Just roll towards me until you're clear." I couldn't hold the bush up much longer. I glimpsed a grin as she rolled beneath me. I checked she was out of the way, then heaved the branch upwards and rolled clear myself. The thorn bush crashed back into position. We lay side by side on the ground.

I studied the surrounding close packed trees. "I don't know how you got in here, but I think the best way back is along the river."

"It's very deep." Saewynn stared into the dark water.

My wet clothes were muddier than they had been before. "I need another dip." She giggled as I lowered myself into the water. I checked my footing and washed off some of the dirt. I held up my arms for Saewynn. "Jump down, I'll catch you."

"You won't fall over again?"

"I promise."

I was surprised at how light she was as she clung round my neck; she couldn't have eaten for several days. We could hear Elfgar's angry voice echoing through the forest.

"We're coming. I've found someone." I carried the girl back to safety.

"Have you found my daughter?" Lord Elfgar strode up.

"I'm afraid not."

He took one glance at the girl in my arms and started to walk away.

"Come on, you've wasted enough time."

"Aren't you glad she survived?"

"It's only a slave, I can get another easily enough." Elfgar turned and shouted at the girl. "Why are you still alive? You should have protected your mistress; died rather than let them take her."

"She was in the forest when they arrived." I felt her arms tighten around my neck. "What was she supposed to do? She would have had no chance against the raiders. Just another carcass to bury."

I faced him over Saewynn's shivering body. "You're scaring her. She's been on her own for days, with nothing to eat. We can't leave her here."

Elfgar was speechless, astounded that I dared to challenge him.

Wulfstan had put away his writing things and pulled down the mint filled cloth from his face.

"We all need a bite to eat. We've had nothing since we left and there's a long journey ahead. We can't fight Vikings on an empty stomach. Bring the girl back to the horses, I'll find some salve for those scratches." I followed him and the others trailed after, leaving Elfgar standing by the water.

"You're not bringing her with us," he thundered.

"She won't be any trouble," Wulfstan called back, "and your daughter will need another woman to look after her, when we've rescued her."

When I tried to put the girl down, she clung to me, her hands clutching desperately at my clothing.

"What's happened to you then?" asked Wulfstan gently. She pressed her face into my shoulder.

I told him that she had been away from the camp when the attack came. "She hid under a thorn bush and got caught. I helped her out. She'll be all right. It's just a few scratches."

"You've got a few yourself. What's your name then?" Wulfstan asked the girl. There was no reply. "Well, little one, do you think you could let go of Byrhtnoth for a moment, so we can treat his wounds?" The girl thought about it then nodded. Once she was standing on the ground, Wulfstan wrapped a cloak around her. "That will keep you warm." He pretended to inspect the scratches on my shoulder. "I think you'll live. You're a bit wet though."

"I'll soon dry in the sun. I slipped over in the river." I winked at Saewynn and was rewarded with a shy smile. "I think we'd better mount up, Elfgar is coming." I lifted the girl onto my horse and climbed up behind her. Wulfstan mounted Sleipnir.

"That's a very ugly horse," she whispered.

"Don't tell Wulfstan, he's proud of his horse. Sleipnir is very clever. Ask Wulfstan later, he might show you some of the tricks he's taught him."

"What happened to Wulfstan's leg? Was he injured in a battle?"

"That's a long story. I'll tell you all about it another time. Where's that food you were talking about, Wulfstan?"

"Did you forget your own food again?" He rummaged in his bag and produced a loaf. He broke it in two and tossed me the larger piece.

"Why bother, when you bring enough for two." I handed the bread to Saewynn. "Eat it slowly," I told her as she stuffed it in her mouth, "you'll be sick eating too much on an empty stomach. And leave some for me."

***

The trail was easy to follow. The raiders had left the way they came; returning to their ships. The dogs caught the scent and we increased our speed.

"Where do you reckon the ships are?" Wulfstan asked.

"We're heading west." I glanced at the sky. "Difficult to tell whether they landed on the south coast or further west."

"Someone along the coast must have spotted them."

"Not if they were dead." They couldn't have killed everyone; someone would have escaped to send a warning. "More likely further west. That means a long ride."

"Unless we catch up with them. They will be moving slowly with all the booty."

I checked Saewynn, who had fallen asleep. "And captives."

"Perhaps she heard something. We'll ask later." We trotted on in silence. "They've kept well out of sight, sticking to the forest."

"They may be Vikings, but they're not stupid. If they travelled in open country, someone would have spotted them."

"I suppose so. I expect they killed everyone in any villages they came across."

"Just so long as I don't have bury any more bodies today." I flexed my shoulders. "It was hard work."

29

I got a campfire going. Wulfstan handed a pair of pigeons to Saewynn. We could always rely on Wulfstan to find us something to eat. Saewynn stared at the two limp bodies.

"What do I do with these?"

"You're a woman, cook them." I was tired and hungry.

"But I'm my lady's maid. I serve only her. There are others to do the cooking."

"You won't make anyone much of a wife." I shook my head.

Wulfstan took the birds from Saewynn and started stripping the feathers.

"Leave her alone, she's only young. There's plenty of time to learn to cook. What do you do for the Lady Elfflaed?"

"I help her with her clothes, I weave cloth and stitch embroidery. She has so many beautiful clothes." Saewynn smiled. "I'm good with a needle. Not that I need to do repairs, she would rather have a new gown than repair an old one. And I help her with her bath. She bathes often." I imagined Elfflaed in her bath.

"Find a stick and put this bird over the fire," Wulfstan ordered me, breaking me out of my dreams. "Anything else?"

"I spend a lot of time combing her hair. It's very long." She raised a hand to her own chopped locks unconsciously. "And I help her with her cosmetics."

"Surely she doesn't need cosmetics?" She was beautiful enough without all that. Saewynn frowned.

"Ignore him, he doesn't know anything about women." Wulfstan passed me the second bird.

"And you do? What have you been getting up to in that monastery of yours?" I speared the bird and handed it back.

"You don't act like a monk." Saewynn looked at Wulfstan with interest.

"I'm not a monk. I'm just training there." He stabbed the sticks forcefully into the ground, angling them so that the small carcases hung over the fire.

"How did you become her maid?" I asked Saewynn, "Do you have any family?"

"I think my parents are dead. I've been in Lord Elfgar's household as long as I can remember."

"Another orphan. You'll fit in well. We're all orphans here."

***

I stripped the last scraps of meat from a bone and tossed it into the fire.

"Better get some sleep. Lord Elfgar will have us up at first light again tomorrow."

"Careful. He's coming." Wulfstan attempted to tidy the heap of feathers surrounding him.

Saewynn moved closer to me as Elfgar appeared out of the darkness.

"Just checking that you're behaving yourselves." He loomed over us. "I don't trust you around women." I tensed but didn't offer a reply. Elfgar focused his attention on Saewynn. "She's not likely to tempt you, skinny little bitch. What happened to her hair?"

"She was stuck in a thorn bush and I cut her out. How else would you expect her to look?"

Elfgar stared down at me for several long seconds.

"Take care. She's my property and I don't want her damaged. I might want her myself some cold night. It would have to be dark, though." He laughed and returned to his own campfire.

"He's gone now. Are you all right?" Saewynn was shaking and tears trickled down her cheeks. I put an arm round her shoulders. "You're safe with us, we won't let him hurt you."

"There's nothing you can do." Saewynn shook her head. "He's right, I'm his property and he can do what he likes."

"Not that, surely?" said Wulfstan, "You're his daughter's maid. Wouldn't she have something to say about it?"

"He's like that with all the young girls. As soon as he notices them, he has to have them. I thought I'd managed to keep out of his way, but now I've come to his attention, that's it." She struggled to stand up. "I wish you hadn't rescued me, I should have stayed where I was, safe. Please, let me go."

"You can't go out there in the darkness. The wolves will find you. You are part of our family now. We fight for each other, don't we, Wulfstan?"

"Yes." He moved round to sit beside Saewynn and patted her hand. "Try and get some sleep. We'll sort things out tomorrow. I'll think of something."

***

Next morning Wulfstan handed Saewynn a bundle of clothes.

"I've been around the camp and explained your problem. Our friends have sworn to protect you. They gave me some clothes as well. You can't stay dressed like that." In the daylight we could see her dress was full of holes. "If we dress you as a boy, perhaps Elfgar will forget about you. Put these on; you can change behind those trees. I'll keep watch." She disappeared into the wood. "Ask

Edward to find her a gentle horse. She should be able to ride on her own, if we all keep an eye on her."

By the time I returned, Saewynn had been transformed. The mixture of men's clothing had turned her into a servant boy.

"It's all wrong, I feel undressed without a skirt."

"Try striding out more. You can walk easier and it will help you to blend in," Wulfstan told her.

She experimented and even ran a few steps. She grinned. "I think I might enjoy being a boy."

Wulfstan produced a greasy woollen hat, its original colour long forgotten.

"Put this on," he whispered to Saewynn, "it is my special magic hat. It will make you invisible."

Saewynn put on the hat and pulled it tight over her chopped hair. A few dark wisps stuck out from underneath. Wulfstan looked her up and down. "I think that will do."

"I thought you said I would be invisible."

"Well... not to me obviously. It's my hat."

"It's a good disguise. The hat is a good idea," I reassured her.

"It's not working," Saewynn said mournfully.

"Of course it works. Byrhtnoth can see you because it's my hat and he's my friend." Saewynn looked sceptical.

Wulfstan took a deep breath. "All right, it doesn't actually make you invisible." He helped her onto a small shaggy pony. "It just stops anyone noticing you."

"Can you manage on your own? I don't mind walking and leading the horse."

"Don't be silly, that would make her even more obvious." Wulfstan handed her the reins. "Just hang on and the horse will follow the others."

"Do you have a weapon?"

Saewynn showed me her small eating knife. "Only this"

"That's not going to be much use," I took out my seax. "You can borrow this."

"And what are you going to use to protect her? We'll find something more suitable later." I sheathed it with relief. What had made me offer it to her? I may be becoming a man but sometimes I still spoke first and thought afterwards.

***

When we stopped to rest the horses, Wulfstan handed the hat to someone else to wear and we led Saewynn into the forest. We found a clearing just out of sight of the others.

"I assume you haven't any experience in fighting?" Saewynn shook her head. Her hair lay flat after being crushed under the hat for hours. When she ran her fingers through it, it stood up in spikes. "We haven't time to teach you how to fight properly. Take my knife and I'll show you a few tricks." His knife was not as big as mine, but just as sharp. "I'll pretend to attack, you try and defend yourself."

I watched as Wulfstan managed to disarm her within seconds. He pretended to hold it to her throat. "If a crippled, trainee monk like me can disarm you, you don't have a chance. If your attacker didn't have a weapon to start with, he does now, and can use it on you." Wulfstan released her. "Don't worry. The first thing to do, if you are attacked, is run away; find somewhere to hide. That's what you did when the Vikings attacked. It doesn't mean you're a coward, it's the sensible thing to do. If you can't run, don't panic. Look around, is there anything you can use as a weapon?"

I pointed out some dead branches and rocks lying around. "If you can't find anything, or you've already been caught, you still have weapons."

"No I don't."

"Yes you do. You have teeth. Anything that comes within reach, bite it and don't let go. You have hands with nails. Pretend you are a wild animal."

"That's right," Wulfstan said, "scratch any skin you find, dig your claws anywhere sensitive. Go for his eyes and rip them out. Stiffen your fingers and poke his eyes out, or up his nose. You get the idea?"

Saewynn thought about it, flexing her fingers. She nodded.

"Good, let's practice that." He shouted as she launched herself forward. "Slowly."

They sparred for a while until Wulfstan grew tired. "One more attack." Wulfstan grabbed Saewynn from behind and pinned her arms to her side. "You can't use your hands or teeth now. Relax, that sometimes puts them off their guard." She slumped in his arms. "But not in this case."

He told me to join the attack. I drew my seax and approached slowly, pretending to look menacing.

"What have you got left?" Saewynn struggled again. "Stop and think." The girl tied to kick back, stamp on Wulfstan's feet. "Ouch. That might work. But what are you going to do about the big knife in front?"

I moved closer, baring my teeth. Saewynn stopped struggling. She leaned back and suddenly kicked out. Her foot caught me straight between the legs. I collapsed on the ground. I had never felt such sickening pain. I rolled into a ball.

There was a shocked silence. Wulfstan released Saewynn and she rushed forward. "I'm sorry. I didn't mean to hurt you. What happened? Is there anything to do?" It was all I could do to shake my head.

"Now would be a good time to grab the knife and cut his throat." I knew Wulfstan was trying not to laugh as he pulled her away. "You have learnt a useful lesson. That's the best way to disable a man." He paused. "Doesn't work if a woman attacks you."

"Why not? I was just trying to knock the knife... Oh!" She realised what she had done and blushed furiously. "Will he be all all right?"

"He'll be fine in a while. Better get back to the others. Don't forget to put the hat on. You will be able to boast that you felled the great Byrhtnoth with one blow. Better not mention it when he's about though."

As she ran back through the trees, Wulfstan said, "You can get up now."

I just swore at him through gritted teeth.

30

The sheet of still water reflected the red and purple sky. Distant trees hung, supported only by their own reflection and the surrounding hills receded into dark night. More water than land, it reminded me of home.

"We can't follow the trail through that."

Elfgar nodded. "We'll camp here for the night. There's no doubt which way they are headed. The boats must have sailed up the Severn."

"From Ireland?" Wulfstan joined us, "or across from Wales?"

"The clothing we took from the bodies could have been Irish." I walked my horse along the edge of the water. "There's space here for a camp. Plenty of grass for the horses."

Elfgar stared into the distance. "We'll catch them tomorrow."

"Unless they've already left." Wulfstan looked for a dry spot to build a fire.

***

Rain fell steadily; water and sky merged into a dense grey nothingness. Those who feared a coming battle said their prayers. Others checked weapons for the final time.

Elfgar paced up and down the water's edge. The grass was trampled and he was oblivious to the water that had collected in the churned ground. The huntsman stood nearby; his dogs crouched behind him, wet and miserable. Everyone waited.

"They've lost the trail?" I broke the silence.

"Of course they've lost the bloody trail. The dogs are useless. No sign of tracks either. I've had men out, up and down the shore." Elfgar looked up at the sky. "This rain has washed away all traces."

"They must have had boats waiting." We stared out across the muddy waters. "They say that King Alfred hid from the Danes out there for months."

"That's a great help. Haven't you got any better ideas?"

"What's that?" I pointed out a hill several miles away. It stood proud from the surrounding waters.

Elfgar peered into the gloom. "That's the Tor."

"There must be a good view from the top." Perhaps we could spot the raiders from there.

"Perhaps," Elfgar said. "There's a monastery nearby. If they haven't been attacked, they may have information."

"Better than standing around here, my lord."

Elfgar's feet were now ankle deep in water. He moved swiftly back to solid ground.

"What are you all staring at? Get ready to leave. We ride for Glastonbury. Somebody get me some dry boots."

Elfhere was at my side as we left the water's edge and rode towards higher ground.

"I hope the Vikings have sacked the monastery."

"Why?" I looked up with surprise.

"They might have got rid of the abbot there: Dunstan. Nobody likes him."

I asked what he had done. I knew some churchmen meddled in politics; perhaps he had annoyed one of Elfhere's relatives.

"Jumped-up little nobody. Managed to worm his way into the

king's court. He arranged some 'miracle' and the king made him one of his advisers." I concentrated on picking the driest route through the boggy ground, not wanting to agree or disagree. "If he is alive, the sparks will fly when Elfgar arrives."

***

The rain stopped as we reached the top of the ridge and a watery sun appeared. Soon we were riding across the lower slopes of the green cone of Glastonbury Tor.

"Is there a path to the top?" I peered upwards.

"There must be." Wulfstan slowed Sleipnir. "I've heard there is a maze and however much you try, you never reach the top."

"Someone must have got to the top. I think there's a building up there." Elfhere pointed. Everyone slowed as we discussed the height and the best way to get to the top.

"We're not going up there." Elfgar quickened his mount. "The monastery is further on."

As the ground fell away, the road passed between buildings and a space that might have been a market place. It was deserted. Not even a dog barked at us.

"Where is everyone?" I heard Edward ask Godric.

"Wouldn't you hide if a group of armed men entered your town?"

"Perhaps they are all at the monastery." Wulfstan pointed. "That must be it there."

A well-maintained wall surrounded a group of buildings. Inside, one building, larger than the others, was being rebuilt, stone replacing the old wattle and daub. Figures moved inside the enclosure. Warily we approached the single entrance, a large stoutly built gate.

Elfgar reined in his horse. "Open in the name of the king."

"Who are you?" A monk appeared on the wall above the gate.

"I am Ealdorman Elfgar. Open this gate at once. We are on the king's business."

The monk scratched his head and looked down on the horsemen below. He took a long look around at the surrounding countryside, before slowly coming to a decision.

"You can come in. The others will have to stay outside. Leave the horses there," he paused, "and your weapons."

Elfgar sat immobile for a moment then dismounted. I handed my sword to Godric, then, with Wulfstan and a couple of the others, joined him outside the gate. There was a lengthy wait, and then the gate gave a loud creak and opened. A head peered out of the narrow gap.

"What are you waiting for? Come in." The gate moved further until there was room for us to enter. It slammed shut behind us.

"Sorry about that. Our gatekeeper is a bit slow. We can't take any chances nowadays. Follow me." The monk led us across a bustling market place. A woman in the doorway of a makeshift hovel glanced up then returned to stirring a pot on a meagre fire. Next door, another paused in her spinning, straightened her back as she inspected us, before returning to her work. A half naked child watched, thumb in mouth as we walked past. There was a group of men standing near some animal pens. They exchanged glances and reached towards absent weapons. Only the sheep and cows ignored us, standing listless and hungry under the hot noon sun.

We arrived at another smaller gate, leading into the main part of the monastery. It was quieter here, and cleaner. An elderly monk tended a small vegetable patch and other monks passed by, faces shadowed by hoods. From somewhere came the sound of a hammer striking metal.

"Please, wait here." The monk showed us into a small building. "I will send someone with refreshment." An empty table stood in the centre of the sparsely furnished room. There was a chair at one end and a bench pushed against the wall.

"We came to speak with the abbot. Where is he?" Elfgar demanded.

"He will be along in a moment." The monk bowed and hurried away.

Elfgar sat in the chair and stretched out his legs. "They have kept away the Vikings. I wonder how they managed that?"

A servant entered with some bread and cheese. He placed it on the table in front of Elfgar. Another carried a flagon of ale. Elfgar grabbed the bread and bit into it. He spat it out.

"I've got better in my saddlebag." He picked up the cheese, sniffed it and threw it back on the table and took a sip from the flagon. "At least this is drinkable." He took several gulps before putting it down. He sat back and closed his eyes. The rest of us, hungry and less fussy, soon polished off the remaining food and drink.

From outside we heard the distant murmur of conversation. The hammering continued for a while and then stopped; a bell started to toll. Elfgar snored and the rest of us exchanged grins. Elfhere went to the open door and looked out. He shook his head and returned to his seat on the bench.

Wulfstan had been sitting quietly staring at the floor. He caught my eye and sat upright. We were the only ones alert when the door was flung open, hitting the wall with a crash.

"Sorry to keep you waiting. No one told me you were here."

Elfgar jerked awake and struggled to stand.

"No need to get up, you must have had a long ride. Someone has brought you refreshment? Good."

The newcomer's eyes swept round the room, settling on the older man.

"Welcome, Lord Elfgar. It's been a long time. What can we do for you?"

The abbot was in his mid-thirties. Mousy brown hair surrounded his neatly shaved tonsure. He was dressed in the dark robes of a Benedictine monk; marked here and there with the small holes caused by proximity to a forge. He had none of the submissiveness of a monk, but exuded a vital energy. He beamed a welcoming smile and waited.

"Abbot Dunstan." Elfgar had made it to his feet. "We are here on the king's business; seeking information about the raiders who landed nearby. We have been following their trail. My daughter has been taken."

"Not the king's wife? I had not heard of this." Dunstan frowned at the news.

Elfgar shook his head. "My younger daughter, Elfflaed. Her travelling party was ambushed and she is missing."

"That is sad news." Dunstan bowed his head. "I will pray for her safe deliverance. You need help? A guide to show you the way?"

"You have had no problems with them?"

"Our walls are strong. The local villages were attacked. Some have hidden in the marshes, others have taken refuge with us."

"You have been lucky. There has been much destruction."

"We prayed and they left us alone." Dunstan shrugged. "And now you have come to destroy them." He turned to me. "You have something to say?"

He caught me unawares. I hadn't said a word; it was if he could read minds.

"Er..." What should I say? "I just wondered," I blurted out the truth, "did you pay them to leave you in peace?"

"That is a very good point. We did offer them money. You think that we shouldn't?" He gave me a pleasant smile, but it exposed slightly too many teeth, sharp and white like some animal.

"If you give them money, they will only come back for more." It was what I had been taught. Elfgar tried to interrupt, but Dunstan raised his hand, bright eyes fixed on my face.

"Perhaps. But we made a decision based on the facts. We did what we had to." He stood, head cocked like a bird studying a worm. "You are Byrhtnoth, are you not?" I nodded. "Several years ago, you begged the Bishop of Wintanceaster for help. How is my

uncle, by the way? I haven't spoken with him since the last Witan."
He studied my face. "You wanted him to help your friend. He was
injured. You were very eloquent. It was a difficult decision; caused
a lot of discussion. In the end I think it was your donation of land
to the church that won it."

"I did what..." I flushed as I realised what I was saying.

"You did what you had to," Dunstan finished my sentence.
"And this must be your friend. Wulfstan?"

Wulfstan nodded. I avoided his eyes. I had never told him
what it had cost me.

"He got you walking then?" Dunstan's eyes took in the twisted
leg and the supporting stick. "You were lucky." His voice hardened.
"What are you doing here with these soldiers? Why are you not in
your cell, doing God's work?" Now he had Wulfstan's attention.
The silence lengthened as Wulfstan considered his reply.

"I have permission to take a break from my monastery. I have
not yet taken my final vows and I have been given leave to consider
the future." I could tell he was trying to keep calm. "In the autumn
I will make my decision."

"There can be no doubt as to what that decision should be,
surely?" The abbot seemed to grow in height. "There can be no
future for you outside the walls of the monastery. You are of great
worth to the church. They have educated you and you must return
their investment." His voice rose. "There is much to be done in the
future. Things have become lax. The church must be cleansed and
rules tightened. You can help with that."

"I will make my own decision, in my own time." Wulfstan's
voice was steady. "As I think you did."

"God told me what to do," Dunstan announced.

"No doubt he will tell me as well."

"Enough of this discussion. We need to find those Vikings."

Dunstan spun at the sound of another voice. "Another puppy
barks. You are?"

"I am Elfhere, son of Ealhelm."

"I have met your father." Dunstan studied him carefully. "Not a pleasant experience."

He looked at Elfgar. "A friend of yours, I think."

"We should be leaving." Elfgar struggled to maintain his politeness.

"Of course. Let me show you to the gate."

"Thank you. I can find my own way." Elfgar stormed out of the room. The others trailed behind.

"A moment please." I paused in the doorway, what did this strange man want?

"You were correct about paying off the enemy, but I knew that the king would send someone to deal with them. And God has sent you. It was only a few old cups and suchlike, but if you come across them, we would like them back."

"I'll do what I can," I promised. We watched the others walk towards the gate. Elfhere and Elfgar were talking animatedly.

"Don't trust him; that son of Ealhelm."

"Elfhere? But he's my best friend, after Wulfstan."

"A man needs all the friends he can get, but beware. Don't believe everything he says." I frowned. What did the abbot know?

31

The guide was small and surly. He said he was from Abbot Dunstan's own estates. They were not far away and he knew the area well.

"You'll want to take your horses?" He sucked on his teeth and nodded. "Better to ride. The water level is going down, but it is deep in places. There are too few boats for all of you." He looked out over the watery landscape. "We will make good time along the high ground, but then the only way is through the marsh." He pointed to a hill that stood at the point where the flooded land merged into the sea beyond. "That's where they are. They call it the Isle of Frogs. The ships are beached on the seaward side. I don't know if they have anyone watching from the top." The guide shrugged. "They have been here some time. Perhaps they have become careless. There is a way to the top of the hill from this side. You should be able to keep out of view."

The guide clambered up onto a shabby mule. Abbot Dunstan appeared on the wall above the gate. He blessed us all before we rode off, towards the distant sea.

***

"We stay this side of the river." The guide led us away from the main flow of water and along banks surrounding small fields. Most contained young trees, with thin trunks and a handful of branches. The remnants of white blossom clung to some.

"The monks dug the fields and drained them. They took cuttings from the best apple trees in the area and planted them here. In a few years there will be enough apples to make cider for the entire community. In time this whole area will be cultivated."

"Very interesting," said Elfgar, shortly, "just get on with the journey."

The guide led us deeper into the marsh, sulkily. The fields ended and we were riding through shallow water. We managed a slow but steady pace, riding in single file. Any departure from the path resulted in a struggle to escape the clutches of the bog. In places, tree trunks had been placed to provide a path across a wetter patch. The horses were uneasy on the uneven surface, where a wrong step could cause a log to shift. Our destination seemed to get no closer.

"Are you sure this is the right way?" Elfgar complained, "You're making fools of us." The water was nearly up to the bellies of the smaller horses. The guide peered at distant landmarks, then made an abrupt turn in the apparently featureless water-scape. He looked over his shoulder.

"If you know better, go ahead."

Elfgar spurred his mount. He had only gone a few yards when his horse stumbled; plunging into deep water. Elfgar hung desperately to its neck. They struggled, churning the murky water. By the time he made it back to safe ground, everyone was splashed with thick, black, stinking mud. The guide waited, just out of range of the chaos. He spat into the water then urged his horse forward.

"Sometimes the direct route is not the quickest."

To add to the misery, it started to rain. Not hard but a steady, soaking drizzle.

"At least it will wash off some of the mud." Wulfstan wrapped his cloak closer around his body.

"And it will hide us from any guards," I replied. "Not that anyone would expect an attack in this weather."

"With all this water the swords will be rusty by the time we get there." Elfhere rode up just behind us. "Are we going to attack them?"

"Not today." I huddled deeper into my cloak. "Is it getting darker? Or is it just the rain?"

Finally we reached dryer land, close to the hill. It was much higher than it had appeared from a distance.

"Split up and hide in the trees. The raiders are camped behind the hill, beside the beach. The main route to the top is from this side. I'll meet you by the path." The guide disappeared into the gloom.

By the time we assembled, it was dusk. The rain had stopped but the darkening sky was still packed with low grey cloud. Water dripped from the trees.

"No talking," Elfgar whispered. "I don't imagine anyone is about in this weather, but we can't be too careful. Leave the horses here." He walked a few steps up at the steep slope. Water trickled down what appeared to be a gap in the ramparts. "The guide says there is a bank and ditch running around the hill. When we get to the top, we split into two groups. You," he pointed at me and some of the others, "circle round to the right. The rest of us will go left. We meet on the far side. For God's sake, keep a eye open for guards."

When we reached the top it was almost completely dark, just a smear of red in the clouds to the west. We moved slowly along the bank. To one side was a broad ditch then the hilltop rose gently beyond. On the other side there was nothing. I could sense the ground falling away beside us; a light breeze lifted our damp clothing. We trod carefully on the short wet grass. No one wanted to find out how far the fall was.

"Anything?" whispered Elfgar when we met again.

I shook my head. There was a glimmer of light as Elfgar wiped his sword on the turf. "Found one man. Wrapped up and asleep. He won't be waking. Check the rest of the summit. There shouldn't be anyone else. We'll set our own guards."

We stood on the top of the bank. The last of the light was reflected in the sea. We could hear it splashing restlessly below. At the base of the hill, the flicker of fires glowing through the trees.

"That's them." Elfgar nodded towards the lights. "We'll decide what to do in the morning.

32

We lay on the short turf, careful not to reveal our presence. Below the blue-green sea glinted in the sun. A hazy outline of distant land wavered on the horizon.

"Wales," whispered someone.

Beneath us, the lower slopes of the hill were covered in trees, separated by patches of meadow. Close to the sea, thin columns of smoke rose and the tops of masts stood, almost invisible.

"How many, do you think?"

"I see two ships, maybe three."

"No more than a hundred men." Elfgar stared down at the hidden camp.

Why hadn't they left? They must have been camped there for a couple of weeks. They usually hit and ran. "What are they waiting for?"

"That." Elfhere had spotted something moving slowly along the coast towards the camp. "Must be the last of the plunder arriving."

"We could send a party down there, between them and the camp." I studied the landscape. "They have to travel through that thick patch of woods." I pointed it out.

"If we attack them there, won't it just alert the main camp?" Elfgar said.

"Not if we plan it well. Kill the guards quickly. Silently. Do you remember that exercise we practised last year?" Several of the others nodded. "Scared the daylights out of those travellers. Not that we killed anyone, that time."

"Then you continue, disguised as Vikings," Wulfstan joined us. "With luck you will be into the camp before they know what's happened."

"The rest of us will circle round behind. Once you have their attention we attack." Elfgar studied the ground below. "It might work. You'll have to move quickly though."

I selected men; those able to run fast and silent, the best shots.

"Sorry Wulfstan. I know you are better than everyone with a bow, but we need to move fast."

"I know." Wulfstan tried to hide his disappointment.

"Can I come?" Somehow Saewynn had wormed her way into the group. "Wulfstan says I'm good with a bow."

"No, you're—" I paused. "You haven't practised this. Anyway, we need someone to protect Wulfstan." I ignored both their outraged expressions and checked everyone had enough arrows. I outlined the plan; confirmed Elfgar's movements. We were ready. I slipped over the lip of the hill, moving silently, dodging from bush to bush.

***

I crouched in the undergrowth, waiting. It had been a mad scramble, running fast, trying to avoid being spotted by both the Viking camp and the raiding party, but we had managed it. I sent Edward to the edge of the wood to scout the approaching group. He'd reported one man leading, mounted on a horse, followed by a small herd of cattle. The Vikings must be expecting a feast tonight. Behind was a group of prisoners, guarded by other warriors and finally a cart, stacked high with pillaged goods.

My men were positioned along the side of the path. All done

in silence; we had practised it many times. I checked back along the path; no one visible. When the procession arrived, I would step out, into the bright patch of sunlight that fell onto the path, and stop them. We would kill all the guards, as silently as possible, and then continue along the path as if nothing had happened. Would it work? I worried I had forgotten something; I thought it all through again. No, I could do no more.

With nothing else to do, I had time to realise that this was not an exercise, a practice with blunted arrows and wooden swords. This was the real thing. We would kill, for the first time, or be killed. There was a tree opposite. Would that be the last thing I ever saw? My stomach churned and the rim of my helmet felt tight round my head. My hand was clenched so close around a spear, my knuckles stood white against the stretched skin. I forced them to relax, finger by finger and watched the blood flow back. I took a deep breath and continued my inspection of the tree. The trunk was gnarled and fissured; twining ivy explored the surface. It was bathed in sunshine and the rough surface would be warm to the touch. I tilted my head to see upwards. The branches were clothed in fresh green leaves; some shone gold in the strong light. High up, hidden from view, a bird sang, sending its liquid notes up, high into the sky. I listened until, abruptly, it stopped. The sound of startled wings crashed through the air. Had I inadvertently moved and disturbed it? Back down the track I heard the alarms of other birds. Then there came the sound of a squeaking wheel. That must be the cart. No voices, but the noise of feet shuffling through the remains of last year's dead leaves. Round the corner came a man on a horse; the rider slumped in the saddle, tired from the journey and looking forward to a meal and sleep. I took in every detail of weapons and armour and adjusted my plans. Slowly the horse came closer. It was nearly here. I gripped the spear firmly, stood up and stepped out into the sunlight.

The spear thudded into the horseman's throat. The impact knocked the rider from his horse, dead before he hit the ground.

I ran forward, grabbed the bridle of the horse, and retrieved my spear. I removed the helmet and tossed the severed head into the undergrowth at the side of the path. I kicked the body after it. I led the horse back along the path. The cattle had stopped; snatching a meal from the woodland greenery. Elfhere was crouched over a body, wiping blood from his knife. I gestured towards the cattle and moved on. I heard a brief clash of swords, a grunt, silence fell. I reached the group of prisoners. Before anyone spoke, I put a finger to my lips. The huddle was mostly women and children. I approached one of the few men in the group.

"Keep everyone quiet," I spoke quickly, "you are free, but we need your help for a short while more. We will attack the Viking camp and destroy them." The man's hair was grey but he looked strong. There was dried blood on his face from a blow to the head.

"Can you fight?"

"I was called to the fyrd in my youth. I can fight."

"Good. Pick out anyone else willing and find some weapons. I'll explain the plan as we walk. We must get moving."

"Will you ride the horse?" Godric distributed weapons taken from the dead Vikings.

"The man had dark hair. I wouldn't pass for him. You'll have to do it." I passed Godric the spare helmet. "Better wipe off the blood first."

The procession reassembled. "Elfhere, get those animals under control."

"I came to fight, not herd cows," Elfhere grumbled.

"You'll be fighting soon enough. Get going."

***

We entered the camp without alerting anyone but soon the Vikings would notice the substitution. I drew my sword, waited. With my other hand I carefully drew a knife and plunged it into the rump of the cow beside me. I shouted and the beast bellowed.

Frightened by the noise, the cattle broke into a run and scattered through the camp. The captives fled back to the safety of the trees. Swords were drawn and arrows thudded into Viking bodies.

I followed the maddened animals. A Viking warrior was knocked aside and thrown to the ground. I glimpsed wide eyes and an open mouth before plunging my sword onto the man's chest. I twisted the sword and ran on. Another man stood before me. I swung my sword and dodged the spray of blood as the head spun away. I raced on.

A man raised a spear in defence but before it had reached the height of his shoulder my sword slashed. Spear and hand spun away. The sword dug into the man's neck and stuck, the dead weight pulling the weapon down. I braced one foot on the body's chest and wrenched it out.

The Vikings were well organised, already forming a shield wall.

I shouted and we rushed to assemble our own line. In the distance I heard a horn. The plan was working. I took my place in the centre of the wall, glanced right and left. Shields locked together. I gave the word. The line moved forward.

Swords beat on shields. One pace. Then another. The two lines clashed together. Every man stared into the eyes of his enemy.

Wisps of smoke drifted across the field. The man opposite me was not much more than a boy. He stared back, panting. I caught a blast of fish breath. I straightened to my full height.

"Get out of my way, you filthy little thief," I shouted down into his face.

Fear appeared in his eyes. I bared my teeth in a triumphant grin. The boy recoiled, stumbled backwards. My sword slid through the gap that appeared between the shields and tore into the boy's guts. His companion tried to close the gap, but he too felt my blade. The Viking defence was falling apart. Behind them, a group of horsemen galloped into the fight and spears caught the sea raiders unawares.

The battle was over. I stood, chest heaving, gasping for breath. Somewhere, the cry of an injured cow mingled with the sound of the fading fight. I glanced towards the slave pen. Already they were free and running towards the trees. I couldn't see Elfflaed anywhere. Perhaps she was in one of the tents scattered round the camp. As I walked towards the largest, a figure burst from the entrance and ran towards me. An unearthly scream rose and fell, mixing with the whistle of the axe he whirled around his head. He spotted me and the axe flew from his hand. I ducked but the weapon caught the side of my helmet. My whole body vibrated with the sickening screech and then the man was on me. He drew a sword. Shaking my head, I raised my shield to deflect the blow and fought back.

We circled, testing each other's strength, searching for a weakness.

"Have you no men, that you send a boy to fight me?" The voice was deep and the accent strange, but I understood the words.

"Man enough for you, ancient." I grinned, for the man was old. Sparse grey hair emerged from under his helmet and his beard, forked and roughly plaited was nearly white. He was richly dressed though, with many rings. He carried more weight than a warrior should, but moved easily as we exchanged blows. He must be the Viking leader, fighting to the death to earn his entry to Valhalla. I could hear shouts of encouragement from my companions, but the old man was alone.

We fought on, neither managing to get the upper hand. My opponent was tireless but gradually I sensed that something was wrong. I was good, but surely this man should have landed a blow on me by now. It seemed he wanted to keep fighting, without actually winning. I tested him, letting down my guard a fraction, inviting a killing blow, but he didn't take the bait. What was going on?

Then I heard the sound of an arrow. The man stumbled. He fell to the ground, the arrow embedded in his leg. I stepped back, confused. Who had interfered in my fight? At the edge of the camp I noticed movement. Wulfstan, mounted on Sleipnir was waving frantically.

I looked towards the sea. While we had been fighting, some of the Vikings had escaped. They had launched one of the ships. It moved slowly away from the shore.

33

Saewynn pulled up my horse.

"Will you ride him in?" She slid to the ground and offered me the reins.

I took one look at the dark swirling waters. He wouldn't go in there without a lot of persuasion. I handed her my helmet and unbuckled my sword. "Look after these." I checked my knife was safe in its scabbard at my waist, and then strode into the water. The ground shelved steeply and within a few steps the water was up to my chest. I gasped at the icy chill then took a deep breath. I dived forward and swam after the departing ship.

I would be an easy target if anyone noticed me, so I headed towards the tall sweeping stern of the ship where I would be hidden. The launch had been hurried, there must have been problems organising the oars as the boat wallowed, side on to the waves. I grabbed a trailing rope and worked my way round the stern to the steering oar. It had been tied up, out of the way, when the boat was beached; no one had thought to lower it yet. I pulled myself out of the water, careful to keep my head below the top strafe of the ship. I clung there for a few seconds, catching my breath. As soon as I appeared I would be spotted. I glanced towards the beach. The ship had already been swept away from the camp. I drew my knife and peered carefully over the edge. My luck was holding; no one looked in my direction. I heaved my body over the edge and crouched in the stern. At the far end of the ship was Elfflaed. She stood close beside a tall man, his bright red hair flared like a torch in the stiff breeze. In the belly of the ship were a group of men; the leader's hearth companions. They had abandoned the oars and no one was attempting to raise the sail. Everyone stared back down the estuary. Had my men launched the other ship? No, they had little experience of sailing a ship of this size. I was on my own. Clinging to the carved word of the stern post, I stood up.

In the distance, approaching at the speed of a galloping horse was a wave. Not a wave like those rocking the Viking ship now, but an enormous, vicious wave. It towered, green streaked with black like a dragon's skin, curling at the top in a boiling froth. The ship was helpless. When it hit, we would be bowled over, the ship ripped to pieces. I tore my eyes from the wave and without thinking, ran the length of the ship. I leaped from bench to bench. One of the attendants turned, but I elbowed him aside, he disappeared overboard. I reached the bow, the tall beast's head rearing above. I ripped Elfflaed from the arms of the red-haired man and jumped onto the gunwale. Grabbing her more firmly round the waist, I felt the ship rise beneath my feet. The wave was nearly on us, streams of white water reached out for us.

I jumped, as high and as far as I could, through the foam and the spray. I glimpsed the rolling water beneath and then we fell; down into the river behind the great wave. The impact knocked all breath from my body. We sank, down and down into the dark depths.

I struggled in the churning water, tossed around, desperate to find the surface. I kept a firm hold on the girl. If I lost her, I would never find her again. I tried to find a trace of light, but everywhere was darkness. Where was the surface? It was impossible to know. I tried not to breath, but water entered my gasping throat. I fought, refusing to let go of life. Then it seemed a voice told me to relax.

I closed my eyes and let my body go limp. We hung in the water. I felt something beneath my feet, something solid in this world of water. I tried to push, but my feet sunk into muddy ooze, drifting weeds twisted round my legs. Desperate, lungs burning, I kicked harder. The river lost its grip. I swam upwards until my head broke the surface, I gulped in mouthfuls of fresh air.

Elfflaed was a dead weight in my arms. Her head flopped and her lifeless eyes stared at nothing. Her mouth hung open, only a dribble of water emerged, no warm breath. She was beautiful, even in death.

I refused to believe she had gone. There was a woman, back when I was young, she had fallen into the river. Someone pressed her chest and she lived. Would it work? I moved my arms until they circled Elfflaed's chest. How slim her body was. I tightened my grip and water spurted from her mouth. I did it again, and again. I felt a shudder pass through her and water gushed from her mouth. She coughed and retched, directly into my face. I couldn't complain. She was alive.

"How do you feel?" Slowly her eyes focused on mine, only inches away. The misty blue froze to ice as she recognised me.

"Who do you think you are? Get your hands off me." Her voice was husky and she coughed again. I averted my face. She struggled, trying to escape my grip.

"Certainly, my lady. Can you swim?"

She realised we were surrounded by empty water. She squealed and wrapped her arms and legs round me. I enjoyed the sensation, but decided it wasn't worth dying for.

"Not quite so tight, or we'll both drown."

I looked around. There was no sign of the ship. It must have been swept far away by the wave, or sunk without trace. The water was still rough; waves picked us up and dropped us again. At the peak of one wave, I spotted a hill rising out of the flat land. Was it the hill where we had spent the previous night? It was land and as good a landmark as any other.

"Can you move round to hold on to my back? Wait until the water is calmer. Now."

"At least I don't have to look at your face." She wound her arms round my neck.

"Not so tight. We won't get far if you strangle me."

"I'll save that until we reach dry land."

"Save your breath." I identified the hill again and started swimming. "Try kicking your legs. It will help to keep you warm."

It was difficult to tell if we were getting closer. Perhaps we were being swept in the opposite direction. If the tide was coming in, at least we wouldn't be dragged out to sea. I kept swimming.

The coast appeared. I stopped and we hung in the water while I inspected what was ahead. Spray was tossed high into the air as waves hit sharp rocks scattered at the base of a cliff. There was no way we could get ashore here. I groaned and changed course, swimming parallel to the coast. We must come to a beach soon; the surrounding land had been so flat. Perhaps we had been swept further than I thought. I was starting to tire. The girl had stopped moving, only the arms locked round my neck gave any sign she was still there. My eyes stung from the salt water, it was difficult to see. Would it be better to stop swimming and drown than reach the shore and risk a violent death on the rocks? I couldn't decide, but I didn't know if I could swim much further. My arms moved slowly as screaming muscles refused to do more. I gasped for air, swallowing more of the salty water. I wanted to give up and sink into the welcoming depths.

I heard a noise above the rushing sound of the waves that had become our entire world. Someone shouting. I raised my head to see an arrow descend rapidly towards us. It plunged into the sea ahead of us. So strange was this sudden appearance that I just watched the wooden shaft bobbing on the surface. It would never support our weight. It had started to float away when I realised there was a rope attached to it. I dug deep for the last dregs of energy and reached for it.

I missed. My numb hand only pushed the arrow further away. I howled with frustration and kicked my legs. I felt Elfflaed stir on my back and her legs moved as well. The rope bobbed closer. My fingers were stiff, unable to grasp the rope. I managed to fling my hand over it and wrapped it several times round my arm. The rope hung slack in the water and then went taut. We moved through the water. I relaxed, concentrating on keeping our heads above the surface.

At the other end of the rope I saw Wulfstan urging Sleipnir along the shore. They struggled through the soft sand as we were pulled closer to the beach. We had been lucky. The cliff rearing up beside Saewynn was at the end of the beach. At its base were the rocks that I had feared would be our fate.

As we got nearer the shoreline, I realised the current was pulling us sideways faster than the rope was dragging us to the safety of the soft sand. We would reach the shore on rough stones littered with larger rocks.

I tried to free myself from the rope, but it was wrapped tight round my arm. My knife was long gone, sunk to the bottom of the sea. There was no time to persuade the girl on my back to let go. I twisted in the water, muscles screaming in protest, until I was on my back. I clutched Elfflaed with my free arm, her head held close to my chest. With my head bent forward to protect her, I waited for the impact. I felt my heels touch bottom. Then my shoulders hit the land. Above the sound of the sea, I heard Saewynn screaming.

34

Without the support of the water, my back dug into the rough surface. I didn't know what was ahead, all I could to do was grit my teeth against the tearing pain. If I hit a rock I wouldn't live long enough to care, so I concentrated on keeping my companion safe. The pressure of the rope abruptly ceased and we stopped. Cautiously I opened my eyes. All I could see was rock. I studied the details, the strands of weed and the conical shapes of limpets, scattered across the surface. Was I still alive? I must be, the pain of my back remained. I tried to blot it out by concentrating on the soft weight of the girl lying on top of me.

Then she moved. My head was jerked from side to side. Sharp shells scraped my cheek; I felt the trickle of hot blood. I welcomed its warmth. I realised that the rough and tumble of the waves had loosened Elfflaed's long blonde hair. We were bound together in its net.

"Get him away from me."

I grunted as a sharp elbow dug into my side.

"Keep still." I stared into the worried brown eyes of Saewynn. "I'll try and untangle you." She gave me a watery smile. "I think we'll have to cut you apart."

"You'll need something smaller than that," I croaked, noticing the sword she brandished. She must have cut the rope with it. She dropped it to the ground. I winced at the loud clang as it hit a rock.

"You can't cut my hair. What will I look like?" Elfflaed protested.

"It will soon grow again." Saewynn had taken out her small knife and frowned at it. "Unless you want to stay there, tied together for life?"

"I wouldn't mind."

I shouted as my head hit the rock again. Saewynn made a decision and I felt her warm hand touch me.

"I'll have to cut your hair close. Lie still."

Wufstan stumbled up, stammering apologies. He knelt on the beach beside us and unwrapped the tight rope from my arm. As he moved it to my side, the blood flowed back. Pain broke through the numbness and I clenched my teeth to drive away this new agony. I closed my eyes and concentrated on the lesser discomfort of Saewynn's hair cutting.

"Use this. It's a bit sharper." Wulfstan handed her his knife.

By the time Elfgar arrived, we had been separated. He dragged his horse to a stop and leaped from the saddle. His daughter stood, wet and shivering, on the sand.

He removed his cloak and swathed her in its folds. "Thank God you're safe."

Wulfstan helped me to my feet. I straightened with difficulty. Elfgar stared at me. "Thank you." He lifted Elfflaed onto the back of his horse and led her away along the beach. Saewynn trailed slowly behind.

My legs shook and I started to shiver. I found a rock to sit on. I wiped my hand across my face and studied the smear of blood.

Then I watched them walk away. Elfgar spoke to Saewynn. She pulled the hat from her head. She stopped and stared at it, and then ran back. She thrust the hat into Wulfstan's hands.

"Thank you. For everything." She reached up and kissed him on the cheek.

"Don't I get a kiss as well?" I asked. She paused, uncertain.

"Girl! Come here!" The instruction echoed down the beach. Saewynn shrugged and gave a sad smile. She ran back towards her master.

"Can't win them all." I shrugged and the pain started again. "Will that horse of yours allow me to ride him back? I'm a bit tired."

Wulfstan didn't reply. He was staring after the small party.

"It's all right, I don't mind sitting here for a while."

***

"Do you want more of this beef?"

I nodded and Wulfstan cut off a lump of the meat and handed it to me. We sat in silence, watching the remains of the Viking ship burn on the beach. Flames leapt into the darkening sky and sparks rained down to be extinguished by the approaching tide. We had found enough wood from the wreaked craft to build a funeral pyre. No one wanted to dig more graves and it seemed the best way to dispose of the dead.

"Elfgar didn't hang around for long." Wulfstan stared out across the water. "I suppose he wanted to deliver the other ship to the king."

"And claim the victory for himself." I wiped the meat juices from my mouth. "Leaving us to deal with everything else. I notice he took everything of value with him."

"Including all the captives."

"He needed them to row the ship. Pity Saewynn had to leave as well. She did well, for a girl. I think you might be in luck there."

"It's not me she likes." Wulfstan sighed.

"She fancies someone else? I hadn't noticed. Anything left to drink?"

"Just some cider."

"That will do." I hefted the small barrel and tipped it, letting the cool liquid flow down my throat.

Wulfstan watched me. "You really don't know, do you?"

I couldn't get rid of the taste of seawater from my mouth. I took another swig. "Know what?"

"It doesn't matter."

Shouts and cheers could be heard from further along the beach. "Elfhere seems to be having a good time."

"Celebrating his victory over the Viking leader," Wulfstan said.

"He still had some fight left? I thought I had disabled him."

"We had. Elfhere finished him off."

"That's not fair. He was a great warrior, protecting his family." It must have been his son I saw on the ship. "He should have been captured. He might have had useful information; why they planned the raid." I thought about it. "There might have been a ransom for him as well."

"Elfhere claimed all his gear."

"It won't do him any good. Not if he got it dishonourably." I leaned back in the sand. "Ouch."

"You haven't opened your wounds again?"

"Stop fussing." I'd drunk so much, I'd forgotten about them. "It's only a few scratches." I took another swig of the cider; it wasn't too bad. "Do you want some?"

"No thanks. I've had enough. So, once again Elfhere gets everything and you're left with nothing. And after doing all the work."

"Reputation is more important than wealth." It was what I believed, but it still stung.

"I suppose so. Some of the others weren't happy with how he behaved."

"That abbot at Glastonbury warned me about him."

"Dunstan? I wondered what you were talking about. Strange

chap. A lot of people dislike him. He inherited a lot of money and thinks he can do what he likes."

"It just means he doesn't have to suck up to anybody." I picked up the remains of the meat, inspected it and put it down. I'd had enough. I reached for the cider again. "I promised him I'd bring back the treasure he was forced to give to the Vikings. I expect Elfgar took that away on the ship. Nothing left here."

"I wouldn't be too sure about that. Remember the cart you ambushed?" I remembered the squeaky wheel.

"When you attacked, it was left in the forest. Everyone forgot it was there."

"We need to check." I tried to stand and collapsed in the sand.

"Everything is under control. I sent Godric to guard it." He watched me with amusement. "I think you've had too much to drink."

"Not enough." I reached for the cider and found the barrel empty. "It's just my legs are stiff after all that swimming."

"You need some sleep."

We watched the incoming tide until it reached the edge of the fire. Steam rose with a hiss. The beach was quiet now, only the gentle lap of waves on the sand. Stars started to appear. As the flames of the fire were finally extinguished, a thin crescent moon shone above the sea. Its reflection created a glittering path across the now calm water.

"What are you going to do now?" Wulfstan sat up.

"Do? I'm going to get some sleep." I spread my cloak out on the sand.

"Not now. The future. You fought, and won, your first battle today. Things have changed."

I thought about it. I suppose they had. "I'll have a place in the king's army now. I wonder how much fighting there will be this summer?"

"What about the sword?"

The sword. I raised my hand. I could almost see the blade shining in the darkness.

"It's time to visit Eadric. What about you? Have you made a decision yet? Will you return to the monastery?"

"I've decided." Wulfstan picked up a handful of sand and let it trickle through his fingers. "I'm not going back. I enjoyed my time there and I've learnt a lot, but I can't spend the rest of my life locked up, time measured by the ringing of bells. Anyway, if today's anything to go by, you need me to patch you up after your battles." He grinned. "And you need someone to record all your gallant deeds. I've already started composing something to be sung in the halls about today. Do you want to hear it?"

"No. I'm going to sleep."

35

"A message has arrived. It's urgent."

I tried to return to the darkness and the enjoyable dream, but it faded away. The insistent voice was real. I groaned, stretched, and then sat up suddenly. Pain brought back the events of the previous day.

Two shapes were silhouetted against the bright morning sun. One was Wulfstan, who was the other? I struggled to my feet; every muscle ached.

"What's the problem?" I yawned. "Don't we deserve some rest?"

"This man has brought a message from Abbot Dunstan." I recognised him now as the man who had guided us through the marsh. "He won't speak to anyone but you."

I looked around. Most of the others were asleep scattered across the beach. Those who were awake looked curiously in our direction.

"I need something to eat." I led the man up the beach to the remains of the beef carcass. "I don't suppose you've eaten either." I sliced off a piece of meat and handed it to him. There was not much left but I found some for myself. I checked no one else was within earshot.

"What's happened?"

"The Abbot of Glastonbury asks that you join him as soon as possible. He is travelling to meet the king at his hunting lodge in the King's Wood." He took a bite of the cold beef and glanced towards the sleeping men. "Elfgar, the lord who led you, has he left?"

I told him he had left straight after the battle; the man lowered his voice. "The abbot has heard rumours that the king is in danger. He needs your men to help protect him."

"Who threatens the king?" The man shrugged. I considered the information. More men were awake now, asking what was happening. They had had enough rest. We were needed elsewhere.

"Get ready to leave," I ordered them, then turned to the man. "Will you be guiding us again?"

"Yes, my lord."

"Not back through the marsh?"

"We head north along the coast. The land is higher there."

As I returned to Wulfstan, Edward ran up. I asked him if Godric was still guarding the cart.

"I think so."

"Tell him to select some of the smaller, more valuable articles; I'm sure he's already had a good rummage through everything. Pack them and load them on the horses with everything else. Leave the rest for the locals; most of it belongs to them anyway. Don't let anyone else see you. Now go."

"What's the rush?" Elfhere wandered across. He was loaded with the booty he had claimed from the Viking leader. A heavy gold chain hung from his neck and several rings encircled his arms.

"I'm surprised you can move with all that dangling off you."

"You're just jealous I got all the spoils. You should have finished him off yourself."

"I had more urgent things to do. Why aren't you getting ready to leave?" Elfhere's companions still sat around the remains of their fire. A jug of ale was circulating.

"They want to know the reason."

"It is enough that I ordered it. Elfgar left me in charge here."

"Just because you rescued his daughter," Elfhere sneered.

I told him he could have done it. "You preferred to stay and kill a wounded man."

"Not squabbling again? I thought we were in a hurry." Wulfstan handed me my sword belt. "What's it all about?"

I drew the weapon and inspected the blade. Elfhere took a step backwards and I slid the sword back into its sheath. I took my time in buckling the belt before replying,

"Abbot Dunstan has requested that we accompany him on a journey."

"If that's all, I think I'll stay here. The less time I spend in that man's company, the better."

"He is meeting the king. We do still serve him, don't we?"

"In that case, I'll put up with the company." Elfhere paused. "Where are we going?"

"I don't know, but if you're not ready in time, we'll leave you behind."

Elfere sauntered slowly away.

"So where are we going?" Wulfstan asked.

"Pucklechurch." I ran my hand through my hair, it felt strange cut so short. "Perhaps Saewynn will be there. We might even reach the king before Elfgar arrives to announce his victory." I grinned at that thought.

"But why the urgency?"

"Abbot Dunstan suspects a plot against King Edmund." My grin faded. "Don't mention it to anyone else. Ah, Godric. Everything packed?" He started to speak. "Tell me later. Are we ready to go?"

***

"You made good time." Dunstan glanced up from a letter he had been studying. As he greeted us, the parchment sprang back into a tight roll.

"Your message sounded urgent. I expected to find you on the

road." I dismounted and tentatively stretched. We had caught up with the abbot on a hill. To the west the river gleamed in the noonday sun; beyond, the hills of Wales were clearly visible.

"We wait for the Ealdorman of East Anglia. There will be warning of his approach; you have time to rest. Have you eaten?"

"We left as soon as we got your message. You said the king was in danger."

"All in good time. What happened to your hair? A close shave in the battle?"

"No. I got entangled with a woman. They had to cut me free."

"Indeed?" Dunstan raised an eyebrow. "I don't think I need to know about that. Have something to drink and tell me about the battle. You were victorious?"

A servant brought me bread and ale. I gave the abbot a report on our ambush and battle.

"Lord Elfgar must have been pleased with your efforts. You say he is returning to the king by ship? Perhaps we will see him sooner than we expected." He frowned and studied his scroll. "You were unable to discover who the raiders were? Why they came to that place?"

"No." I took another swig of ale. "We disabled the leader, but he died before I could question him. Elfhere killed him and claimed all his gear."

"Just for the booty? Or something else?"

"What other reason could he have? There was a young man, perhaps a relative of the leader. He perished on the ship. We didn't find his body." Why was the abbot so interested?

"I will send out messages, in case he is found. It was probably just a random raid from Ireland, although a bit early in the season for that. Your man wants you."

Godric waited nearby. I spoke to him then presented a small bundle to Dunstan.

"You asked me to retrieve the articles you were forced to give to the Vikings. Elfgar took all the valuables we found at the camp, for safekeeping he said. I expect he will return the abbey's possessions to you personally. Please accept this small token of my thanks for the help given us by your guide."

Dunstan unwrapped the cloth. There were a handful of rings and a cross. It was only a few inches tall but beautifully worked with several inlaid jewels. Godric had chosen well.

"I don't know where it came from, but it should be returned to the church."

"I thank you. It is a very fine piece. I hope you kept some treasure back for yourself." The abbot gave me an appraising glance. "You should receive payment for your efforts. Fame is good, but gold proves your worth."

I told him that we had taken our share.

"Good. Athelstan is late. We should make a move. If you are rested?"

***

"Have you found out what is going on?" Elfhere urged his horse level with mine.

"Ealdorman Athelstan is coming. Duncan was waiting for him, not us."

"What's he doing so far west?" Elfhere frowned. "He doesn't usually move far from his own lands."

"Perhaps he has something to discuss with the king. Doesn't his wife foster one of the king's sons? Perhaps he is ill or there is some problem."

"The younger son, Edgar. He is with the king; the king's wife wants to get to know her stepchildren. There is no sign yet of her having any of her own."

"It's early days." I gave him a curious glance. "How do you know all this?"

"Someone must have mentioned it. More to the point, why don't you know? You're interested in her sister."

186

"I don't think I've got much chance there." Especially not after nearly drowning her.

"You never know. Kill a few more Vikings and she might take more of an interest." Elfhere laughed and dropped back to his place in the column.

"You should listen to him, you know." Wulfstan had been listening. "We're not boys any more. If you want to get anywhere, you need to pay more attention to what's going on. What's the point of being a warrior if you don't know who you're supposed to be fighting for."

"We fight for the king. That's simple enough."

"Perhaps."

***

The sun was low in the sky when Athelstan and his men caught up with us. He joined Abbot Dunstan at the head of the column. I watched the animated conversation; heard my name mentioned. What were they talking about?

Darkness descended. I was nearly asleep in my saddle when I found the Ealdorman riding beside me.

"It's not far now, then we can rest. Didn't we meet a few years ago? You were still training then. Now, the abbot tells me, you have been defending the shores of our country. You must tell me about it later."

He spurred his horse back to the head of the column. I recognised him now. He was older; there was more grey in his hair than when we had conversed at the king's table. Why had he remembered me?

36

It seemed I had barely lain down to sleep before someone shook me awake. We had arrived late at the small hall. It was used only occasionally, when the king was hunting in the area. Everyone was asleep and we bedded down wherever we could find space.

In the weak dawn light I saw Ealdorman Athelstan leaning over me. Immediately I was alert.

"What has happened?"

"Nothing. I hope nothing will."

I sat up. Aches from the long ride had been added to my discomfort; but at least my back felt less sore, the scratches must have scabbed over. No one else was awake.

"What do you want with me?" In the distance I heard voices. A dog barked and someone quickly hushed it. Athelstan sat back on his heels.

"Abbot Dunstan has heard rumours of a plot to kill King Edmund. We don't know who, or why. That is what I am here to discover." He checked no one was listening. "The king has decided to go hunting this morning. It's a last minute decision so I'm sure no attempt will be made on his life. Will you join the hunt? Keep close to the king. Tell him about your recent fight with the Vikings, he'll enjoy that. Make sure he's safe."

I moved to wake Wulfstan, asleep nearby. Athelstan gripped my arm tightly. "Tell no one. We don't know who can be trusted."

"But you trust me?"

"Yes."

I reached for my weapons.

"Good hunting." Athelstan walked rapidly away. I stood for a moment, yawning, then headed towards the group of men gathered outside the hall.

"Morning Byrhtnoth." One of the king's attendants recognised me. "Where did you appear from?"

"We arrived late last night." I yawned again. "Too late for the meal. Is there get anything to eat now?"

The man pointed to a servant moving through the crowd. "I could do with something myself." We dodged through the stream of excited hunting dogs. "Anyone else from your party joining us?"

"I don't think so. They were all sleeping soundly when I left. What are we after this morning?"

"Anything we can find. The king's mother arrived yesterday and he's trying to avoid her. If Edmund's got anything to do with it, we'll be out all day."

"Oh good." I groaned. At least it would wake me up.

Edward appeared with a large, well-rested horse. What was he doing up so early?

"Yours was exhausted. This is from Athelstan." The animal was eager for some exercise. Edward helped me mount.

"Give him my thanks." I struggled with the powerful beast, before getting him under control. "Tell the others I'll be back later."

I identified the king's horse. It was a flashy chestnut, easy to spot among the others. The dogs and their handlers moved away into the trees. A servant handed the king a hawk. It fluttered its wings before settling quietly on his wrist. There was a brief consultation with the head huntsman and then the king followed the dogs into the forest. His friends and attendants clustered closely around him. I followed on behind.

***

The sun warmed my back and the gentle motion eased the stiffness of my muscles. My immediate hunger had been satisfied. I looked forward to fresh meat at the feast later. I checked the position of the king and moved closer. I relaxed in the saddle, but watched everything.

We moved silently through the forest, the dogs questing ahead. A bird was disturbed. It flew up into the clear blue sky. A decision was made; a hawk was loosed. The king had first choice but allowed other men a turn at the smaller targets. Everyone watched the hawk fly high. The bird hovered against the bright sky, barely moving. Suddenly, wings closed, the hawk dived, claws outstretched to grasp its prey. I had no hawk. I searched faces for suspicious glances, but all appeared concentrated on the hunt. Servants collected the rapidly accumulating corpses.

Fewer birds appeared and we moved to a thicker part of the forest. It grew darker as the trees closed in. The hunters strung out along a narrow track. Everything was quiet. If I were to plan an attack on the king, this is the place I would chose.

An animal appeared on the path ahead. A wild boar, a large sow, her teats hung low under her belly and piglets clustered around her. She stood, unafraid, glaring at the men before her with angry red eyes. The king called for his boar spear, his eyes never leaving the animal. A servant placed it in his waiting hand. The king urged his horse forward, expecting the sow to run. She stood foursquare before him, head swinging from one horseman to another. He rode closer but still she refused to move, just lowered her great head, as if considering whether to charge or not.

The king's horse stopped, upset by the heavy musky scent. The king lifted the heavy spear, and then plunged it into the animal.

His aim was true. The sow dropped to the ground, dead. There were no cheers or shouts of congratulation. This was not sport but an execution.

The piglets scattered. The hunters followed, chasing the small striped shapes into the surrounding woodland. Shouts and instructions echoed through the trees. Branches snapped and leaves shuddered, as horses blundered through. The piglets scurried here and there, then doubled back. Spears sped through the air. Only King Edmund remained on the path, staring down at the dead pig. I did not join the others. My job was to keep guard, to watch.

Servants rushed forward to deal with the carcass. The young men returned from their chase and tossed small bodies to the ground. One had injured a piglet. He paraded up and down with the small animal on the end of a spear. The king raised his head from his contemplation of his kill.

"We ride on. There is a place ahead where we will stop for refreshment." He looked with distaste at the squealing piglet. "Finish off that animal. We are here to kill, not torture."

The man apologised. He lowered the spear and cut the piglet's throat with a sharp knife. Blood sprayed, catching the sun like a rain of jewels, splattering the king. There were gasps and Edmund scowled at the man, then kicked his horse along the path. We followed him, well aware of this sign of ill omen.

Servants had set up a camp in a grassy glade. There was a seat under a canopy for the king, and a bench with bread and wine. The birds caught earlier in the day were already cooking over a small fire. One of the piglets was quickly butchered and added to the heat. Men sat around discussing the details of the hunt and passed around a drinking horn. I took only a sip and passed it on. I sat at the edge of the clearing, leaning against the trunk of a large tree. I rubbed my eyes. They still stung from the seawater. Was that only two days before? I was confused by the lack of sleep. It was peaceful here. Surely it wouldn't do any harm to rest my eyes for a moment. The voices faded away.

"Byrhtnoth!" I jerked awake. I was the centre of attention.

"Are we boring you?" King Edmund addressed me.

I struggled upright; felt a twinge of pain as scratches pulled at my back.

"I apologise. I have been somewhat lacking in sleep recently."

"And may we ask what has been keeping you from your bed? Some willing girl perhaps?"

"The Lady Elfflaed." I regretted the words as soon as they left my lips.

"My wife's sister?" Edmund raised a curious eyebrow. "You do aim high."

"Nothing like that." I shook my head to clear it. "There was a raid, deep into Wessex."

"Why was I not told of this?" The king jumped up, looking from one man to another. There was no reply.

"Ealdorman Elfgar sent a message. Perhaps it didn't reach you?"

"We have been travelling recently." The king sat back in his chair. "Tell me about it."

"There was an attack on a group of travellers. Elfgar's daughter was among those captured. We followed and found them on the coast, a day's ride south of here. We fought and destroyed them."

"And rescued the girl?"

I nodded. "She was taken on one of the ships. It tried to escape." How to explain it all? "I followed and brought her back."

"I thought there was a whiff of the sea about you. So you travelled here to tell us about this great victory? Why did you not mention it earlier?"

"I thought you had received the news. The Lord Elfgar took one of the ships. I expected to find him here already."

"Another person we have managed to avoid today." Edmund laughed. "You have done well. You must join us in our campaign this summer."

"There is to be fighting this year?" someone asked.

"There is always fighting in the north," the king said. "Perhaps we can arrange a marriage between this brave young man and the Lady Elfflaed." He inspected my travel-stained clothing. "Though I doubt you can afford her. I had to give her father a gold hilted sword for her sister, and a large bag of silver."

"Was she worth it?" someone called, cheekily.

"Well, her sister is the pretty one." He winked at me. "But she came with much land." The others cheered and started to debate the merits of different women of the court.

"So why did you come here?" the king asked me.

"It was the Abbot of Glastonbury." I thought quickly, not sure what to say to the man I was protecting. "He asked me to come. I don't know why."

"Ah, Dunstan. He must have had his reasons. I wonder what they were?"

A huntsman interrupted the conversation.

"A stag has been spotted," Edmund shouted, "the hunt continues."

I walked slowly to my horse. The other men spoke to me, asked questions, offered congratulations. I was part of the group now, no longer standing at the side watching. I should have been celebrating, but I was just too tired. There would be no rest yet.

37

The large stag hounds strained at the leash, ears cocked, sensing their time was coming. The deer was sighted, wandering alone through the trees. We moved into position. The plan was to drive the deer back towards the hall, perhaps kill it in full view of the visitors there.

The stag walked slowly, snatching a bunch of fresh new leaves from the trees, or lowering its head to graze the succulent spring grass. It had no antlers, they lay somewhere deep in the forest; cast off now their need was over. He was old, and thin from the past winter, but well muscled, the stumps of new antlers already emerging. By autumn he would be armed to fight for his share of the hinds. His ruddy coat gleamed in the dappled sunlight and the long hair that garlanded the strong shoulders was streaked black. He stopped, head up, alert. Something had disturbed him. Had a twig snapped under a horse's foot? Perhaps he caught the drifting scent of man or dog. His head turned in our direction. Then he was running. He disappeared into the trees.

No need for silence now. The dogs were released and streaked across the abandoned clearing. The horsemen followed, shouting and screaming. Birds flew, sounding alarms. Other forest animals beat a hasty retreat from the chaos. The stag ran fast through open glades, then used thicker cover to change direction. The dogs followed hard on his heels. The mixture of brown and black, grey and white, streamed behind like a comet's tail. The riders spread out. Each taking what they thought was the easiest route, trying to anticipate which way the stag would run. I ignored the animal. I followed the man, the king.

We burst out into an area of heath and the horsemen tightened up. We were close to the hall. One more patch of woodland and the stag would be brought to bay on the lawn beyond. Everyone strained to be first to the kill. We entered the darkness of the final patch of forest, slowing only slightly. Weaving round the trees, jumping obstacles and crashing through bushes. One horse reared when a bird flew up under his nose, depositing his rider on the ground. Someone caught a glimpse of reddish hide, tried to follow, and found themselves alone. The dogs, silent so far, slowed. They scattered, whining in frustration, casting around for any scent.

A deer burst out onto the green sward, the king close behind. I was his shadow. People emerged from the hall, shouting and pointing. The deer stopped. It was not the stag, but a hind, trembling in terror. The king pulled his mount to a sudden halt. Along the edge of the trees, other hinds emerged, some with their spotted fawns. The dogs harried at their heels. Horsemen emerged, circling in confusion.

King Edmund was the first to realise what had happened.

"Crafty devil. He's doubled back." Far away, a horn sounded. "Someone's spotted him. Quick, collect the dogs." The king dragged his horse round and plunged back into the woodland. Some riders shook their heads and sat watching as the others followed the king. I wished I could stay with them. With a sigh, I raced after the king.

We chased him back across the hearth. The pace was slower now. Even the mighty stag was tiring. Some of the dogs were still in pursuit. They followed the prey into the forest again. Huntsmen had remained behind. They knew this stag of old; he had been hunted many times and always escaped. They knew the land as well as him and subtly herded the animal to a rocky area. Soon we were threading between high rocks. Hooves clattered on stony ground. Dogs barked. I followed the king round a bend and suddenly, there was the stag. Cliffs towered above him. There was nowhere to run. He was trapped.

The hounds gathered round, snapping at his legs, jumping for his throat. The stag kicked out. One of the dogs caught the blow. There was sharp yelp and blood stained the ground. One of the dog handlers arrived and called off his pack. They retreated out of reach of the savage hooves, whining and snapping.

The stag stood, legs spread, head down. His tongue spilled from his mouth and spittle dripped on the ground. His chest heaved as he dragged the air into his lungs. Then he raised his head, unwilling to meet his death in such a submissive pose. The king selected a spear, short but with a heavy blade, sharp and deadly. He balanced it in his hand, considering the options. He looked round. I was there, at his shoulder. Other men were arriving, jostling for position in the cramped space. He handed me the spear.

"He is yours, if you can take him."

There were whispers as the king drew his horse back, leaving me to face the stag alone. I adjusted the spear, finding the perfect place to grasp it. I raised it above my shoulder, registered the ache in my muscles and compensated for the weakness. My eyes blurred, the wind from the fast ride had irritated my sore eyes. I blinked and searched the stag's body for the vital point. I noticed the sweat streaked hide and the marks of old wounds, some from spears like this, others the results of battles, with other stags, in the autumn mists. The animal moved, as if presenting his heart as a target. I pulled back the spear and in the split second before I loosed it, saw the muscles bunch. Anticipating the impact? As the spear hung in the air between us, the stag jumped.

Not forwards, to attempt escape through the men clustered

ahead, but upwards, as if he had grown wings. The spear skittered harmlessly along the brown hide, leaving a thin trail of blood, before dropping to the ground. The heavy animal hit the rock face with a loud thump. His forelegs found a narrow ledge, invisible from below and his hind legs scrabbled at the hard surface, sending down a shower of stones on the watchers beneath. I ducked and watched as he somehow found purchase. He moved upwards, around another rock. With a flick of his tail he disappeared, leaving only a smear of blood on the rock.

"Well," the king broke the lengthy silence, "I've never seen anything like that before."

I dismounted to retrieve the king's spear. Edmund watched me. "Bad luck." I handed it back. He turned and rode away. As I returned to my own horse, I heard a noise. I traced the weak whimper to a dog lying to one side. It was the one that had been kicked by the deer. As I bent down to help, one of the hunt servants approached.

"Don't worry, I'll sort that out." He drew a knife from his belt.

I stroked the soft black fur. The dog, a bitch, was much smaller than the other hunting dogs. She must have been with the men in the forest and joined the hunt in the final stages. She would never have kept pace from the beginning. Blood covered her head and one ear hung by a shred of skin. One of her front legs was broken. It might be repaired. I made a snap decision.

"I'll take her. I know someone who might be able to repair the damage."

"She'll never be worth anything, even if the leg mends."

The bitch's russet eyes stared up at me, pleading for her life.

"It doesn't matter. Have you got something to tie round her head? We might be able to save the ear."

The servant gave in and helped me to wrap up the animal. I remounted and the man passed her up.

"She'll probably be dead before you get her back to the hall. At least the king survived."

I started, what did this man know? I looked back up the track. I was neglecting my task.

"Not that king. Him." The servant pointed up the rock face. "We call him the king of the forest. He's lived to run another day. Perhaps he'll sire more young bucks before your king hunts him again."

As I rode to catch up with the rest, I made the black bitch more comfortable against my chest. She raised her head and licked my face.

38

Where had I slept the night before? The borrowed horse had been led away. The bloody bundle in my arms was still warm; I felt the faint patter of her heart against my chest. She had whimpered as I dismounted, clumsy from tiredness.

"There you are." Edward had found me. "Everyone has been searching for you. Are you wounded?"

"It's just a dog. It was injured. I thought Wulfstan could... Where is he?"

"Everyone is talking about a flying stag. Did you see it?" What was he talking about? I followed him to a long building and ducked my head under the low lintel. The room was nearly empty. I saw Wulfstan and Godric at the far end. I found my bed and sank down onto it.

"Where have you been?" Wulfstan hurried over. "We were worried when we found your bed empty this morning."

"I went hunting."

"Why? Didn't you have enough riding yesterday?" I couldn't explain, I gave him the bundle.

"She's injured. Can you do anything?" Relieved of my burden, I lay back and closed my eyes.

"You can't sleep. The feast is about to start." Wulfstan

unwrapped the dirty cloth and inspected the animal. "I should be able to set the leg, it's a simple break. What happened to it?"

"She came off worse in a fight with a stag." I dragged my weary body upright. "Careful with her head, the ear is nearly off."

"Was that the flying deer?" Edward asked eagerly.

"I'll get Saewynn to sew that back on. She's good with a needle."

"Elfgar is here then?"

"They arrived earlier." Wulfstan gently inspected the dog's head. "The scalp is cut as well. That accounts for all the blood. Godric, find some water. Then help him dress."

I attempted to remove my filthy tunic.

"He'll need a wash as well."

I felt brighter after Godric had poured a bucket of cold water over me. He rubbed me down with some straw, like some docile horse. Dressed in my best tunic, I watched Wulfstan deal with the injured bitch.

"Will she be all right?" I pulled a comb through my wet hair.

"She should be fine. She'll have a few scars; I don't know if I can save the ear. What was a little thing like that doing, tackling a stag? She must be very brave." He stroked the thin body. "Carry on. You can't be late for the feast. I'll join you later."

The hall was busy. Men gathered, exchanging greetings and catching up with the latest news. Colourful banners hung from the walls, competing with the rich clothing on display below. Servants threaded their way through the throng, arms full of loaves for the table. I caught a glimpse of Elfgar across the room. The man reluctantly acknowledged my presence. Elfflaed ignored my wave and turned to her companion. Nothing had changed there, then.

I found Athelstan and gave him a short report on the day's events.

"Thank you." His eyes were constantly moving across the crowd. "It was probably just a rumour, but anything can happen during a hunt; a convenient accident." People were sitting down.

"The king should be safe here. No one would try to murder him in his own hall." He led me to an empty place on the bench. "There's a good view of the top table. Watch out for anything suspicious."

My job was not over yet. I hoped I could stay awake. I poured a cup of ale from a nearby jug. The cool liquid soothed my throat; I must avoid the mead this evening. I began eating as soon as the food arrived, I hadn't realised how hungry I was. They brought in the sucking pigs from the hunt. They had been cooked quickly. As one of the participants in the hunt I was awarded a potion. The skin was crisp and golden, scattered with herbs. As I pierced the meat with my knife, a trickle of blood oozed from the meat. I recalled the spray of blood that had stained the king's clothes. Was it really a bad omen?

I studied the top table. King Edmund, of course, was in the centre, seated in a large chair. Next to him was a woman. Her chair was smaller than the king's, but richly decorated. She was dressed in purple and gold. Necklaces hung from her and rings glittered on her fingers. She ate little, but her hands moved constantly, perhaps to demonstrate her wealth. She tapped on the board to emphasise a point and plucked at the sleeve of the king to get his attention. He had his back to her, deep in conversation with Abbot Dunstan. The woman was older than she appeared. She must be Edgiva, Edmund's mother. No wonder the king had been so keen to spend the day hunting.

Where was the king's wife? I spotted her squeezed in near the end of the table, next to her father, Elfgar. It looked like she was complaining about something and Elfflaed was trying to calm her down. I compared the two sisters. The king had been right; Ethelflaed was not nearly as pretty as her sister. He had said he would arrange a marriage between us; he must have been joking. I could never aspire to the hand of the daughter of the richest man in the land. I attempted to make conversation with my neighbours, but was too tired to make sense of what they said. I was relieved when Wulfstan arrived. I moved up to make room.

"Any food left?"

"Plenty." I pushed the plate of pork towards him.

"I've left the dog with Saewynn. She's sewing her up. I've sent some food for them both. Are you sure you don't want this, it's very good?" I said I'd had enough. "Are you going to tell me what's going on?" Wulfstan lowered his voice, but the noise in the hall was rising. The edge had been taken off appetites and drink was flowing. I checked no one was listening.

"Lord Athelstan woke me early. Said there was some plot against the king. He asked me to accompany Edmund on the hunt. Make sure he was safe. He wouldn't let me tell anyone, even you."

"I knew it must have been something important. You look tired."

"I am. Keep talking to me, or I'll fall asleep here. He asked me to watch for anything suspicious during the feast."

"Here? No one's going to try anything here. That was a good trick."

"What? I didn't notice." I was watching the audience, not the acrobats. Checking who was paying attention. Who wanted to kill the king?

The scop tuned his harp. The mead horn started to circulate. I watched the ebb and flow of the servants. They cleared dishes, brought more food, refilled jugs. One caught my eye. He was less servile than the others. He held his dark head high, as if he considered the feasters his inferiors. I watched him move up and down the hall; noticed how he lingered too long near the top table.

"I know that man from somewhere." I nudged Wulfstan.

"Who?" I pointed him out. "Never seen him before. You've probably noticed him around the court. He stands out from the others, though."

The noise level rose as more alcohol was consumed. It was time for the women to retire; the men would continue until the drink ran out, perhaps all night. I watched Eadgifu lead the way to the door, attendants fussing around her. Ethelflaed and Elfflaed followed slowly, side by side, talking animatedly. What was it that women talked about, when men weren't there? I listened as two warriors argued about the tactics of some long ago battle. I dragged my attention away. Where was the man I had been watching? He was directly opposite, leaning over the board to refill some cups. A sudden draught caught the fire, sending a flame high in the air. The light turned the servant's hair a brilliant red. I recognised him.

"The ship. He was on the ship." I gripped Wulfstan's arm.

"Who? What ship?"

"The servant. He was one of the raiders. He's changed his hair, but I'm sure it's him."

We watched the man saunter towards the door, following the women.

"He was on the ship with Elfflaed." I stood up. Athelstan looked curiously in my direction.

"Tell them what's happened. I'll follow the man."

I hurried towards the door, pulled Godric from his seat near the bottom of the board. In the doorway we collided with a man entering. I apologised, searched the pile of weapons for my seax. Armed, we burst from the hall. We were blind in the darkness. Which way to go? I caught the sound of a woman's laughter.

"Over there."

Away from the hall, it was easier to see. We saw a couple, close together. An argument. I recognised Elfflaed's raised voice. I ran towards them.

"Leave her alone."

The second figure spun round. I caught a look of hatred. The man disappeared into the darkness.

"Catch him," I shouted to Godric.

"Are you all right?"

"Of course I'm all right," Elfflaed said, "what do you think you're doing?"

"But, wasn't he...?" I stopped, confused.

"He was one of the raiders. He cared for me, protected me. You killed his father; you nearly drowned him. He came here to check that I was safe. It was very brave of him." She turned away. "He came to say goodbye. Before he returned to his own country."

"I'm sorry. He got away." Godric emerged from the darkness.

"It doesn't matter. It was a mistake."

"A mistake?" Elfflaed's voice rose. "You're the mistake. Your parents made a mistake by having you. Whoever they were." She stalked away.

I'd really had enough now. I just wanted to sleep.

"Well, that didn't go well." Godric lowered his weapon. "Let's get back to the hall, we need a drink."

As we walked back towards the light of the hall, the noise from the building changed. The convivial hubbub usual at this late stage of a feast had disappeared. Shouts of alarm were punctuated by screams.

"Murder!"

39

I pushed through the knot of people in the doorway. Armed guards fought against the flood of feasters trying to escape. I ran up the centre of the hall, where the acrobats had performed earlier. I dodged past the great fire. It was dying now, casting shadows on the walls. Devils seemed to writhe and cavort with figures from the wall hangings. I reached the far end, searched the faces. Everyone was focused on the floor beyond. I leaned across the disordered table.

King Edmund lay on the floor. For a moment I thought he slept, but open eyes stared blindly up at the roof beams overhead. A patch of blood bloomed on his chest. One hand clutched at the wound, as if to force the heart to beat again. Nearby another body lay, face down. There was more blood here, splattering an anonymous brown cloak, and soaking into the reeds beneath. A guard sat nearby. Blood dripped from a hastily wapped cloth around his arm.

"What happened?"

"It was a messenger," Athelstan said, "he approached the king. No one noticed him draw a knife. Everyone was watching you. There was a scuffle and the king fell."

"It was my fault."

"Of course not. The assassin took advantage of our distraction."

I ignored his consoling words. I knew that I had failed.

"Yes, it was your fault," Elfgar said, "if you didn't spend your time chasing girls, you would have been here to protect your king. I saw you follow my daughter."

It was too much. I spun to face Elfgar.

"If you had more control of your daughter, she wouldn't get into trouble. Then she wouldn't need to be rescued."

In the quiet of the hall someone stifled a nervous laugh.

"You can't talk to me like that." Elfgar stepped towards me, face flushed.

"Perhaps he was part of the plot."

The suggestion slithered down my back like an icy draft, coming from a man I'd not seen before.

"He spoke to the assassin as he left the hall. Was he giving him his instructions? I have been informed that this man has been following the king all day, waiting his chance."

It was the final straw. I swung round, seized the man by the front of his tunic and dragged him across the table. Bowls of food scattered and drinks were upset. Wine and mead spread across the board. They dripped to the floor below, merging with the pool of blood.

"How dare you say that?" I shouted into his face, only inches away. The man's watery blue eyes widened and his pasty skin paled.

"Nobody accuses me of that. Nobody. I would never do anything to harm the king. Take back those words or they will be the last you speak."

I raised my hand, still clutching the seax, towards the man's throat. Somewhere, far off, I heard shouting. Hands grabbed me, trying to pull me away. I directed all my rage and frustration at him. I cannot remember the words I shouted. Something hit the side of the head. My grip weakened. The seax spun away, out of reach. The man collapsed across the table.

The blow drove all anger from me.

I recognised him now. I had seen him before. This thin sickly man was Eadred. He was Edmund's brother. And he would be recognised as king, probably the next day.

I watched, in a daze, as attendants helped the new king upright and brushed the remains of the feast from his clothes.

"I apologise for my behaviour." What else could I say?

"Get out."

I shook the men from my arms. I walked down the hall, looking neither right nor left. I held my head high, focused on the black shape of the open door. I awaited the blow of a spear in my back or the sound of a sword slicing towards my neck, but all was silent.

I walked out, into the darkness. I kept on walking until I found a place darker than anywhere else. I'd done everything wrong but I was too tired to even think about that now. I lay down and curled into a ball. I saw an image of the horror on Wulfstan's face, before a wave of black sleep arose and drowned me.

40

The sun was high in the sky. Where was I? Why had nobody woken me? I was tucked in a narrow space between a fence and a building. I could hear the quiet movement of horses and smell the distinctive mixture of hay and dung. I was behind some stables. How had I got here? Had I drunk too much the night before?

Then I remembered.

I must leave. There was no sound of a search; everything was quiet. From far away came the sounds of distant singing. It must be the funeral mass for the king. I might have time to collect some of my belongings before anyone realised I was still here. I took a cautious glance round the edge of the stables, no one in sight.

As I ran silently to the visitors' hall, I considered my options. Which way to go? After the recent battle, I would not be welcome in Ireland, so west was out. South, across the seas to Frankia? Where would I find a ship? I remembered the stay with Coela, years ago. Perhaps I should go to Lundenburh and get lost in the teeming streets.

By the time I reached the empty hut, I knew there was only one way to go. North. If I was lucky I might find a new lord to serve, to fight and die for, or robbers might kill me on the road. I didn't really care. I stuffed some clothes into a leather bag. There was not much. I retrieved my sword from beneath the mattress. What had happened to my seax? Someone would have claimed it. I would miss it. As I lifted my shield from where it hung on the wall, I heard a noise.

I'd forgotten the dog. She was curled up in a basket on Wulfstan's bed. I bent and stroked the skinny curved back; the thin tail beat once. Dark eyes gazed up from a clean bandage around the narrow head. She would survive.

"I can't take you with me," I told her, "you'll be all right with Wulfstan, he's good with animals." I heard the door opening and stood up slowly. I hoped I wouldn't have to kill one of my friends.

Saewynn stopped when she saw someone was there, then rushed over when she recognised me.

"Everyone was so worried when you disappeared. Are you all right? I brought some scraps for the dog."

"I'm leaving." I picked up the bundle and hefted the shield onto my back.

"Where are you going? When will you return?"

"I won't be back."

"Why?" The girl followed me towards the door. If she didn't know, someone would explain it to her.

"I must get away before anyone notices me."

"Have you got any food?" I hadn't thought about that. "Wait here. I'll find something from the kitchen."

"Not here. Someone might come."

"They won't be back for ages. They're choosing the new king. Edmund's sons are too young. They will decide on Eadred."

I flinched at the name. "Meet me behind the stables. Be quick, I can't wait long." I peered out the door; the coast was clear.

***

I was ready to leave when Saewynn appeared round the corner.

"There's a large piece of ham and a chunk of cheese. The bread

209

is fresh this morning, it should last a few days. The leather bag is filled with the best ale."

I thanked her and she watched as I packed the food and tied the bundle tightly.

"Do you really have to leave? Where will you go?" I didn't reply, what could I say?

"Will I see you again?" She wiped away some tears, and then she hurled herself into my arms. I hugged her and buried my face in her dark fragrant hair.

"Take me with you. I won't be any trouble."

I released her and forced a smile.

"They'd really be after me then. I threaten the king, and then steal a slave. You'll soon forget me." I smoothed her hair. "It's growing longer."

"So will yours."

I tossed the bundles over the fence. I grabbed the top of the wooden barrier and pulled myself up.

"Look after Wulfstan and the others. Tell them I'm sorry I let everybody down."

SUMMER 946

41

Saewynn rubbed her eyes on her sleeve and walked slowly back to the hut. She stopped at the entrance to pick up the fallen bowl and went to feed the dog. When the food was gone, Saewynn wiped her greasy fingers on her skirts.

"That's all for now, little one." The animal's dark eyes peered up into hers. "I'll try to bring you more later."

The dog looked towards the door and whined.

"He's gone. He said he wouldn't be back." She stroked the smooth black fur as the dog rested her head in her lap.

The men arrived back from the chapel, breaking the silence. Wulfstan sunk down onto the bed beside her. He bent and rubbed his leg.

"Too much standing around. Always makes it ache. You must get back to your mistress. The witan will start shortly and she'll want to look her best."

Saewynn wondered how to break the news, but before she could, Wulfstan noticed the empty space where Byrhtnoth's shield had stood.

"He was here. Where is he?"

"Gone."

"Where?"

"I don't know. He said he was sorry he had let everyone down." Saewynn buried her face in her hands. "I don't think he's coming back."

"Of course he'll come back." Wulfstan put his arm round her shoulders. "He can't leave like that. Where will he go? What will we do without him?"

Others gathered round, asking questions. Saewynn shook her head.

"Good riddance, I say," Elfhere smirked, "it was impossible for him to stay, after what he said to the king."

"He's not king yet," Wulfstan said.

"He will be. Who else is there? Edmund's sons are too young. I'm glad Byrhtnoth left quickly. We may survive the ignominy with him gone."

A few agreed; others protested. With Byrhtnoth gone, Elfhere would become their leader.

"Pity he didn't take this smelly animal with him." Elfhere nudged the basket. The dog gave a low growl. "Vicious little bitch." He drew his knife. "I'll put an end to her noise."

"No!" Wulfstan caught his arm. "Leave her alone. She's my responsibility now, until Byrhtnoth comes back."

"Hobble back to the monastery then, both of you," Elfhere sneered, "I'm off to acclaim the new king. Who's with me?"

"What's going on here?" The room darkened as Ealdorman Athelstan filled the doorway. "Where's Byrhtnoth? Is he here?"

"No. He left," Wulfstan said.

"Why has he done that? I need his support in the witan. It would be his first time. No one else here is qualified to vote, I suppose?"

"I own sufficient land to take part," Elfhere boasted. "Byrhtnoth has dishonoured us and fled."

Athelstan inspected Elfhere, from his clean soft boots to his carefully combed hair. "At least Byrhtnoth knows what honour is. You serve your father, I think."

"Of course."

Athelstan turned to Wulfstan. "Abbot Dunstan has requested your help. He is short of clerks."

Wulfstan nodded and reached for his writing bag.

"What is that woman doing in here?"

Wulfstan told him she had brought food for the dog. Athelstan approached the basket. The dog raised her head and moved her tail.

"Is that the dog Byrhtnoth rescued? Look after it. And you, get back to the kitchen or wherever you belong."

Saewynn bobbed her head and hurried out.

"If Byrhtnoth returns, send me word." Athelstan strode out of the room.

***

"Where have you been? Quickly, pin my veil," Elfflaed snapped, as soon as Saewynn entered the room. "The meeting will be starting soon. I must look my best."

"You always look your best, my lady." Saewynn took the silver pins and carefully positioned them in the snowy white linen. "There, perfect."

"Where is my blue cloak?"

"Did you lend it to your sister? She needed something to wear at the feast last night."

"Of course. I wonder what will happen to her now her husband is dead. I expect our father will marry her off to someone else, although not to the new king, the church would not approve. Perhaps I shall have him instead. Is that allowed? I must ask a priest." She nodded at her image in the mirror. "Yes, that will do. Where have you been all this time?"

"Byrhtnoth has gone," Saewynn blurted out the news.

"Where? Is it to do with the king's death?"

Saewynn nodded. "He feels responsible."

"He insulted the new king. I wish I'd seen it. Something exciting happens and I'm not there. I'd love to have seen that young man taken down a peg or two. How do I look?" She stood up and smoothed her gown over her hips. Nothing kept Elfflaed from contemplating her appearance, not even the murder of her sister's husband.

"Wonderful, my lady. Good enough for a king."

"Of course."

***

The hall was filling up. The guards on the door, alert after their mistake of the previous night, were careful to relieve everyone of their weapons. One richly dressed man argued that his knife should not be left at the door, but it soon joined the mounting pile. The top table remained in place but the benches had been pushed against the walls. The royal chair stood empty, awaiting the new king. Clerks sat in the places usually occupied by great men and Abbot Dunstan bustled between them, checking inkwells were full and blank parchment was ready. He stopped in front of a pile of old documents and sorted through them, unrolling one to scan the contents, then another. From her position behind Elfflaed, Saewynn saw Wulfstan and gave a small wave. He acknowledged her presence and continued his job, sharpening goose feather quills.

The crowd in the body of the hall moved restlessly; a continual ebb and flow as men met, spoke and moved on. The great ealdormen, clad in their costly fabrics and glittering jewels, stood, staking their claim to a position in the hall, as near to the top table as possible. They eyed their enemies, assessing their wealth and the number of their supporters. They also checked the ones they called friends. Allegiances changed quickly at a meeting like this. Saewynn watched Elfgar, her master. He was closest to the table, explaining something to Dunstan, who shook his head and moved away. Another man approached Elfgar, bowing to the richer man. At the second man's shoulder, Saewynn recognised Elfhere. He lingered there with an ingratiating smile. The second man introduced him to Elfgar, who acknowledged him graciously and exchanged a few words. The other man must be Elfhere's father. He was an Ealdorman in Mercia and had the same smooth polished appearance as his son.

Nearby, Ealdorman Athelstan of East Anglia watched Elfgar and his group, before continuing his own conversion. Why was he interested in Byrhtnoth? Was he a relative? He was tall, like Byrhtnoth, but then many of these families were descendants of the Danes who had invaded the eastern lands long ago.

"Stop dreaming and fetch me some wine." Elfflaed's voice was sharp. "Take some to my father as well." Saewynn hid a smile, as she hurried to the jugs waiting at the side of the hall. Her mistress was upset that the men were more interested in politics than in admiring her.

***

The witan went on for hours. The churchmen talked at great length, mainly to each other and in Latin. Documents were flourished, discussed and discarded. Blank parchments were covered in small black words. Great men spoke, stating their cases, jostling for position, arguing or agreeing, depending on their alliances. Saewynn passed the time watching the few women in the room. Who was wearing what? Which style of gown was most in favour? What colours would suit her mistress? Elfflaed spoke to her occasionally, commenting on some point that had been made or how handsome a young man was.

It ended with the outcome everyone had expected. Eadred would be king. A date was set for his coronation. Messengers were sent out to tell the country of his accession. Great men swept out of the hall, angry at the outcome or eager to get home. Others stood around, loath to leave, celebrating their success.

"I must rest before the feast tonight. What do you think I should wear?"

"I know just the thing, my lady. We'll need your blue cloak back from your sister, though."

"Fetch it."

42

A welcoming brazier glowed in the corner of the women's hall and refreshments were laid out on a low table. Saewynn could not see the blue cloak; perhaps it was in Ethelflaed's chamber. She scratched at the door and, hearing no answer, pushed it open. She looked round, it seemed that the two sisters were alike in their untidiness, although the king's wife had fewer clothes. Saewynn felt sorry for her; better to be the daughter of a rich father than the neglected wife of a king. Perhaps she hadn't pleased her husband. Saewynn paused in her search. How did one please a king, or any man? She wondered how she might please Byrhtnoth. She blushed and concentrated on the pile of clothes.

She spotted the distinctive bright blue cloak and picked it up. She heard a sound from the outer room. The door banged back against the wall. Someone had entered.

"No one is here. We can talk in private."

It was the loud, commanding voice of Eadgifu, the king's mother. Saewynn felt she should make herself known but it was too late. A man replied. She couldn't make out the words.

"Shut the door. Why can't you do what you are told?" She must be talking to a servant. The man's reply was muffled, but it sounded like Eadred, the new king. It was impossible to leave now. Saewynn must keep quiet and hope they left quickly.

"I told you to leave everything to me. I could have arranged things better than that, and at the right time."

"I was tired of waiting." Eadred's voice was louder now, anger taking over from the whining complaints. "His sons were growing. I wanted my turn. You said I would be king."

"But why do it like that?" The queen's voice filled with scorn. "In the middle of a feast. Why not quietly, a sudden illness or a hunting accident?" The king's reply was too quiet to hear. "If you want to use an assassin, pick one you can trust to do the job properly."

"At least I managed to put the blame on that boy, the one Athelstan picked to protect Edmund."

"You did well there. What was his name? Byrhtnoth? What happened to him? Did you get rid of him?"

"No. He disappeared." Eadred sounded disappointed.

"He won't show his face around here in a hurry. We can easily get rid of him if he does. What's that noise?"

Saewynn had been unable to stifle her gasp. She would be discovered. They wouldn't hesitate to kill her.

"Did you check no one was here?"

"You said it was empty."

Saewynn slipped onto the bed, pulling the blue cloak over her.

"Check the rooms," Edgifu commanded.

First one door opened, then the next. Saewynn closed her eyes tightly.

The door of the room opened. Perhaps they wouldn't notice her.

"This one's empty." Saewynn relaxed.

"Wait, someone's asleep."

Saewynn thanked him for the suggestion. She opened her eyes, blinking.

"Lord Eadred. What are you doing here? Where am I?" She looked at the blue cloak, clutched tightly between her fingers. "I came to collect my lady's cloak. I was so tired. I sat down for a rest. I must have fallen asleep. Is it late? I must go."

She was struggling upright when the king's mother appeared at the open door. "Oh, my lady, you're here as well. I'm so sorry, I must go." Saewynn stood up and tripped over the long cloak. She sprawled onto the floor. She crawled towards the door, bobbing her head repeatedly. "Sorry my lady, sorry."

Edgifu disappeared from the doorway. "A stupid servant girl." She hissed at the king, "let her go. Are you all right, my dear?" She spoke to Saewynn with a voice like molten honey. "Don't you know Lord Eadred is now king?"

"Are you, my lord?" Saewynn forced her eyes open in amazement. She bobbed her head again.

"Surely you must know. Weren't you at the Witan?"

"I was there for a while, but I had work to do. Congratulations, my lord."

"Oh, go away. I have a headache."

Saewynn backed towards the door, bobbing her head and clutching the blue cloak. Eadred watched her go, a satisfied grin on his face. As Saewynn made her escape, she heard the low voice of Edgifu.

"We'll discuss this another time."

***

Saewynn ran. She found a place out of sight. She leaned against a wall, shaking. The words ran through her head, terrifying her. She bent over and was sick. Had they believed her? Should she tell anyone what she had overheard? Who? Would they protect her? She took a few deep breaths. Keep calm. Act as usual. Don't attract attention. She still clutched the blue cloak. Her mistress must be wondering what had happened to her.

Saewynn straightened her back, wiped her mouth with the back of her hand and walked slowly out of her hiding place.

Elfflaed hardly glanced up as she entered the room.

"You found the cloak? Put it away now; I've decided to wear something else this evening."

"Yes, my lady. It has become creased. I'll hang it up." She hung it over the clothes pole, smoothing the thick woollen fabric, composing her face. "Shall I help you with your hair?"

"Find me the white veil. Is it back from the laundress?"

There was a light tap on the door and Saewynn jumped. Lord Elfgar impatiently asked his daughter if she was ready.

"Just coming."

"Excuse me, my lady. Do you need me at attend you at the feast? I feel unwell."

Elfflaed looked at her maid properly for the first time.

"You are a little pale. Tidy up here before you go. No need to wait up for me, find somewhere else to sleep. And don't come back until you feel better, it might be something infectious." She swept out of the room.

Saewynn sunk down onto the bed, her legs unable to support her. She had never felt so alone, not even when she had been trapped in the forest. This time there would be no Byrhtnoth to save her.

Perhaps Wulfstan could help. He was always full of good ideas. Saewynn went to the door. Night was falling and torchlight glowed from the hall. Men and women approached, attracted by the promise of food and entertainment. In the distance she heard singing, monks assembled for another service. Perhaps Wulfstan was with them. She glanced back at the cosy room behind her. Elfflaed could put her own clothes away. Shocked by her rebellious thoughts, Saewynn shut the door firmly behind her.

***

It was dim in the chapel, the monks silhouetted against the flickering light of candles. Saewynn found a stool and sat down to wait. A priest moved to and fro at the far end. It must be the Abbot of Glastonbury. She remembered him talking to Byrhtnoth when they stopped there. Was it only a few days ago? She didn't understand the words but the singing and chanting were restful and she relaxed. She felt safe here. The service finished and she stood up. The movement attracted the attention of the abbot. He bent and spoke to someone. Heads turned towards her. Perhaps she shouldn't be here. A gesture from the abbot told her to stay. She waited and recognised the limping figure of Wulfstan.

"Has he come back?"

Saewynn shook her head. "Something has happened, I don't know what to do, who to tell." She tried to hold back her tears.

"It's all right." Wulfstan put a supporting arm round her. "Tell me what happened, I'll help you, whatever it is."

The monks, heading towards the door gave them curious glances. One whispered to his companion, who sniggered a reply. Wulfstan frowned at them and they hurried out. Dunstan approached and shooed the men out the door.

"What's the problem? Can I do anything?"

"I don't know," Wulfstan said.

"Don't go," Saewynn begged Dunstan, deciding suddenly to trust him too. "You need to hear this as well. It's important."

"Let's find somewhere more comfortable." Dunstan led them to a small hut nearby. He poured some ale into a cup and handed it to the girl. "Now, what's this all about?"

The words spilt out of Saewynn. How she had gone to find the cloak. How she had been trapped in the side room.

"I didn't mean to listen. They started talking before I could escape."

"Of course you didn't." Dunstan's voice was quiet and soothing. "Go on."

Saewynn repeated everything she had heard. The admissions, the threats and how she had pretended to be asleep.

"That was quick thinking."

Saewynn gave Dunstan a grateful smile.

"This is terrible. Something must be done. The witan should be recalled."

"Be still, Wulfstan. I had suspected this."

"But..." Wulfstan stood, ready for action.

"Sit down. We need to think this through." Dunstan paused. "What happens if we accuse Eadred of this crime? It is this girl's word against that of the king and the king's mother. Who will they believe?"

"I can't do that." Horror spread across Saewynn's face.

"Of course you can't." Dunstan patted her hand. "The important thing is, we know the truth. This fact can be put away and used when appropriate. The children are in danger?"

"Not immediately, but they plan something."

"It is clear. We must protect the children. Make sure one of them at least grows up to become king." Dunstan stood up. "Eadwig is safe for the time being, far away. Edgar is here. I will speak to Ealdorman Athelstan; his wife fosters the boy. We must get him away to East Anglia as soon as possible. He will be safe there."

"What about Saewynn?" Wulfstan moved closer to the girl. "She's in danger too. If the king's mother discovers she heard the conversation..."

"I'll arrange something, keep her out of the way for now."

Wulfstan nodded.

43

"Do you still have those boys clothes that I gave you?" Wulfstan asked.

"I think so. We haven't stopped long enough to sort out the luggage."

"Won't Elfflaed worry if you suddenly disappear?"

"I told her I was sick; that I didn't want to go to the feast. She thought it might be something serious. Told me not to come back this evening."

"That's useful."

"This is where she is lodged. Wait outside, I won't be long."

Wulfstan was still wearing a monk's robe. He pulled up the hood and clasped his hands together as if praying.

"Found them." Saewynn emerged from the hut.

"There's not much." Wulfstan looked at the small bundle that Saewynn clutched to her chest.

"I'm a slave, I don't have much." She stopped. "If I disappear they'll search for me. I'll be a runaway."

"We'll sort it out." He patted her shoulder. "I'll give you my magic hat again." Saewynn gave a nervous giggle. "I'd better get ready to travel as well."

"Where are you going?"

"I'm coming with you. What else am I going to do? Go back to the monastery?" He remembered the beach, discussing the future with Byrhtnoth; how they would travel and have adventures. It had all vanished, now his friend had gone. "I've nothing else to do." They walked in silence. "Wait here." Wulfstan pushed open the door, then beckoned to Saewynn. "All clear."

Wulfstan pulled out his bag and started rummaging through it. Byrhtnoth's dog was curled up in her basket, splinted leg sticking out. She raised her head.

"What's going to happen to her?"

"Who? Here's your hat." He handed it to Saewynn. "Oh, the bitch. I suppose we'll have to take her as well. She won't last five minutes here."

Saewynn smiled for the first time that evening. "She's still Byrhtnoth's dog though. We'll look after her for him."

"Of course." Wulfstan gathered his clothes together and stuffed them into the bag. "I've not got much more than you."

"You've dropped something." Saewynn reached under the bed and pulled out a bundle of cloth.

"That's not mine. It belongs to Byrhtnoth." They both stared at the dirty garment, "He must have thrown it there when he washed after the hunt. It's not fit for anything but rags now."

Saewynn took the cloth and smoothed it out. At some time, long ago, it had been a rich brown but with repeated washing had faded to a dull sandy colour. Old tears had been carefully repaired but other, newer rents were visible. The back of the garment was shredded, streaked with dried blood. It must be from when Byrhtnoth and Elfflaed were dragged from the sea. The wounds would not have healed yet. He hadn't said anything. But then, she had hardly spoken to him since then. She buried her face in the material. It smelt of blood and the salt tang of the sea, but mostly of sweat, his sweat. She breathed in the scent. Wulfstan turned away and continued packing.

Saewynn noticed more blood, a large patch on the front of the tunic. Her heart lurched, then she realised it was the dog's blood. He had carried her when he returned from the hunt. She looked down.

"I'll use it to line the basket. She will need some padding if she is to travel with us." Saewynn bent and draped the old tunic over the animal and tucked in the edges. The dog sniffed the material and looked up at Saewynn. They would both remember him.

***

In the hall, Dunstan and Athelstan talked, voices drowned by the noise of loud conversation around them.

"You will leave quickly?"

"As soon as possible. Perhaps tomorrow." Athelstan stuck his knife into a gobbet of meat from the dish in front of him." He raised his voice. "The hunting has been good here." A man sitting nearby nodded.

"There will be good hunting in the north this year; the new king will be tested early in his reign."

Athelstan agreed. "One might almost think they knew that King Edmund would be taken from us."

"A plot?" The man frowned. "Surely not."

"Someone must have paid that assassin. I wonder who?" Athelstan chewed his meat thoughtfully.

"You will take the girl with you?" Dunstan whispered. "She needs protection. We must keep our witness safe."

Athelstan took a sip of ale.

"She is maid to the Lady Elfflaed. I will speak to Ealdorman Elfgar about her."

"He mustn't suspect anything."

"You don't get to be Ealdorman of East Anglia by being stupid."

"Of course not. I apologise."

"Or Abbot of Glastonbury either." They exchanged a friendly smile. "How are you getting on with draining your marshes? I plan to increase production in the fens. Do you have any advice?"

For a while they discussed ditches and pumps.

"And the boy, Wulfstan, you will take him too? We need someone reliable to write letters."

"He can tell me all about drains. Stop worrying, the scop is tuning his instrument. I wonder what he will find to sing about our new king?"

Later, as he returned to the hall after relieving himself, Athelstan met Elfgar. "My lord, a word with you."

"What do you want?" Elfgar had been drinking heavily.

"Nothing serious. Your daughter, Elfflaed, has a maid, I don't know her name, good with clothes?"

"What do you know about her?" Elfgar's eyes narrowed in suspicion.

"Nothing. It's just that my wife asked me to find a good seamstress while I was here. She can't find anyone suitable in East Anglia. You know what women are like." He rolled his eyes and Elfgar grunted. "Do you think your daughter would let her go? I'll pay a good price."

"I'll speak to Elfflaed. She's fond of the girl, but she might be prepared to let her go. For the right price." Elfgar's eyes gleamed at the mention of money.

"Thank you." Athelstan watched him return to his seat.

***

"I know she's useful, but it might be better to get rid of her. All that fuss with the raiders. The less people know about that, the better. We must protect your reputation, my dear."

"I was becoming bored with her. I need someone with more experience in these things." Elfflaed raised a hand to touch her veil, checking it hung smooth and unwrinkled. She thought how ill Saewynn had looked. "In fact, get rid of her now. She might damage my clothes if she knows she is to be dismissed."

Elfgar stared at his daughter. It was many moons since she had agreed with him without argument. He hurried off to find Athelstan before she changed her mind.

44

Wulfstan watched as the soldiers manoeuvred the travelling cart out of yet another rut in the road.

"I don't know why they had to bring that thing," commented Saewynn, "it slows the journey."

"Some women prefer to travel in comfort."

"Comfort? They tried to make me ride in it. I'd rather walk."

"Instead, you've got your pick of the spare horses." Wulfstan glanced at her mount, "Isn't that Byrhtnoth's horse? He's a bit big for you."

"Poor thing. He hasn't had much exercise." She tugged on the reins as the large stallion protested at the wait. "I can manage him."

"So I see. You're starting to become quite a good horse boy. Having any problems with the others?"

"No. I think they've forgotten I'm a girl."

"You'd better get back, we're on the move again."

"What's Athelstan worried about? He's getting very agitated."

"I'll speak with him. Stay here." Wulfstan urged Sleipnir forwards, past the swaying cart, towards the head of the column.

"Excuse me, my lord. Is there a problem?"

"I don't know." Athelstan scanned the thick trees lining the road. "They should have been cut back. They're too close. I can't see anything." He studied the empty road ahead. "I've been expecting an attack for days. Everything appears quiet but someone is out there."

"You sent men to search," Wulfstan pointed out, "they found nothing."

"A determined gang can disappear in woodland like that."

"Robbers? Or someone else?" Wulfstan could see no more than a few feet into the thick barrier of leaves. Athelstan was right; anyone could be concealed in there.

"Why did they let us go so easily, without any attempt to seize the boy? It will be today. I'm sure of it."

"Why today? We are deep into your territory now?"

Athelstan nodded. "But soon we will reach the flat lands, away from the trees, exposed. They will have missed their chance. They must attack today."

The warm summer's day seemed to grow cooler and Wulfstan shivered.

"Don't worry. I have a plan." Athelstan smiled.

***

"Right. Off that horse, you're travelling in the wagon," Wulfstan told Saewynn.

"I told you it made me sick, all that swaying backwards and forwards."

"You'll do what I say."

Her eyes opened wide in surprise. Wulfstan whispered a few words, Saewynn nodded and slid down from the tall horse. She ran to catch up with the wagon. With a scowl back at Wulfstan, she swung herself inside.

It wasn't long before her desperate voice emerged from the closed wagon.

"Stop. Let me out. I'm going to be sick." Other women shouted and the wagon slowed. Before it came to a stop, a shape leapt from the vehicle and disappeared into the bushes. The sound of retching could be heard. Wulfstan trotted up.

"I'll deal with her." He poked his head into the wagon. "Is the boy all right?" There was a brief conversation. "Carry on."

The driver whipped the oxen and the wagon jerked into movement. Wulfstan waited at the side of the road until most of the procession had passed.

"All clear. You can come out now."

Saewynn emerged. Clutched to her chest was a bulky bundle. It started moving and a tousled head emerged.

"Do it again!"

"It was fun, wasn't it? Perhaps later?" Saewynn passed the small boy up to Wulfstan, who rapidly wrapped his cloak around him.

"I got him out of the wagon." She grabbed a handful of her horse's mane and pulled herself onto his back. "What do we do now?"

"Edward. Leave the baggage pony with us. Go and fetch Godric. He is towards the head of the column." The boy handed over the leading rein and urged his horse into a trot. He squeezed past the other travellers.

"Can you carry this on your horse?" Wulfstan raised the lid of the basket and Saewynn lifted out the dog. She laid her across her mount's back.

"She wants to get down and walk." Saewynn held the struggling animal.

"She'll have to stay there. We might have to ride fast. She can walk a few steps, but would never keep up. Right, young man, in you go." Wulfstan dropped the boy into the empty basket. "Keep your head down."

"It's all part of the game," Saewynn told him, "you must hide from everyone."

"We'll let you out soon." Wulfstan pushed down the grinning face and closed the basket. "Good job he's small for his age."

"What's going on?" Godric had returned with Edward. "Is the horse lame?"

"No." Wulfstan checked everyone was out of sight. "Our plans have changed. Ealdorman Athelstan is expecting an attack. When it happens we leave." They rode slowly along the path. "We head north," he waved at the trees on their left. "Make a note of any tracks running in that direction."

"Where are we going?" Saewynn was struggling with the squirming dog; the stallion disliked the extra passenger. "You take her." She thrust the animal at Wulfstan.

"Byrhtnoth's village. It's not far." Wulfstan stroked the dog and she soon quietened. "Byrhtnoth was safe there, he said, so the Aethling should be as well. Not too fast. We don't want to catch up with the others. How does he know so much about Byrhtnoth?"

"I wondered that. He was concerned when Byrhtnoth..." Saewynn fought to slow her horse. "When he disappeared."

"The Ealdorman never visited the village that I noticed."

"I'd forgotten you came from the same place, Godric."

"Me and Edward, both. It will be good to go home for a while. Do you hear anything from your sister, Edward? How long is it now since we left?"

The boy thought. "Must be four, five years?"

"Enough of the reminiscences." Wulfstan frowned. "Can you find your way back?"

"Of course." Godric glanced at Edward and shrugged. The boy nodded confidently.

"Good. I think we're on our way." They heard shouting ahead; the hiss of arrows followed by the sound of clashing swords.

"We passed a gap in the trees not long ago." Saewynn dragged the big stallion round and raced back. She turned off the road, the others not far behind. Godric slashed at a sapling as he passed and it fell across the gap, disguising their exit.

They rode fast through the trees, slowing their headlong rush only when Wulfstan decided they were out of range of the attack.

They waited for Edward to catch up. As he stopped, the basket lid opened and Edgar's head appeared.

"More! More!"

"Are you all right?" Wulfstan approached the panting pony.

"Fun! More?"

"Only if you're good. You have to hide." He closed the basket, checking that the lid was fastened. He leant down and whispered, "Keep very quiet. The bad men are still around."

"Over there." They had stopped at the edge of a clearing. Godric pointed to the far side. A man stared across at them. He was roughly dressed and carried a small bundle. He was unarmed, an ordinary traveller.

Before anyone could speak, Saewynn kicked her horse into motion. Released, the stallion hurtled across the grass. Holding the reins in one hand, she drew a seax from the scabbard hanging from her waist. Waving it in the air she shouted. She reached the traveller and pulled violently on the horse's mouth, causing it to rear. Giant iron shod hooves hung high over the man's head before thumping back into the turf. Horse and girl screamed in unison as she swung the seax down towards his face. The man dived to the ground, before scrambling back into the thick bushes. They listened to his stumbling progress as the horse stamped the ground and tossed his head.

Saewynn sheathed the seax and walked the horse back towards the others.

"Sorry. I didn't kill him. Shall I go after him?"

"That won't be necessary." Wulfstan was the first to break the shocked silence. "I don't think he'll be coming back."

Godric and Edward sat, mouths hanging open in astonishment.

"So, which way do we go?"

LATE SUMMER 946

45

I was tired of walking. The day was hot and the sun beat down. There was an oak tree in the distance. It stood alone, apart from the forest. As I got closer it filled my vision. I entered the dark shade with relief.

Dried leaves and the remains of last year's acorns crunched underfoot. Deer must have visited, to feed on the lower shoots, leaving empty space beneath the twisted branches. A small brown bird inspected me with bright eyes, before fluttering up into the dense green canopy. I circled the massive trunk. The bark was rough; mottled grey and green like the scales of a mighty dragon. I found a place between two giant buttresses and dropped my pack with relief. I shrugged the heavy shield from my back and propped it against the tree. Above, the branches arched like a roof just above my head. I had my own hall. It was the only one I had now.

Many travellers had stopped here; the marks of their fires were visible on the ground. I cleared a space and gathered a pile of dry twigs. A dead branch hung from the green covering. It would have been too high for most men to reach, but I pulled it down. It caught for a moment, then, with a snap, it fell. A rain of twigs and leaves landed on my head. I picked up the remains of a birds nest. I arranged the twigs in a pyramid over some dead leaves, leaving room to insert the nest later. Larger twigs went on top. I broke the dead branch into pieces and piled them nearby. I struck a flint several times until one of the bright sparks caught the cloth. As it glowed red I placed it carefully in the nest, carefully folding over the edge, encouraging the flame. When it grew warm, I pushed it into the pile of sticks. Soon the fire was burning merrily. I added pieces of the dead branch.

I skinned the hare I had caught earlier in the day and balanced it over the fire. I shook the leather bag. Not much left. I would need to find water tomorrow. The ale that had filled it was long gone. Saewynn had cried when she gave it to me. What had happened when they discovered I had gone? Had the dog survived? I pushed the memories away; they were no longer my concern. I pulled a piece of meat from the carcass. It was nearly cooked. I chewed the tough stringy meat. The animal must have been old; I would not have managed to catch it otherwise, but it was better than nothing. I sat and watched the bright slanting rays of the sun creep their way under the edge of my leafy roof.

I woke suddenly. Everything was bathed in bloody red. The fire had died, but was stained by the crimson disc of the sun balanced on the horizon. The dragon skin of the trunk at my back appeared to run with blood and the leaves above shimmered black and red. I heard the sound of a heavily laden cart approaching, rumbling over the dry ground. I drew my sword, ready to meet whoever was coming. I lowered it. It was no cart but the sound of distant thunder.

I walked out from beneath the tree. Heavy black clouds were piled up all around, only a bloody streak of clear sky where the sun had set. A flash of lighting flickered on the underside of the dark blanket. The reflected light of the sun coloured the clouds; red, orange and a sickening brown. Far away I noticed a shadow of falling rain. There would be no problem finding water the next day.

I watched the spectacle until I felt my hair start to rise. I dropped the sword and moved away. The tree reached up into the darkening sky, nothing taller. It had turned from protection into a trap. I moved further away. A few fat drops of rain fell, bouncing on the dry dusty ground and disappearing. They fell faster, becoming a solid sheet of water. Had I ventured too far from the tree? Made myself a target instead? The sky lit up with a flash brighter than any fire. The crash of the thunder rolled across the land like the meeting of two gigantic shield walls.

I crouched down to make myself a smaller target. Perhaps I sent a plea to Thunor, the old god of storms. There was another, brighter flash, a great roaring crash and something hit me, hard.

***

I woke to cold and dark. I was on my side, face resting in a pool of water. The ground beneath was soft and damp. I recognised the tree where I had camped. It looked different now, silhouetted against a clear star filled sky. How long had I been lying here? My left arm, trapped beneath my body was numb. I longed to stay there, to sleep longer, but water irritated my nose. I watched the bubbles in the water as I exhaled. I must move, before I drowned. Was it possible to drown in a puddle of water?

I attempted to get up. I couldn't move; something pinned me to the ground. Had my arm sunk into the mud? I placed my free hand flat on the ground and pushed harder. Whatever clung to me surrendered my body and I sat up. With release came great pain. I bent forward until the dizzy sickness subsided. Had someone ripped off my arm? Tentatively I explored. It was there, but hung numb and useless at my side.

A tingling told me that feeling was returning, but a greater pain drowned it out. My whole body hurt, as if an enraged ox had trampled it into the earth. I struggled to my feet, and then sank to my knees fighting against blacking out. I concentrated on the pain, where was it worse? My left shoulder. I shivered, the pain

239

increased. I needed to find shelter, quickly. I struggled upright and shuffled towards the sword. Carefully, I bent to pick it up. Using it for support, I made my way slowly back to the tree.

The tree was injured too. It must have been lightning, but it was as if a giant axe had struck it, slicing down through the trunk. The white scar gleamed in the starlight. One great bough lay across the ground, surrounded by leaves and broken branches. Plenty of firewood now, but it would be impossible to light a fire one handed. The thought of never holding a shield again rose up – I thrust it away.

I needed to assess the damage. I sat on a branch and reached to touch my left arm. Ignoring the pain that shot through my body whenever I moved, I ran my hand up the arm. I closed my eyes to better imagine the contours of my own body. I felt a trickle of hot blood. Was that a bone sticking out, near the shoulder? It didn't feel like bone, the surface was rough, fibrous. I opened my eyes, trying to work out what had happened. In the darkness they focused on the pale scar of the oak tree. I understood.

The tree had exploded. Pieces of wood had shot out, like a hail of arrows. I touched the splinter in my shoulder. How big was it; a finger's width? I pulled it, gently. I gasped as the pain intensified. Worse, I had felt the movement within my body. I reached back until a finger touched the wood. It protruded several inches and I could tell that end was thicker.

It must have hit from behind, passing through my shoulder and emerging from my arm. I did not know what damage it had done in its passing. Feeling had returned to my left arm, but I was unable to move it. To pull the piece of wood out from the front would tear my shoulder apart. I would never carry a shield, or anything else, again.

It had to be extracted from behind. I knew, from the size and angle, that I could never do it myself. A skilled leech or healer might do it without causing more damage. Where would I find someone like that? My eyes searched the foliage as if one hid there.

I felt other, smaller, splinters in my side. I could do nothing more. I lowered my battered body to the ground. I was so tired. Should I lie down to rest? Animals – wolves and other predators – would soon catch the scent of blood on the wind. I sat upright, sword gripped in my bloodied hand and waited.

46

By the time dawn came, I knew I had to deal with the injuries myself. Every movement caused the splinter to pull on my shoulder. It would be impossible to walk any distance. Perhaps another traveller would visit the tree. Would that person be friendly or kill me for my sword? How long would I have to wait? I was hungry. The hare had been my first meal for days. I had avoided villages where I might have bought food. Water had been easier to come by, but there was none here. The bag was empty and the parched land had quickly swallowed the heavy storm rain. I chewed some leaves from the tree, but the bitter taste made the thirst worse.

Carefully I pulled the smaller splinters from my side and back. Most of the wounds were superficial and any bleeding quickly stopped. I tried again to reach the larger piece of wood. Although my fingers touched the surface, there was no way to pull it free. I chewed one of the fragile bones discarded the night before. Could I somehow cut off the protruding stump of wood and pull it out? Oak was hard. How long would it take to cut through that thickness with an axe. I studied my eating knife. That would take even longer. I imagined the pain.

I stabbed the knife into the ground in frustration. It hit a tree root and bounced back. The sudden jarring made me scream with pain. I stared at the knife as my breathing returned to normal. I couldn't pull out the splinter, but was it possible to push it out? It was the only option.

Moss grew on the trunk of the tree. I pulled some off and placed it in a neat pile. I ripped my tunic into strips using my knife and teeth and lay them ready. I stood and studied the rough surface of the tree; recalled my position when the lightning had struck. I hunched forward until I felt the pressure within my shoulder ease. I leaned close to the tree until the tip of the splinter nearly touched; my weight supported by one hand. I raised my face to the leafy canopy and muttered a prayer. To God or one of the old gods? Perhaps the tree itself, I don't remember. I checked the shard of wood was perpendicular to the solid trunk. I turned my head towards the sun soaked land beyond the tree. Before I could change my mind, I dropped the supporting hand.

***

I returned from blackness to pain. My cheek pressed tight against the tree. Right hand clutching the trunk, my fingers dug deep into the bark. I tried to move. I was pinned against the tree. Had I driven the splinter back into the tree? No. That was impossible.

I ignored the pain, exploring other sensations. Blood ran down my back. The dragging feeling had gone. Either I had succeeded, or would shortly die from blood loss. I freed my right hand. The nails were broken and bloody. Keeping the rest of my body motionless against the tree, I reached back. No wooden spike, nothing but blood pulsing lazily. I held my breath. I pushed again against the trunk. This time the tree allowed me to escape. I collapsed onto the ground, crawled to the moss and piled most of it onto one of the strips of cloth. I lay down, shoulder pressed into the soft bundle. I had no energy left for more. If fate wished, the blood would stop and I would live.

***

The sun was high. I was alive. I found the ends of the cloth and tied them across my chest. I sat up, head swimming. My shoulder throbbed with pain but the bleeding appeared to have stopped. I stood up, leaned against the tree for support. My arm still hung useless, every movement painful. I strapped it, bent close across my chest. Painfully and slowly, I collected the remains of my belongings together.

I wanted to stay, rest in the shade of the great tree. It was impossible. My mouth was as dry as a shrivelled corpse. I must find water soon or all my effort would be wasted. Where was my shield? I had propped it against the tree. It must be under the fallen branch. I needn't worry about leaving it behind. I picked up my sword belt. It was difficult to buckle with only one hand but I finally managed it. I was still reluctant to leave. The bloody imprint of my hand on the trunk waved me farewell. I acknowledged its salute. Which way to go? North still? It was as good a direction as any.

***

Beyond the shade of the tree, the heat of the sun hit me. A dark line of green ahead suggested more trees, even forest. There would be water there, somewhere. I kept my eyes fixed on it and plodded forward. With one arm out of action, my pace was uneven, with every step my shoulder throbbed with pain. I pushed it into the back of my mind and concentrated on putting one foot in front of the other. It seemed I walked for hours, but the sun hardly moved.

***

The silence was broken by the harsh sound of crows. Where? I saw nothing but the flat expanse of dry grass. Behind me, the stricken oak was small on the horizon, the trees ahead no nearer. The sound came again, above. A kite soared, motionless in the heavy air, forked tail sharp against the dark blue sky. His wings tilted to avoid attacks from a group of noisy crows. He maintained position directly over my head. I tried to shout defiance; I was not dead yet. Only a croak as harsh as the crows emerged. I looked to the trees ahead. There must be water there. I continued to walk.

***

The forest was thick, a solid mass of hectic green. A barrier to further progress. I leaned against the nearest tree to rest. I felt a trickle of moisture down my back. Sweat or blood? Did it really matter? One was as dangerous as the other. I saw no way through, left or right. I listened for the sound of running water. All I heard was the pounding in my head. I went left. At least the sun was on my back rather than glaring into my eyes.

***

I almost missed the path. I stumbled at a dip worn by many feet. I noticed the gap in the trees, narrow and winding. At last, an entrance into the forest. I let my sore eyes adjust to the darkness. It was silent. The sun was high. Birds were resting from the heat of the day. The scent of the forest was overpowering after the dry dusty air outside. As I walked deeper, the path underfoot became soft with a thick layer of leaves, fallen over many autumns. The smell of rotting wood mingled with that of fresh new growth. From somewhere the scent of some unknown flower filled my senses and then was it was gone. There was still no sound of water.

***

I followed the path as it wove its way through the trees. When it divided I chose a way at random. It joined other paths, some wider, some narrow. I tried to select the wider paths but they ended suddenly and I would retrace my steps. After a while I stopped thinking and just walked. What did it matter?

***

I entered a glade, carpeted with fresh green grass. There must be water here. I picked a spot where the grass was thickest. The ground was hard. I hacked at it with the point of the sword. Close to the roots of the grass, the soil was damp. I smeared some on my neck and face to cool the heat that consumed my body. It soon dried and crumbled away. I dug deeper, but the earth was stony and without moisture. I think I dozed for a while, then dragged myself upright and continued to walk.

***

Sometimes I recognised a tree, or a particular bend in the path. I refused to accept I was lost. My vision blurred with the pain in my head and I stopped, waiting for it to clear. The light under the trees began to dim. I could not see the sun, but knew the long day was ending. I searched for a place to stop. Why hadn't I stayed in the grassy glade? Which was the right way? I knew I was lost.

***

I found a patch of moss. As good a place as any to stop, perhaps there would be water. The moss was only a thin covering over large rocks. There was no water but the moss felt cool against my hot body. I sat against the largest of the rocks. For a while I was at peace; the ache in my shoulder faded and tired muscles relaxed. I closed my eyes.

***

Everything was cold and black. I searched for my cloak. I couldn't find it. Had I left it somewhere? I couldn't remember. The movement caused the pain in my shoulder to return. I touched it gently. It was hot and swollen. I would die unless I got help soon, perhaps even if I found help.

The forest was noisy now with the sounds of life, the rustling of small animals as they foraged through the leaf litter. An owl hooted overhead and I heard the almost silent beat of its wings. It became aware of my presence and disappeared to hunt elsewhere.

There were unidentified noises; shrieks and grunts as hunter sought hunted. And found them. I raised my head as I caught the sound of a wolf, howling into the darkness, far away. There was a reply, closer. Were they following my trail? Would they catch my scent in the still air?

Perhaps they were not wolves, but the evil barghests, that people spoke of in whispers around the winter hearths. Giant animals, half goblin, half wolf, they would tear me apart in seconds with their teeth and claws. I would not hear them coming, nor see them in the dark.

I remembered the thrill of the stories in the safety of the hall, but they had given me nightmares in the night. There was one story, my favourite, which had scared me the most: The tale of the great monster that crawled out of the bog. It took men by the handful to consume in its watery lair. The boys spent many hours discussing which of the bogs or lakes around the village was the home of this evil creature.

In our games I always played the hero who killed the monster, but in the night I screamed as it crept closer and closer, searching for a victim to drag down into the cold dank water. Those nights my mother got no sleep.

I almost wished the monster would come now. At least I could grab a sip of water before I died. Shivering, I curled up, the sword within reach of my hand.

As I drifted into sleep, I remembered that a sword had been useless against the beast.

47

Every movement caused the pain to flare in my shoulder and disturb my sleep. I sensed eyes watching from the darkness and felt the touch of crawling beasts on my body. I could not tell dreams from waking. Strange distorted animals crawled up trees or flitted about my head. Cries echoed through the forest. It was only when the first glow of light touched the sky and the sounds of night were drowned by the first notes of bird song, that I sunk into a deeper sleep.

The light was not bright; the sky was veiled by thin cloud. Branches moved in a gentle breeze. Cool air caressed my body. I was surprised that I was still alive; perhaps I wasn't. I lay still, afraid to move, and watched the movement of the trees. I listened to the whisper of the wind through the branches.

If I was dead, this pleasant place was not heaven, but hell. Why else did the wind sound so much like running water? Forever out of reach. I closed my eyes. Perhaps I would sleep again.

The sound was insistent. I listened to it, separating the different threads of sound. There was the rustling of the leaves, the steady scrape of one branch against another, a sudden burst of song from familiar birds. Beyond that, something else, the cool sound of running water. I kept my eyes closed, moving my head in one direction, then another. I located the sound. It was carried on the wind, and it was close. Why hadn't I heard it yesterday? Because the forest had been still and windless?

I struggled to my feet. My head throbbed with pain, almost drowning the complaints from my battered body. I grasped the sword, dug it into the ground and leaned on it for support. I faced the breeze and the sound of the water. I opened my eyes to check the direction, compared it with the light patch of sky that indicated the position of the sun. I didn't want to go astray if the wind stopped. I took a step, then another. I could almost smell the water on the breeze. I tried to hurry, but stumbled and nearly fell. Take it slowly. I struggled through the forest, hacking at undergrowth with the sword, using it as a crutch as I walked.

I emerged onto a wide, well-trodden path. Opposite were more trees and beyond them was the water, a substantial stream from the sound. I no longer needed the wind as a guide. I had found the life saving water. I crossed the path and through the long grass that lined it. I parted the branches and there it was. I stood at the top of a steep bank, just below was the water. Desperate now, I searched for a way down.

"Take care. The water is deep there."

I ignored the voice. There had been voices in my head for some time. I had learned to ignore them.

"Are you deaf? The water is dangerous. If you fall you will drown." The voice was louder. I raised my head.

Across the river was a woman. She sat on a rock, combing her long wet hair. She wore a thin white shift, which clung to her damp body. I blinked. She was still there. She must be the spirit of the river. Would she demand a gift to let me drink? What could I offer her? I bowed my head in respect.

The woman stood up and approached the water. It was shallow that side and her long white feet sank into the gravel of a small beach.

"You are injured." It was a statement rather than a question, but I nodded. "Wait there. I will send help." She hurried up the bank, gathering a bundle of clothes.

My eyes were drawn back to the water. So close, and I was so thirsty.

"I said stay there. Do you want to drown? Someone will come soon." She disappeared into the trees and I collapsed on the bank. My legs dangled over the edge. The water was still several feet lower. I watched as it flowed swiftly past. She had said it was deep, but how deep? If I jumped, would I drown as she had said? If it was shallow I might break a leg. Had I imagined her? Perhaps she had tricked me? Left me to die of thirst in sight of plenty. I was unable to lower myself into the water, not with one good arm. Could I swim if it was deep?

If no one came, I would jump, regardless of the consequences. I stared into the water, noticed how the ripples moved and sped downstream and the sparkle as the sun caught them. At the far side, the water was slower; moving in eddies where it kissed the bank. Nearby a willow branch dipped into the water, rising and then falling with the current. I watched entranced. Time stood still.

I was interrupted by voices. I crawled back to the road. I dragged myself upright against a tree and raised my sword. My hand shook with the weight and I reluctantly lowered it. I awaited my fate.

A woman appeared first, not the woman from the river, older. A nun. Behind came two men, old, roughly dressed, slaves or servants. One carried a length of wooden fencing.

"You are in a bit of a state, aren't you?"

I tried to rely, but only a croak emerged from my parched throat. I tried again, pointing at my mouth and then at the river.

"Thirsty are you?" At last. "Good thing I brought this water bag with me."

I stepped forward to grab it from her.

"Not so fast, just a small sip. Too much will make you ill." She took a small cup from her robes, poured some water and handed it to me. I drained it and held it out for more. The woman frowned but added a few more drops. I swilled it round my mouth before swallowing.

"Thank you." She nodded with satisfaction.

"Can you walk?" I took a step and my legs collapsed. The woman caught me expertly by my right arm. She took my sword and handed it to one of the men. "Don't worry. You'll get it back." The other man brought the hurdle. He placed it on the ground and the woman lowered me on to it. She laid the sword at my side.

The whole world spun as the men lifted me.

"Careful. He's suffered enough, without you two throwing him around."

I closed my eyes.

48

We crossed a bridge; I heard the river rush beneath. A heavy door opened and closed and I was laid on a table. Gentle fingers removed my clothes. I tried to struggle when they cut away the bindings round my shoulder. The nun placed a hand on my chest.

"We will be as careful as we can, but we must see what the damage is."

I gritted my teeth. Someone held my arm in position as they rolled me onto my stomach. The nun tutted and sent for warm water. I stiffened as they peeled away the blood soaked bandages.

"It's a bit of a mess." The voice was close beside me. "Can you hear me?" I looked into clear grey eyes. They were familiar. It was the woman I had seen beside the river. Her hair was covered now, like the older woman. She smiled.

"Do you know how you came by this injury?"

"A tree... oak tree. Lightning."

"There was a storm passed over, two nights back? Would that be it?"

"Perhaps." Was it only two nights?

"And you've been walking since then?"

"I needed water. I couldn't find any."

"You are a very brave boy."

"I tried to remove the branch. I couldn't reach it." I blinked to get rid of the moisture that filled my eyes.

"It's all right. Judging by the size of the wound, you got most of it out. There may be some left behind. It must be cleaned." She gave instructions and someone left the room.

"It will be painful. I will give you something to make you sleep."

"I don't need it." I could stand the pain. I had lived with it. It was part of me. "I won't make a noise."

"It is no disgrace to shout, but it is for our benefit, not yours. You cannot help but struggle, then we might do more damage than we need."

Someone handed her a small horn cup. She held it to my lips.

"No." The woman raised dark eyebrows. "Will I lose my arm?" I had to know the truth.

The woman touched my cheek. Her fingers were soft and cool.

"I will not lie to you. We cannot tell what will happen. We can only pray to God for your recovery."

"If I lose my arm," I faced the possibility, "you must let me die."

"Why should you want such a thing? People survive great injuries and lead a useful life thereafter."

"Not me." I stretched out and grasped her shoulder. "Promise."

"All right, I promise. Drink this."

I swallowed the liquid in one gulp. It had a bitter taste. The woman pushed a strip of leather between my teeth.

"It will prevent you biting your tongue." I felt her hand stroke my hair.

***

"If you are going to thrash about, we will have to bring the men to tie you down."

Where was I? I seemed to be anchored at the bottom of a green sea. I blinked to clear bleary eyes, found I was in a room. There was a window, almost covered with green foliage. The sun was low; dawn or dusk? Reflected light flickered round pale walls. I was lying on a high bed propped up on soft pillows. I became aware I was naked beneath a light covering. I moved my head and met the eyes of an elderly nun. She sat on a stool with a pile of sewing on her lap.

I recognised her. "On the road. You rescued me."

"My name is Edberga. How do you feel?"

How did I feel? I recalled little of what had happened, only the terror I had felt, but I would not admit to that. Then I remembered the tree. I checked my arm. It was still there. I breathed a sigh of relief. It was still strapped to my body, but the dressings were clean and tidy. There was no pain, but I obeyed the woman's first instruction and kept quite still. "I don't think I feel anything."

She appeared satisfied with my reply. She gathered up her sewing and dropped it into a basket. She stood up with a groan, a hand to her back as she straightened.

"Better than me, then." She approached the bed and placed a hand on my forehead. "The fever has passed."

"I'm thirsty."

"Of course." She fetched a jug from the darkest corner of the room and poured me some water. She held my head as I drank. "It was fresh from the spring this morning."

"What spring?" I relaxed against the pillows.

"The spring of St Mildgyth. It has healing powers. That is why our community is here; why you were sent here."

"Nobody sent me. I was lost."

"God sees everything and everyone. He sent you to us. Can you move your fingers? Your left hand? I assume your right hand is fine, judging by the way you clung on to your sword."

Where was it? Desperately, I looked round the room.

"It is safe." The nun laughed. "Now, can you move those fingers?"

I studied my hand. It was untouched. My nails were longer than usual; I had been lying here a long time. I concentrated and a finger rose. I let it fall. I tried the others, one by one, then the thumb. It was stiff but moved.

"Very good." She took both my hands, raised the right one. "Grip hard." My fingers closed around hers, but were unable to grip as hard as I would have wished.

"Don't worry. You are still weak from the fever. Now try the other." It looked helpless, emerging from the bindings. I tried to grip her hand, but when I tried to exert any pressure, the ache in my shoulder, that I had nearly forgotten, returned. I released her hand.

"It hurts? That is good. It would be worse if you felt nothing at all. Sleep now." She glanced towards the darkening window. "It is night. We will continue tomorrow."

***

We continued the exercises and every day my hand became stronger. Edberga refused to remove the bindings. It would take time to heal the torn flesh.

Finally, one day, she removed the pad from my back and studied the scar. I wondered what it looked like. It didn't matter, as long as I regained the use of my arm.

"It is healing cleanly and fresh air will do it good."

Had I left anything in the wound?

"One tiny splinter. That's what caused the swelling and the fever."

"It must have been a difficult job to get it out. Who did it?"

"Who did it? I did. Who else?"

"But you're..."

"I'm what? A nun?"

"I was going to say, a woman."

"Well spotted," Edberga said dryly as she sat down on her stool and took up the never-ending pile of sewing. "You men, with your big weapons, slashing and hacking at bodies. You don't realise, with our smaller hands, expert at needlework," she picked up her mending, "we are better at the delicate work of stitching you back together."

"I hadn't thought about it."

"That's the problem. Too much fighting, not enough thinking."

"Perhaps." I lay back on the bed. It was peaceful in the room, but boring. I asked if I could begin to practise with my sword. "I'll only use one arm."

Edberga shook her head and continued to sew.

49

I felt more comfortable once I was allowed to dress and move about. Edberga had repaired most of my clothing and what was beyond repair was replaced from a collection kept for the poor. I was forbidden to leave the room. I watched the shadows move across the walls and thought about my future.

"The Lady Edith will come to speak with you later. She will decide what is to be done with you, if the bindings can be removed."

"Can't you do that?"

"I only advise. She decides everything that is done here. You have been treated as we would treat any visitor to our community. Now you are about to join the world again, we must determine your position. You must not lie to her, she knows everything."

I awaited this ogre with trepidation. How could a woman, even a nun, make such a decision about my future? When the door finally opened, a slim figure slipped into the room. Her hair was covered with a veil and her body swathed in dark cloth. A wooden cross on a leather thong hung from her neck. She looked so different from the lithe young woman beside the river, but I would have recognised her anywhere.

"You are the Lady Edith?"

"I am."

"I wasn't sure you existed. When I saw you," I glanced towards Edberga, "walking by the river, I thought you were something I had dreamed."

"I often walk there, early in the morning, to pray and clear my mind for the day ahead." Her face coloured slightly and she pulled her veil to shield her face from the older woman. "God must have sent me, for if I had not been there, you would surely be dead by now."

"I am grateful." I looked down at my arm. "I hope that I am."

"You are alive, that is all that matters."

"Does it?" If I lost the use of my arm, I would have no life. "You are young for your position. Have you been here long?"

"Forever. I came with my mother when I was a child. Then she..." she paused as if uncertain what to say, "she left, I stayed. I had no choice, I've been here forever."

"It was God's will," Edberga said, "he brought you to us, to learn and then to lead us.

"Of course."

"My mother died when I was young. It is hard to lose someone at that age. I think I still search for her, in other women." It was one of the many things I had thought about while lying ill. "You remind me of her." I laughed.

Edith raised dark eyebrows. "That should help you answer my questions honestly. First, your name?"

I had invented stories to explain my presence, but I knew I could not lie to this woman. I gave my name and my position in the royal court.

"Why were you wandering alone, without servants or companions? Were you attacked?"

"I have walked alone for a long time."

"Are you an outlaw?" Edith frowned. "Are we in danger?"

I told her she was safe. "I did a terrible thing. You will cast me out when you hear what I have done."

"You are too young to have done something evil. Perhaps you

should tell us what happened and let us decide. We can go to the chapel if you prefer."

"Here is fine." I picked at a piece of loose thread from my bandages.

"The king who died recently."

"King Edmund? We said many prayers for his soul. They say he died in some brawl. Did you kill him? No, they said the assassin was killed. Were you involved?"

"I might as well have killed him. I let him die."

"Tell me what happened." Edith's voice was gentle.

"I was told to guard him. I was tired. A battle, travelling, I had little sleep. I was distracted." I raised my head. I wasn't making excuses; I just wanted her to understand. "I wasn't there. My lord died and I was not there. I should have protected him, died for him, but I am still alive."

"Who commanded you to do this thing?"

"Lord Athestan, Ealdorman of East Anglia." Edith nodded slowly. "Do you know him?"

"No matter. He should have chosen someone else. Someone more able."

"I was able. I should have done my duty."

"No-one can do a job properly if they have not slept. It is not your fault."

"There is more," I said quietly.

"More? Tell me everything."

"I was angry, confused. Someone accused me of being distracted by a woman. I wasn't, I thought there was someone, suspicious, following her. I made a mistake. Then the king's brother, Eadred... "

"The present king."

"I suppose he is. He accused me of being part of the plot. I was angry. I attacked him, laid hands on him."

"Oh dear." She frowned. "Why would he say that?"

"There have been rumours," said Edberga.

"Hush. So that is why you left?"

"I left early the next day, without any farewell." I remembered Saewynn, crying. "I had let down my lord, the King; my companions and my friends. My shame would not let me stay. I had no destination. The north was as good a direction as any. My ... no matter, that is not important. I avoided people and human habitation. I have no lord, and no future. I arrived here." I looked round the quiet room. "I don't even know where here is."

"We are not far from Tamworth, the old capital of Mercia," Edith told me. It didn't really interest me. What did it matter where I was?

Edith spoke quietly to the other nun then she placed a gentle hand on my injured shoulder. "I must think on this. We will talk again. Edberga will remove your bindings and see how you have healed. It will be painful, I think." She walked towards the door and pulled it open. "I will pray for you."

***

I sat on the bed as Edberga unwound the clothes that had kept my arm immobile for so long. Unsupported, it hung lifeless at my side; something apart, useless. The nun moved the arm slowly back and forth.

"Not bad." She nodded. "Lie down."

As I stretched out, face pressed into the mattress, I remembered the last time I had lain like this. I stiffened in preparation for the pain.

"Relax. How can I judge your condition if you fight me?" My arm hung down, towards the floor. It swung when she pushed it gently. I felt the movement in my shoulder, but no pain.

"Can you touch the floor?" I stretched, but my fingers were reluctant to move.

"Other side." I turned onto my back. I must hang my arm off the side of the bed, but I knew this was going to hurt, a lot.

Edberga grasped my arm and slowly lowered it.

"I told you to relax."

"I'm trying." I closed my eyes, tried to think of something else. All I could see was the Lady Edith, sitting beside the water, combing her hair.

"Very good. You can sit up." She moved behind me and ran her hands over my shoulder, exploring the bones and muscles. The prodding grew rougher. Strong fingers dug into my flesh. I flinched when she found some nugget of pain. By the time she stopped, I felt I had spent hours in a shield wall, sweat ran down my body.

"We need a drink after that." Edberga poured two cups of water from the jug. She sat next to me and we sipped the cool liquid.

"Well?" I wanted the silence to continue forever, but I had to know the verdict.

"It will take a long time, as long again as you have been strapped up, perhaps longer. But my job is done."

"What do you mean?" Was it the end? She could do nothing more for me?

"It means, my boy, that as far as I can tell, you will make a complete recovery."

"Are you sure?"

"Nothing is completely certain in this life. Who knows what the future holds? But now it's up to you."

I gulped down the rest of the water, then hid my head in my hands; both hands I soon realised. The pain, the worry, the despair was over. I lifted my head and, with a slight flinch, straightened my back.

"I don't know how to thank you." How do you thank some who has given you back your life?

"It's what I'm here for." She took the cups back to their place by the jug.

"It was hard work. I don't want you to spoil it. You must take things slowly, build up your strength gradually." She told me what exercises to do and why not to over do them. "You will need plenty of food to build you up. I'm afraid you will have to work for that now. You will live with the men and help them with their work. I will instruct them what you are capable of." She anticipated my next question. "I will keep your sword for the time being. It would be too much of a temptation." Perhaps it would, but without that I was still half a man.

"Patience. The time will pass. Get dressed and I'll show you your new home."

***

I was given a pallet in the hut occupied by the two old men. They spoke little. I never discovered if they were brothers; they looked and sounded alike, strong like oxen and as stupid. They were too old to be a threat to the nuns, but young enough to do the work too heavy or unsuitable for women.

Their hut was outside the monastery enclosure close to the narrow plank bridge that was the only entrance. I quickly discovered that the small community was sited on an island. The river split then came together. There was a small mill; now and then visitors would arrive with a bag of grain to be ground. The nuns took a share of the flour as payment. A strong back was needed to haul the sacks and in time, as my shoulder mended, this became my job.

The men spent a lot of time in the forest. They gathered withies from the stools of willow along the riverbanks. Soon I was strong enough to help cut the thin stems. The nuns wove baskets from them. They also made fish traps to set in the fast flowing river. I helped to set them out and haul them in. We ate a lot of fish at the monastery.

Eventually my sword was returned. It was in a sorry state, covered in dried mud and grass. The point was blunt and the edge was nicked along its length. The surface was pitted with rust. I was ashamed to claim it as mine. How carefully I had cleaned it every time it had been used; now it was useful only to dig the fields. I must work hard to get it fit to use, then I could fight again.

I got into the habit of visiting the far end of the island, where I had first seen the Lady Edith. Not in the morning, never then, but in the evening, when I knew everyone would be assembled in the chapel for vespers. After a day's work in the hot sun, I would swim in the river. I found the water supported my body and I could exercise without pain.

I took a few of the long poles used for supporting plants in the garden, and sharpened the ends into points. I hardened them in a small fire; there were no spearheads to be had in the monastery. I practised throwing them at trees, first close and then further away until my aim improved.

I spent long hours cleaning and sharpening the sword until it gleamed gold in the low evening sun. The first time I tried to swing it, at a slender sapling the height of a man, I thought the blade was damaged. But it was I who was damaged. Lack of strength and practice had sent me back to the state of a beginner.

I slashed at the sapling again and again, until it was a pile of shredded wood on the ground.

I would improve.

I must improve.

Without my battle skills I was nothing.

50

"You've left one. Shall I cut it down?"

We were working in the forest, cutting firewood for the winter. The men had left one sapling standing.

"No, gotta leave him to grow big."

"Not many oaks here," the other man said, "don't waste good wood on fires."

"Aye, save him for building."

"I saw an oak, a big tree. It was struck by lightning." I touched the scar on my shoulder. "It was how I was injured. Don't know where it was." I selected another tree and prepared to swing the axe.

"Oak," one of the men said.

"Aye, oak." The other nodded thoughtfully.

"Aye." The first man grinned, displaying a selection of random teeth, before bundling up a pile of sticks.

They didn't speak much, and when they did I rarely understood what they said. I swung my axe into the trunk of the next tree.

***

Early next morning they shook me awake. Outside, an ox was harnessed to a cart. The men climbed up and pointed to the flat bed of the cart. It contained a selection of axes and a saw. I climbed up and sat on a pile of ropes.

I asked where we were going; the only reply was a grunt. I made myself comfortable. No doubt I would find out when we arrived.

The cart wound through the forest. The sound of the river died away and silence surrounded us. The path rose and the ox slowed. There was a jolt and the cart emerged from the forest. The view was open now. Tall grass moved like the sea, seed heads rattling in the breeze. The cart continued up a hill, the surface smoother under the feet of the plodding ox.

"That's it." I pointed. "That's the tree." The men raised their heads from their contemplation of the ox's tail.

"Oak," said one.

"Aye, oak," replied the other.

As we got closer, the damage to the giant oak was obvious. Most of the tree still stood but its symmetry had been destroyed. On one side the sky was empty, where it had once been filled with dense green foliage. Across the ground stretched a long bough, surrounded by brown dead leaves. The cart stopped and we sat and took in the scene. One of the men pointed at me.

"Lucky." I agreed. How had I emerged alive from this devastation?

One man jumped down and unhitched the ox. It moved away and started ripping at the tall grass. The other man inspected the wood lying on the ground. He cleared away some of the dead foliage for a better view. He made a decision and after a discussion, accompanied with much waving of arms, they collected axes from the cart. They removed the small branches from the bough, piling them carefully to one side. They decided where to divide the skeleton of wood that remained. Two men at a time could work on the tree, first one axe and then the other.

I took my turn. My shoulder ached, but no more than my back and the rest of my body. The day was cloudy but still warm and soon sweat ran down our bodies. One of the men called a halt and I collapsed onto the ground. We passed around a large skin of water. Bread was produced, together with strips of smoked fish. Soon we were back at work. We didn't stop until late afternoon.

The main bough lay on the ground, long and straight. The men admired the wood; calculating how many planks they would cut from it. Were they planning to cut it there? I was sent to fetch the ox. Several branches were piled together. They made a substantial load. The men argued how they were to be arranged, but eventually both were happy. The ox was harnessed to the logs and one man led it down the hill, sweeping a wide path through the grass. We watched the slow progress for a while before returning to our labour, removing surplus bark from the main log.

I stood on top of the log, hacking down at the final strands that attached it to the trunk. I stopped to ease my aching back. As I bent to continue, I noticed something. I jumped down and cleared away the branches. It was my shield. I had left it leaning against the trunk. I seized the rim and pulled. It didn't move. I scraped at the dry earth with the axe, but, close to the massive trunk, the ground was hard as iron. My companion came to inspect what I had found. He pulled me away.

"Tomorrow. We sleep now." I realised that dusk was falling.

We finished the bread and drank most of the remaining water and I lay down next to the shield. I stoked the crescent of smooth wood that was all that was visible. Was it still intact under the oak?

**

The second man returned early the next morning. He had brought both the monastery's oxen, yoked together. Thick ropes dragged behind. It took a long time to attach the ropes to the fallen branch. We cut grooves to stop the ropes slipping and removed more bark. Finally we were ready. The oxen were urged forward. The ropes tightened. Nothing happened. There were more adjustments; obstacles were removed from the path. There was more shouting at the great beasts. Finally, with a jerk, the log moved. It slid forward, gouged into the soil and halted. The ropes were rearranged and the oxen strained forward again. The log moved slowly, then a bit faster. The men nodded and broke into broad smiles.

"You stay." He pointed at me. "Guard the wood. Back later."

I watched the massive log move slowly down the hill. A furrow in the dark soil marked its passage. I tidied the chaos left behind and loaded some of the bark into the cart. It would be sold to the tanners in the town. Then I collected the axes and started to sharpen the blunted blades.

I couldn't put the moment off any longer. I walked to the trunk of the oak tree, to the remains of my shield. There was not much to see. The log had dragged what was left several feet before abandoning the shattered pieces. The boss was twisted out of shape and almost flat; it had received the full weight of the fallen bough. Most of the boards were smashed to splinters. I picked up the remains and brushed off the soil. I slipped my hand through the familiar grip and curled my fingers round the leather padding. I lifted the shield as if in defence. The section that I had spotted the previous night fell to the ground, leaving me clutching only the deformed shield boss and the section of wood between it and my hand.

I let it drop. My shoulder was able to lift a shield, but I had no shield to lift.

***

It was late when I heard the voices. Strangers, they made more noise than the silent men from the monastery. I picked up the largest of the axes.

"We didn't know anyone was here." The men stopped abruptly.

"Didn't you notice the cart?" I waved the axe in its direction. The men stepped back. There were three of them; they appeared to be innocent travellers. They had no obvious weapons, but I was taking no chances.

"We thought it had been abandoned."

I didn't reply.

"We were planning to shelter here. Spend the night."

"It's starting to rain," added another, "there's plenty of room for all."

I stepped away. Beyond the shelter of the oak, a light drizzle fell. There was no sign of my companions returning.

"There is a monastery. That way." I gestured with the axe. The travellers flinched, eyes fixed on the sharp blade. "You can get shelter there. Just follow the path. It's not far."

"Thank you, we will follow your advice." They hurried away, looking back to check I was not following.

When they were out of sight, I went and sat down, back against the trunk of the tree.

"Just the two of us again." Above, leaves rustled in the breeze. "Just don't fall on me this time." I relaxed and closed my eyes.

*****

The old men were back early next morning, with the oxen.

"Should finish today."

We gathered the rest of the larger branches into a load to be pulled by one of the oxen. The cart was piled full of bark and the most useful of the brushwood. The axes were stowed away. One of the men picked up the remains of the shield. He turned it over and over in his hands before peering up at me from beneath bushy bows.

"Maybe use this." He tossed it onto the cart.

All that remained was a layer of dead leaves. The livid white scar that marked the spot where the tree had split was fading. It was if nothing had ever happened there.

I walked behind the laden oxen, picking up anything that fell off. I glanced back only once. The oak tree stood alone, upright once more.

51

Rain had swollen the river, and while we had been away the fish traps had filled. I spent several days in the cold water, collecting fish and preparing them for smoking. I wasn't getting any fonder of fish. In the evenings I still took my sword to the end of the island. I was back training, as I had done for most of my life, but there was no one to spar with, to practise different blows, to test my skills. For the first in a long time, I wondered what my friends were doing.

There had been fighting in the north. Had they been there, been injured? Wulfstan must have returned to his monastery. Had he taken his vows after all? It was not my concern. I stabbed the sword into a figure stuffed with straw. I had made it to practise with; if I stayed much longer I would need a replacement. I cleaned the sword and slid it back into the sheath. I stripped and waded into the river, swimming upstream against the current. This time I went further than I had gone before. I reached a section where the water foamed white through sharp fanged rocks. I clung to a thin branch of willow. What lay beyond? The narrow leaves slipped through my fingers and I let the river carry me back to the island.

I sat on the small stony beach, shivering as the cool evening breeze dried my body. What should I do? Could I stay here? I glanced at the pile of clothes. The smell of fish hovered over the shabby, patched garments. I imagined growing old, eventually replacing the other men, working for the nuns.

They wouldn't let me stay. There had been complaints that I was distracting the younger women of the community, despite my efforts to keep out of the way, eyes to the ground if I encountered anyone. It was an easy decision to make. I would leave, soon, when I had decided which way to go.

Someone was approaching. I quickly dressed, and pulled my sword closer to my hand. One of the old men emerged from the bushes and I relaxed. The other followed him, carrying a shield. He handed it to me.

"Had some spare wood. Mended it."

"Blacksmith in town straightened out metal," the other said, "didn't take long."

I touched the polished boss. It reflected the shimmering light of the river.

"Found some paint. Change if you want."

A green cross divided the surface. The quadrants between were painted a vibrant blue.

"Cross for the monastery."

"And the island, blue for the river."

"It's beautiful." I slipped my hand through the handle, the old familiar grip. I raised my arm. I was complete again.

"I don't know what to say."

The men backed away, alarmed. "No need to say anything."

"Just a small job." They turned and disappeared between the trees.

I stood for a moment, inspecting the shield. I walked back to where my sword lay and buckled the belt round my waist, adjusting it until the hilt hung close to my hand. I picked up the shield, admiring the bright colours again, and drew the sword. I practiced with both, coordinating the rise and fall of the shield with strikes of the sword. I moved round the space, splashing through the shallow water, leaping over rocks. I swung the sword at hidden enemies and hid from secret attackers behind the shield. Then I stopped. I threw back my head and screamed a challenge to the darkening sky, beating the sword against the shield. Newly roosted birds flew up in panic. A nearby crow replied to my shout with a hoarse cry and flapped away through the trees. My teeth were bared in a triumphant grin.

I dropped my head; had they heard me back in the monastery? Breathing heavily I carefully cleaned the sword and slipped it back into the sheath. Carrying the new shield on my arm, I walked slowly back through the gathering dusk.

It was nearly dark when I reached the monastery. The rain had made the path slippery. I took the route through the cluster of huts occupied by the nuns. No one would be about at this time. I was nearly at the gate when a light appeared. The Lady Edith carried a flickering candle in a raised hand. I stepped forward to apologise for my presence, but the peaceful expression on her face turn to a look of fear and horror. She dropped the candle and ran swiftly away. I heard the slam of a door and the sound of a latch falling.

When I got back to the hut, the men were already asleep, snoring loudly. She'd not raised the alarm, despite her look of panic. I propped the shield against the wall and unbuckled the sword, laying it beside my pallet. I stretched out in the darkness. I didn't know what to do. Eventually I slept.

***

"The Lady Edith wants to see you."

"I am sorry. I scared her last night. I shouldn't have been inside the fence."

It was close to the noonday meal when Edberga found me. I had been watching the men split oak branches into planks. They pored over the wood, tracing the grain, calculating exactly the right spot to insert the wedge. Then they called me to wield the axe. Sometimes one blow was enough and the trunk would split along its length.

I dropped the axe and brushed chips of wood from my clothes.

"It's not that. Well, not exactly. Your shoulder has recovered, judging by the way you were swinging that axe."

"It aches a bit now and then, but I'm getting plenty of exercise.

Edberga stopped and inspected me, head to toe.

"You've put on weight. All muscle though. Are you getting enough to eat?"

"Plenty. I wish it wasn't always fish though."

"Yes." She smiled. "That's the problem with a religious life. How high can you raise your arms?"

I raised them both and clasped my hands above my head. Then I stretched up, plucked a leaf off the tree above and presented it to Edberga.

"That seems satisfactory. I think we can say you have recovered."

"What does she want?" We had reached the enclosure.

"I don't know, but it's something important, she was awake all night, praying."

What had I done wrong? I couldn't imagine how I had offended her.

"She's in the garden." Edberga gave me a push in the right direction.

52

I walked between small beds of vegetables and flowers. A few of the nuns looked up as I passed, but returned to their labourers when they saw the prioress was watching. She smiled when I stopped in front of her. I apologised.

"I think I frightened you last night."

"It is nothing. I thought I saw... someone else. You are looking well."

"Thank you, my lady. Edberga tells me I am recovered." I knew what would happen now. "You want me to leave."

"Not just yet. Let us walk, I have more questions for you." We inspected the plants in silence.

"When we spoke before, you mentioned your mother. Do you remember her name?" Why did she want to know? I thought back.

"I don't believe I do. At that age..." I had barely reached seven summers, "she was just my mother."

"Of course. You said she had grey eyes, and long fair hair." Had I told her about the hair? Perhaps when I was ill. I sometimes dreamed about my mother.

"She combed it out at night. It looked white in the firelight. During the day it was plaited and hung over her shoulder, like a thick rope. People told her that it was wicked and she should keep it covered, I don't know why. I loved to touch it. I'm sorry, you don't want to know that."

"Your father. What happened, do you remember him?"

"They say his name was Byrhthelm. People say that I resemble him. Whether he is alive or dead, I know not." If he still lived, I am sure he would have returned.

"The sun is getting hot. Let us walk in the orchard, it is shady there." She walked towards a small gate and pushed it open. The grass was green and lush under the trees. A small gaggle of geese hissed and flustered, then lost interest. Beneath some of the trees apples lay, small and green. Edith walked to the nearest tree and inspected an apple hanging low on the branch. The green was tinged with pink.

"It will be a good harvest this year. The rain came just in time to swell the fruit." She looked up, her cheek flushed pink like the apple. "My mother's name was Leofflaed. She was a relative of the Ealdorman of East Anglia."

"Athelstan?"

"You said you met him recently." I nodded. "She was sent to Mercia, to marry. She was very young. The marriage was not a success. Her husband, my father," her lips curled in a grimace, "tired of her. He wanted to wed another, so he sent her here. I came with her." She looked round at the peaceful scene. "It has been my only home." Why was she telling me this? I followed her into the shadow of the next tree.

"We were happy." She turned away, towards the tree. "Then, one day, he came." She paused, frowned and continued. "It was stormy. The apples had long been picked and stored. He and his companions took shelter. The storm continued several days. Then it was over. He left. He took my mother with him." She looked down. "I never saw her again."

"I'm sorry."

"Sorry?" She spun round. The anger I had seen last night

276

flared, then her eyes flooded with tears. "They said his name was Byrhthelm." I thought I had misheard.

"What did you say?" She must have confused the name.

"Your father stole my mother from me."

"That means?" My head spun, I could not work out what had happened.

"Yes, little brother, I am your sister." She took my arm and led me through the orchard. We stood beside the river and I stared into the glittering water.

"I knew it, even before you said his name. I remember her hair too. The curl at the end that I twisted round my finger."

"Sometimes she cried when I did that. She must have missed you very much." I grasped her hand and squeezed it tightly. "Are you certain of this? Half the women in England have hair like that." I remembered the slave girl in Lundenburh. Now I understood why her death had upset me so.

"You told me his name," Edith's voice broke through my thoughts. "And last night, when I saw you, emerging from the dark. It was him, coming with his weapons to destroy my life again. When were you born?"

"In the summer, sixteen years ago. I was seven the year of the Battle of Brunanbugh. That was the year she died."

Edith counted the years on her fingers. "That would agree." She giggled. "Do you realise, you might have been conceived on this very spot?" She clapped her hand to her mouth, horrified by what she had said.

Embarrassed, I stared down at the ground. Small flowers scattered the grass. Here? "In winter? In a storm?" We stared at each other. We started to laugh. I had a sister.

I picked her up and swung her round before depositing her back on the ground. "I've never had a sister before. I don't know how to behave."

"I've never had a brother. Aren't they supposed to look after their sisters?"

"I don't know. I've never had anyone to look after before. I had a dog once, but that was only for a day or two. I wonder what happened to her?"

"I've just remembered." Edith started giggling again. "That storm, it snowed. Everything was frozen solid, ice and snow feet deep."

"Very hardy people, my parents." It was the only thing I could think of to say.

"Come on," Edith wiped away tears of laughter. "That was the bell for the midday meal. We can discuss this later."

As we walked towards the hall, I dropped Edith's hand.

"I don't think we should mention this to anyone, just yet."

"No." Edith adjusted her veil. "You know who must know about all this? Who can confirm everything – or not?"

"Yes. The Ealdorman of East Anglia."

"Athelstan."

53

"I have decided that I wish to visit my close relative, Ealdorman Athelstan. There are family matters to discuss. I will not be away for long. Lord Byrhtnoth, now thankfully recovered, is travelling to his own lands in East Anglia. He has agreed to be my escort. It is not necessary to inform the Bishop. Edberga will take charge while I am absent, I will be back before you have noticed I've gone."

"What are you doing? You cannot go, just like that. Surely you must get permission?" Edberga followed her out of the chapel.

"If I have to ask permission, time will pass. Summer will be ended and it will be impossible to travel."

"But with him? What will people say?"

"If I am to travel, I need someone to protect me." She told Edberga that I was a relative. "Who here is more suitable?"

"Why is it so urgent? Why now? You are needed here."

"No I'm not. Everything runs perfectly smoothly. If it was you who were leaving, dear Edberga, there would be a problem." Edith paused and looked around. "I have spent all my life here. Never travelled further than the local town. Never experienced the world. Now is the time."

Despite her eagerness, it took several days before we were

ready to leave. A horse had to be found, a gentle mare, suitable for a nun to ride, but strong enough to carry provisions too. We expected to spend the night at local halls, or monasteries. If we found no shelter at the end of the day, a tent would be needed. I was used to sleeping anywhere, but Edith would need privacy. As a nun, she had few personal possessions, but she must take gifts for the Ealdorman.

I stood and watched as more was added to the load, then added my bundle of homemade spears to the horse.

"I'm not sure there's going to be room for you to ride," I whispered to Edith as she studied the horse with trepidation. "Have you actually ridden before?" Edith shook her head. "At least you will have plenty of padding." I folded my cloak and hung it over the saddle. "Up you get." I lifted her onto the mare. "Don't worry about the reins. I'll lead her, you just hang on."

Edberga bustled through the crowd. She clasped a large bundle to her ample bosom. What else did we need to take?

"Are you sure you'll be all right?" Edberga asked. "Take one of the men with you."

"I don't think so." Edith looked towards where they stood, side by side. "I'm taking their assistant away, I don't think either could manage on their own."

"If you insist." Edberga thrust the bundle at me. "This is for you. If you are to protect my lady, you need protection yourself."

I unwrapped the bundle. It was a heavy padded coat, layers of material and wool, stitched tightly together, the next best thing to a coat of mail. It must have taken her a long time.

"Once you got out of bed, I didn't have much else to do. I had to keep making it bigger, as you recovered." I tried it on. "I put an extra layer in the shoulder, just in case."

"It's perfect. I don't know how to thank you; for everything." I gave her a hug.

"It was nothing. Just doing my duty." She flustered like a hen disturbed from her nest.

"I promise I'll bring her back safely."

"You better had, or you'll wish you'd died in the forest."

I swung my shield onto my back and waved to the two men. "Thank you."

They looked embarrassed. Their heads bobbed in unison and two mouthfuls of uneven teeth grinned at me.

"Thank you all." I looked round the group of nuns and servants gathered to see us off. "I don't know what to say."

"How about goodbye?" Edith answered dryly.

"Yes, my lady." I grasped the bridle and urged the horse into motion. Edith wobbled and grabbed at the shaggy mane.

"You'll soon get used to it." I waved a final farewell and we clattered over the little wooden bridge. It was reinforced with fresh oak, my final job.

***

The day was dry and warm, with a hazy sky blocking the heat of the sun. We skirted the nearby town, to join Watling Street.

"They say that it travels straight, all the way to London. Then on to the coast." I guided the horse up a bank and onto the uneven rocky surface. "We should make good time now."

"Only giants could have built something so marvellous." Edith swayed in the saddle and then regained her upright pose. "I have decided that riding a horse is not very comfortable."

"You'll get used to it." I strode on, causing the mare to speed up.

"Not so fast, that's even worse."

I slowed down again. It was going to be a long journey.

We stopped the night at a small hall close to the road. The family knew of the monastery and we were made welcome. Edith nearly fell when I lifted her from the horse. Perhaps it would be better if she walked for some of the time.

Next day, the road continued, up a hill and down the other

side. I soon discovered that Edith was no more used to walking than riding. When the way was steep, she struggled, breathless, demanding to stop every few steps. Down hill, when I tried to speed up, she complained her feet hurt. One night, we swapped some of our stock of smoked fish for some strong boots. I would have offered her mine and walked barefoot, but I knew they would be much too big. It worked for a while. The hills were smaller and the pace increased.

We came to a place where a stream crossed the road. Once there had been a bridge, but it had been washed away when the river flooded, taking much of the road with it. Someone had built it long ago, but no one had maintained it for a long time. We paddled through the mud and shallow water. The horse slid on the wet rocks. Soon another hill rose before us.

"I have a blister." Edith sat down on a stone at the side of the road. There were worn letters carved on it, indicating the distance to some unknown place. She untied her boot and inspected the large blister on her heel. "There's one on my other foot as well."

I lifted her back on the horse. We would climb this hill, the biggest so far. Then find somewhere to stop.

It was nearly dark when we reached a settlement. Buildings lined the side of the road. There were lights in some houses and drunken shouting drifted from one of the doorways. I picked one of the quieter houses that looked more respectable than others. I offered the rest of our dried fish for a bed for the night. Edith was nearly asleep when I lifted her off the horse. I laid her on the bed and covered her with a blanket. I unloaded the horse and gave it a quick brush and some fodder in the stable.

By the time I finished, Edith was fast asleep, fully dressed. I removed her boots and begged some water from the householder. I gently washed my sister's feet. I dried them and wrapped the blisters in a clean piece of linen. Edith moaned in her sleep. I lay down on the floor beside her. We could not go on like this.

54

I was up early. The road ran straight through the small town and on into the distance. A wall, half derelict, surrounded it. Some of the buildings, those closest the road were of stone as well. It had been built at the same time as the road, for the same purpose it served now, catering for the travellers that passed this way. I sipped from a jug of ale and talked with some of those travellers. Where had they come from? Where were they going? And which was the best way to go? Some were suspicious, but others gave helpful information.

When Edith emerged, hobbling in her boots, I was ready to go.

"Have you eaten?"

"There was some gruel, but it was cold. I didn't fancy it."

"Here." I handed her the piece of bread. "It's a bit dry, but fine if you dip it in the ale." I took another sip and handed her the jug. Over the rim, she stared at her mount with distaste.

I told her not to worry. I took my cloak and threw it over the horse's back. There were some spots of blood on the saddle, from where her legs had chafed. She hadn't mentioned it. She had suffered rather than complain. I should have noticed.

"Only one more day."

"Are we nearly there?"

"No, we're going to have a break. The road heads south, but we need to go east. That road goes to Hamtune." I pointed towards a track that left the main road.

"There's an abbey there. You can rest and recover from your blisters." I would find a different way to travel. Perhaps rig up some kind of cart. "Take off those boots and load them on the horse, I got rid of the rest of the fish, so there's plenty of room."

Edith stood in the dust in her bandaged feet while I mounted the horse.

"Take my hand." I pulled her up and sat her sideways on my lap, her head rested on my shoulder. I put my arms round her to hold the reins. I wasn't sure how long the animal could bear the extra weight, but it was worth a try.

"Can you get your veil out of my face?" She smoothed it down and I smiled down at her. "Comfortable?"

"Very. Why didn't you do this earlier?"

"I didn't think it the right thing to do. Riding through the countryside, cuddling a nun."

***

A palisade crowned the top of the hill, the wood fresh and yellow. It was on the disputed border between Mercia and the Danelaw and was regularly burnt. Now it was in English hands again. The mare staggered to a halt at the gate. I was walking again, supporting Edith, who slumped in the saddle. Her eyes were closed and her face pale.

"This is the Lady Edith, prioress of St Mildgyth's. She is ill and seeks help."

"What's wrong with her?" A bored guard barred our way. "Can't let her in if she has something serious."

"Just tired. She insisted on this journey, but she is unused to travelling. She needs to rest a few days."

"You may enter. The abbey's not far, just carry on up the road."
The reluctant horse tottered onwards.

The abbey was a building site. New walls rose above the chaos
of scattered rocks and burnt beams. Workmen shouted as stones
were hauled slowly into the air. In a nearby shelter I heard the
now familiar sound of axe on wood. A young monk hurried past.
I caught his arm.

"Who's in charge? My lady needs somewhere to rest. Do you
have somewhere she can stay?"

"I don't know. I'm new here." The monk looked round the
area helplessly.

"My lady travels to visit the Ealdorman of East Anglia. She is
a close relative." I emphasised the words.

"Oh. I'll find the abbot for you. Wait here."

I lifted Edith from the horse. She leaned against me.

"Where are we?"

"Safe. They are finding somewhere for you to rest." I looked
around at the chaos of dust and noise. "It may take some time."

The monk brought a tall man with whispy white hair.

"I am Abbot here. Ealdorman Athelstan visited only a few
weeks ago. He came with the bishop to inspect our work." We
watched another stone rise up the walls. "He told us we were
working too slowly."

"My lord, this lady is the prioress of St Mildred's Well, near
Tamworth."

"I have heard of it," the abbot said, "they say that miracles are
worked there. I must visit some time."

"She needs help," I reminded him – why was this so difficult
for these monks to understand? "She is tired and must have rest
before we continue our journey."

"Of course. Follow me." He led us though the space that was
to be the abbey nave. Behind was a scattering of rough wooden
buildings. The abbot showed us to a small hut that stood away
from the others.

"I'm afraid it's not much. Accommodation is limited here, but she will be safe. I will send a woman to attend her." He noticed my sword. "We will talk later. Please join me at my table."

***

"You live well." I leaned back, my immediate appetite satisfied.

"I find that men work better when they are well fed. Some wine?"

"No thank you, I prefer ale." I watched the monks and workmen sitting together, shovelling in the rich vegetable stew. "There are some that would not agree with you."

"If God provides us with our daily bread, then I feel we should share it with all."

I took another chunk of the coarse brown bread and agreed. He asked why we were travelling to visit Lord Athenstan.

"A family matter. Lady Edith took it into her head that she must go herself. She didn't realise how tiring travel can be."

"Is she feeling better?"

"Much. We will continue when the blisters have healed. Perhaps I can find a cart for her to ride in; we can't go on as we are."

"That will be very slow. The roads are not good and the land less settled. It has been fought over for so long." The abbot took a small sip of his wine. "Have you considered a boat? Many people travel on the river here. It flows towards the coast of East Anglia." I had seen it as we came up the hill. It might be the best solution.

"I will ask around for something suitable leaving in the next few days. More stew?"

"Thank you. I think I can manage a bit more."

***

"You're looking better."

"I just needed a good sleep." Edith was watching the building

286

work. Her feet were raised on the bench, modestly covered by her skirts.

I found room beside her and leaned back against the wall of the hut. It was warm in the sun. "How are the blisters?"

"Improving, but it will take a few days before I can walk properly. When do we have to leave?" I could hear her voice shaking.

"Don't worry, I spoke to the abbott. He's found us passage on a ship. The river goes all the way to the east coast. No more walking."

"Oh, thank you." She gave a relieved smile. "I don't think I could have managed much more."

"I've had to sell the mare, to pay for the journey."

"Thank the Lord. I never want to go anywhere near a horse ever again."

"You'd rather walk?" I teased her, "Or do I have to carry you everywhere?"

"I've been a bit of a nuisance, haven't I?" She hung her head.

"Not at all. I've bought you a present," I produced a pair of shoes. "For when I'm not around to act as your mount. They're my old ones, so they're well worn in. They were starting to get tight and were full of holes." My feet must have grown recently. "I found someone to patch them up, they lined them with sheep's wool. No more blisters."

Edith tried on the shoes. "They fit exactly, and so soft. How did you know how big my feet were?"

"I had to wash them the other night. You were asleep I think. I'm sorry."

"I wondered who had done that. Don't be sorry." Edith kissed my cheek. "Thank you, brother."

It must have been the first time anyone had kissed me since I was a child. It felt strange. I would have to get used to it.

"I had some new boots made for myself. They didn't have any big enough."

Edith told me to stand up and tilted her head.

"I think you've grown taller."

"Must be all the exercise. And the fish. Although we don't have any left."

"Oh dear." Edith frowned. "Well, if we are travelling in a boat, there should be plenty of fish."

"Good." I grimaced. I'd hoped I wouldn't have to eat any more dried fish, for a very long time.

55

"I didn't realise how much that horse carried." I struggled with a multitude of different bundles. "Do we really need all this stuff?"

"Yes. We can't leave it here anyway."

"Let me help." The monk I had spoken to when we arrived rushed up and took the small bag that Edith carried. He strolled beside her through the gate and down the hill, asking her if she was recovered.

"Thank you for your concern. My br— my man found me some shoes lined with wool. Much more comfortable."

"We have many good shoemakers here. People are returning to the town, now the fighting is over."

"Is it?" I interrupted. "Is the fighting over?"

"We have a new king now. He is a great warrior and has extended the land of England far into the north."

"Not what I heard." I rearranged my burden. The monk ducked as the bundle of spears swung round and nearly hit him.

"How far is this ship?" Something fell to the ground with a metallic clang. Edith tried to hand it back to me, but caught my expression and tucked it under her arm.

"Not far now." The monk pointed out the river and the fleet of ships moored along the quay.

We stopped by a broad shallow vessel, stacked high with large bundles.

"Wool from the sheep on the abbey's estates," the monk informed us. "It is collected here and sent down river to be sold. We get a better price there. This boat is one of the last of the season. You were lucky to catch it."

"Where shall I put this?" I dropped everything onto the wooden planks of the dock.

"They didn't say anything about a monk." A heavyset man was watching us from the boat. "More trouble than they're worth."

"The monk's not coming," I was glad to tell him, "it's just the lady and me." I asked if he was the captain.

"Name's Osric. Don't know about the woman, but looks like you can handle yourself. Can you row?"

"If I need to."

"Good. There's space for you at the bow."

I lashed the leather tent across to create a private space for Edith and stowed the rest of the belongings inside.

"Shall I carry you on board?" I held out a hand.

"I think I can manage." She stepped from the quay onto the edge of the ship and jumped down to stand beside me. She thanked the monk for his help.

A boy untied a rope and jumped on board with it. The captain pushed the boat away from the dock with a pole and the third member of the crew let down the sail with a rush of heavy cloth. The captain took the steering oar and the boat moved slowly out into the river.

"I smell sheep." Edith wrinkled her nose.

"What do you expect with all this wool. Does it offend you?" I was rearranging our possessions to make more room.

"You won't notice it after a while." The boy sat on top of the bundles, eyes wide as he watched us. "There are worse cargos."

"Come here," Osric shouted from beyond the billowing sail, "leave our guests alone." The boy waved and crawled nimbly away across the sacks of wool. Edith disappeared into the shelter.

"Are you comfortable?"

"There's not a lot of room, but I can manage." She stuck her head out. "It's better than walking."

The ship moved fast with the wind behind it. The river was swift flowing here and the creamy crest of the water was only inches below the gunwale.

"It's not going to come over, is it?"

I stood beside the bow post. No savage beast head here, just some roughly carved decoration.

"The captain knows how to load a boat. There won't be any waves, unless there's a bad storm. If that happens they'll tie up at the bank. Just relax and enjoy the ride."

The hills grew lower. As the river entered the flatter landscape, the wind died and the sail hung limp.

"The river will take us now." The captain adjusted the steering.

I joined him at the stern. "How long will the voyage take?"

"As long as the river wishes." Osric shrugged. "The summer was dry and the river is low. Let the nun pray for a wind, or rain to swell the waters."

"Why not use the oars?"

"There are places on this river where we have to row, you as well if you want to get anywhere. Enjoy the rest while you can."

Village children watched as we sailed past, some waved, but most just stood. In the fields, harvest had begun. Rows of labourers marched in line, stooping and swinging in unison as the tall stalks fell before them. More came behind stacking the stems.

The land grew wide with fewer people, just a shepherd watching over his sheep, fat from the rich grass. Elsewhere, cattle, gathered at the water's edge, raised their heads. They followed the slow progress of the boat with curious eyes, until something scared them and they retreated in panic, trampling through the pasture before stopping to watch again.

At night we stopped well away from any habitation, the captain finding a convenient post to tie up the boat.

"You know the river well." I watched the well-practised manoeuvre.

"Been going up and down all my life, first as a boy, like the young 'un, then as mate, learning the bends and the currents. Now I've got my own boat. One day they'll bury me on the bank and my ghost will watch the generations come and go."

"Are there ghosts?" Edith's worried eyes searched the surrounding landscape.

"None as will hurt you, Lady."

We cooked a meal on the bank nearby, watching the sky display its colours; red, orange and purple as the sun slowly set. As the light faded, we boarded the boat to sleep, snug between the bales of wool.

56

The river widened, sprawling across the countryside in giant loops. We would travel for hours only to find we were close to where we had started.

Edith spotted a patient heron, motionless in the reeds. The boat came too close and the bird heaved its body out of the shallow water and flapped slowly away.

"There, a kingfisher."

"Where?" I opened my eyes.

"You missed it. They fly so fast. I saw them often, back at the monastery."

"Nowhere to hide out here. There's a hawk." I shaded my eyes from the sun and watched it circle high above, searching for a meal. It hung in the sky, motionless, before plummeting to the ground. It rose with a bundle of fur clutched in its talons. It circled once, flew off towards a patch of trees, far away. I watched for several minutes before I realised we had stopped moving.

"Do we need to get the oars out?" I shouted towards the stern.

"Think we might. I need some exercise."

The mate took over the steering and Osric removed the plugs from each side of the boat. He handed me an oar and poked the other out through the boat's side. He sat down on a chest, and peered over the packs of wool.

"Let's find out if you're any good."

I nearly ran the boat into the bank to start with, but soon found my stroke and the boat moved faster through the water. I had not rowed since I was a boy and the action was different from my recent axe work. My arms and shoulders began to ache, especially the one that had been injured, but I carried on until Osric called a halt. I collapsed, gasping for breath. Osric removed the oar from my clenched hands and stowed it away.

"Well done." He gave me a pat on the back. "We're back in the current now. You can take a break."

I leaned over the side and dangled my throbbing hands in the cool water. I scooped up handfuls and poured it over my head. I made my way back to the bow and slumped down beside Edith.

"Easier than riding?"

***

I was unable to sleep. The blisters I had got from rowing itched. I'd kept them hidden from Edith; I knew she would make fun of me. There was no moon and the stars were hidden by thick cloud. I stared up into the darkness. I could see nothing with my eyes open or closed.

Somewhere a bird of the night called wistfully in the darkness. A sudden breeze rattled the nearby reeds. I heard the whisper of the water as it caressed the hull. Nearby Edith breathed gently. At the other end of the boat, snoring broke the silence, there was a grunt and it was quiet again. There was splash as some animal slipped into the water or a fish jumped.

Then I heard the sound of wood against wood. It was followed by a whisper. It was close. I felt the slight tilt of the boat as the weight shifted. I shouted as I fumbled for my sword. Edith gave a startled scream and I heard a low voice.

"A woman. Find her."

Everything was black. I heard the stealthy sound of footsteps.

"Keep quiet," I hissed to Edith.

The footsteps stumbled and a rough male voice swore. I crouched down, low against the ship's side. The man reached me, thought I was another obstacle. My sword shot upwards before he moved, through his stomach and into his heart. There was a grunt and a splash as I heaved the body overboard. I froze and listened for the other intruder.

"What's happened?" The voice came nearer. The second man kicked the same obstacle as the first. I remembered the chest I had sat on as I rowed. I knew his position exactly. Ignoring shouts from the stern, I ran forward and slashed my sword, right and left. There was a sudden spurt of hot blood. I reached forward, grasped a handful of greasy hair. Another swipe of the sword separated head from body. I threw it away. It landed with a squelch in the mud. I vaulted the body and heard scuffling ahead: two men, uncertain of what to do. There was a high-pitched scream from the back of the boat, then silence. I listened. The men were climbing over the side; I heard them land in a small boat. Someone charged towards me, panting. I recognised Osric's voice.

"It's me." I handed the captain my sword. It would be unwieldy in a small boat. I drew a knife, small but sharp. "I'm going after them." I heard the splash of an oar, no attempt at silence now. I launched myself into the dark, landing heavily in the boat. My foot found a rotten plank and cold water gripped my leg. I lost my balance and fell against someone. We grappled. The boat tipped back and forth. I smelt the stench of stale beer. I plunged my knife into the man's neck. His grip weakened and I punched him hard in the stomach. The man collapsed into the bottom of the boat. The water turned warm with blood. The boat tipped as the other man tried to escape. I lurched towards him and sunk the knife into his back. He fell away and I heard the gurgle as he sank into the water.

I struggled, my foot stuck in the bottom of the boat. The cold water rose up my leg, pulling me down.

"Are you all right?" I heard Osric's worried voice just above.

"Give me your hand. I'm stuck in the boat." There was a touch on my face and I grasped the captain's arm. I felt a sharp pain as my ankle was pulled through the broken wood, then I was back onto the ship.

"Is everyone safe?" I could hear Edith crying in the bow.

"A few scratches. It was bit confused. We killed one between us."

"There are more." I cocked my head towards the land and the sound of pounding feet.

"They're running away. Don't think they'll be back, but I'll shift the ship away from the bank." A rope parted and the ship moved. "Here's your sword." Osric folded my fingers round the hilt. "Are you injured?"

I stood up unsteadily. My foot held, no serious damage there.

"I'm fine. I'll tell the woman she's safe." I shuffled along the ship and bumped into the chest. I promised myself to move it out of the way.

"It's too dark to do anything now. We'll sort everything out tomorrow. Get some sleep. I'll keep watch." I listened as Osric's footsteps retreated and went to reassure my sister.

57

"Wake up. Please wake up," Edith screamed and tugged at my arm. I pushed her away and reached for my sword.

"Where are they?" I peered into the mist that blanketed the river. The sky was pale and the sun had not yet risen.

"I thought you were dead. You were so still and..." Edith waved her hand towards me, my clothes were soaked in blood.

"That's not mine." I lay back down, closed my eyes and told her to wake me when the day has properly started.

"You might be badly injured. You could be bleeding to death."

"If I haven't died yet, another hour or so isn't going to make any difference." I tried to slide back into the pleasant dream she had dragged me from.

"Please. I have to check." Edith was crying. "I don't want to lose you now."

I gave up the idea of getting more sleep. The boat was moored, motionless, in the centre of the river. The mist was clearing and reeds appeared on the bank. Somewhere, a bird experimented with a few notes, then after a pause continued with a longer phrase. A dark head appeared in the water and headed smoothly towards the bank, followed by a formation of ripples. An otter, home after a night's fishing. The slender body slid out of the water, glanced back towards the boat and disappeared into the darkness that lingered beneath the reeds.

"That's a good idea." I walked to the edge of the boat and lowered myself into the river. I gasped at the cold then dived down into the silent water. It was not far to the bottom, where weeds waved gently in the current. I swam above them until I could hold my breath no longer, then surged up through the silver barrier above. I shook my head, the spray of drops pattered like rain on the surface. I waved at Edith who had been scanning the surface anxiously. I dived again, then drifted, arms outstretched and eyes closed. I swam to the stern of the boat, stopping to exchange a few words with Osric. Then I swam lazily back to where Edith waited. I climbed back into the boat. Water ran from my body to form a puddle on the boards.

"Better?"

I gave her a broad grin and stripped off my wet clothes. I wrung them out, with an extra rinse in the river for an especially stubborn bloodstain.

"You're bleeding." Edith pointed.

I glanced down at my chest. I didn't remember being wounded in the fight, but a thin red line was clearly visible.

"It's just a scratch. It isn't even bleeding." I noticed something else. "Now, that is bleeding."

The puddle of water that had collected at my feet was rapidly turning from pink to red.

"Sit down," Edith shrieked and pushed me to the deck. She grabbed my foot, supporting it on one of the packs of wool.

"Don't move." She dived into her shelter. "Sister Edberga gave me some supplies in case of accidents." She rummaged through her luggage. Osric wandered up. I rolled my eyes and Osric nodded. He handed me the damp tunic I had abandoned on the deck and I wrapped it round my foot.

"What are you doing?" Edith emerged, flushed.

"Stopping the bleeding. Once that's done, you can sew it up or bandage it; whatever is needed."

"Sew it up?" Edith's face paled.

"Only if it doesn't stop bleeding."

We sat and watched the cloth. It became pink, but no darker. The bleeding had stopped.

"You enjoy this," Edith said sharply.

"Enjoy what?"

"All this. Fighting, killing people." She shuddered.

"Why not?" I shrugged. "It's what I do; protect my country, friends – my sister – from danger. It's a simple choice. If I don't do it, others will suffer."

"I hadn't really thought about it before." Edith slowly unwrapped the cloth. "I've been shut up in the monastery so long, I don't know how the world works."

"It's not the monastery. You're a woman. You're not expected to know about these things."

"Perhaps I should." She dabbed at the deep gouges that stretched up my leg. "How did you do this?"

"It was the thieves' boat. The bottom was rotten. When I jumped in..."

"You jumped into their boat? In the dark?"

"As I said, when I jumped in, my foot went through the bottom. I killed the men." I hoped they were dead. "The boat started to sink. I'd have drowned if Osric hadn't pulled me out." I looked at Edith's shocked face. "What's the matter?"

"Nothing." She inspected my injuries. "I don't think it needs stitching."

"Just bind it up then." I twisted my ankle to view the damage.

"Keep still!" Edith picked up a pot of ointment and smoothed some on the wounds. She took out her spare veil, smoothed it out with regret, giving it a lingering glance before she ripped it into strips.

"You're shivering. Put that cloak round you, you'll catch cold."

"It's just the wind." The reeds at the edge of the water were rustling. Small waves appeared on the surface of the river and the boat rocked. Osric and his mate rushed to the sail, raising it to catch the breeze.

"No rowing today," he shouted towards us.

"I'll come and give you a hand." I began to get up.

"No you don't." Edith held me down. "You will stay here, with your foot up, and rest. You've done your job. Let them do theirs."

58

"If this wind continues, we should reach Medeshamstede tomorrow." Osric watched the sail billow. "Our voyage ends there, on the edge of the fens. Where do you travel from there?"

"I'm not sure." I glanced at Edith. We had planned to visit Ealdorman Athelstan, to discover more about our mother. But home was so close, if it was still my home. "There is a place near Ely. We might stop there."

"You'll need a small boat if you want to navigate the fens." Osric watched the passing countryside. "Prepare to drop the sail, we are near the bridge." The mate and the boy rushed to obey. "The old bridge carries the north road across the river. The mast must be taken down. I will find a boat for you when we get to Medeshamstede."

I thanked him.

"No. Our thanks are due to you. We would all have been killed in our sleep if you had not been there. We owe you our lives."

"It was nothing." I returned my attention to cleaning my sword.

***

The sun was sinking low at our back when I smelt the distinctive taint of the fens across the flat land and heard the distant whisper of the sea.

"I don't really know you at all, do I?" I had sensed Edith watching me. I continued staring into the distance.

"We've been travelling for days. You must know me by now."

"It's all so strange. All my life I've been alone and then I discover I have a brother. We spoke about our mother, but I don't know anything about your life, what you were like as a boy, who your friends are. Do you have a girl who loves you?"

"No girl." I sat down beside her as the darkness closed in. "No friends either now, no one. Except you." I patted her hand. "Or have you changed your mind about wanting a brother?"

"Of course not. You have a home out there." She took my hand. "Is it still your home?"

"I don't know. I lived there for seven years and then I left." I had told her that much. "I went back again. Four years ago? The Lord Toli was dying; he died soon after I arrived. You might have met him; I think he served my father. The place is mine now, at least it was. Perhaps the king has given it to someone else. There will be people there who knew your mother. They can tell you about her life better than I can."

"I would like that."

"Then we will go there. They cannot turn away travellers, whoever owns it now."

59

We arrived at Medeshamstede early next morning. The river beneath the low hill was packed with boats. River transports like ours, larger sea-going ships and fishing boats, full of fish. Cargos were loaded, unloaded or transferred from ship to ship. We halted as an unwieldy ferry was being punted slowly from one side of the river to the other. Apprehensive grooms clung to nervous horses, while their well-dressed riders gathered on the bank, waiting to continue their journey.

Osric sailed slowly down river, searching for a berth. Unsuccessful, we rowed back and after exchanging shouts with another captain, we tied up alongside him.

"It's a busy place," Osric said, "we will have to wait to unload. If you want to break your journey, the monastery is up there." He pointed towards the top of the hill.

"They're rebuilding, like Hamtune."

"The Danes destroyed all the religious buildings. It didn't stop trade though, it's busier than ever."

I decided to continue our journey. It was still early and we'd had plenty of rest. There was no point in carrying everything up the hill and back again.

"You offered to find us another boat?"

"I'll send the boy." He spoke to him and the boy nodded. He jumped from our boat to the next and then onto the quay. With a wave he disappeared into the crowd.

"It's so busy." Edith had been watching the activity.

"The main road to the north, Ermine Street, crosses the river here. Everyone has to pass through the town." I pointed out a sleek warship gliding through the water, powered by many oarsmen. "That must be the water reeve, checking the ships on the river and people crossing." The boat made an efficient stop by the ferry. Words were exchanged and the horsemen were waved on. "They will have spent the night in the town. Word will be sent to the king about who is travelling his land."

"I know. We were supposed to do the same." I hadn't thought about that. Had news of my travels been reported? Edith laughed at my concern. "Don't worry, who would we have told? We didn't know who you were. Was that why you travelled through the forest?"

I hadn't really thought about it. "I just wanted to be alone, avoid everyone. Looks like our transport has arrived."

We threw a rope to the boy, who fastened the small boat against the hull and clambered back onboard.

"It's very small," Edith said, "is it safe?"

"It will be fine. It's made to travel the fens. I used them all the time when I was a boy and survived." I climbed in and inspected the boat. "No rotten boards." I grinned at her. "Pass everything down."

"How much do I owe you?" I asked Osric. I reached into my pouch, hoping there was enough money left.

"You saved our lives. You are my friend now and I don't charge friends."

I clasped the captain's hand and thanked him.

"Just make sure you return the boat. It belongs to my cousin. Mention my name, it will find its way home. If you need a trip back up river, I'd be glad to take you. There's more rowing in that direction."

I laughed and stepped into the small boat. I held out a hand for Edith. "Don't be scared, it's perfectly safe. Just keep your weight in the centre."

As she climbed down, the boat shifted. Edith sat down in a hurry.

"Comfortable?" I caught the rope from Osric and pushed the small boat away from the shelter of the ship's side. I gave a final wave and took up the oar. It dipped into the water and we moved away.

"There's a bucket there." I pointed it out. "If we sink, you can use it to bale." Edith's eyes opened wide and she looked back towards the safety of our temporary home.

"Don't worry. I'll protect you."

We threaded through the mass of shipping, following the river downstream. When we had left the town behind and the water was less busy, I raised the small triangular sail. The boat speeded up and I relaxed, using the oar only to correct our course.

The river widened and land disappeared under the spreading water. Soon only the patches of reeds and tree lined banks indicated the course of the river.

"How do you know which way to go?"

Osric had given me instructions. "It's very simple. We continue until we meet another river, joining us from the south. We sail up that river. The village is on the bank; I'll tell you when we get there. If we miss the river we'll end up at the sea."

"What do we do if that happens?"

"Well, it depends."

"Depends on what?"

"On whether the tide is coming in or out. If it's coming in, we can get back. If it's going out..." I paused to adjust the sail.

"What will happen if the tide's going out?"

"Oh. We'll sail away and never be seen again. Perhaps we'll freeze to death in the far north, or be swallowed by a whale, like Jonah."

"You're teasing me." She thought about it. "Aren't you?"

"It's not going to happen, we've found the second river." I studied the water and told Edith to hang on. She clutched the sides of the little boat. I watched the surface of the water and the surrounding landscape. I studied the pattern of ripples on the surface of the water ahead. I passed Edith the end of a rope.

"When I give the word, pull on that as hard as you can." I dug the oar deep into the water. "Now!"

Edith pulled the rope and the mast swung round. The sail hung loose then caught the wind and filled again. The boat tilted violently, then righted. We were sailing south now, instead of east.

"That went well." I relaxed back onto the bench. "You might like to bale out some of the water."

Edith picked up the bucket. I thought she was going to throw it at me, but she noticed the water lapping around our feet. She started to bale.

As we sailed south, I wondered what sort of reception we would receive.

"Is something wrong?" Edith asked.

I shook my head and watched the river ahead.

"Is that where we're going?" She pointed across the expanse of water to a large island rearing out of the landscape.

"That's Ely. It's not far now."

The island disappeared as the river curved. We passed a village. No one was about. I took down the sail and we glided on. Trees lined the bank and I studied them carefully. I changed the angle of the oar and we slid through the trees into a secluded pool. Gently the bow of the boat touched a muddy beach. I jumped out of the boat and pulled it further up onto land.

"We've arrived."

60

I lifted Edith out of the boat and carried her to a drier patch of ground. When I put her down, she staggered and nearly fell.

"The ground is moving."

"We've been on the water for days. You'll soon be back to normal." I put an arm round her shoulders and we followed a narrow path through the trees.

"Aren't we going to unload?"

"Not yet." I didn't know what sort of reception we would get. I told her to make sure she knew the way back if anything happened to me. I made sure my sword was ready.

"Nothing's going to happen."

"You're too innocent. You shouldn't trust everyone."

"No. I met you and look what happened? Dragged half way across the country, crippled by a horse and nearly drowned. I want to go home."

I looked at her in horror. What had I done? I started to apologise then realised she was laughing. "Just keep close to me."

We walked beside the river until we reached a small meadow. A hut stood alone, surrounded by a low fence. In front of it, standing at an angle, was a rough wooden cross.

"A church, a good sign." Edith crossed herself. "Although it doesn't look as if it's used much." She gave me an accusing look. I explained I had not been there for many years.

We followed the path past the church. The sun was getting low and shadows lay long across the ground. Houses were just visible ahead and to the right the ground rose gradually. At the top of the hill, figures were silhouetted against the glowing sky. I shaded my eyes, but it was impossible to recognise the distant shapes.

"Harvesters." They still had much to do, as far as I could tell. We walked slowly along the path until there was a movement on the hill. Someone was pointing. I dropped Edith's arm and waited.

A dark shape broke away and hurtled down the hill towards them, a long shadow racing before it. I pushed Edith behind me and drew my sword. A dog slid to a stop, tumbling a couple of times before righting itself. It sat, panting, and raised one front paw, tongue lolling from its mouth. One ear was erect – the other hung down, almost covering one pleading eye.

"You survived then?" I slid the sword back into its sheath. I couldn't believe this was the dog I had left behind, so many months ago. How had she remembered me? I picked her up. She squirmed in my arms, stretched to lick my face. The thin tail whipped back and forth.

"Someone's glad to see you." Edith came and patted the animal.

"We called her Leola. It means swift, like a deer, but you can change it if you want."

Saewynn's clothes were dusty; the old boy's clothes we had used to disguise her. What was she doing here?

"Is Elfflaed here?" She wouldn't be working in the fields; perhaps she was at the hall.

"I left her service. It's a long story. Welcome back. Who's that?" She stared at Edith.

"This is Edith. I am escorting her on a visit to Lord Athelstan, her relative."

"I am pleased to meet you," said Edith. "Why are you dressed like that, my dear? It is not suitable for a woman."

"Everyone is needed for the harvest." Saewynn turned back to me. "Are you staying long?"

"You've cut your hair again."

"It's easier." She ran a dirty hand through her untidy sweaty locks. "Too hot for that silly hat."

"Is Wulfstan here as well? I thought he would be back in his monastery."

"He's at the hall. Eadric is getting old. He's teaching Wulfstan to run the estate. Someone had to take control, with you being... away."

"Welcome home, my lord." Edward joined Saewynn on the path. "My lady." He gave Edith a curious glance. "Welcome to the village."

"Thank you, Edward," I said. "You're here as well. That means Godric must be around somewhere."

"He's just taking..." Saewynn gave him a sharp kick on the shin. "He's busy. He'll be back later."

I frowned. Edward flushed and Saewynn maintained an expression of fierce innocence.

"No doubt you'll tell me what's going on later. Edward, we've left our boat down by the chapel. Bring it round to the hall." I put down the dog. She stood close beside me. "Leola?" She raised her head. "It's a fine name and she recognises it. No need to change it." I smiled at Saewynn. "You'll have to tell me everything that's happened, but first we need some refreshment. It's been a long day." I took Edith's arm. "It's not far to the hall." We walked slowly along the path towards the distant buildings.

***

A large crowd had gathered near the hall. The boat had been pulled up onto the beach and Edward was directing some men to carry our baggage up to the hall.

The place looked more prosperous than on my previous visit. The huts were well-thatched and small productive gardens flourished between them. I acknowledged some faces I recognised. The thatch on the hall was old, but I noticed the hole I had asked to be repaired had been patched. The door opened and Wulfstan limped out into the evening sunshine.

"Welcome back, my lord."

"It's good to be here." What else could I say? Did he blame me for leaving, without even saying goodbye? Did he hate me? Why was he here? I stared across the space between us, trying to read his expression.

Hild emerged from the hall carrying a jug. She poured mead into a horn cup and presented it to me. I swallowed the smooth liquid in one gulp.

"We need to talk." Wulfstan walked back into the hall. I thanked Hild and introduced her to Edith.

"Please bring her to the hall when she is refreshed." I took a deep breath and followed Wulfstan into the hall.

"Well?" Wulfstan waited for an answer.

"I'm sorry."

"Sorry? You leave like that, without a word. Abandoning everyone who depended on you. Disappearing without a trace. No one knew if you were alive or dead. Where have you been?"

"You know why I had to go. I failed everyone, the king, my lord, and my companions. I couldn't face anyone; see the contempt in their eyes, especially yours." I walked towards the door. "We'll go as soon as we've rested."

HARVEST 946

61

"Sit down." Wulfstan pulled out a bench. "Why did you feel you had to go? Just because of some argument with Eadred?"

"I was responsible for the king's death. I was ordered to protect him and I failed." I turned away. Why didn't anyone understand? I had no choice but to leave.

"The king had other men to guard him. He was in his own hall, surrounded by guards. They all failed to prevent his death. No one blames you. You're not that important, however much you think you are."

It couldn't be as simple as that. "What about the new king?"

"Eadred? He's got other things to worry about."

"What's happened?"

"We can talk about that later. I think the villagers have waited long enough for their meal. You're home now, that's all that matters." Wulfstan stood up and threw his arms round me. "You've grown. Are you ever going to stop?" What had that got to do with anything?

The hall filled quickly and I walked to my seat at the top table. Leola lay down beneath the chair as if it was her natural place. I stroked her soft head.

"You said you had a dog once, to care for." Edith took the seat beside me. "Seems she is caring for you." Leola wagged her tail. "At least she likes me."

"Has someone upset you?" I looked round the hall, people were settling into their places. "Who was it? I will punish them."

"Nothing like that, just that there are so many people I don't know."

"Wulfstan. Come and sit beside the Lady Edith. You should have a lot in common. She is prioress of St Mildgyth's, near Tamworth. Wulfstan is my oldest friend," I told her. "He has spent time in a monastery in Wessex. I thought he had returned there, but it appears that he has interested himself in managing my estate."

"It is good to meet you. Byrhtnoth has told me so much about you. Tell me why you decided to leave the monastery."

"Thank you, Hild." I dipped my hands into the bowl of water and dried them with a cloth, "I apologise for arriving unannounced."

"I'm sorry my lord, we have nothing better than pottage. There will be a feast in a day or so, to celebrate the harvest. I'm glad we can also celebrate your return. You've been away a long time."

"Too long." A small boy appeared from behind Hild's skirts. "Hello who are you?"

"That's my dog." The boy pointed at Leola. "Give her back."

"I'm afraid she belongs to me," I told him.

Hild tried to drag the boy away.

"I told you before. She's not your dog. You know you were only allowed to play with her until her master came back. Now he has."

"Don't like you." The boy backed away as I stood up. "I'm not scared."

"There you are, you young rascal, you know you're not supposed to be in here." Godric rushed up. "I'm sorry, my lord. I'll take him away."

"Hello Godric. I was wondering where you were hiding." I

crouched down and spoke to the boy. "Don't be scared. You have cared for her very well. She is very obedient, did you train her?"

"Yes, I did." The boy puffed out his narrow chest. "Saewynn helped – and Wulfstan, but I did most of it."

"You are very clever. In the future, when I have lots of dogs, you can train them all. Perhaps you can have one of your own then. Meanwhile, we will share her. You can look after her when I'm not here. Agreed?"

The boy frowned. He stuck out his bottom lip, but then he grinned. "All right."

"Come on." Godric cleared his throat. "Time for your bed." The boy took his hand and allowed himself to be led away.

"Determined lad. He should go far." I sat down and took up a spoon. "Is he yours?" I asked Hild.

"Oh no, my lord." She blushed. "Just a visitor. He'll be gone soon."

"Are you all right?" Wulfstan was coughing over his own meal.

"Tell you later," he managed to say.

"Give him some more ale, Hild. This food is very good."

The meal was short. The villagers were tired from their work in the fields; they soon went to their own huts, or prepared to bed down in the hall.

"You can sleep in the chamber." I took Edith's hand and led her to the door at the back of the hall. "Edward has brought everything from the boat. You should be comfortable. If you need anything, I'll be close by."

"We've slept in worse places." She leaned forward. "Why haven't you told anyone? About us?"

"It never seemed the right moment."

"You should do it soon. People are getting the wrong idea."

"What do you mean?"

"Never mind." She reached up and kissed my cheek. "You'll soon find out." With a final mischievous glance, she opened the door and closed it firmly behind her.

When I returned to the table, there was a strange expression on Wulfstan's face.

"What's wrong now?"

"It's none of my business." We were interrupted by a commotion at the entrance to the hall.

"Where is he? Why did no one tell me he was back?"

Eadric shuffled up the hall. He had aged. He was even thinner than he had been and his back was bent, no longer stiff and upright. As he came closer I noticed his eyes were milky white.

"Eadric. It is good to meet again. Someone told me you were sick; I intended to visit you tomorrow."

"It is my job to be there to welcome you." The old man's head turned towards me. "I must speak with you."

I stepped down to meet him. I took his arm and guided him to a seat. I put a cup of ale into his hand.

"Drink that and we will talk. How are you? Not as sick as I was told."

"Not sick, just old. My eyes are useless; I see only shapes moving in the darkness. You have grown, I can tell that."

"It's been a long time; four years or more."

"As long as that? I lose track of the days." Eadric sipped his ale. "This has improved. I heard you were doing well, until you disappeared. What happened?"

"Another time. It's getting late and we must sleep."

Eadric nodded. He cocked his head. "Is Wulfstan there?"

"I am."

"How is the harvest going? Is it all gathered yet?"

"Not yet, another day, two perhaps. The weather is set fair."

"Good." Eadric took another sip of his drink and replaced the cup carefully on the table. "Take me back to my bed."

62

"We must talk." Wulfstan was already sitting at the board when I woke. I stretched. It was late; the hall was nearly empty. I hadn't realised how tired I had been last night.

Hild brought a fresh jug of ale and filled our cups.

"Thank you. Please tell the Lady Edith when she wakes, that I will be back later."

"Yes, my lord." She walked stiffly away. I watched her go.

"What's the matter with her?"

"Come on. I need to check on the horses." Wulfstan rose and headed for the door. I called Leola from her search among the floor rushes. We followed him along a path into the woods.

"I arrived just in time. Eadric had let things go. Not his fault. You saw last night that his sight is going." I nodded. "His mind is still sharp, so he gets frustrated at times. It's been a good summer and the crops have yielded well. God willing, the grain will be in soon." Wulfstan checked the sky.

"That's good. But why are you here?" He hadn't had an interest in farming before, but then, he wanted to learn about everything. "Godric and Edward I can understand, this is their home. And why is Saewynn here?"

We reached the paddock. Sleipnir trotted over and Wulfstan stroked his nose.

"You brought my stallion." I noticed the big animal. He had ignored our arrival, as usual. "You must have had a problem travelling with him."

"Not really, Saewynn rode him most of the way."

"Saewynn? She could barely ride a horse back in the spring. Now she's riding Thunor and working in the fields." I gave him a sideways glance. "Are you and she...?"

"Certainly not. And if we were, it's no concern of yours. Not anymore."

"I think you'd better tell me what's going on." I led the way to a fallen tree and sat down. "This needs chopping up for firewood."

"I suppose we're all here because of Saewynn. She overheard a conversation." Wulfstan lowered his voice and checked there was no one about. "There was a plot to kill King Edmund. His brother, Eadred was involved."

It explained a lot. I had thought about it so often and wondered why he had tried to blame me. He had been putting people off the scent.

"Perhaps. We didn't know what to do. Saewynn was in danger. If anyone discovered what she knew... You weren't there. We went to Athelstan. He was very good, took on your men as his own, until you returned. He paid Ealdorman Elfgar for Saewynn and we all travelled with him to East Anglia. His foster son, Edmund's son, Edgar, was in danger. We brought him here. You met him last night."

"That boy." The colour drained from my face. What had I said?

"Yes. You promised to make him your kennel boy." Wulfstan laughed. "If he ever becomes king, unlikely because Eadred is still young, I'll try not to remind him of that."

I leaned back, trying to make sense of what had happened.

"What have you been doing?" Wulfstan seemed unable to control his curiosity. "I wouldn't have imagined you carrying on with a nun. You do know it's against the law?"

"What do you mean? What nun?" I stared at him in confusion.

"You and Edith. It's obvious something is going on. Even Hild noticed. Why do you think she was so short with you this morning?"

Everything became clear. I burst out laughing.

"You didn't think...?" I shook my head. No wonder I had got some strange looks.

"Well, it was suspicious. You arrive together, just the two of you. I thought you must have run off with her. Come here to hide, like the rest of us. What's it all about?"

I rubbed Leola's ears, still chuckling. "It's very simple. Edith is my sister."

"Your sister? But you don't have any relatives. You're an orphan, like me. How did you meet?"

I told him about walking away. "I decided to go north, to find out what happened to my father." I told him about the accident, and my despair. I showed Wulfstan the scars.

"That's nasty, you were lucky not to die."

"I thought I would lose my arm, I didn't want to live."

"I know," Wulfstan said quietly. I nodded.

"Someone's done a good job on it. Was that Edith?"

"No that was Sister Edberga, and St Mildgyth," I explained about stumbling on the monastery and the slow recovery. "It wasn't until later, when Edith and I talked, that we realised we had the same mother. Don't tell anyone. We need to find out more about what happened. Our mother was a relative of Athelstan. He must know the truth."

"If your mother was a relative, that means you're a member of his family. No wonder he was so annoyed when you left."

"Was he? I thought he was angry because I'd failed in my duty."

"This needs some serious thought. Are you sure you don't want to tell anyone else?"

"Not yet. I want Edith to meet Eadric. He must remember something about her, our, mother. He was servant to Lord Toli, who served my father. Perhaps he'll finally tell me more about him." I stood up to leave. Leola jumped up and followed close at my heel.

"Before you go. If you don't want people to talk, you'd better act more formally with Edith." I acknowledged the words, before striding back along the path.

***

"Hild has been telling me about the chapel we passed yesterday. It has not been used for a long time."

"There must have been a priest there at one time." When I had been young, one had come from Ely to celebrate Christmas, Easter.

"It should be used more often. I will inspect it, and it must be cleaned." Edith asked Hild to find someone to bring brushes and cloths.

"Of course, my lady." Hild hurried out.

"You realise a lot of the people round here follow the old ways?" Although we were so close to Ely, many clung to an older faith. The coming of the Danes had not helped.

"All the more reason for the church to be active. It must act as an example. Will you accompany me?"

"The servant will show you the way. You wanted to speak to Eadric." I lowered my voice. "About our mother. I will bring him to the church. It might encourage him to tell the truth."

"Does he not speak truly?" Edith frowned.

"Not always. I will meet you there later."

"I think you have been talking to your friend."

"Wulfstan? He said we have been giving the wrong impression. I told him the truth."

"Poor Byrhtnoth, always jumping in with those big feet of yours, never thinking about the consequences. How is your foot, by the way?"

"It's fine, thank you." I headed towards the door, her laughter ringing in my ears.

"Good morning." I ducked my head under low lintel of Eadric's hut. "Are you comfortable here?"

"No, but it's better than being in the hall. People will keep moving things around in there and I can never find anything. They bring me my food regularly. That Wulfstan has got things organised, for all he's a cripple."

"Wulfstan is my friend. I am sure you have taught him everything you know."

"Not everything." Eadric tapped his nose and cackled.

"No. Some things should not be told to everybody. Or at the wrong time."

"I can see you understand, now."

"That is why I returned." Surely I had earned my father's sword by now? "I have brought someone to speak with you." The old man swung his head around. "She is down at the chapel. She wants to hear about her mother, my mother. Do you remember?"

"Of course I remember. My eyes may be dim, but my brain is still sharp." His tongue as well. "I remember everything."

"Will you come to the chapel, or shall I bring her here?"

"Is the sun shining? I won't go out if it's raining."

"It is a beautiful day." I offered him my arm. He took it reluctantly

"All right. Don't want to trip over and make a fool of myself."

As we walked slowly along the path, I described what I saw: the glitter of the sunlight on the river, the heavy foliage of the trees that was becoming tired and drab.

"It will be winter soon. Doubt I'll see another summer."

"I'm sure you will. The harvesters are up on the hill. There will be plenty of food this winter, plenty of stories round the hearth fire."

"I feel the cold too much, I know my time has nearly come."

"Do you have the cloak I gave you? It belonged to Lord Toli."

"I have it still, it's getting threadbare but it still serves."

"That was a long time ago. I'll find you a better one."

"Not so long when you get to my age. You're a good lad. You could have fought against me, but I think you understood how things should be."

"Perhaps. I know more now."

"That is as it should be. Now tell me what you have been doing. Young Wulfstan told me much, but then you disappeared. What happened?"

63

"Hello old man. It's been a long time." Edith rose from a stool and offered it to Eadric.

"It has indeed." I led him to the stool. "You are the child? Come closer."

The floor of the church had been swept and cobwebs removed from the lower walls. A clean white cloth covered the rough stone that acted as an altar, no one looked closely at the pictures that were carved there. Edith had placed her crucifix on the cloth.

"It wasn't my fault. I was against it from the start," Eadric whined.

"I know." Edith took one of his hands and cradled it in hers. "You were the only one who took any notice of me, tried to talk to me."

I leaned against the wall to watch.

"It wasn't for your sake," Eadric said sharply, "it was all wrong; wrong for him and wrong for her. I knew the first time they met there would be a problem. I tried to persuade him to move on. It would have been all right if he had taken his pleasure and left. It had happened often enough." He turned his head in my direction. "No angel, your father. You should know that. We couldn't leave. I've never seen snow like it. It was as if something trapped us there and wasn't going to let us go until it was too late. He didn't force himself on her; she was as keen as him." I could see this upset Edith. "Perhaps she felt it was her last chance of a life, perhaps it was love. I wouldn't know. All I can tell you is that when the snow melted; it went as quickly as it came, we left and she came with us."

"Leaving me behind." Tears trickled unchecked down Edith's face.

"I'm sorry. I could say that your mother decided you would be safer left behind. It was still winter after all and travelling was hazardous. To tell the truth I think she had forgotten you existed." He reached out and rested a hand on her head. "She remembered later and she regretted leaving you every day." Silence fell. I watched a patch of light move across the floor.

"What happened next?"

"Always impatient." Eadric gave a bitter laugh. "You happened next. They travelled, hiding from her husband's family. He didn't want her, but he didn't want anyone else to have her, or her lands. When her time was near they had to stop. They came here. He owned this land and was protected by her family. He was here when you were born." Eadric closed his eyes, looking back into the past. "He held you in his arms. You were so small; almost fitted into one of his hands." I looked down at my own hands. "Yes, big like you he was. He was so proud of you. Then he left."

"Why? Where did he go?" I leaned forward, eager to learn, at last, what had happened to my father.

"I don't know. He talked about going to sort things out, he didn't say how. It was summer by then. He had to leave; he served the king. They say he was sent into the north, some negotiations. He left us behind, Lord Toli and me. We were to protect you, and your mother. We never heard from him again. If only he hadn't left his sword behind. Without that he was unprotected."

"Why did he do it?" It was something I had never understood. Why would a man abandon his land, his family, but leave his sword?

"He had given it to you. I was there, we all were. He held you in his arms, you were a month or so old, and offered you the sword. You tried to grasp it. He held his hand over yours on the handle. He told us that the sword was yours. He made us swear on the blade that we would protect you, and the sword. We were to guard you both until you could wield it yourself. You cried when he tried to take it away."

"I always knew it was mine."

"The time has nearly come for you to receive it."

"When?" I longed to hold it again.

"Soon, very soon. Then my life's work will be done." Eadric struggled to his feet. "I have spoken enough. My throat is dry. Take me back."

"Are you coming?" I asked Edith as I took his arm.

"No. I'll stay here for a while. I need to think, and pray."

***

We met Hild on the path, carrying two buckets of ale. They looked heavy. I offered to help.

"It's not your job, my lord, I can manage." But she lowered her burden to the ground with relief. "It's for the harvesters. They need a break."

"I need a drink as well. Been doing a lot of talking." Eadric found a wooden cup and handed it to the girl. She dipped it in the liquid and handed it to him.

"I was planning to see how the harvest is going. I'll give you a hand." I asked Eadric if he could find his way back.

"Do you think I don't know this place like the back of my hand. I can find my way anywhere." I watched him hobble off, picked up the buckets and followed Hild up the hill.

"What has he been telling you?"

"Oh, this and that. Things about the village."

We reached the top of the hill and the workers stopped work.

They gathered round, dipping their cups and drinking gratefully. Bread was brought out and we sat down to eat. Most of the grain had been cut, the sheaves stacked at regular intervals across the field. Saewynn flopped onto the ground nearby. I passed her a cup of ale, and she downed it greedily. She had been gathering and tying the stalks in neat bundles and was covered in dust. She wiped the sweat from her sunburned forehead and reached for a chunk of hard bread.

"Hot out here." Saewynn just grunted through her mouthful of bread. I tried again. "Will you finish today?"

"Perhaps." She accepted another cupful of ale and sipped it more slowly. "The sun is good for drying the sheaves. We can start bringing down the ones we cut earlier."

"You've become quite the expert, but it's hard work for a girl."

"I'm as strong as a boy." She gave me a fierce look. "Anyway, they've got young children working up here."

"Only collecting the gleanings." I watched some of the men sharpen their sickles, before returning to the patch of grain still standing. "I'll give you a hand."

"You can't do that. You're the lord, you don't work in the fields."

"If I'm the lord, I can do what I like. Anyway, I need the exercise." I stripped off my tunic. A breeze cooled my body through the thin linen undershirt. I wouldn't risk using the blades, not without some practise first, but I could help collect some of the sheaves.

Saewynn shrugged and led me to the furthest field. She showed me how to arrange the individual sheaves into a stable load and tie them with a rope of twisted stem. She helped to lift it onto my back.

"Where do I take it?"

"Just head back to the village. Wulfstan will show you where to stack it."

Some of the harvesters gathered to witness the strange sight of the lord loaded like a packhorse, but the novelty soon wore off and they bent to their own work.

"Don't forget to come back for the next one," Saewynn shouted after me, "there are plenty more to be moved."

64

"That's the last one." I dropped the bundle of sheaves and stretched. I was hot, sweaty and my back ached.

"I heard the cheering as you came down the hill. Put it over there, it needs to dry out before we put it with the others." Wulfstan pointed to a covered area.

"It's been a good harvest. Will there be enough to last the winter?"

Wulfstan scribbled a few figures on a wax tablet and nodded. "I'll confirm it with Eadric, but I think so." He watched me trying to brush the dust from my clothes. "Get cleaned up. Hild will be annoyed if you delay her feast. She's been preparing for weeks."

I walked back through the village and down to the river. All the workers had gathered there. Some stood in the shallows, scooping up water in buckets and pouring it over their heads. Others had swum out; ducking under the water to remove the layer of dirt and sweat that covered their bodies. I waded into the water. It was cold but refreshing.

"First one to the far side gets an extra cup of mead." I dived forward, quickly followed by a group of older boys, arms flailing and feet kicking. They strung out and I slowed, letting one of the others win. We gathered on the far side, catching our breath and arguing about the result.

A group of girls had gathered and were obviously discussing us. One of them called across the water.

"A kiss for the first one back."

We struck out across the river. One boy, smaller than the others, was having problems. Spray kicked up from the leading boys was hitting him in the face. His head sunk under the water and he reappeared, spluttering.

I grabbed him and cleaved a path through the rest of the swimmers. As we neared the edge, I pushed the boy ahead. He was first to touch the bank. He scrambled out and rushed to the group of girls to claim his reward.

The girl who had made the promise sauntered slowly towards the water, hips swaying.

"You cheated." She looked down at me and smiled. "You could have won easily. Didn't you want a kiss?" She pouted full red lips.

"Perhaps later." I winked at her. "Hey, who are you splashing?" I grabbed one of the boys and ducked him underwater. Others joined in and soon everyone was splashing about. I picked up one of the smaller children, swung him to shrieks of excitement and threw him far out into the river. Soon everyone wanted a go.

"Don't you want anything to eat?" Hild stood on the bank, hands on hips, disapproval battled the smile on her face.

"Come on, fun's over." I peeled off a child hanging round my neck and heaved myself out of the water. "Sorry, Hild."

I passed the tables that had been set out on the open space near the river. Jugs were standing ready amongst bunches of flowers and corn. I grabbed one and took a large mouthful of ale. I noticed Hild eying me. I replaced the jug and moved on, savouring the smell of roasting meat that hung in the air. The heavy wooden chair had been dragged out from the hall. Someone had hung my new shield from it. My heart sank. The fun was over. I had to take my place as lord. I walked slowly back to the hall.

It felt oddly empty without the benches. The hearth was cold and filled with grey ash. Edith sat in the corner. She had found a loom from somewhere and was arranging the warp threads on it, pulled tight by the hanging weights. I felt guilty at leaving her on her own. I gave her a quick wave and opened the door to the chamber. I rummaged in my chest until I found a clean tunic and struggled into it. The evening was warm, but I must wear my cloak, it would be expected. I dragged a comb through my damp, tangled hair. Anything else? I picked up my sword belt. It was the symbol of my authority. I buckled it reluctantly round my waist. I drew the sword and inspected it. There was a touch of rust, I hadn't cleaned it properly after the fight on the boat, but it would do for now. Eadric had said nothing since our conversation in the chapel. Would I ever see my father's sword again?

There was a tap on the door. It was Edith.

"Are you ready? Everyone's waiting."

"Will I do?"

Edith adjusted the folds of my cloak. "Very impressive."

I took her arm and we headed for the harvest feast.

***

We were served the best pieces of meat. A young pig had been slaughtered and the flesh was tender, the skin crispy. Waterfowl had been trapped in nets and roasted. Fish, large and small had been fried or boiled in pots with different seasonings. There was the usual pottage and even a small bowl of fresh peas, picked before they dried. And of course there was bread, warm from the oven and made from the newly harvested wheat.

I held the large round loaf and broke it into pieces. Edith spoke a brief prayer over it and it was passed along the board. I took a large bite and nodded in appreciation. It tasted so much better when you had helped to harvest it.

"I'll have a bit of everything please, Hild. I'm starving."

"All at once, my lord?"

"Whatever you've got." I held out the wooden plate.

The noisy conversation died down as each villager tucked into his or her favourite dish.

"What's that noise?" Edith asked as she separated the flesh from the bones of a small fish.

I raised my head from the plate and listened. "Sounds like horses."

Godric had also noticed the sound. I gave him a signal and he swept up Edgar. The boy held a chunk of bread in one hand, a half chewed bone in the other and a surprised expression on his face. They disappeared into the surrounding woodland. I didn't know where the hiding place was, but it looked a well-rehearsed action.

I stood up slowly. Leola had been curled asleep beneath my chair. She woke and we walked to where the road entered the village. I waited, hand resting on the hilt of my sword. It was probably some travellers passing through. Where were they going at such speed? The horses arrived fast and pulled up quickly when they saw us waiting. They milled around in the road. The leader walked his horse forward.

65

"Elfhere. Making an entrance as usual?" I didn't want to deal with this, not now, in front of everyone. I scanned the faces of the other horsemen, nodding to those I recognised.

"We wondered if we would find you here." Elfhere jerked his reins, causing his horse to toss his head. "We were in the area and I remembered you talking about this place. We are in need of a bed for the night." He was already dismounting.

"Of course, you are welcome." They were visitors. I must be polite. I told Edward to take the horses. "You arrive at a convenient moment. We were sitting down to our meal, a feast to celebrate the harvest. Please join us." I led them down towards the table. The villagers craned forward to identify the new arrivals. Word spread that the visitors were friends and some returned to their meal.

Hild waited with a bowl. A servant poured water for the travellers to wash their hands. I saw her blush when Elfhere complimented her on the flowers in her hair.

Godric appeared and I met his eyes. The boy was well hidden, one less thing to worry about.

"Godric will collect your swords. They will be safe until you depart."

"That won't be necessary. This is a simple meal in the open air. And we are all friends, aren't we?" Elfhere put an arm about Hild's waist, holding her a little too close. "I'm ravenous after that long ride."

I let them keep their swords. I hoped it wasn't a mistake, but I didn't want to appear unwelcoming. "Where have you come from?" I led him to the table.

"We are returning to the king's court. The fighting is finished for this year. But you already have a guest at your table."

"This is the prioress of St Mildryth's." Edith greeted the visitors. "She is travelling to visit relatives in East Anglia."

"I know the place. You have come a long way from Mercia. But you are too beautiful to be hidden away in a monastery, perhaps we can change your mind about that," he leered at Edith.

"I don't think so." She returned to her seat, next to my chair and Elfhere slid onto the bench next to her. I watched the new arrivals find places at the long boards. Some of the villagers moved to sit on the ground nearby. Saewynn had disappeared. She must be with Edgar. I didn't think Elfhere would recognise the girl, but she was safer out of his way. I stared at my plate; I was no longer hungry. I broke off a piece of bread. It was no longer warm but I put it in my mouth. It stuck in my throat.

I listened as Elfhere talked to Edith about Mercia. Who did she knew in the area? I drained a cup of ale and looked round for more. Hild had brought the mead horn. I took it from her and took a deep draft. She whispered for me take it easy, that there might not be enough to go round. I ignored her. The warmth of the liquid spread through my body and I took another sip before passing it to Edith. She shook her head. I offered it to Elfhere.

"You won't find better in the king's hall. Hild makes it herself."

"It is very good." Elfhere inspected Hild over the rim of the horn. Slowly he licked his lips. "I'm sure you're good at everything you do." Hild smiled nervously.

"Don't you ever give up, Elfhere?" I asked.

"Of course not. We've been away fighting." He passed the horn to the next person, but not before admiring the decoration and, I imagined, assessing its worth. "We've not seen many women. Not willing ones anyway." He winked at Hild. She shifted uncomfortably.

"Leave her alone," I snapped.

"Sorry. Belongs to you, does she? Surely you won't miss her for a night? Remember that whore, in Winchester, before we went north with the king?" Elfere spoke to one of his men. "Some of the lads hadn't been with a woman. We decided they needed to do it before we went into battle; no one wants to die without experiencing that." He grinned at me.

"Of course not." I didn't want to talk about it but I couldn't stop his gloating.

"We promised her a gold ring if she'd do us all. She didn't half shout when we turned her out afterwards with nothing; told her she hadn't been enthusiastic enough."

"I've still got the scars where she tried to fight me off," someone shouted, I didn't recognise him.

"It wasn't fair. She needed the money, she had a baby."

"Was it yours, Redwald?" I recognised him, he'd always been a shy boy.

"No." He flushed. "Someone said her body was found in the river the next day."

"Hope she took the child with her. Don't need any more beggars on the streets." Elfhere turned to me. He had a strange glint in his eye. "She said it was all your fault."

"Me?" What trouble was he hatching now?

"Told everyone the great Byrhtnoth had let her down; promised to look after her. Must admit, I didn't know you had it in you." There was more laughter from his men. "But she was insistent; offered to fight us when we didn't believe her. Not that she was in much of a state to do anything by then, she could hardly stand."

Was it the same girl? The thief I had given food to, years ago. She had been right. I had let her down. So concerned with my own future I had forgotten hers. Another person I had let down.

"I don't remember anyone like that." Elfhere noticed my hesitation. I knew I would pay for it.

"How did the fighting go?"

"Same as usual. Tramping all over the countryside. Kill a few of them, lose a few of ours."

"I noticed there are some missing faces. Not many of our friends left. I thought the group would last longer."

"It was your fault." Elfhere glared at me. "You left, things fell apart. I tried to keep everyone together, but some left to find new lords."

"Not my fault if you lost control. Where has that mead got to?"

I saw the horn had reached Wulfstan, who sat further along the bench. He got up and brought it to me.

"Hello, Elfhere, what have you been up to?"

"Well, if it isn't the cripple. Thought you would have shuffled back to your monastery when your protector ran away." He turned back to me. "Remind me, coward, who is your lord now? I didn't notice you fighting in the north."

"I left because..." What could I say? "I made a mistake. It was unforgivable. I thought I had brought dishonour on the group. It seems that I was wrong." I lifted my head and met his eyes. "You managed that." I saw the anger flash across his face.

"That shouldn't stop you fighting for your king." His smile returned.

"I was ill." I concentrated on the pile of crumbs on the table. "It took a long time to recover."

"Pity." Elfhere spoke under his breath. He noticed the faces turning towards us. Silence spread down the table. He seemed pleased with the audience and grinned like a wolf closing in on his prey.

"The Lady Edith," I tried to distract him, "is prioress of the monastery where I recovered." She gave me an affectionate smile. "I am accompanying her on her visit to Ealdorman Athelstan. He will accept my service."

"It's true." I felt Wulfstan's hand on my shoulder. "He told me so, many months ago."

"Are you talking about this whore?" Elfhere placed his hand on Edith's thigh. She tried to push him away but he squeezed tighter. She looked at me for help.

"This woman belongs to my family. Her mother was a whore and she is a whore. Why else would she ride unaccompanied across the country with you? I'm taking her back where she belongs."

Curious faces turned towards Edith and whispers spread down the table.

I jumped to my feet. The heavy wooden chair thudded to the ground behind me. Leola leapt clear and fled. I reached for my sword. I drew it from the scabbard. The sun glinted on the sharp edge.

"Get your filthy hands off my sister."

There were gasps. Elfhere sat back and folded his arms.

"I said her mother was a whore. What does that make you?"

66

I stalked to the hard flat ground beside the river, my sword clenched tight in my hand.

"Tell them to put down their swords. This is between you and me, no one else."

Elfhere shrugged and ordered his men to sheath their weapons. I glared at Godric until he reluctantly slid his away. I swung my sword, to release some of the tension. Elfhere attacked without warning. I defended myself.

Round we circled, testing each other. We had fought so many times, first with wooden sticks, then with blunted blades. We knew every trick the other used, how a blow would be repulsed. I had grown taller since we last fought. We probed carefully, becoming accustomed to the different angles. The swords moved faster.

"Remember, I always win."

"Not always," Elfhere spat back.

"Usually." I attacked, pushing him backwards.

"Things change." Elfhere swung his sword down and I dodged aside. "I've leaned new tricks." The clang of blades rang through the warm air. The sun was getting low. We circled to keep it from blinding us.

"And you are injured."

I stepped back. How did he know? In the heat of the fight I had forgotten. Now I remembered. I felt the weakness in my shoulder, the memory of the pain. My confidence slipped away. I lost the smooth flow of the sword, unable to stop protecting my weaker side. I felt the prick of Elfhere's blade to my sword arm. I backed away. I heard, as if from a great distance, the change in the shouting. I saw the flash of Elfhere's grinning teeth. I felt soft ground beneath my feet. I must be close to the river. I must not let myself be trapped. As I leaped towards Elfhere, my foot slipped. I fell, twisting in the air to avoid my opponent's sword, landed on my back, all breath knocked out of me. I raised my sword to ward off the fatal blow I knew was coming. I watched the blade descend and felt the impact through my body as the swords met. There was an unearthly screech and the sound of shattering metal. There was a splash as half my weapon disappeared into the river, leaving me clutching the hilt and a few inches of blade.

Time stopped as I looked up into Elfhere's triumphant eyes. Was this to be my death? On my back in the mud? I felt a moment of regret. I had let everybody down, again. I watched the shining blade descend. Let it be quick.

A shape hurtled between us. Leola's teeth fastened on Elfhere's sword wrist. Her long legs clawed at his body. I watched as Elfhere shook his arm. The dog bit deeper, small drops of blood flew through the air. I saw Elfhere reach for the knife at his belt. I remembered I still held the useless sword hilt. I hurled it with all my strength. It hit the knife as it was raised it to gut Leola, knocking it from Elfhere's hand. The river received another offering.

I crawled away, searching for another weapon – a stone, anything to defend myself. If it was my time to die, I would die on my feet. As I struggled upright I heard a yelp and my dog sailed through the air, landing with a splash in the water. I watched long enough to see her dark head resurface, then faced Elfhere.

I stepped backwards under the force of the hatred on my

opponent's face. Elfhere sucked his injured wrist. When he lowered his sword to attack, blood was visible on his clenched teeth.

"Why?" I might be about to die, but wanted to know the reason.

"Because you're in my way," Elfhere spat out the words.

I backed away. I heard someone shout my name. I dare not take my eyes off Elfhere's face. Eadric appeared. He thrust a sword into my empty hand. I caught a glimpse of the shimmering blade I remembered from long ago.

The old man stumbled. Elfhere's bloody sword emerged from his chest. Eadric collapsed on the ground.

I screamed in anger. I felt the power of the sword flow through me. I saw nothing but Elfhere. I stepped over the body before me and attacked with a flurry of blows. The sword seemed a continuation of my arm, knowing where to strike before the thought was made. We fought back up the slope. Elfhere was tiring, but I felt filled with energy. He stopped and lowered his sword.

"It's not fair, you cheated."

I stopped in confusion. What did he mean? I felt a blow on the back of my head. I fell. I saw Elfhere's foot on my sword, my father's sword.

"But I cheat too," the words followed me into the darkness.

67

My head pounded. I tried to move but the world span dizzily. I was violently sick. The sickly taste of mead told me I had drunk too much. What had happened?

"Make him stop. It smells bad enough already," a voice spoke out of the darkness.

"Where am I?"

"An outbuilding. Pigs were the previous occupants." Wulfstan was close beside me. "How do you feel?"

"Terrible. What happened?"

"Someone hit you. Do you remember the fight? With Elfhere?"

I groaned, I remembered. I struggled to stand.

"Don't bother. We've tried to get out. The door is secure and there's a guard outside."

"Godric? Is that you? Who else is here?"

"Edward. And some of the other men."

"And Eadric," Wulfstan added.

"He's alive?"

"Only just. He refuses to die until he's spoken to you."

He always was stubborn. "Where is he?"

There was a dull red light seeping through cracks in the hut wall. Dark shapes moved and then I was kneeling beside Eadric.

I found his hand and clasped it in mine. It was cold and sticky with blood. I heard a whistling sound as the old man struggled to breath. Elfhere's sword had gone through his lung. I was amazed he was still alive.

"Hello old man."

"Byrhtnoth?" Edric's voice was a whisper. I squeezed his hand. "Should have given you the sword earlier."

"It was the right time."

"Did my duty." Eadric coughed and I knew there was blood on his lips.

"Always. Sleep now, you will feel better tomorrow."

"No." He fought against the blood that bubbled from his mouth. "Find your father."

"My father is dead." That is what everyone said. "Isn't he?"

"Alive." He gripped my hand. I was surprised at the strength he still had. "Promise."

"I promise. But where is he?" I sensed, rather than saw, the final gush of blood from Eadric's mouth. The hand I held became limp.

"He has gone." I found Eadric's face and closed his eyes with gentle fingers. I bent and whispered to him, "I swear I will find him, even if I have to search the whole world." I straightened up. "First I have to get out of here."

I went to the door and hammered on it. I kicked at the thick boards, but it remained firm.

"Keep the noise down," the angry voice of our guard, shouted back. "I'm missing the fun, stuck out here. I could throw this torch in there and leave you to burn."

"Told you so." Who said that, I wondered, as I slumped against the door? In the distance I heard the sound of drunken shouting. The sky lightened for a moment as someone added fuel to the fire, down by the water. "I expect they'll let us out in the morning. Don't suppose there'll be any food left. I never got any of that roast pork."

"Shut up." I resumed my place on the floor. Silence descended, somebody snored. At the back of the shed came the sound of scratching.

"That's all we need," I said, "you'd have thought the mice would be busy with all that grain in the barn."

"I don't think its mice." Wulfstan shuffled over to the wall. We heard the sound of muffled conversation. "It was Saewynn," he told me when he returned, "she's got a plan."

***

We crouched in silence behind the door. We heard Saewynn arrive. She offered the guard some bread. We heard her laugh.

"What? Now?"

That was the signal. I pounded on the door again. The others shouted. When we stopped, all was quiet. Then the latch rattled and the door slowly opened. Saewynn stood in the doorway. She handed me something. I felt the familiar shape of my seax.

"I haven't held this since..." I remembered it skittering away in the struggle. "Since the king died."

"We found it later. Kept it for you."

"What did you do to the guard?" I prodded the large shape stretched out on the ground.

"Loom weight." She raised her hand containing the heavy, round stone. "Looks just like a piece of bread in the dark." She reached into her basket and produced several knives from under the bread and handed them out as the men emerged from the hut. "I found these in the kitchen. Hild keeps them sharp."

"Where are the women? Have they locked them up somewhere else?"

"No. They're down there." She pointed to where flames flickered in the distance.

"My sister as well?"

"What sister?" Saewynn frowned. "You don't have a sister."

"Edith, the nun. She's my sister." I gripped Saewynn's arm. "Where is she?"

Saewynn glanced again towards the fire. A terrified scream cut through the night air. I started to run.

68

I paused in the darkness, just outisde the bright circle illuminated by the blazing fire. Elfhere's men were seated on the benches. They were shouting and beating cups on the tables. There were girls from the village there, some drunkenly joining in with the shouting, others cowering in the grip of some man. I saw a girl, the one I had promised to kiss. She was huddled on the ground, clothes torn and tears steaming down her face. She saw me waiting in the darkness. She turned her head away.

The others arrived. I gave them instructions; disarm the carousing men first, kill only if necessary. I searched for Elfhere. He was directly opposite, the focus of all the shouting. He was on top of a table, struggling with a woman lying beneath him, their shapes distorted by the heat from the fire.

I moved fast. I leaped across the fire to reach the couple. I flung myself on Elfhere, grabbed his hair and wrenched back his head. Edith, eyes wide in terror, shuffled backwards from beneath Elfhere. She clutched her disordered clothing around her. I held the edge of the seax against Elfhere's throat. He tried to struggle but I kneed him in the back. Soon he was immobile, face to face with his victim.

"Are you...? Did he...?" Edith drew up her knees and hugged

her arms round them. Our eyes met and a silent message was exchanged.

"No." Her voice cracked. She gulped in air. "No! He did nothing." She spoke out, for everyone to hear. "He is not man enough to harm any woman."

"That is a good reply." I grinned and tightened my grip on Elfhere's hair. "I need not kill him." I brought my mouth close to his ear. "Not yet."

I checked my men had taken control. Everyone was quiet, watching the three figures poised on the table. I had an audience.

"We cannot kill him, but he must be punished. He has attempted to rape a nun, a violent crime against the church. He has looked upon the nakedness of my sister. He must be punished," I shouted the last words for all to hear.

"How should he be punished?" I asked Edith. Half her face glowed red from the fire, the rest was shrouded in darkness. "It is your choice."

I changed my grip, wrapping one arm around Elfhere's neck. I handed the sharp knife to my sister. "What shall we do to him?"

Edith took the knife. Her hand shook slightly. In the light of the fire it seemed to run with blood already. She studied the man's body exposed before her. She hesitated.

"Perhaps we should castrate him, cut off what has offended you."

She reached forward until the sharp point touched the pale white belly. The blade moved lower, leaving a thin trail of blood, until it reached the sparse curling hairs. She paused.

"You've seen it done to animals, when the colts become geldings?"

Edith nodded, a smile spread across her face, the knife moved.

"Oh dear. The boy has pissed himself." I spoke so everyone could hear. There were laughs from the spectators. Comments were made about Elfhere's prowess, or lack of it. I returned my attention to Edith. She had retreated with an expression of distaste.

"Perhaps not. It would be something easily hidden, except if he married." I laughed. People were offering suggestions now.

"Something more visible, so everyone would know of his crime. Cut off his ears? No, his hair would cover their loss. His nose though, he couldn't hide that."

Edith lifted the knife.

"Why not cut out his tongue. He prides himself on his eloquence." I felt Elfhere's muscles clench as he clamped his teeth together. I whispered in his ear again, "Do you think I wouldn't break your teeth to reach it?"

Edith's hand was steadier now and the blade weaved like a snake in front of Elfhere's face.

"The eyes. A good choice – one or two? Just one would slow down his fighting skills; both would make a cripple of him. How do you fancy being a cripple, Elfhere? Do you want to feel what it's like to be worthless?" I tightened my arm round his throat as he tried to break free. There was no pain in my shoulder now.

Edith dropped the seax onto the board.

"I don't know. Sorry, I can't do it." Tears filled her eyes and streamed down her face.

"It's all right," I told her gently, "that's what you've got me for." I picked up the knife and inspected the edge. I was pleased someone had kept it sharp. I stood up, lifting Elfere with me. We faced the crowd.

"I've had enough of this game." I lifted the saex and slashed it across Elfhere's face. The wound stretched from close to one eye, across his mouth and stopped below his ear. The skin split like a ripe plum and blood spurted. Some drops reached the fire and fizzed in the flames. There was a sigh from those who thought I had cut his throat, but when I threw him down onto the ground, he crawled away from the heat of the fire. He tried to pull up the trousers that shackled his ankles, but I jumped down and aimed a kick at the bare exposed arse, shifting him a few feet towards the road.

"If I find you on my land again, I'll kill you." I stepped

towards him. Elfhere kicked off his obstructing clothing and ran. He looked back only once. His ruined face now smeared with dust as well as blood, he held the flap that had been his cheek with one hand. His words were mangled but his eyes were clear with hatred.

"I won't forget this," I think he said.

"Neither will anyone else." I laughed and walked away.

I went to Edith, picking up my cloak that had been abandoned on the ground. I wrapped it gently round her and beckoned Hild who stood nervously nearby.

"Take her somewhere safe." I walked to the fire and the people who stood there, transfixed by the violence they had witnessed.

"If any of his men wish to go with him, leave now." Several faces, unknown to me, exchanged glances, and slunk away. "The others may rest here for tonight. If you wish to remain to serve me, we will discuss it tomorrow." I walked over to the board and found a cup half full of ale. I drained the contents. Most of the village still stood, waiting for instructions.

"Go to your beds, we'll clear up in the morning." People drifted away, talking quietly.

"Place those strangers under guard," I told Godric, "but treat them well. They're not to blame for picking the wrong leader." As I walked slowly back to the hall, Leola trotted up. I bent and stroked her.

"Where have you been hiding? I wonder who taught you to attack like that?"

Wulfstan waited at the entrance to the hall. He was staring in the direction Elfhere had taken.

"You should have killed him."

"I know." I shrugged. "But he used to be our friend."

69

I stopped at the entrance to the hall.

"Do you remember, all those years ago, when we first met, outside the doors of the king's hall? I was so alone."

"Me too, but you seemed to know what you were doing."

"I didn't. But we did it together."

"You leading, me following."

"No, you pushing from behind. Now I have so much. Friends – you, Edward, Godric – did I ever tell you I was once scared of him?"

"You? Scared? Never."

"I was scared today, terrified I would lose everything. I have family, a sister, what if I had lost her?"

"But you didn't. Come on, let's get some sleep."

"Friends, family, this place." I stared out into the darkness. "What more could anyone want?"

"A sword?"

"Yes, the sword. I wonder what happened to that?"

Historical Note

It is very likely that Byrhtnoth, Ealdorman of Essex, would have disappeared into the mists of history, if it had not been for his death, fighting bravely for his country against invading Vikings.

The Battle of Maldon, in 991AD, was one of the noble failures that the British love so much – we lost the battle but fought well, gloriously. Men fought at their leader's side, then, inspired by his death, died to avenge him.

It probably didn't happen like that, but by the start of the 11th century, after years of peace, when England was experiencing the threat of invasion, some nameless poet thought it would make a good story, a story to inspire a new generation.

Again, it is luck that the poem survived, copied over the years until it has come down to us, not complete, but with enough inspiring speeches to stir the heart.

But how much do we actually know about Byrhtnoth?

Byrhtnoth was in his sixties when he died. He was buried at Ely Abbey, and reburied in the cathedral. His bones were found in 1789 during restoration work. His height was estimated at 6ft 9in and his head was missing, hacked off by the Vikings. We know the name of his father but not his mother. He had a wife, perhaps a daughter. He had connections with Ealdorman

Athelstan, called Half-King, of East Anglia, second only to the king in power.

Everything else is conjecture. Where, and when, was he born? How did he become a man great enough to marry a relative of the king?

Into this gaping hole I have set my book. I have taken his year of birth to be 930AD, when the final battles were being fought to unite the land that became England. He lived through the reigns of the grandchildren of King Alfred: Athelstan, Edmund and Eadred. The latter two appear in this book, together with King Edmund's son Edgar, who would later become King Edgar the Peaceable.

King Edgar's son was King Ethelread the Unready, for whom Byrhtnoth died at Maldon.

Byrhtnoth would have worked with Dunstan (later St Dunstan) to reform the church, but that came later.

In this book all kings, queens, ealdormen and bishops are historical. The death of King Edmund happened as written, but who was responsible and Byrhtnoth's part in it, if any, is speculation.

The Viking raid, Byrhtnoth's village and Edith's monastery are all fictionial, as are Byrhtnoth's friends and companions, except for Elfhere.

Elfhere was later Ealdorman of Mercia. He and Byrhtnoth were on opposing sides after the death of King Edgar. Did their rivalry start when they were children? Who knows.

And the sword? Well every warrior needs a sword. The poem tells us that Byrhtnoth carried a "bright bladed sword... golden hilted" when he died. It doesn't say where it came from.

Acknowledgments

I never meant to write a novel, especially not one set in the (so called) dark ages, although I have read historical fiction all my life. As a genealogist and local historian, I have a hundred stories to tell, but that would be via non-fiction.

It was with the aim of sharpening my writing ability that I joined a writing class at the Percival Guildhouse, an Adult Education Centre in Rugby. I'm not sure how I ended up in the Writing Fiction class, but as the weeks passed, Byrhtnoth took over. It was with the encouragement of our tutor, Gill Vickery, that I continued to write. I can honestly say that I would never have done it without her.

I must also like to thank all the students who have shared the class with me, listening to me reading out passages (sorry about the violent bits!) and encouraging and inspiring me. Special thanks to David Boulton for advice on medical matters and horses.

Halfway through the book, I became stuck. I didn't know what I was writing, or why. Thank goodness for the Arvon Residential Course I took in summer 2015. Those few days at The Hurst were an emotional roller coaster. I nearly gave up, but with help I made it through in one piece. Thank you to Arvon for running such life changing events, the other historical writers that attended (and still keep in touch) and most important, the tutors, Manda Scott and Karen Maitland, especially Karen for sometimes appearing at just the right moment to nudge my book in the right direction.

Thank you for all the authors out there, too many to mention, writing blogs, or passing on information via Facebook and Twitter to help struggling writers to fulfil their potential or just cheer them up.

Many thanks to all the other Dark Age writers from whom I have learned so much, including Matthew Harffy for writing such fantastic books that they make me want to give up, but then make me try harder (and for letting me hold his seax). And Cliff May, who read the book.

Thank you to Cathy Helms of Avalon Graphics for my beautiful cover, even if we couldn't find exactly the right sword. And The Book Guild for publishing my book.

I must make my apologies to members of the Rugby Family History Group and the Rugby Local History Research Group, for not replying to e-mails quick enough and neglecting to do things I should have done. Little did you know I was living in the 10th century most of the time!

Finally, thank you to my family.

To my parents who encouraged me to read and didn't think it unusual to fill a holiday suitcase with books instead of clothes.

To my sons and grandson, for giving me a small insight into the life of boys.

And most of all, thank you to my husband, despite making it into print before me (non-fiction, so it doesn't matter), for putting up with me, and not, I hope, being too jealous of Byrhtnoth.